Praise for *Fast Track*

'Stephen Leather writes really exciting action thrillers.
It's like being there yourself'
Chris Ryan, author of *Zero 22*

'The fast-paced action scenes are expertly choreographed;
the description of settings – from the luxurious bars where
Ankara's gangsters gather, to Dubai's glittering skyscrapers –
is brisk and richly detailed. Leather knows the inner workings
of the security services. But beyond the enthralling storyline
he also asks some tough questions about contemporary
Britain – without preaching'
Financial Times

Praise for Stephen Leather

'Packed with intricate detail on the intelligence services and
written with Leather's familiar gusto, it hurtles off the page,
grabbing the reader by the throat'
Daily Mail

'Leather once again delivers high-octane thrill-a-minute action
that reads like a pitch for a Netflix series'
Irish Independent

'Entertains and whisks the reader along at a
breath-taking pace'
Shots Magazine

STEPHEN LEATHER
FAST TRACK

HODDER

First published in Great Britain in 2021 by Hodder & Stoughton
An Hachette UK company

This paperback edition published in 2022

1

A CIP catalogue record for this title is available from the British Library

Paperback ISBN 978 1 473 67207 9

Typeset in Plantin Light by
Palimpsest Book Production Ltd, Falkirk, Stirlingshire

Printed and bound in Great Britain by Clays Ltd, Elcograf S.p.A.

Hodder & Stoughton policy is to use papers that are natural, renewable
and recyclable products and made from wood grown in sustainable forests.
The logging and manufacturing processes are expected to conform
to the environmental regulations of the country of origin.

Hodder & Stoughton Ltd
Carmelite House
50 Victoria Embankment
London EC4Y 0DZ

www.hodder.co.uk

FAST TRACK

'Cheeseburger or Big Mac?' The Deliveroo driver opened his back carrier. There were three McDonald's bags sitting on top of a C8 CQB carbine with a flash suppressor on the end of its ten-inch barrel. 'I've got two cheeseburgers but only the one Big Mac.'

'Are you serious, Jack?' said Alan Sage, who was sitting astride his Honda PCX 150 scooter. He was also wearing a Deliveroo jacket and had a C8 in his back carrier. The CQB was shorter than the average carbine, making it perfect for close protection work and for fitting into a Deliveroo carrier box. 'How did you get time for a Mickey D run?'

'There was a drive-through on the way. Do you want one or not?' Jack Ellis was one of Sage's closest friends. They had been on SAS selection together twelve years earlier and had buddied up on missions around the world. He was tall and lanky with piercing brown eyes and a drooping moustache that even he admitted gave him the look of a Seventies porn star. He had picked up the nickname 'Thing One' to differentiate him from his twin brother, Joe, who had joined the regiment a year after Jack and was promptly designated 'Thing Two'. Both had served with distinction in the Parachute Regiment's Fourth Battalion.

'Hell yeah,' said Sage. He held out his hand and Ellis gave him one of the bags.

'There's fries in there, too.'

'You're a star,' said Sage. He was in his late twenties, a former Para who wasn't long back from a mission in Syria so his skin was dark from the desert sun. He hadn't bothered to shave his

Stephen Leather

beard as there was every likelihood that he would be back some-where hot and sunny within the next few months.

'Don't I get one?' asked the third member of the group. Jeff 'Mutton' Taylor had been in the SAS for more than two decades, usually serving as patrol medic on overseas operations. He was short and squat with powerful arms that came in useful when he performed his party trick – fifty one-armed press-ups at double time. He had been with Sage on the Syrian mission but had shaved his greying beard as soon as he'd returned to the UK, leaving him with a patch of pale skin around his mouth and chin.

'Mate, you should be thinking about a salad rather than a burger,' said Ellis. 'You're the only man I know who can spend a month in the sandpit and come back fatter than when he went in.'

Taylor slapped his expanding waistline. 'This is fucking muscle, mate. And it's a proven scientific fact that the average McDonald's salad has more calories than a burger.' He held out a gloved hand. 'But I'm not greedy, I'll take a cheeseburger.' He was sitting on a scooter painted in the livery of the DHL courier company and had a matching helmet perched on one of his mirrors.

Ellis tossed him the bag.

The earpiece in Sage's ear crackled and all three men tensed. 'Victor One is approaching the Oxford turn-off,' said a female voice. 'Stand by, stand by, stand by.' There were two women sharing the comms but they used a single call sign, Charlie One.

The SAS troopers and their scooters were in the back of a removal van heading south on the M40, following two vans – codenamed Victor One and Victor Two – each with two men in the cab and four jihadists armed with Kalashnikov assault rifles in the back. The vans had started their journey at just before nine-thirty, departing from an industrial estate to the west of Birmingham. The warehouse the jihadists were using had been under surveillance by MI5, but according to the female analyst who had briefed the SAS team, they didn't know where the jihadists planned to attack. The analyst had also admitted that MI5 didn't know how many other potential terrorists were involved, so the decision had been taken to follow them to their intended destination rather than to arrest them at the warehouse. Which was why the three SAS troopers were in the removal van with their scooters and carbines. With no way of knowing which city was the intended target, the plan was for the trucks to ferry the scooters to where they would be needed.

The two vans were being followed by MI5 surveillance experts in a variety of vehicles and there was an MI5 helicopter watching from high up in the sky.

The operation was being run from a control centre in MI5's headquarters in Thames House. They were handling all comms. Despite there being Counter Terrorism Specialist Firearms Officers on the operation, the police top brass weren't involved. The CTSFOs had been assigned to MI5 for the duration of the operation. Sage wasn't sure why the cops had been kept out of it. It felt to him like an error of judgement. Once shots were fired people would be reaching for their phones and calling nine nine nine and if an armed response unit turned up, there was every chance they would misread the situation.

Once the two vans had turned onto the M40, London had seemed the obvious choice but Oxford was still a possibility.

'Victor One is remaining in the middle lane and not indicating,' said Charlie One.

Sage didn't know if either of the women on the comms were the same one who had handled the briefing at six o'clock in the morning. She hadn't given her name, but then spooks almost never did. She was in her forties and had a menacing stare as if she was daring them to look anywhere but at the maps and photographs she'd put up on a large whiteboard. There had been more than twenty men and women gathered together in the abandoned factory building that had been used to prepare for the operation. There were nine bikes being used by six SAS troopers and three CTSFOs from the Met, with drivers for the three removal vans that were being used to ferry the bikes. Each driver was accompanied by an armed CTSFO and there were six surveillance vehicles, all driven by unarmed MI5 surveillance experts.

'Victor One has passed the Oxford turn-off,' said the woman in Sage's ear. 'Victor Two is in the middle lane and not indicating.'

'Looks like London, then,' said Taylor. He unwrapped his burger and took a big bite. 'I knew it was going to be London.'

'They've got to cover all bases,' said Sage. 'We'd all look like tits if we were waiting for them in London and they attacked Milton Keynes.'

'Milton Keynes is a shithole,' said Taylor. 'Nobody would miss it if they wiped it off the map.' He shoved a handful of chips into his mouth.

'Victor Two has passed the Oxford turn-off,' said the woman. Sage looked at his watch. Central London was about sixty miles from Oxford, about an hour and a half at the speed they were travelling. His gut told him that was where the jihadists were heading, but once they reached the capital it was anyone's guess what their ultimate target would be.

'So how long have you known this young lady?' asked Dan Shepherd as he slowed the BMW X5 and turned into Brighton Marina.

Liam laughed. 'Dad, you sound like something out of a Jane Austen novel.'

'I wondered if this was a roundabout way of asking for her hand in marriage, except that you're approaching the wrong father. You realise that it's her dad you're supposed to be asking?'

'You are mad,' said Liam.

'Seriously, this is the first of your girlfriends that I've been introduced to. So I'm assuming she's special.' He found a parking space and guided the SUV in.

'Yeah, she's special,' said Liam. 'Her brother Ant is in my unit. We had a family day last year and she turned up with her mum and we hit it off.'

Shepherd noted that Liam hadn't contradicted him when he'd referred to her as a girlfriend. 'No father?'

'Their father got that long Covid thing. He was in ICU for a couple of months and he's at home now but he's still not well.

That's why we're here. It's his boat and he says it has to be taken out regularly. He says they're like dogs, they have to be exercised.'

They climbed out of the SUV. They were both wearing jeans and waterproof jackets and trainers. The weather forecast had been good for the day with no rain but it could still get chilly out on the water. Shepherd opened the back and took out a blue and white cooler.

He locked up the car and they walked through the marina. 'You've been on the boat before?'

'A couple of times. She offered at the family day and I had some leave due. I came down with Ant and had a great time. Then last month I came down from Yeovilton on my own.' Liam flew Wildcat helicopters for the British Army's Air Corps 659 Squadron based in Yeovilton in Somerset.

'Ant's her brother?'

'Yeah, Anton. We went through training together and now we're in the same unit.'

'Which one's Maverick and which one's Goose?'

Liam laughed. 'It's not *Top Gun*, Dad. And we don't fly together. But yeah, if it was *Top Gun*, he'd insist on being Maverick. He's thinking of transferring to the Apache.'

'That's a hell of a machine,' said Shepherd.

Liam shrugged. 'I'm happy with the Wildcat,' he said. 'The Apache is awesome but at the end of the day it's just you and the co-pilot looking for things to shoot at. Anton is mad keen, but then he's been playing *Call of Duty* since he was a kid. I like the Wildcat because there are always other people involved. You're moving them around or rescuing them or transporting stuff that people need, or doing reconnaissance or fire control and command and control. We've got missile capability and a door gunner so we can shoot if we have to, but that's not our prime mission.'

'You're enjoying it, obviously.'

'I love it. I love everything about it. I love the flying but I love being part of a group, you know? It's like we're in a gang, and we all take care of each other.'

Shepherd nodded. 'Like a family.'

'Yeah. That's what it feels like. I mean, I know you did your best after Mum died but we never really had a family, not a real family. You were my dad and all, but you were away a lot.' He saw Shepherd's face fall and he put his arm around him and squeezed. 'I'm not getting at you. You were a great dad. You still are. I mean, how many kids grow up with a real-life hero for a father? But I was on my own a lot of the time, and now I'm not.'

Shepherd knew exactly what Liam meant. The SAS had become his surrogate family and in many ways it still was. It had been more than twenty years since he had left the Regiment but his closest friends were still from those days, and he had never felt safer than when he had been surrounded by his SAS comrades.

'They're talking about sending me to Belize later this year, so that'll be fun.'

Shepherd laughed. 'Yeah, I've got fond memories of my time in Belize – not.'

'That's right, that's where the SAS does the jungle phase of selection, isn't it?'

Shepherd nodded. To join the elite Regiment, recruits were tested to their limits, physically and mentally. For every one hundred applicants only about eight were allowed to wear the coveted beige beret. The first phase – endurance, fitness and navigation – was usually called 'the hills stage' because it took place in the Brecon Beacons in South Wales. Candidates had to carry weighted Bergens over a series of timed marches. The hills stage was physically demanding but at least you could prepare for it. The second phase – jungle training – was actually much harder. Candidates were helicoptered into the Belize jungle and had to live in four-man patrols for several weeks, surviving and patrolling in wet and miserable conditions on minimal rations. The third and final phase was escape and evasion followed by tactical questioning. It was back to the Brecon Beacons where the recruits had to survive in the open for up to three days, before being interrogated and subjected to near torture. The recruits weren't physically tortured but they were treated roughly, forced into stress positions and deprived of sleep. It wasn't pleasant, but like most troopers Shepherd had found it a lot less stressful than the jungle phase.

'And that's where you got your nickname, of course,' said Liam.

Shepherd grinned. 'Yeah. Funny how it works. You eat one tarantula for a bet and you get a nickname that sticks with you your whole life. How about you? Did they give you a nickname?'

'They tried to call me Sheep-Shagger but I nipped that in the bud.'

'That's normally for the Welsh. You're not Welsh.'

'Shepherd. Sheep-Shagger.' He laughed. 'Like I said, I nipped it in the bud, but I ended up with Skills.'

'Skills? How does that work?'

'Liam. So Liam Neeson, right. And in that movie *Taken* he says he has a particular set of skills, remember? So when I was being trained, one of the instructors said I needed to work on my hovering skills and someone did that Liam Neeson quote and the next thing I know I'm Skills.'

'Better than Sheep-Shagger.'

'Definitely.' He pointed ahead of them. 'There she is.'

Shepherd wasn't sure if the 'she' referred to the yacht or the girl but he looked in the direction Liam was pointing.

The yacht was gleaming white with a single mast and two wheels at the stern and two narrow windows in the hull. The girl was a tall West Indian with shoulder-length frizzy hair and bright red lipstick that matched her nail varnish. She was wearing light blue jeans with ripped knees and a dark blue Cambridge University sweatshirt with the sleeves pulled up. She waved when she saw Liam and he waved back.

They walked along the jetty towards the yacht and by the time they reached it she had jumped down and was waiting for them. Liam hugged her and she put her arms around his neck and kissed him on the lips.

Liam broke away first, his cheeks reddening. 'Dad, this is Naomi. Though you probably guessed that by the PDA.'

Naomi laughed. 'He really hates public displays of affection.' She held out her hand. 'Pleased to meet you, Mr Shepherd. Liam talks about you all the time.'

He shook her slim hand. Her skin was soft and her nails were long and slightly pointed. They definitely weren't a sailor's hands. 'Great to finally meet you,' said Shepherd. 'Liam has told me next to nothing about you.'

'Dad!' Liam turned to look at her with imploring eyes. 'That's not true. Really. It's just that I'm not at home much and he never calls me.'

'I was joking, Liam,' said Shepherd. He grinned at Naomi. 'And call me Dan. Thanks so much for inviting me. It's been a while since I've been on a yacht.'

'So have you sailed before?'

'Actually I had my first serious sailing lesson out of this very marina a few years ago,' said Shepherd. 'My boss at the time took me out. It was a Catalina 375, if that means anything.'

'Nice boat. Fibreglass, made in America, twelve metres. This is a bit smaller. It's a Jeanneau Sun Odyssey, just under nine metres. My dad bought it ten years ago and I helped him sail it over from France.'

'Liam says your dad's not well. I'm sorry about that.'

'He's okay, I guess. He just gets tired and he doesn't sleep well. If he just stays in the house and lets Mum take care of him, he's fine. But even a short walk has him short of breath. So he makes me take the boat out every couple of weeks. They have to be used or they start to seize up.'

Shepherd held up the cooler. 'We brought food and I wasn't sure where you stood on drinking and sailing so there's wine, beer and soft drinks.'

'Have you ever known a sailor who doesn't drink?' she said. 'I'll put it in the galley.'

She climbed onto the deck and held out her hand. He gave her the cooler and she headed down a hatchway. As she disappeared from view, Shepherd looked over at Liam and nodded his approval.

Liam laughed. 'You're mad.'

'She's lovely.'

'Yeah, I know.'

Liam climbed onto the boat and Shepherd joined him. 'She obviously likes you.'

Liam opened his mouth to reply but shut it when Naomi reappeared. She had put on a blue fleece over her sweatshirt and tied her hair back. 'I had a peek at the wine,' she said to Shepherd. 'Nice choice. I've put it in the fridge.' She climbed through the hatch and closed it. 'So this boss of yours, how much did he teach you?'

'Really just the basics. Mainly went through the terminology. Leeward, windward, tacking, jibing, halyard, downhaul, the kicker, boom yang, backstays.' He laughed. 'It was like learning another language.'

'He must have been a good teacher, you seem to have remembered it all.'

'Dad's got a trick memory,' said Liam. 'He remembers pretty much everything he sees or hears.'

'What do they call that?' asked Naomi. 'Eidetic memory, right?'

'That's it,' said Shepherd. 'I certainly never forget a face or something I've been told.'

'And you can imagine what a pain that is when you're growing up,' said Liam. 'Difficult to pull the wool over the eyes of a parent who remembers every single thing you've ever told him.'

'I wish you remembered everything I told you,' said Naomi. 'He's not a great student. Put him at the controls of a helicopter and he's a happy bunny, but tell him to pull on the downhaul and he stands there like I've asked him to pat his head and rub his stomach at the same time.'

Liam laughed and gave her a hug. 'I'm trying,' he said, 'I just get frustrated at travelling so slowly.'

'I know,' she said. 'You feel the need, the need for speed.' She patted him on the cheek. 'Okay, so you get the engine started and head out of the marina. Dan, do you want to cast off the docklines?'

Shepherd threw her a mock salute. 'Aye aye, captain.'

'Victor One is approaching the end of the motorway,' said Charlie One in Sage's ear. 'We're about to encounter London traffic so all Foxtrots prepare to disembark.' Foxtrot was the call sign of the bikes, presumably F for Follower but he hadn't asked for an explanation. He was Foxtrot 6, which was all that mattered. Ellis was Foxtrot 5 and Taylor was Foxtrot 4.

'Victor One and Victor Two have now left the motorway and are heading east on the A40.' There was then a flurry of instructions as the controller ordered several of the vehicles to move in front of the vans. They all had the call sign Sierra, which Sage assumed came from Surveillance. The radio then fell silent for several minutes and Sage figured she was on another channel arranging more coverage in the city.

Taylor had a mobile phone showing Google Maps clipped to his handlebars and he peered at it. 'RAF Northolt coming up on the left,' he said. 'Possible target.'

'Nah, they've got armed guards and these jihadi bastards only ever shoot at civilians,' said Sage. 'If anyone ever fires back they piss themselves.'

Taylor laughed. 'Yeah, I hear you,' he said. 'We were in Iraq a few years back helping the cops with their training programme. Every time their guns went bang they flinched and closed their eyes. They're not great when things go bang. So what do you think?'

Sage shrugged. 'Like the secret squirrel woman said at the briefing, they prefer shopping malls, lots of civilians and little in the way of security. Or a shopping street. Oxford Street is damn near perfect. They could start at one end and in a hundred yards kill dozens of people.'

'If it was me, I'd take the bastards out now,' said Ellis. 'Waiting until they come piling out of the vans is cutting it too close.'

Taylor nodded in agreement. 'We should have gone in when they were in the warehouse. Throw in a few flash bangs, go in guns blazing, and Robert's your father's brother.'

'Nah, I get why we're letting them run. Like she said, they don't know who else might be involved. There could be more than one cell and if we take out this one, the other cell could carry on. This way we can assess the target and keep an eye out for other attackers.'

Ellis gulped down a chunk of burger. He rarely chewed his food, he ate like a dog, biting and swallowing in one smooth movement. 'I didn't get that,' he said. 'They've got their under-cover guy, Tango One, but he doesn't seem to have a clue as to what's going on.'

'Because he's low down on the totem pole and they're giving him the mushroom treatment,' said Sage. 'You have to look at the position he's in. If they even suspect that he's an informer, can you imagine what they'd do to him? He's not going to put himself at risk by asking too many questions.'

'Mate, he can't even tell us what the target is,' said Taylor.

'They probably haven't told any of them,' said Sage. 'Probably only the drivers know. These guys are pretty clued up on security. We think of them as ragheads and camel jockeys but these are the bastards that pulled off Nine-Eleven and Seven-Seven.'

'So where do you think they're headed?' asked Ellis.

Sage took a bite of his burger as he considered the question. Unlike Taylor, he didn't need to consult a GPS to know where he was and where he was heading. Navigation and map-reading had always been his strengths and his knowledge of London was as good as any cab driver's. 'Like Mrs Spook said, somewhere with a lot of people who can't shoot back. The way we're heading we're going to pass through White City and then the Westway leads to Paddington. The station's a perfect target. Of course if they head south from there, then we've got Hyde Park, Mayfair, Westminster.'

'The Houses of Parliament again?' said Ellis.

'Doubtful,' said Sage. 'They've beefed up security since that lone wolf attack in 2017.'

'Yeah, but at least they blew that raghead away,' said Ellis. 'I heard that there were twenty rounds in him by the time they'd finished.'

'He wasn't a raghead,' said Sage. 'He was a Brit convert.' Adrian Russell Elms was a cocaine user and violent criminal who had become a Muslim and taken the name Khalid Masood before driving his car into crowds of pedestrians on Westminster Bridge, then running towards the Houses of Parliament and stabbing an unarmed police officer to death. 'Also he was acting alone. Just a nutter with a car and a knife. What's happening today is a totally different ball game. These guys are well organised and armed, and probably fought with ISIS overseas. That's why we're on the case.'

'Yeah, Mrs Spook was a bit vague on that score, wasn't she?' said Taylor. He shoved a handful of French fries into his mouth and continued to chew and talk. 'How did they get into the country in the first place? None of them are Brits, right? All hardened ISIS fighters by the sound of it.'

'She said the guys doing the driving were British born, but the ones in the back are from overseas,' said Ellis.

'Obvious, innit?' said Taylor. 'They've been pouring in from France, packed onto small boats. Border Farce meets them and brings them in and then checks them into the nearest Premier Inn. They turn up with no passport or ID and no one gives a fuck.'

Ellis nodded enthusiastically. 'It's a laugh, it really is. I mean how hard can it be to put someone who arrives in this country illegally behind bars until it has been proved beyond any doubt who they are? If they're genuinely fleeing for their lives, all well and good. But if there's any doubt, you keep them under lock and key, end of. Instead we give them houses and money and put them in our schools, and then when the shit finally hits the fan we get called to clear up the mess.' He looked at Sage and Taylor in turn. 'Well, am I right or am I right?'

'You're not wrong,' said Taylor.

Ellis looked expectantly at Sage, waiting for him to agree,

but as Sage opened his mouth, the woman came in over the radio.

'Victor One and Victor Two are still heading towards central London, now on the Westway,' said the voice in Sage's ear. 'And to confirm, we have no intel on any further targets. So far we have only Victor One and Victor Two as target vehicles.'

'How would they know?' asked Ellis.

'They'll be monitoring mobile phone traffic,' said Sage. 'If they were planning to meet up with other units, they'd have to talk to them.'

'If they know that for sure, we should take them out now,' said Taylor. He screwed up his burger wrapper and tossed it into the corner of the van.

Sage knew that Taylor was right. The longer they held off from confronting the jihadists, the more chance there was of civilians getting hurt. But they were just pawns in this game, all the decisions were being taken back at MI5's headquarters and no one was asking the troops for their opinions.

'Alphas One, Two and Three, prepare to disembark Foxtrots,' said Charlie One, using the code signs of the three removal vans.

'Here we go,' said Taylor. He grabbed his helmet and pulled it on.

'We will carry out the disembarkation in stages,' said the woman over the radio. 'Alpha Three first, followed by Alpha Two and Alpha One. All Foxtrots to head east on the Westway. All Foxtrots respond in order now for comms check.'

Sage pulled on his helmet and adjusted the strap. They were in Alpha Two.

'Foxtrot One, check.' A West Country accent over the radio. It was one of the CTSFOs, a new face to Sage. The CTSFOs were cops, and while they didn't come close to the SAS's fitness standards, they were pretty much their equal when it came to handling their weapons.

'Foxtrot Two, check.' A Scouser. SAS. A relatively new recruit that Sage had only met once before in the barracks. His nickname was 'Grassy' so Sage assumed his family name was Fields or Meadows or something grass-related.

'Foxtrot Three, check.' A Brummie. Another CTSFO, a big bruiser of a man who dwarfed his bike. His name was Michael Burton and Sage had trained with him at the SAS's barracks in Credenhill two years previously.

'Foxtrot Four, check,' said Taylor.

'Foxtrot Five, check,' said Ellis.

'Foxtrot Six, check,' said Sage.

The three other bikes checked in, nine in all.

'Alpha Three, pull over,' said the woman.

The removal vans had been fine for following the trucks on the motorway but they were too big to use in the city. Once the bikes had disembarked, the removal vans would leave the surveillance up to the Foxtrots and the Sierras.

'Alpha Three has pulled over,' said Charlie One. 'Opening rear door now.'

In less than a minute Foxtrots Seven, Eight and Nine had checked in and confirmed that they were mobile. Then the driver of Alpha Three confirmed that the truck was on the move again.

'Alpha Two prepare to pull over,' said Charlie One. The removal van slowed and juddered to a halt. Sage started the engine of his scooter and Ellis and Taylor did the same. The rear door rattled up and the driver and the front-seat passenger, both burly men in brown overalls, pulled out a ramp and lowered it to the ground. There was a queue of cars behind the truck and several started to pound their horns angrily. Taylor drove down the ramp first, followed by Ellis. Sage brought up the rear.

Taylor pulled a sharp turn around the truck and sped off down the road. 'Foxtrot Four is mobile,' he said over the radio.

A white van swerved from behind the removal van to overtake and the driver pounded on his horn and swore angrily at Ellis. Ellis had to brake sharply to avoid a collision. The white van roared off. 'Arsehole,' muttered Ellis. He accelerated away, notifying the controller that he was mobile.

More vehicles were following the example of the white van

driver, pulling out and venting their frustration with their horns. Several drivers gave Sage the finger but he just smiled and waited for a gap in the traffic. 'Foxtrot Six is mobile,' he said, then pulled out after a Mercedes sports car and accelerated past the removal van. The driver and his mate pushed the ramp back and hurried to the cab accompanied by a cacophony of angry horns.

'Do you want to get the wine, Dan?' asked Naomi. She was standing by the starboard wheel having brought the yacht onto a course parallel to the shore, now about three miles off to their left. 'And Liam, can you bring in the sail just a bit.'

'Sure,' said Shepherd. He ducked down through the hatchway and down a couple of steps into the main cabin. It was spotless, all polished pine and stainless steel. There was a compact galley to his left with a small fridge and he opened the door. The wine and beer were there, along with the sandwiches and snacks they'd bought from a Marks and Spencer outlet on the way to Brighton. There was a tray tucked in next to the microwave and he pulled it out and placed the food and drinks on it, along with three wine glasses. As he picked up the tray he noticed two envelopes on top of the microwave, both addressed to Kingston Clarke, sent care of the marina office, presumably Naomi's father.

He carefully carried the tray up the steps and onto the deck. The boat had slowed and Naomi had activated the autopilot. She helped Shepherd put the food out on a small table and pulled a Swiss Army knife from the pocket of her fleece. She flicked out a corkscrew and handed it to Liam. 'Can you do the honours?'

'Happy to,' said Liam, and he deftly pulled out the cork. Shepherd couldn't help but notice how easily the girl was able to get them to do what she wanted. It just seemed natural to carry out her instructions, especially as she always asked with a smile and a sparkle in her eyes. She would have made a good Army officer, he realised. She had a natural confidence without any trace of arrogance and he could easily imagine men following her into battle. Liam poured the wine and Naomi raised her glass. 'As my father always used to say, may the warm wind at your back not be your own.'

Shepherd and Liam both laughed and drank.

'I heard a good toast a while back,' said Shepherd. 'Here's to lying, cheating, stealing and drinking. If you're going to lie, lie to save the life of a friend. If you're going to cheat, cheat death. If you're going to steal, steal the heart of the one you love. And if you are going to drink, drink with friends both old and new.'

Naomi grinned and raised her glass to him. 'I love that. Can I borrow it?'

'I stole it from someone else, so feel free.'

Naomi held the tray out and Shepherd took a sausage roll. 'So what do you do, Naomi, for a living?' asked Shepherd.

She laughed and flashed Liam a sly look. 'So you really told your dad nothing about me?'

'He's away a lot. And he's not on social media.'

Naomi looked at Shepherd. 'Really? No Facebook, Twitter, Instagram?'

Shepherd shook his head. 'I'm not a fan. If I want to talk to Liam, I call him.'

'Which isn't very often, to be honest,' said Liam.

'What about calling on WhatsApp? Or Messenger?'

'I prefer the old-fashioned way,' said Shepherd. 'Why do you ask?'

Naomi sipped her wine. 'Because social media is what I do. Brand awareness, mainly. We have a company that raises brand awareness for individuals and companies, mainly by setting up and running social media accounts.'

'So you're an influencer?'

'Not really. But we do run accounts for influencers. We're more behind the scenes.'

'And who do you mean by "we"? You have a company?'

'Dad!' said Liam. 'This isn't an interrogation.' He smiled at Naomi. 'He used to be a cop. He can be a bit accusatory when he starts asking questions.'

Shepherd laughed and held up his hand. 'Sorry, Liam's right. I'm just interested, that's all.'

'That's okay. There are three of us at the company. We met at university.' She pointed at her sweatshirt. 'We all met and talked online and it was only after a few weeks that we realised we were all at Cambridge, albeit at different colleges. We were all pretty active on social media and had lots of followers between us, and we realised that we could use our knowledge of how it works to help other customers. We started the business when I was in my second year and by the time I graduated we were turning over six figures.'

'That's good,' said Shepherd.

'Six figures a month,' she said, raising her glass to him. 'And we're doing even better now. Perversely Covid was good news for us because we all worked from home anyway but the lock-downs meant more people were staying at home and using social media.'

'Sounds fun,' said Shepherd.

'Oh it is. We break new products, promote services, and we handle the Twitter, Instagram and Facebook accounts for quite a few household names.'

'She's brilliant at it, Dad,' said Liam. He ripped open a pack of Marks and Spencer pork pies, pulled one out and bit into it.

'And is your father in the marketing business?'

Naomi shook her head. 'Dad, no, he's a property developer. He'd done really well converting pubs into apartments, right across the country. He's slowed down a lot since he got ill, but his team are going gangbusters. Pubs are closing left and right and he can often buy them for a song.' She took another sip of wine. 'And what about you, Dan? What do you do? Liam is always vague when I ask him about your work.'

'I'm a civil servant,' said Shepherd. 'Home Office. It's really really boring and mainly involves me sitting at a desk studying spreadsheets.'

'You don't look like a man who spends all his life behind a desk.'

'I run a bit, and use the gym.' He patted his own stomach.
'Got to keep fit, right? What about you? What do you do for
fun?'

'I ride, when I can. And I play badminton. I keep trying to
get Liam to play but he says it's a game for sissies.'

They laughed and chatted about sport as they drank and ate.
Shepherd didn't like having to lie to the girl but he had no choice,
which is why he had changed the subject so quickly. Anyone who
had served in the SAS would rarely admit to an outsider that
they had been in the Regiment. And MI5 officers were only
allowed to tell their closest family members who they worked for.
He liked Naomi but she was an outsider and that meant he had
to lie to her. She wasn't the first nice person he'd lied to and she
certainly wouldn't be the last. Lying went with the turf. Though
to be fair, he would also lie to save a friend.

Alan Sage accelerated past a taxi and then moved over to the
left. The target vehicle was three cars ahead of him, a dark blue
van with the name and logo of an Indian restaurant on the side.
It was Victor Two. Victor One was about ten cars ahead. Victor
One was a white van in the livery of a boiler repair company.

The two vans had driven down the Westway until it had crossed
Edgware Road and become Marylebone Road. Traffic had grown
heavier and the vans were crawling along. The bikes could have
weaved in and out of the traffic but they held back. They had
driven past Madame Tussauds and then turned south when they
reached Warren Street Tube station, driving down Tottenham
Court Road.

Sage knew that if they continued south they would reach the
junction of Oxford Street and New Oxford Street, a perfect
jumping-off point for an attack on defenceless shoppers. The
woman on the radio had the same thought. 'Victor One and
Victor Two are approaching Oxford Street so would all Foxtrots
move closer,' she said.

Sage accelerated and got to within three car lengths of Victor
Two.

'Victor Two is closing up on Victor One,' said the woman's voice in his earpiece.

'Driver of Victor One is using his mobile,' growled a Scottish voice. It was Joe Ellis, AKA Thing Two, who had been in the Alpha Three truck. Sage was tempted to suggest they pull the driver over and charge him with using his phone at the wheel, but he knew that MI5 didn't share the SAS's cavalier sense of humour so he held his tongue.

'Victor Two driver is also using his mobile,' said one of the CTSFOs over the radio.

Sage would have bet money that the two van drivers were talking to each other, which meant they were getting close to their intended target.

'Victor One is approaching Oxford Street,' said Charlie One. 'All Foxtrots on maximum alert.'

Sage smiled to himself. He doubted that any of the Foxtrots would be on anything less than full alert. His own heart was pounding as if it was about to burst out of his chest and he had to force himself to take slow, deep breaths.

'One hundred feet. Eighty feet. Sixty feet. Forty feet. Twenty feet. Victor One is crossing Oxford Street. Victor Two is also crossing Oxford Street.'

So Oxford Street wasn't the target. But Shaftesbury Avenue, heart of the capital's theatre land, was approaching and Leicester Square was coming up on the right, an area of London that was always packed with tourists. Beyond Leicester Square was Trafalgar Square.

'Foxtrot Seven is overtaking Victor Two,' said one of the CTSFOs.

'Foxtrot Six move to behind Victor Two,' said the comms controller.

'Foxtrot Six moving behind Victor Two,' confirmed Sage, accelerating towards the van as the CTSFO accelerated away on his Addison Lee courier bike.

They crossed over Shaftesbury Avenue. Then they passed by Leicester Square. Both vans were slowing. Was Trafalgar Square the target? It had been one of a number of possibles put forward during the briefing. More than ten thousand protestors were expected to attend an anti-government demonstration, though the MI5 analyst who had conducted the briefing had acknowledged that most ISIS attacks in the capital in the past had not been political and the Trafalgar Square demonstration was just one of more than a dozen possibilities.

Sage hadn't been at all impressed by the quality of the intelligence they had been given that morning. The spooks had a man on the inside, designated Tango One and currently in the rear of Victor Two, just a few feet ahead of him. Tango One was wearing a distinctive black beanie with a white Nike swoosh and a green parka and they were under strict orders not to shoot him. Or at least not to kill him. If their own lives were threatened, they were authorised to return fire but they had to wound and not kill.

Tango One hadn't even been able to tell his handler the geographic area that was to be attacked, never mind the specific target. Tango One was also unable – or unwilling – to tell them how many attackers there would be or how many vehicles would be involved. The MI5 analyst had identified twelve tangoes and two vehicles but had stressed that there could well be more taking part. That was why the operation had been allowed to run as far as it had. If MI5 had known for a fact that there were only twelve tangoes, then they would have taken them out the moment they had picked up their weapons.

As they had been walking over to their bikes after the briefing, Sage had snatched a few words with Jack Ellis. He had been equally unimpressed with the MI5 analyst. 'Fucking secret squirrel bollocks,' had been his verdict.

Sage had agreed. It was all very well saying that continued surveillance was necessary until they had evaluated the full extent of the terrorist attack, but the simple fact was that when the tangoes emerged from their vans with their guns, the likelihood was that they would start firing immediately. The team would have only seconds in which to react, and any hesitation would lead to civilians being caught in the crossfire.

The National Gallery was coming up on their right. The gallery was at the north of Trafalgar Square and all traffic was being diverted to the left, around St Martin-in-the-Fields church and along Duncannon Street. Victor One made the turn. There were two Deliveroo bikes tucked in behind the van.

Victor Two indicated and turned left, following Victor One.

'Victor One and Two are preparing to stop,' said Charlie One in Sage's ear. Presumably they were monitoring the conversations between the two drivers. 'All Foxtrots on high alert, please.'

Sage smiled at the 'please'. The SAS weren't much for Ps and Qs. Just get the job done with the minimum of fuss and fuck the pleasantries.

An Uber Eats delivery bike drew up on Sage's right. He glanced over and the driver nodded. It was one of the CTSFOs, Michael Burton. He was wearing a black full-face helmet. Like Sage's it was lined with Kevlar and the visor was bullet-proof plastic. His jacket bore the logo of the delivery company. He was wearing a Kevlar vest under his jacket and his carbine was in his delivery box.

'Foxtrot Eight is overtaking Victor Two,' said Burton over the radio and he accelerated.

The vans were slowing now.

'Foxtrot Six, move ahead of Victor One and Victor Two,' said the controller in Sage's ear.

Sage frowned. If the vans were indeed pulling over, then it would make more sense for them to fall back and to be ready when the jihadists exited their vans. The logistics of the operation were being controlled by MI5 and Sage had felt that had been a mistake. Spooks might be good at gathering information and running agents, but when it came to organising a gunfight it was the SAS who were the specialists. There had been no SAS officers at the briefing and it had been made clear that the troopers were just hired hands there to follow orders and work alongside the CTSFOs.

'Foxtrot Six overtaking Victor Two,' said Sage. He twisted the accelerator and went by the van. Out of the corner of his eye he saw the driver looking around. A bearded Asian, mid-twenties, wearing dark glasses and a white skullcap.

There was a black taxi tucked in behind Victor One. The driver was an MI5 surveillance expert and was unarmed. His passenger was an SAS trooper by the name of Brendan 'Dobbo' Dobson who had a Glock pistol under his black leather jacket and a C8 carbine on the floor by his feet. Dobbo was a recent recruit to the Regiment, barely into his twenties, but had already acquitted himself well in several missions, including a bodyguarding operation in Qatar when the Regiment had been tasked with defending a Sheikh who was close to signing a five-billion-pound defence contract.

The van ahead of Sage indicated and pulled over to the side of the road. Sage had no choice other than to go around.

'Victor One is stopping,' said Charlie One. 'No sign of any further target vehicles. All units prepare for contact.'

Sage braked, then drove up onto the pavement. He jumped off the bike and hurried around to the rear. Two men in suits carrying briefcases walked by and one of them saw him pull the carbine from the box. 'What the fuck!' said the man.

'Armed police,' growled Sage. 'Get the fuck out of here.'

The two men hurried away. Sage heard the taxi cab screech to a halt, and the sound of the doors of the vans being thrown open. He ran down the pavement. Dobbo was getting out of the cab, his carbine in his left hand. He grinned at Sage and slammed the door. The MI5 driver had dropped down in his seat. 'It's clobbering time,' said Dobbo.

'Contact, contact, contact,' said Charlie One in Sage's ear. She sounded totally calm, but then she wasn't the one being shot at.

As they started down the pavement towards the two vans, they heard the pop-pop-pop-pop of a Kalashnikov being fired on fully automatic. The driver of Victor One saw them coming and his mouth opened in shock. The passenger was also a bearded Asian and he had a Kalashnikov in his hands. He snarled and tried to bring his weapon to bear on Dobbo and Sage but there was no room to manoeuvre and Sage had all the time in the world to put two shots through the windscreen and into the man's head.

The driver was raising his hands but Sage didn't care whether he was surrendering or lifting a weapon, they were in full kill mode so he didn't hesitate to put two shots in the man's chest.

Dobbo had kept on running so he reached the rear of Victor One first. Two of the jihadists had jumped out. One had made the rookie mistake of keeping his finger on the trigger and his weapon was still firing wildly up in the sky. The second jihadist had ducked down with his back to the van, clearly unsettled by the shots. Dobbo put two shots in the head of the man firing his weapon and the pop-pop-pop immediately stopped as the Kalashnikov fell to the tarmac. The dead jihadist pitched forward, his head a pulpy mass. Sage put two rounds in the chest of the second man and he pitched forward and fell on top of his weapon.

The remaining two jihadists in the van started to swing up their weapons but Burton appeared in the middle of the road with an HK MP5 in his hands. Burton fired twice at the man on the left and both shots hit the man in the chest. The nine-millimetre rounds made the man stagger back but didn't take him down, so Burton fired again, stepping to the side to keep Dobbo and Sage out of the line of fire. Dobbo fired at the jihadist on the right at the same time and both jihadists slumped to the floor of the van.

Sage heard more shots around Victor Two but they were all the double cracks of C8 carbines. He and Burton ran towards the second van. The driver and front-seat passenger of Victor Two were dead in their seats, covered in blood and cubes of broken glass. Two dead jihadists lay on the ground. Sage ran wide to get a better view of the inside of Victor Two. Just as the occupants came into view Dobbo jumped back as a Kalashnikov fired and the round hit Burton in the centre of the chest. The CTSFO grunted and took a step back. The vest would save his life but a Kalashnikov round at close range was nothing to laugh about and his MP5 fell from his hands.

Sage moved into a crouch and took two quick side steps. His mind was racing as he assessed the situation facing him. Two men. One was wearing a bomber jacket and jeans with an ISIS scarf tied around his head. He was whooping with excitement, a crazed look in his eyes. The other was wearing a black beanie with a white Nike swoosh and a green parka. Tango One. The informant. He was holding a Kalashnikov but had the barrel pointing at the roof of the van.

Sage fired twice at the man in the bomber jacket. The first round caught him in the neck and the second in the chest.

Tango One screamed in terror, threw his weapon onto the floor and dropped to his knees.

Ellis and Dobbo hurried over, their weapons pointed at Tango One's chest. 'Down on the floor, now!' shouted Dobbo.

Sage rushed over to Burton who was lying on his back, gasping for breath. 'You okay, mate?' asked Sage.

Burton nodded but couldn't speak. Sage patted him on the shoulder.

Two CTSFOs were bending down to check the bodies at the rear of the van while Ellis fixed Flexicuffs around Tango One's wrists. The man began to protest but Sage told him to shut the fuck up. Dobbo tossed him a black canvas bag, which Sage pulled over the man's head before dragging him to his feet.

Ellis and Dobbo helped Tango One out of the van and dragged him to the taxi where the MI5 driver was emerging cautiously from the footwell.

MI5 director Giles Pritchard smiled with relief. 'Well, I think we all deserve a pat on the back, don't you?' he said. 'I don't mind telling you that I had my reservations about allowing the operation to run as far as it did, but we seem to be vindicated.' He put his hands on his hips as he stared over the top of the metal-framed spectacles that were perched on his hawk-like nose at the large screen that dominated the wall. It was showing an aerial view from the helicopter that had shadowed the two vans on the drive from the Midlands. Once the vans had stopped, the helicopter had swooped down to provide a real-time bird's-eye view of the jihadists being dealt with.

'It couldn't have gone better,' growled Ken Reid, MI5's head of Technical Operations, Analysis and Surveillance. His dour Aberdeen accent always made him sound depressed, even when he was celebrating a victory. 'Drinks all round tonight.'

They were in a windowless operations room down the corridor from Pritchard's office in Thames House, not far from Lambeth Bridge. There were half a dozen pods in the room each with multiple screens, and several larger screens on the walls. Reid was in one of the front pods, wearing a headset. Sitting in the pod next to Reid was his equivalent from MI6, Martin Williams, bald and bearded. Unlike Reid he wasn't wearing a headset as he was there mainly as an overseer and as a courtesy to MI6 who had been running Tango One. 'Bloody good work,' said Williams. He stood up and stretched. 'And special thanks are due to Mo Uthman, of course, without whom none of this would be possible.'

A thin pale-skinned Asian man wearing a grey suit that looked a size too big for him raised a spindly hand in acknowledgement. Uthman was in his mid-twenties, with a close-cropped beard and black hair that glistened as if it had been oiled, and was the officer who had been running the agent designated as Tango One in the operation.

There were four other people in the operations room. Standing with his back to the wall, by the door, was Major Allan Gannon. The SAS veteran was in his early fifties, just a couple of years younger than Pritchard, square-jawed and with close-cropped hair and a nose that had been broken several times during an illustrious special forces career. He was wearing a dark blue suit and a red tie, but even in the civilian clothing there was no mistaking the man's military bearing. 'Your team did everything that was asked of them, Major, please pass on my heartfelt thanks.' The Major flashed him a tight smile.

Pritchard nodded at a man in his thirties wearing a black blazer and black jeans who was sitting in one of the pods. He was

Inspector Craig Bird from the Met's Specialist Firearms Command. 'And if you could pass on my respect and thanks to your officers, Inspector Bird.'

'Will do, sir,' said Bird.

Sitting in the pod next to Bird was Frank Russell, one of MI5's Metropolitan Police liaison officers. Russell had retired as a Chief Superintendent after a thirty-year career with the Met. He was about the same age as Pritchard, but whereas Pritchard's slicked-back hair was starting to grey, Russell's was jet black and always looked as if he had just stepped out of a wind tunnel. Like Pritchard he'd hung his jacket on the back of a chair and rolled up his shirtsleeves. 'Frank, I need you to get onto the Met ASAP and let them know that we've just carried out a successful operation and that we'll be doing whatever cleaning up is required.'

Russell tapped the earpiece through which he was monitoring Met radio traffic. 'The calls have started coming in and two Trojan units are on the way.' The Trojans were the Met's armed response units, spread out across the city ready to respond to firearms incidents.

'Obviously the priority is to stand them down. No ambulances, either, we'll be wanting to do our own forensics on the bodies.'

Russell picked up a phone.

Pritchard went over to the pod occupied by Diane Daily. She was often called Scaley Daily by her colleagues – but never by Pritchard – as she had served five years in the Royal Corps of Signals before joining MI5. Royal Signals soldiers were referred to as Scaleys, or Scaley Backs, because back in the old days they had to use primitive transmitters with massive batteries which would leak and scar the backs of the operators. Communications had come a long way since those early days and while Daily was only in her twenties, she was one of MI5's top communications specialists. Standing next to the pod was Donna Walsh, who headed up MI5's London surveillance operations. She wore dark-framed glasses and her chestnut hair was pinned back from her face. Walsh and Daily had been running comms for the operation and it had been a difficult task from the outset. London seemed to have been the destination, but even that wasn't guaranteed as the jihadists could easily have headed south to any of the towns on the coast. Once the vans had left the motorway and started driving through London, the surveillance had simplified and Walsh had been able to bring local assets and CCTV coverage into play, but then it had become a much more cat-and-mouse game with the knowledge that when the vans did eventually stop, they would have only seconds in which to react. Walsh and Daily had shared the radio work as the vans had driven down the M40 and both had been calm and near unflappable throughout, but Daily had taken over once they had reached central London.

Daily rubbed the bridge of her nose. 'That was challenging,' she said.

'You were brilliant,' said Walsh, patting her on the shoulder.

'When they were getting ready to stop, I almost lost it.'

'Nonsense,' said Walsh. 'You had everyone just where they needed to be. Training is going to be using this for years to come, it was pretty much perfect right from the moment they left the warehouse.'

'Donna's right,' said Pritchard. 'It was textbook.'

'Giles, we've got some crowd movement still going on,' said Reid, gesturing at the main screen.

Pritchard turned to see what he was pointing at. Once the shooting had started, people had panicked and started running away from the gunfire. But the square had been so crowded that the demonstrators were soon bunched together and running had been impossible. People were still moving south, heading towards the Strand and the River Thames beyond. The people nearest the shooting could see that there was no current danger and so had taken out their phones and were videoing. But those in the centre and north of the square were still panicking, pushing and shoving to get away. 'They'll calm down soon,' said Pritchard.

'We were lucky there wasn't a stampede,' said Reid.

Pritchard wrinkled his nose. The crowds were still pushing to leave the square. Some headed east down the Strand, others were hurtling down Northumberland Avenue and Whitehall to the river. Police officers in fluorescent jackets had formed a line across Whitehall in an attempt to block their progress but the crowd broke through.

Pritchard looked over at Russell, who had just come off the phone. 'Frank, see if there's anything you can do to control the—' He was interrupted by a flash of light on one of the screens. Almost immediately there was a billowing cloud of smoke that enveloped the Strand around Charing Cross Station. There was no sound but it was clear that there had been a massive explosion.

Williams staggered back as if he had been punched. He put his hand on his chest and began gasping for breath.

As the smoke began to disperse they could see dozens of bodies on the ground and dozens more casualties wounded and bleeding. Those that could began running back towards Trafalgar Square.

Williams groped in his trouser pocket, pulled out an asthma inhaler and started sucking on it greedily.

Pritchard put his hands on his head, unable to comprehend what he was seeing. He shook his head, trying to clear his thoughts. The helicopter swooped down towards the Strand, giving them a clearer view of the carnage. It was clear that there had been a major explosion outside the station. Pritchard's mind was whirling. This was no longer an MI5 operation, Downing Street and the Met would be taking over. MI5 don't have the resources to deal with a terrorist incident on this scale.

Russell was staring open-mouthed at the screen showing the view from the helicopter. Pritchard went over to him. 'What the fuck just happened?' whispered Russell.

'It looks like a car bomb,' said Pritchard. 'Or a truck. We'll need to check the footage. The helicopter should have caught it and there'll be CCTV footage. Frank, you need to talk to the Commissioner and let him know that we need to be involved at every step of the investigation.'

'Do you think the bomb is connected to the operation?' asked Russell.

Pritchard grimaced as he considered the question. It could have been a coincidence that a bomb went off just as the jihadists had mounted a Marauding Terrorist Firearms Attack (MTFA), but that was highly unlikely. But assuming the two events were connected, there had been a major failure in intelligence and someone was going to have to answer for that. He was just about to reply when there was another massive explosion, this time at the entrance to Whitehall. If anything it was even bigger than the first and the cloud of smoke obliterated Admiralty Arch and the main Foreign Office building.

Williams had his inhaler back in his mouth. The room had gone completely silent as everyone stared at the main screen. The helicopter had gained height and the two clouds of smoke were both visible on either side of the screen. The smoke was clearing outside the station and even more bodies were visible, many of them in pieces.

'What the fuck?' gasped Pritchard.

The crowd was pushing northwards now, trying to escape the explosions, but there were still people pushing to get away from the shooting and when the two surges met, people were forced to the ground and trampled on. There was no sound to go with the images on the screens but it was clear that people were screaming and panicking.

The police who had been there to control the demonstration were also panicking, running around shouting and waving but with no coherent plan.

'Who's Gold Commander for policing the demonstration, Frank?' Pritchard asked.

'Superintendent Ron Carroll,' said Russell.

'Well he needs to get a grip on the situation,' said Pritchard. He stared at the screen, a sick feeling in the pit of his stomach. The dead and injured were being trampled on by those trying to escape. Several police officers in fluorescent jackets were running down Whitehall, away from the carnage. Others had fallen to their knees, tears streaming down their cheeks. He shook his head in annoyance. The police needed to start guiding people away from the square, ideally to the north, and they needed to at least try to calm people down.

There were now two clouds of thick grey smoke blowing across the square. A single ambulance came into view. It stopped and two paramedics climbed out. They looked around, clearly wondering where they should start. There were more than a hundred people on the ground, many of them clearly dead but the rest badly injured and in need of urgent attention. If Ron Carroll had been doing his job properly, he would have already declared a major incident and called for every ambulance in the city to be diverted to Trafalgar Square, along with every available police officer. Roads would need to be closed, the areas around the explosions sealed off as crime scenes, and names and addresses of witnesses recorded. But from what Pritchard could see on the screens the police were running around like headless chickens. He took a deep breath. Dealing with the crowds and the casualties wasn't his job and it was pointless to start second guessing those who were supposed to be handling it.

He looked over at Martin Williams. The MI6 officer shrugged at the unasked question – what the hell has happened? They both looked at Mo Uthman, who was now standing with his back to the wall, his arms folded across his chest. He looked as if he was about to throw up. He saw that everyone was staring at him and his eyes flashed defiantly. 'What?' he said. 'You think this is my fault?'

'No one is saying that, Mo,' said Williams. 'But something has clearly gone very wrong.'

'When was the last time you were in contact with your agent?' asked Pritchard.

'This morning. At just after six. I got a text saying everything was going ahead.'

'Those were his exact words?' asked Pritchard.

'No, of course not,' snapped Uthman. 'I'm not stupid. If there was a problem or a delay he would text me with the word supper. If everything was okay he'd use the word breakfast. The message said he was going to be eating breakfast later.'

'And then nothing?'

'The plan was always that they would leave their phones behind in Birmingham. They all used burner phones so they might even have destroyed them.' He looked up at the main screen showing the view from the helicopter, which had descended to get a closer look at the carnage. He shuddered and looked away.

'When did you last have a face-to-face?' asked Pritchard.

'Two days ago, in Birmingham. We had a pre-arranged meet in a McDonald's.'

'And he was fine?'

'He was apprehensive, obviously. He didn't want to go through with it. He couldn't understand why we weren't arresting everybody.'

'Apprehensive because of the forthcoming attack, or because he was worried about being discovered?'

Uthman frowned. 'What do you mean?'

'It's not a difficult question,' said Pritchard. 'Was he worried that the cell was going to realise that he was betraying them? Or was he worried about taking part in the attack?'

Uthman sneered at Pritchard. 'Why the fuck does that matter? He was nervous. I calmed him down. I explained that we needed the operation to go ahead and he agreed to do it. I went through what he was to do and explained that so long as he was wearing his Nike beanie and parka nothing would happen to him.'

'And did he mention explosives at any point?'

Uthman pushed himself away from the wall, eyes blazing. 'What? Why the fuck would you ask me a question like that?'

'Mo, calm down,' said Williams quietly.

Uthman turned to glare at him. 'Calm down? Calm the fuck down? You can see what he's doing here, he's trying to dump the blame for this on me.' He looked back at Pritchard and pointed an accusing finger at him. 'What do you think? That he told me that they were planning to detonate two car bombs and I what, I forgot? I forgot to pass on that rather important information.' He shook his head angrily. 'Who the fuck are you to talk to me like this anyway? I don't fucking work for you.'

Pritchard's eyes narrowed. 'You need to calm down, young man, and remember who you're talking to.'

'Who am I talking to? I'm talking to the man who presided over one almighty cock-up, that's who I'm talking to. This is your fuck-up, not mine. It was your men on the ground, I was only running the agent. And I wasn't running him for you. I was running him for MI6. I don't answer to you, I answer to Melissa Schofield. You don't have any right to put me through the third degree.'

'Mo, please, you need to calm down,' said Williams. 'Getting angry isn't going to solve anything.'

'Don't fucking tell me to calm down!' shouted Uthman. 'Can't you see what's happening here? He's going to burn me at the stake for this. There are people still dying out there and he's looking to hang the blame on me.' He jabbed his finger at Pritchard again. 'It's because I'm Asian, isn't it? I'm Asian and they're Asian and something has gone wrong so now let's blame the Asian because let's face it they're all the fucking same, aren't they? Well fuck it, you're not going to railroad me.'

He headed towards the door. Pritchard stood where he was, his jaw set tight. Williams called after Uthman but the MI6 officer ignored him, yanked the door open and practically ran out of the room.

Williams headed after him but stopped when his mobile burst into life. He took it out and checked to see who was calling. 'Melissa,' he mouthed to Pritchard, and took the call. Melissa Schofield was the chief of MI6, the Secret Intelligence Service. Uthman was right, he worked for Schofield and not Pritchard, but Pritchard doubted that the MI6 chief would be any happier about what had happened. Schofield rarely left the MI6 head-quarters building at Vauxhall Cross, on the south side of the Thames. She had been watching the operation from there and obviously would be looking for answers. And at the moment, Pritchard had none.

As Williams cupped his hand around his phone and lowered his voice to talk to his boss, Pritchard looked back at the main screen. Two more ambulances had arrived. The square was emptying and the police finally seemed to be getting their act together and were directing people away from the square, mainly to the north, either side of the National Gallery. He shook his head in amazement when he saw there were people moving among the dead and injured, not helping but videoing and taking photographs on their phones.

Major Gannon joined him, walking so softly that Pritchard was only aware of his presence when he appeared at his shoulder. 'This is not something we've seen from ISIS before,' said the Major quietly. 'There's a military precision about this. And the timing was almost perfect in terms of maximising casualties.'

'That's what I was thinking,' said Pritchard.

'How did we not know about the explosives?' asked Gannon. 'I thought the whole cell was under surveillance.'

'So did I, Major,' said Pritchard. 'So did I.'

Martin Williams turned down the volume of the television and tossed the remote onto the coffee table. Sky News was on and they were bringing in a succession of so-called experts, none of whom had a clue what had happened but who were clearly being paid by the word. Two of the 'experts' had referred to the Real IRA and waffled on about Irish independence post-Brexit and another had used ISIS and Al-Qaeda interchangeably as if they were the same thing. 'Where do they get these people from?' he muttered.

'They've got to fill air time and anything will do,' said Melissa Schofield, who was sitting in a winged leather chair looking through French windows at the garden. 'Nature and the media abhor a vacuum.' Schofield was in her fifties, her greying hair had a lustrous shine to it and she usually had a half-smile that many an opponent had misread over the years. She looked at her watch, a rose gold Rolex. 'Martin, do me a favour and give Ken Reid a call. Make sure that they really are delivering Abbas as they promised.'

They were in an MI6 safe house in Hampstead, awaiting the arrival of Mo Uthman and for MI5 to deliver their agent, Abdul Abbas, who had been taken from Trafalgar Square in a black cab. Schofield wasn't happy about leaving MI6 headquarters in Vauxhall Cross, but following the bombings a crowd of photographers and TV crews had gathered outside and she didn't want Uthman or Abbas or anyone else involved in the operation to be spotted. She had left the building in the back of a courier van and planned to stay in the safe house for the next few days. She had already phoned Mo Uthman and given him the address of the safe house. Uthman was jittery and that was to be expected, but Schofield had managed to calm him down. Uthman was young and relatively inexperienced but had done a first-class job shadowing the jihadists when they had come over from Calais and set up in Birmingham. He was clearly worried that he was going to be blamed for the bombings, but Schofield had assured him that he was worrying unnecessarily. Schofield had been watching over his shoulder every step of the way and he hadn't put a foot wrong. What had happened was a tragedy, but it wasn't Uthman's fault. Abbas would need to see a friendly face when he eventually arrived at the safe house, so Uthman had to be there.

'You think they might renege?' asked Williams.

Schofield waved at the television. 'I hope not, but someone is going to have to take the blame for that and Abdul Abbas might well know what went wrong. Whoever has Abbas controls how his information is released.'

Williams stood up and made the call, but before Reid could answer, two young men in dark suits appeared carrying trays. One had four mugs on it, the other two plates of biscuits, a milk jug and a sugar bowl. Williams headed out into the hall to continue the conversation.

'We found biscuits,' said the man carrying the tray with the mugs. Stephen Collins was in his thirties, tall with soft features and a voice so feminine that he was often mistaken for a woman on the phone. He was one of MI6's top analysts with an encyclopaedic knowledge of fundamentalist terrorism.

His colleague with the biscuit tray was Peter McKie, one of MI6's's surveillance experts. Early on in the operation McKie had been in Birmingham leading one of three teams that had been running 24/7 surveillance on the jihadists. McKie was a former Metropolitan Police surveillance expert who had retired after almost thirty years' service, deferred his pension and started doing exactly the same work for MI6 at an improved salary. His left hand was badly scarred, the result of an acid attack when he was a beat cop in Tower Hamlets, and he usually wore a black glove to hide it as people had a tendency to stare when they first saw it.

'Excellent,' said Schofield. 'Too much to hope for Hobnobs, I suppose?'

'Chocolate bourbons and plain digestives,' said McKie.

'Better than nothing, I suppose,' said Schofield. 'Which coffee is mine?'

'They're all the same, ma'am,' said Collins. 'Your call.'

Schofield leaned forward, poured plenty of milk into one of the mugs, then picked it up and took a chocolate bourbon. She was just settling back into her chair when Williams returned from the hall. 'He should be here in the next ten minutes,' he said. 'There was some traffic hold-up, but he's on his way.'

'Excellent,' said Schofield.

'Ken says that they haven't told Abbas about the bombs,' said Williams, sitting back down on the sofa. 'They got him out of the square and off to an MI5 safe house before the bombs went off. They haven't told him, to see how he'd react. So far it looks as if he assumes that it's been a successful operation. He keeps asking when he'll get his British passport.'

'Right, well when he gets here we'll continue in that vein,' said Schofield. She looked over at McKie and Collins who had taken their coffees over to a dining table. 'Stephen, Peter, we don't let Abbas know about the bombs. I'll tell him when I think the time is right.' The two men nodded.

The doorbell rang. Williams got off the sofa and went into the hall. There was an intercom unit on the wall with a screen showing the view from a CCTV camera covering the front entrance. 'It's Mo,' said Williams.

'About bloody time,' said Schofield.

Williams opened the front door. Mo Uthman was there wearing a dark green beanie hat and a black North Face jacket. He had a Nike backpack over one shoulder and he unslung it and held it across his chest as he walked inside. 'Hi, Martin,' said Uthman. 'I'm sorry about before. I shouldn't have lost my temper the way I did.'

'We were all under a lot of stress,' said Williams, closing the door. 'Where did you go?'

'I walked around for a bit, then I went home. Then Melissa phoned me. Is she here?'

Williams pointed at the living room door. 'In there.'

Uthman took a deep breath. 'Is she angry with me?'

Williams smiled. 'You know Melissa. She never loses her temper.'

Uthman nodded and took a deep breath. Williams patted him on the shoulder. 'She doesn't blame you for this. She really doesn't.'

Uthman exhaled. 'Okay,' he said. 'What about Abdul?'

'He's on his way. And just so you know, he hasn't been told about the bombs.'

'Why not?'

'Just in case he's in any way involved. We'll be talking to him at length, and if at any point he shows that he knows that there have been explosions, that'll be a red flag.'

'Martin, Abdul is our guy,' said Uthman earnestly. 'He has been right from the start. If it wasn't for him, we wouldn't even know about that cell. He's put his life on the line for us.'

'I understand that.'

'And now you're treating him like a suspect.'

'No, he's being brought here for a debriefing.'

'Except you're hoping to trip him up. Abdul deserves better than that.' He shook his head fiercely. 'This is just unfair.'

'It's a debrief, Mo. We need to know what went wrong and Abdul might be able to help us with that.' He patted him on the shoulder again. 'We'll get through this. All of us. We just need to keep our cool. Okay?'

Uthman nodded. 'Okay, Martin. Yes. I hear you.' He forced a smile. 'Thanks. And again I am so sorry about the way I behaved over at Thames House.'

Williams took his hand off Uthman's shoulder, patted him on the back, and guided him into the sitting room, where Schofield was dipping a biscuit into her mug of coffee. She smiled when she saw Uthman. 'Mo, good man, sit yourself down.' She looked over at Collins. 'Any chance of a coffee for Mo?'

'Of course,' said Collins.

'I'm fine,' said Uthman, sitting down in an armchair and placing his backpack on the floor next to him. Williams went back to the sofa.

'So, here we are,' said Schofield. 'It's been one hell of a day, obviously.'

'Melissa, I have no idea what happened. This has just come out of the blue.'

'Well hopefully Abdul will be able to cast some light on it,' said Schofield.

'He couldn't possibly have known about the bombs,' said Uthman. 'If he had known, he would have told me.'

'I understand that, Mo, but there is no doubt that the bomb attack was linked to the firearms attack. The bombers knew where the armed jihadists would be and that they would drive the crowd towards the south of the square. The bombers knew exactly what was going to happen. The question is, how did they know?'

'I have no idea,' said Uthman. He frowned. 'Are you saying this is my fault? That I should have known that there were going to be bombs? How am I supposed to have known that? I was running Abdul and he didn't know, I'm not bloody psychic.'

'No one is blaming you, Mo,' said Schofield.

'That Giles Pritchard was,' said Uthman. 'He's definitely got it in for me.'

'Well I'm not Giles Pritchard,' said Schofield. 'Nobody here has got it in for you.'

'I was the one who identified this cell, and I was the one running Abdul,' said Uthman. 'If there was someone else planning a bombing campaign linked to my cell, surveillance should have picked it up, right?' When no one answered, Uthman looked over at Peter McKie. 'You were on surveillance, Peter. Did anyone, ever, mention bombs?'

'No,' said McKie, clearly reluctant to be drawn into the conversation.

'And they didn't mention Trafalgar Square, did they?'

McKie shook his head and looked away. 'No,' he said.

'Exactly,' said Uthman. 'Surveillance didn't hear anything about explosives, and neither did Abdul. As I said, I'm not psychic.'

'Please, Mo, there's no need to be defensive. We're just trying to find out what happened. Obviously if you had known there were going to be explosives you would have told us. And if Abdul had known, he would have got word to you. But clearly someone knew that your cell was going to be attacking Trafalgar Square and had the two bombs ready to go. That suggests they had plenty of time to get their explosives together and to get their vehicles prepared. So the big question is, how did they know when apparently the cell didn't?'

Uthman shrugged. 'Like I said, I'm not psychic.'

'Well let's see what Abdul says when he finally gets here.' She looked at her watch. 'Which hopefully won't be too long. Are you sure we can't get you a coffee, Mo? Or a soft drink?' She looked over at Collins. 'Are there soft drinks in the fridge?'

'Coke, Fanta, and water,' said Collins.

'There you are, Mo. Plenty to choose from.'

Mo shook his head. 'No, really, I'm fine.' He leaned towards her. 'You think Abdul has been lying to us?'

'I don't know what to think. That's the purpose of this debrief. Either Abdul didn't know about the explosion, or he knew and didn't tell you. If at any point he reveals that he knows about the explosions, then we know it's the latter.'

'He was setting us up, is that what you're implying? He was using us? Which means he was using me?'

'It's a debrief, Mo. There's no point in second-guessing what will or won't happen. We're just going to sit down with Abdul and go through it with him.'

The doorbell rang and Schofield smiled. 'Speak of the devil.'

Williams pushed himself up off the sofa and went out into the hallway. 'It's him,' he called.

'I think I will get myself a drink,' said Uthman. He went out into the hallway and along to the kitchen while Williams opened the front door. Williams brought Abbas into the sitting room where Schofield, Collins and McKie were getting to their feet.

Abbas had the hood of his parka up and he kept his head down as he shuffled into the room.

'Abdul, there's no need to worry,' said Schofield. 'You are among friends here. We just need to talk. Why don't you sit down?'

Abbas looked around, then sat down where Williams had been sitting. He pushed back the hood of his parka and looked around. 'Where is Karif?'

Karif was the name Uthman had been using to run Abbas. MI6 officers rarely if ever used their real names when handling agents. 'Karif is in the kitchen getting a drink,' said Schofield. 'My name is Angela, I'm Karif's boss. We just need to ask you a few questions about what happened today. Okay?'

Abbas nodded. 'And then I can get my passport? And a house? Karif promised me a house. In London.'

'We'll start making the arrangements once we've finished our chat,' said Schofield. 'Now, are you okay if we record our conversation?'

'Sure,' said Abbas.

Collins took a small digital recorder from his pocket and walked over to the coffee table. He switched it on and placed it in front of Abbas. As he straightened up, his head exploded and blood and brain matter splattered across the carpet. Schofield's mouth fell open in surprise and then everything went black.

Naomi picked up the bottle and went to pour more wine into Shepherd's glass but he moved it away and shook his head. 'One's enough for me, I'm driving,' he said.

'I'm not,' said Liam, holding out his glass. Naomi poured in the last of the wine. The yacht was still on autopilot, heading on a course parallel to the coast slowly and steadily. They had finished most of the snacks and were preparing to head back to the marina when Shepherd spotted a helicopter heading towards them from the mainland. It was at about a thousand feet and descending in the clear blue sky.

Naomi shaded her eyes with her hand as she squinted up into the sky. 'That's not one of yours, is it, Liam?' she said.

Liam shook his head as he peered upwards. 'It's a Sikorsky S-92, with the Coastguard.'

'It's coming this way,' said Naomi. She looked around. 'I don't see anyone in trouble and there haven't been any emergency calls on the radio.'

The helicopter was still descending and heading in their direction.

'What do you think, Liam?' asked Shepherd.

'No idea. They're definitely coming this way.' He looked over at Naomi. 'We're not doing anything wrong, are we?'

'It might be the wine,' she said, holding up the bottle. 'They might be coming to breathalyse us.' She laughed when she saw the look of confusion flash across his face.

Liam grinned sheepishly when he realised she was joking. 'Good one,' he said.

The waves around them began to flatten under the downwash from the rotors, then the helicopter went into a hover about a hundred feet above them. They craned their necks to see what was happening. A side door opened and a crewman in bright orange overalls and a white helmet appeared. He leaned out and then began to drop down on a winch.

'What is going on?' asked Naomi. 'I'm going to heave to, to make it easier for them.'

As the crewman got closer to the deck, Shepherd and Liam moved apart to give him room. He was turning slowly as he descended and was talking into his radio mic, obviously giving instructions to the helicopter.

The crewman landed, his knees flexing to absorb the impact. He was in his late twenties, not much older than Liam, with freckles across his nose and pale eyebrows. 'Daniel Shepherd?' he shouted, above the noise of the helicopter.

'That's me,' said Shepherd.

'You're wanted in London, now,' he said. He unclipped a harness from his belt.

'No problem,' said Shepherd. He raised his arms as the crewman attached the harness. 'Sorry about this, Naomi,' he said. 'I'll have to love you and leave you.' Shepherd fished his car keyfob from his pocket and gave it to Liam. 'Hopefully see you back in London.'

'What's going on?' shouted Liam.

'No idea. I'm sure they'll tell me when I get there.'

The crewman finished attaching the harness and clipped it to his own. He gave it a couple of tugs to check that it was secure, then used his radio to tell the helicopter crew that they were ready. The line tightened and the crewman wrapped his arms around Shepherd.

Naomi looked at Shepherd in amazement as his feet lifted off the deck. 'Dan, what exactly is it you do for the Home Office?' she shouted.

Before Shepherd said anything he was yanked up into the air. The crewman grinned at him. 'You okay?' he shouted above the noise of the turbines.

'All good!' Shepherd shouted back.

'You look like you've done this before.'

'It's not my first time!'

The winch hauled them up as the helicopter turned back towards the mainland. There was a second crewman waiting at the doorway and he helped Shepherd inside. He unclipped him from the crewman and helped fasten him into a seat. The second crewman closed the door and sat down. Shepherd didn't bother trying to speak, the noise of the rotors and turbines was near-deafening. They were flying over land now and climbing.

The first crewman gave him a headset and Shepherd pulled

it on. The earphones were snug and the noise-cancelling kicked in. 'Thanks for the lift, guys,' he said. 'Does someone want to tell me what's going on?'

'There's been an incident in London and you're needed back ASAP,' said the crewman.

'How did you know where I was?'

'We had a GPS location so I'm guessing they tracked your phone,' said the crewman. 'We had orders to pick you up and take you to London Heliport. There's a bike waiting for you there.'

'What's the incident?' asked Shepherd.

The pilot cut into the conversation. 'Two bombs have exploded in Trafalgar Square,' he said. 'The square has been sealed off and they're still dealing with the dead and injured. It's bad.'

Shepherd stared out of the window as they continued to climb over Brighton, heading north. Nothing he had been working on involved bomb plots or explosives and there had been no chatter to suggest that a major incident was being planned. Large-scale explosions were generally the work of the IRA and Muslim terrorists and both had been quiet during the Covid pandemic. Shepherd wasn't sure why it had been necessary to summon him in on his day off, but he was sure he'd find out soon enough.

London Heliport was eighty kilometres from Brighton and the Sikorsky covered the distance in less than twenty minutes. As the helicopter flew over south London towards the Thames, Shepherd asked if they could do a quick detour over Trafalgar Square.

'I'll have to check with air traffic control, sir,' said the pilot.

'Any pushback, explain that it's an MI5 flight,' said Shepherd. 'Roger that, sir.'

Pushback or not, the helicopter was given clearance to fly across the river and do a circuit over the square. The pilot dropped down to a thousand feet and went into a tight turn, giving Shepherd a view of the square below. Police barricades had been set up on the roads leading to the square and the only people moving about were police or ambulance personnel. There were two blackened areas to the south of the square and several dozen bodies still lying on the ground like broken dolls. Paramedics were trundling trolleys to ambulances waiting outside the square. There was a line of ambulances down the Mall, and slightly shorter lines of emergency vehicles down Whitehall and the Strand. In all there must have been more than thirty ambulances in attendance. More were coming and going but there were no sirens or flashing lights so they were clearly no longer dealing with casualties.

There were craters in the blackened areas that must have been twenty feet across. The bombs had probably been in vans or cars, and the metal and glass would have turned into deadly shrapnel that had ripped through the crowds. There were so many blood-stains around the square that Shepherd wasn't able to count them.

'How many died?' asked Shepherd.

'Sixty-five was the last number I heard,' said the pilot. 'Hundreds more injured.'

'Has anyone claimed responsibility?'

'They're saying ISIS.'

Shepherd gritted his teeth as he stared down at the carnage. What sort of animals would do something like that? And what did they hope to achieve by killing civilians? It defied under-standing. How many families had seen their lives changed forever by the bombs? People had lost loved ones, others would be struggling with disabilities and injuries for decades to come. And for what? He felt his heart start to pound so he took slow deep breaths to calm himself down. Anger wouldn't solve anything.

He sat back in his seat as the helicopter finished its turn over the square and headed back to the river. The pilot began the descent as he flew along the Thames to the London Heliport at Battersea, not far from his apartment. The helicopter circled the heliport and then landed. There was a high-powered Yamaha motorcycle parked by the main building. A man in black leathers wearing a full-face helmet was standing looking at the helicopter, holding a white crash helmet.

'I guess that's my ride,' said Shepherd, unfastening his harness. He took off his headset and handed it to the crewman who was sitting opposite him. 'Thanks for the lift, guys.' He opened the door and jumped out, bending at the waist as he jogged under the still-turning blades. The motorcyclist handed him the helmet without a word and climbed on. Shepherd pulled on the helmet, snapped down the visor and buckled the strap before getting on the back of the bike. The engine roared into life and they sped off.

The biker was clearly a professional, weaving in and out of the traffic as they sped over Battersea Bridge and east along Chelsea Embankment and Grosvenor Road. He delivered Shepherd to Thames House in about half the time a car would have taken. He took the helmet from Shepherd and drove away without a word.

Shepherd went inside, passed through security and headed up to Giles Pritchard's office. Amy Miller, his secretary, was at her desk and she asked him to wait as Pritchard was on a phone call. She waved at a chair but Shepherd didn't want to sit. 'I'm okay,' he said.

'He won't be long,' Amy said. She was in her sixties, with her hair tied back in a tight bun. She always had the look of a stern headmistress but her background was far more interesting than a career in education – she was rumoured to have been one of MI6's top agent-runners in East Germany before the Berlin Wall was torn down.

Shepherd stood looking out of the window until she told him that he could go through. Pritchard was standing behind his desk, his shirt collar unbuttoned and his White's tie at half mast. He ran a hand through his hair and forced a smile when Shepherd walked in. 'Sorry about the short notice but it's all hands to the pumps,' he said. 'Where were you?'

'I was on a yacht off Brighton with my son,' he said. 'Father-son bonding.'

'I'm sorry about that,' he said. 'But you've heard about the explosions in Trafalgar Square?'

'I flew over on the way,' he said. 'It looks bad.'

'It is. Really bad. Sixty-six people dead, several hundred more injured. The explosions seem to be connected to the undercover operation that you were briefly involved in. Remember that MI6 officer who was running the jihadist who came over from France?'

'Mo Uthman? Sure.' Shepherd didn't bother hiding the contempt he felt for the man.

Pritchard held up his hands. 'I know you two didn't get on, and with hindsight maybe you were right. Uthman continued to run his man after you left the operation and today we followed a group of twelve armed jihadists, including Uthman's agent, from Birmingham. Your Credenhill colleagues were involved, under the supervision of your old friend Major Gannon, and we had CTSFOs in attendance. We assumed we were dealing with a relatively straightforward Marauding Terrorist Firearms Attack, and initially that assumption appeared valid. We took down the jihadists and Uthman's agent was removed successfully. It looked like a complete success and then two bombs went off. The first was outside Charing Cross station, which started people stampeding back into the square and then there was a second – larger – bomb detonated in Whitehall. It was a bloodbath.' He shuddered at the memory.

'And the whole thing was co-ordinated?'

'No question about it. The first bomb went off in the path of people fleeing from the shoot-out and the explosion drove everyone back towards the second bomb. The technique that the IRA used to use in the bad old days.'

'And Uthman's agent didn't see it coming?'

Pritchard sighed and sat down behind his desk. 'If he did, he didn't pass that intelligence on to Uthman.'

'And what does Uthman say about that?'

Pritchard looked pained. He leaned forward and linked his fingers on the desk. 'It gets worse, Dan,' he said quietly. 'It gets a lot worse. The head of Six was furious, obviously. She demanded to see Uthman and the agent at a safe house in Hampstead. We delivered the agent, Uthman turned up to meet with Melissa

Schofield and Martin Williams and two of their analysts for a debrief and there was another explosion.'

'What?'

'Everybody in the house was killed except for the agent, who apparently escaped before the explosion. The Press has been told it was a gas explosion, but it was a bomb.'

Shepherd shook his head. 'So what the hell is going on?'

'That's what we need to find out,' said Pritchard. 'This has obviously all been carefully planned. The guns, the bombs, and the attack on the safe house. A lot of time and effort went into this.'

'Did you get a chance to talk to Uthman?'

Pritchard shook his head. 'He pretty much ran out of the operations room once the bombs had gone off. He was pretty sure he was going to get the blame.'

'Well that's a foregone conclusion, isn't it? His agent was clearly in on this from the start. They played Uthman like a one-string fiddle. I knew there was something wrong about his agent. But Uthman was too busy bigging himself up to notice.' He saw the baleful stare that Pritchard was giving him and he folded his arms. 'I know, I know. Hindsight is twenty-twenty.'

'We need to be moving forward on this,' said Pritchard. 'There's nothing to be gained by saying you were right. Though right you obviously were.'

'Do we know where the explosives came from?' asked Shepherd. 'Please don't tell me that Uthman arranged for the explosives and the guns.'

'We don't know,' said Pritchard. 'This was supposed to be a joint MI6–MI5 operation but they kept their cards close to their chest and we know next to nothing about what was going on behind the scenes. They needed us to run the surveillance and takedown today because they don't have the resources, but we were very much in the dark about what else had been going on. And they closed ranks as soon as the shit hit the fan. Melissa Schofield wouldn't answer the phone and Martin Williams was out of the office not long after Uthman left.'

'Why didn't you hang on to the agent?' asked Shepherd. 'You could have interrogated him.'

'He was MI6's agent so I could hardly refuse to hand him over. Much as I would have liked to. It was pretty clear that Schofield was looking for a way for MI5 to take the blame for what happened because the PM is going to want somebody's scalp for this.'

'You said everyone was killed in the safe house with one exception,' said Shepherd.

Pritchard nodded. 'Indeed. MI6 don't know this but shortly before the explosion, the agent was seen leaving the house.'

Shepherd frowned. 'By who?'

'By the driver who had delivered him. Our guy. He didn't leave straight away. He says he was having a cigarette but we checked his phone and he was on a call to his mistress at the time so he was definitely there. He saw the agent leave through the back garden.'

'And he didn't think fit to tell anyone?'

'The way he tells it, he was considering his options when the house went up.'

'Do his phone records confirm that?'

'They do, yes.'

'So what do we think? That the agent set up the whole Trafalgar Square fiasco? I'm going to start using his name, this "agent" thing is getting tiring. His name is Abdul Abbas. So do we think that Abbas set up the bombings in the square and then somehow arranged for the safe house to be attacked, killing the senior MI6 staff?'

'It's a possibility.'

'And if we can prove that, it'll take the heat off MI5, I suppose.'

Pritchard smiled thinly. 'It's more a question of finding out what happened and why,' he said. 'We'll have to move quickly, obviously. We've spoken to Border Force and Abbas's picture and details are at all ports and airports, and the Eurostar. He'll probably assume we'll do that, which means he's likely to have gone to ground. That being the case, we might be able to track him. He left the house on foot, there's CCTV coverage all around that part of London. You've seen him, you've spoken to him, I can't think of anyone better suited . . .'

'. . . to play bloodhound?'

'Exactly,' said Pritchard. 'What I don't want is any form of public manhunt because that will open up a can of worms I'd rather it stayed firmly shut. This needs to be below the radar.'

'And if I find him?'

Pritchard looked pained. 'Please don't say "if", Dan. Let's not jinx it before we even start.'

'When I find him, then,' said Shepherd. 'What do we do?'

'We'll question him. Find out what the hell happened.'

'And what about the police investigation?'

'They'll be investigating the bombings. And we'll be as helpful as we can about the shootings. But they won't be looking at the Hampstead safe house and they won't be aware of Abbas. They don't know who the occupants of the house are; with the amount of damage done identification is an issue. I'm going to have to consult with Number Ten to see how we handle that, but at the moment we are trying to keep MI5 and MI6's involvement out of this.'

'And this safe house? One of ours or one of theirs?'

'Theirs,' said Pritchard. 'The only reason we are aware of it is because we delivered Abbas there.'

'I wonder why they didn't pick him up themselves?'

'At Trafalgar Square, you mean? There were no MI6 personnel there.'

'Afterwards. Once we had him. Why didn't they collect him?'

'It was all a mad rush,' said Pritchard. 'It was quicker and easier for us just to drop him off. We had him in one of our safe houses and we delivered him to Hampstead.'

'And the driver?'

'Solid as a rock,' said Pritchard. 'He's been with us for years and before that was a Royal Protection officer.'

'I'll need to talk to him.'

'Of course.'

'Was anyone with him when he dropped off Abbas?'

'No, there was no need. He was working for us – well, by that I mean he was working for Six, obviously. He wasn't a suspect, they wanted a debrief on their ground and that made sense because they know him and we don't.'

'They didn't want anyone from Five in on the debrief?'

Pritchard looked pained again. 'I was told that it would be better under the circumstances if he was surrounded by friendly faces. With hindsight, obviously, we were lucky that there weren't any MI5 personnel on the premises.'

'Sure, but you can see what was going on, right? They were getting ready to cover their own arses.'

Pritchard nodded but didn't say anything.

Shepherd gritted his teeth. 'People dead in the streets and they wanted to play politics,' he said. 'Unbelievable.' He shook his head sadly. 'Somebody needs to pay for this.'

'And someone will,' said Pritchard. 'But the priority now is to find Abbas.'

'MI6 won't be happy when they find out that you know he's alive and didn't tell them.'

Pritchard shrugged. 'I'll cross that bridge when I get to it,' he said. 'But to be honest, the last thing on my mind at the moment is whether or not MI6 is happy with me or not.'

'Did Abbas have a phone?'

'In Birmingham, yes. But they all gave up their phones when they got into the vans.'

Shepherd narrowed his eyes as he considered his options. 'I'd like to bring in outside help,' he said.

'I'm not sure that's a good idea.'

'My old pal Jimmy Sharpe is with the National Crime Agency so he has a warrant card and has the cop gravitas that a lot of our people lack. I worked undercover with him for the Met and SOCA, but prior to that he was a full-on detective so he knows the drill. If we're going to be asking for CCTV footage, his warrant card will make things much smoother.'

Pritchard nodded slowly. 'And how much of what's happened does he need to know?'

Shepherd grinned. 'Razor is as trustworthy as they come, and takes no nonsense from anybody. If I'm your bloodhound on this, he's your Rottweiler.'

Shepherd heard a horn beep three times and he looked around. A dark green Jaguar was parked on the other side of the road, its indicator lights flashing. Jimmy Sharpe beamed at him from the driving seat. Shepherd looked left and right, jogged across the road, and climbed into the passenger seat. Sharpe was wearing a dark blue suit over a blue shirt and red tie. He had put on a few pounds since they last met and his hair was greyer, but he had the same mischievous smile on his face. 'So why is it I only hear from you when you need something?'

'Didn't you get my Christmas card?'

Sharpe snorted. 'I'm just saying, the odd social call would be nice.'

'Razor, the whole Covid thing put paid to a trip to the pub. You're not in my support bubble.'

'Until you need help.'

'Well, yes. All right, I promise you, after this is done, dinner's on me.'

'The Delaunay?'

'Yes, The Delaunay.'

'Can I have lobster?'

'Bloody hell, Razor, I just need your help, I don't want to sleep with you.'

'And what's with the casual attire?' said Sharpe. 'I feel over-dressed.'

'I was on a boat when the shit hit the fan.' Shepherd looked around the car. It smelled new and the interior was gleaming. 'This is nice.'

'Jaguar F-PACE, no idea what that stands for, it's a nice motor.'

'Forty grand?'

Sharpe chuckled. 'Give or take. My uncle passed away. He'd never had kids and I was his closest relative.'

'Sorry for your loss.'

Sharpe shrugged. 'It wasn't really a loss, to be fair. Hadn't seen him for going on thirty years. He got Covid and I couldn't have seen him even if I wanted. But he left a will and gave everything to me. A couple of hundred grand once all his bills had been paid. So I treated myself.'

'Why not?' said Shepherd. 'You can't take it with you.'

'Well Uncle Willie certainly couldn't,' said Sharpe. 'Right, where are we going?' He moved his hand towards his GPS but Shepherd shook his head. 'I'll give you the directions,' he said. 'Hampstead. Did you hear about the house that blew up? Gas explosion.'

Sharpe shook his head. 'The only thing on the news today are the bombings in Trafalgar Square. That's what this is about, right?'

'Unfortunately, yes. Head for Hampstead Heath, it's not far from the Vine pub.'

Sharpe put the SUV in gear. As they drove north towards Hampstead, Shepherd brought him up to speed on what had happened at Trafalgar Square and later at the Hampstead safe house.

'Why weren't you at the takedown?' asked Sharpe when Shepherd had finished. 'Getting too old for the action man stuff?'

'Thanks for the vote of confidence,' said Shepherd. 'Nah, I got taken off the case a few months ago.'

'You couldn't get on with the Uthman guy?'

Shepherd looked across at Sharpe. 'Why do you say that?'

'Just the way you talk about him. No love lost, right?'

'He was just wrong for the job,' said Shepherd. 'He ticked all the right boxes. Asian. Graduate. Speaks English, Kurdish and Arabic. Said all the right things at his interviews. They rushed to sign him up and then fast-tracked him. At MI5 and MI6 they start the new recruits slowly, training them on the job. You'd have to be there five or six years before they'd even consider to let you start running an agent, never mind recruiting one. But

Uthman was over in Calais within months with a brief to spot ISIS fighters trying to make their way over to the UK. To be fair to the guy, he managed to get his claws into Abdul Abbas pretty quickly. Of course, maybe that's a red flag in itself.'

'What was Abbas's story?'

'He was a Syrian student from a wealthy family and they had paid smugglers to get him out of Syria to France and they were funding his attempt to cross the Channel. Abbas told Uthman that a group of wannabe jihadists had approached him. They were planning to cross the Channel in a small boat like so many asylum seekers, but once they reached the UK they had instructions to go underground and carry out high-profile terrorist attacks. Abbas was horrified by what he heard, but he didn't let on. He made a call to the British Embassy and they passed him on to Uthman. Uthman encouraged Abbas to stay in with the guys, and eventually he became a fully-fledged agent. I got the impression that Uthman had promised him citizenship but he was always vague about what promises he'd made to Abbas.'

The Vine pub was ahead of them and Shepherd pointed which way Sharpe should drive.

'Anyway, Abbas and the jihadists make it across the Channel and get to Birmingham where they lie low. Uthman kept in touch with Abbas and gets enough intel to identify the guys who are supplying the cell with weapons. We bust them and Uthman poses as an arms dealer. That's when I got involved. Six doesn't have the authority to run a major operation on British soil so the head of MI6 approaches my boss and he agrees to help. I pose as an arms dealer with Kalashnikovs from Serbia and we arrange a meet and hammer out a deal for ten AK-47s. All good, everything went as planned, and then just as we're about to leave, Uthman starts talking about explosives, about how I could get grenades and Semtex and all sorts of shit. And he suggested that I knew people who might be interested in financing their group. I was gob-smacked. It came out of the blue, but was as if someone had flipped a switch in his head and he couldn't stop talking.'

'Nerves,' said Sharpe.

'Maybe. But he didn't seem nervous. He did have this nervous tic, though. A tell. When he was unsure of himself and tried to make things up, he'd tug at his earlobe. I spotted it the first time I met him and I pointed it out to him but he wouldn't listen. He was full of himself, didn't think an old fart like me could teach him anything. So he puffs up his chest and carries on like he was some sort of terrorist mastermind. And they were eating it up. I tried to cool things down but he wouldn't let me talk. I mean, Razor, he was barely out of short pants and I've been working undercover for going on twenty years. I tell you, if I'd had an AK-47 in my hands I'd have shot him there and then.'

Sharpe chuckled and Shepherd gestured for him to take a right turn.

'I don't say anything to him, but when I got back to Thames House I complained to my boss. I got taken off the case. It was as if I was the one in the wrong, you know? Okay, I get that he was the main point of contact for Abbas but the guy was dangerous. I was told that MI6 were backing him one hundred per cent so I was thanked for my contribution and told that my services were no longer required.'

'And this chicken has now come home to roost?'

'Either Uthman was lied to, or the agent was being lied to, but either way dozens of people are dead and hundreds are in hospital.' He pointed at a house in the distance. 'That's it,' he said.

'The patrol car and the cop standing by the gate is the clue, I suppose,' said Sharpe, with a grin. He pulled over at the side of the road.

There was another car parked nearby, a large black Lexus. There was a balding man in a grey suit behind the wheel, blowing smoke through the open side window. 'That's Rob Gilkes, the guy who dropped Abbas off today,' said Shepherd. 'Can you have a word with the cop, I'll talk to the driver.'

Sharpe nodded and climbed out of the SUV. He walked over to the house, taking his warrant card from his pocket. Shepherd went over to the Lexus. Gilkes climbed out and flicked away what was left of his cigarette. 'How are you doing?' asked Gilkes.

He raised his right hand and then lowered it as if he wasn't sure whether he should be shaking hands or not. When Shepherd didn't offer to shake, Gilkes settled the matter by putting his hands in his pockets.

'So you dropped the agent off at what time?' asked Shepherd.

'Just after three o'clock.'

'And what time did you see him leave?'

'No more than five minutes later.'

Shepherd looked over at the house where Sharpe was saying something to the uniformed cop. 'From the back of the house, right?' From where they were standing, all they could see was the knee-high wall topped with railings, the gate where the cop was standing, and the front of the house, a two-storey Victorian detached house with large chimneys. 'Where were you?'

Gilkes pointed to the right of the gate. 'I pulled up there. I escorted the principal to the front door and he went inside. I went back to the car and lit a cigarette.'

'And used your phone?'

Gilkes winced. 'They checked, yeah?'

'People died, of course they checked.'

'So you know, then. I was talking to the girlfriend. There was only an hour or so to go on my shift and if I headed back right away, there was a chance they'd give me another job so I didn't rush.'

'I'm not with human resources,' said Shepherd. 'I just want to know what happened.'

Gilkes nodded. 'I had a fag and I spoke to the girlfriend. I arranged to go over and see her after work. As I was talking to her, I saw the principal leave by the back door.'

'Alone?'

'Yes. Alone.'

'And how was he when you drove him?'

Gilkes frowned. 'In what way?'

'Was he happy? Sad? Nervous?'

'Well not happy, obviously. Not after what had happened. He looked worried. He was biting his nails.'

'And when you handed him over, was he searched?'

'They shut the door so I couldn't see. Do you mind if I smoke?'

'Go ahead,' said Shepherd. 'Show me where you were earlier.'

Gilkes lit a cigarette as they walked to the gate, where Sharpe and the cop were now laughing, best of friends. 'It hasn't been classed as a crime scene so Dave here says we can have a look around if we want,' said Sharpe.

'There doesn't seem to be that much damage from the outside,' said Shepherd, looking up at the building. 'Have SOCO been?'

'Been and gone,' said Sharpe. 'They're waiting on builders to come in and make the site secure, so until then Dave is on guard duty. Front door is open if you want to go inside.'

Shepherd turned to look at Gilkes. 'Hang on here, we'll just be a couple of minutes.'

'No problem,' said the driver.

Sharpe pushed open the front door. Shepherd's eyes immediately began to water and he had the urge to sneeze. There was ash speckled across the wall to his left but everything was dry. 'So the fire brigade weren't here?' he asked Sharpe.

'According to Dave they turned up not long after the explosion but there was no fire. Just a lot of damage.'

'So they know that it wasn't a gas explosion?'

'I guess so.'

To their right was an open doorway. The door itself was hanging off its hinges and the wood was ripped and torn. Shepherd looked into the room. It had probably been a sitting room but everything in it had been reduced to rubble. The windows had been blown out and a cold wind was blowing in from the garden. The ceiling was blackened and ripped apart, as were the wooden floorboards. There were some pieces of what had once been furniture lying next to the blackened walls but pretty much everything in the room had been destroyed. There wouldn't have been much left of anyone who had been in the room at the time.

'This was one serious bomb,' said Sharpe.

'Yeah,' said Shepherd. 'And it looks as if it was loaded with shrapnel which ripped everything apart. I'm guessing they used a commercial explosive, enough to kill everyone in the room but not bring the building down.' Whatever sort of bomb it had been, it had obviously been professionally prepared because the damage was spread equally around the room. 'Did your pal Dave tell you if they took any bodies away?'

'No bodies, just bits of stuff in evidence bags. Probably enough to carry out DNA analysis but not much more than that. What do you think this was about, Spider? Did they know that the agent would be here?'

'I don't think the jihadists are smart enough for this,' said Shepherd. 'They ended up buying their AK-47s from me, I don't see how they could have got hold of explosives of this quality.'

'You can buy anything on the black market these days. Semtex. C4.'

'But you need the right contacts. And they didn't have them. At least not when I met them.'

Shepherd left the room and headed outside. Sharpe followed him. Gilkes was standing by the garage, still smoking. 'We'll have a quick look around the garden,' Shepherd said to the cop.

He motioned for Gilkes to join them and he walked over, his cigarette cupped in his hand. 'Show me where you were standing when you saw the guy leave.'

'Over there,' said Gilkes, gesturing with his cigarette. He took them out through the gate and along the pavement, looked back at the house, then took a few more steps and stopped. 'Here,' he said.

Shepherd joined him. From where they were standing they could see about a third of the garden, a hedge at the back and a wooden shed.

'And it was definitely him?' asked Shepherd.

'Definitely,' said the driver. 'Blue jeans, and one of those green coat things with a fur-lined hood.'

'A parka?'

'Yeah, a parka.'

'Hood up or down?'

'Up.'

'And was it up in the car?'

'Yeah, like he was hiding.'

'And when he was in the car, did he have a phone with him?'

'I didn't see one. He just sat staring out of the window.'

'Was he carrying anything? A bag? A parcel?'

'No. Nothing.'

'And he left after five minutes, you said?'

Gilkes shrugged. 'No more than five minutes. Four maybe.'

'And how long after that before the explosion?'

'About another two minutes.'

'And what did you do? Did you call three nines?'

'Of course not. I called the office.'

'And after the call, who got here first?'

'What do you mean?' He flicked ash on the road and took a long drag on his cigarette.

'Did Five get someone here? Or did the police or fire brigade arrive? I'm assuming the neighbours would have dialled three nines even if you didn't.'

'It all happened very quickly,' said Gilkes. 'I think the fire brigade were here first but there was no fire. Then our guys turned up in a British Gas van. Then the cops. I was told to get the hell out of Dodge and I went home.'

'You weren't debriefed?'

'I was told to stay home and I stayed there until I got the call to come here and talk to you.' He took a final pull on his cigarette and flicked it into the gutter. 'Am I in trouble, here?'

'If anything we're grateful for you seeing what you saw,' said Shepherd. 'Without you clocking Abbas leaving we'd have assumed they were all dead in there. Okay, let's see if we can work out where he went.'

The three men went back into the garden and around the house. The grass was littered with broken glass from the sitting room windows. 'The bomb was inside,' said Sharpe. 'It wasn't thrown in.'

'You noticed that?' said Shepherd. He grinned. 'You ought to be a detective.'

'Well if your guy didn't take it in with him, and it wasn't thrown through the window, it must have already been inside.'

'Yeah, it looks that way.' Shepherd looked at the driver. 'Show me where he went.'

Gilkes walked across the grass carefully, then stopped and looked around. 'This is where I saw him first.'

Shepherd looked at the back of the house. The only way out was the kitchen door and that couldn't be seen from the road. He went over and turned the handle. It wasn't locked. 'Okay, which way did he go?'

Gilkes pointed to the shed. 'Over there.'

'Did he walk or run?'

'He walked. With his head down.'

'Purposefully?'

Gilkes frowned. 'Purposefully?' he repeated.

'As if he knew where he was going?'

'I'm not sure. He walked in a straight line.'

'Show me.'

Shepherd and Sharpe followed him as he walked slowly across to the shed. 'Then he walked behind it,' said Gilkes.

He stepped to the side so that they could walk past him. There was a hedge behind the shed, separating it from the garden of the neighbouring house.

'Could he have got through?' asked Sharpe.

'He was thin enough,' said Shepherd, kneeling down. He examined the soil and nodded. 'Yeah, he crawled through.' He straightened up. 'Okay, Rob, we're done. We'll take it from here.'

'You're sure? I can stay as long as you need me.'

'No, we're good.'

'And you're serious about me not getting a bollocking for this?'

'You didn't do anything wrong. You delivered him in one piece and once he went through that door he was no longer MI5's responsibility. I get that you should have gone back to base straight away and that they don't like personal calls being made on work time, but if you hadn't stayed we'd never have known what we know.'

'It's just that they haven't told me when I'll be on duty again.' He shrugged. 'I keep expecting them to call and tell me to pick up my P45.'

'I think they just wanted to keep you on ice until I could debrief you,' said Shepherd. He patted the man on his shoulder. 'Don't overthink it.'

Gilkes thanked him and walked back to the gate.

'Does this guy have a mobile?' asked Sharpe. 'GPS would make this so much easier.'

'I'm afraid not. They were all made to leave their phones in Birmingham and the driver didn't see him with one in the car.'

'That's a pity.' Sharpe pointed at the hedge. 'You're not expecting me to crawl through that, are you? This is a seven-hundred-quid suit.'

'And very nice it is, too, Razor. Very sharp. No pun intended.'

'And these shoes weren't cheap.'

Shepherd laughed. 'Why don't you collect the car and drive around? I'll meet you over there.'

Sharpe grinned. 'That works for me,' he said.

As Sharpe walked back to the house, Shepherd got down on his hands and knees and forced his way through the bottom of the hedge. It was a tight squeeze but he managed it. He crawled through into next door's garden, then straightened up and wiped his hands on his trousers. He looked up at the house. There were two windows on the upper floor, blinds down in one, curtains open in the other.

A glass-sided conservatory had been built on the rear of the building. Inside were towering potted ferns around rattan furniture. The kitchen appeared to be empty and Shepherd walked across the lawn towards the path that ran around the house. As he got closer to the conservatory he saw movement inside and he froze. A grey-haired man in a corduroy jacket and a wool tie stood up from a high-backed rattan chair, holding a pipe in one hand and a newspaper in the other. His mouth fell open as he stared at Shepherd. Shepherd stopped and raised his hands to show that he wasn't a threat. The man walked over to a door and slid it open. 'Can I help you?' the man said in a tone that suggested that it was the last thing he wanted to do. He had the voice of a maths teacher and had his head back as he looked down his nose at Shepherd.

'I'm sorry,' said Shepherd. 'I'm with the police.'

'Well you don't look like a police officer,' said the man. 'What do you think you're doing in my garden? This is private property, you have no right to be here.'

Jimmy Sharpe appeared at the side of the house. 'I'm sorry, sir, we're involved in an ongoing investigation.' He walked over to the sliding door and showed the man his warrant card.

The man frowned as he stared at the card as if he was trying to memorise everything on it. 'Is it to do with the gas explosion earlier today?' he asked.

'Were you here when it happened?' asked Sharpe.

'I was at school,' said the man, and Shepherd smiled as he figured he'd guessed his profession correctly.

'Was there anyone at home?' asked Sharpe.

The man shook his head and gave the warrant card back to Sharpe. 'My wife's a nurse, she won't be back for another hour or so.'

'I see you've got a CCTV camera on the side of the house, covering your driveway,' said Sharpe.

The man nodded. 'There was some vandalism in the street a few months ago, an officer from our Neighbourhood Policing Unit couldn't offer us extra foot patrols but he did suggest we got a camera installed.' He wrinkled his nose. 'It makes you wonder why we pay council tax, doesn't it? There weren't any staff shortages during Covid, were there? Hassling dog walkers and stopping us hugging our parents. But tell them that someone is going around scratching cars and do they even bother sending someone around? No, they don't.'

'Do you record from the camera?' asked Shepherd.

'It's downloaded to the internet automatically. And gets stored there. For a month, I think.'

'It would be really helpful if we could see the footage from earlier today,' said Shepherd. 'Obviously we're interested in the time when the explosion occurred.'

The man frowned. 'Do you have a warrant?'

'No. No warrant.'

'I thought you needed a warrant for something like that?'

'Strictly speaking, yes,' said Shepherd. 'And we could get one easily enough, we'd just have to bother a judge and they really don't like being bothered.'

Sharpe took out his wallet and opened it. He fished out a business card. 'What I can do for you is to make a note on the Police National Computer that you, at this address, were helpful to a major inquiry, and that note will flash up in the future if you have a problem. A speeding ticket or a parking offence, anything like that. When your details are checked they'll see the note and they'll hopefully cut you some slack.' He grinned. 'It's not exactly a get-out-of-jail-free card but it's the closest we've got.' He handed over the business card. 'If you want to confirm who I am, there's a number on there you can call and someone at the National Crime Agency will vouch for me.'

'That's like the FBI, right?'

'As good as,' said Sharpe.

The man studied the card, and then nodded. 'I guess it wouldn't do any harm,' he said.

'Here you go, the one in the Greenpeace mug has sugar in it,' said Mr Hargreaves, putting a tray down on the desk. They were in his study, a box room with a desk, filing cabinets and a large day planner on one wall, and a single window over-looking the rear garden. Karl Hargreaves was indeed a maths teacher who taught at a local secondary school and worked as a private tutor on the side. He had been surprisingly helpful once he had seen Sharpe's NCA card and had even provided a plate of McVitie's chocolate digestives along with the two mugs of tea.

'You're a star, Mr Hargreaves,' said Shepherd. He was sitting on a high-backed orthopaedic chair moving the mouse with his right hand as he reached for a biscuit with his left. Sharpe had pulled up a stool and was sitting at Shepherd's shoulder.

'Is it any help?' asked Mr Hargreaves, bending down to look at the screen.

The CCTV footage was downloaded in real time to the security company's server and could be viewed once a username and password had been typed in. The picture was in colour and of very high quality. The camera was aimed at the driveway and would capture anyone entering or leaving. 'It's perfect, thank you,' said Shepherd.

They had started watching from the time that the MI5 driver had said he had arrived at the house. The driveway was empty. A young woman with a pitbull on a lead walked by, left to right. Then another woman walked right to left pushing a baby in a stroller.

'There he is,' said Sharpe, pointing at the screen.

Abbas appeared at the bottom left of the screen. He was walking briskly but without appearing to be rushing. He had his hands in his pockets, his hood up and his head down but the camera angle meant they were only ever going to see his back anyway.

'He came through my garden?' asked Mr Hargreaves.

Shepherd wanted to tell the man to give them some privacy but he had been more than helpful and he didn't want to appear churlish. Besides, they needed to keep on his good side because they didn't want him going to the media with his story.

'It appears so,' said Shepherd. Abbas walked to the gate and turned left, heading in the direction taken by the woman with the stroller. He kept his head down as he walked quickly along the pavement. He wasn't looking around and Shepherd had the impression that he knew where he was going. Once he had disappeared from view, Shepherd clicked the mouse to play the video in reverse.

'Who is he?' asked Mr Hargreaves.

'We're not sure,' lied Shepherd. 'He might have been a homeless person sleeping rough in the garden shed. At the moment we just want to check that he's all right.'

Shepherd let the video rewind until Abbas had vanished. He took out his mobile phone, then clicked the mouse and used his phone to record the picture on the screen as the figure walked back down the driveway and along the pavement.

He clicked the mouse and switched off his phone camera once Abbas had disappeared down the pavement.

'It was a gas explosion, right?' said Mr Hargreaves. 'That's what they said on the radio.'

'That's what we were told,' said Sharpe.

'Was anyone hurt?'

'I'm not sure,' said Sharpe. 'We have just been told to check up on this guy. The explosion is being looked at by a different department.'

'Well he looks just fine, doesn't he?' said Mr Hargreaves. 'Not hurt at all, I'd say.'

Shepherd stood up and put his phone in his pocket. 'Thank you for your help, Mr Hargreaves,' he said. 'We'd obviously prefer it if you'd keep this to yourself.'

'Who would I tell?'

'Well, hopefully nobody,' said Shepherd.

Sharpe stood up, sipped his tea and grabbed a couple of biscuits, then Hargreaves showed them out of the front door.

'Nice to have a member of the public who actually is helpful and supportive,' said Sharpe as they reached the pavement. 'I was expecting the worst, him being a *Guardian* reader and all.'

'And chocolate digestives. That's got to be a first.'

Sharpe popped a biscuit into his mouth and looked down the road as he chewed and swallowed. 'So what do you think?'

Shepherd shrugged. 'Assuming he isn't planning on escaping on foot, there are three options, I guess. If this was planned, then Abbas is heading for an RV where he'll be picked up. Option two, he's running scared and will flag down a taxi. Option three, he uses public transport, which means bus or Tube.' He frowned as he called up a mental map of the area. 'The nearest Tube station heading in this direction would be Tufnell Park. Or if he changes direction and heads down Highgate Road, then Kentish Town isn't too far. Give me a minute, will you?'

Shepherd took out his phone and called Pritchard. 'I need CCTV checking at two Tube stations,' he said. 'Who can I use?'

'I'll get Donna on the case,' he said. 'Let me talk to her and she can call you back on this number.'

Shepherd ended the call. Sharpe was looking down the road. 'Are you okay to walk and come back for your car, or do you want to drive ahead and park?' he asked Sharpe.

'Let's both walk,' he said. 'Two sets of eyes are better than one.' He popped his last biscuit into his mouth and they headed down the road.

As they reached an intersection, Shepherd's phone rang and he took it out of his pocket. It was Donna Walsh. He quickly explained that he needed her to check CCTV footage at the two Tube stations. 'I'll send you a video of him in Hampstead taken a few hours ago. And I'll probably have a few council and company cameras that we'll need to access.'

'No problem, Spider, I'll be here as long as you need me,' she said.

Shepherd sent her the video that he'd taken from the computer screen, and put his phone back in his pocket. 'What do you think?' he asked Sharpe.

'Straight on is the obvious choice,' he replied. 'Depends whether he's running anti-surveillance or not.'

'The hood up and head down suggests he's aware of cameras, but then why would he have taken the route he did through the gardens? He might just as well have gone out of the front of the safe house.'

'Maybe he saw the driver. Maybe he assumed there'd be surveillance at the front of the house. Maybe he panicked.'

'He didn't look as if he was panicking on the CCTV,' said Shepherd. 'He seemed to know where he was going.' He rubbed his chin. 'If he knows we'll track him, then he'll do everything he can to throw us off the track.' He pointed down the road.

'Let's try straight ahead. We'll check the first available CCTV and then we'll know if he turned off or not.'

They continued down the road. They reached a filling station and stood together checking for CCTV cameras. The system was more concerned about monitoring the cars at the pumps than it was about passing pedestrians, but one of the cameras on the roof was pointing towards the road. They went inside and asked to speak to the manager, but the bored gum-chewing woman at the cash register said he wouldn't be in until later that evening.

Shepherd asked if they could take a look at their CCTV footage and she frowned as if he'd asked her to solve a quadratic equation in her head. A customer came in to pay for his fuel and they stood back while she dealt with him, then Sharpe took over, showing her his warrant card and asking her in his sternest voice to call her manager. She used her mobile to make the call and then sullenly handed it to Sharpe. Sharpe explained who he was and what he wanted. The manager wasn't as cooperative as Mr Hargreaves had been and insisted on calling Sharpe's office to check his credentials, but having made the call he was as nice as pie and asked the cashier to let them into his office.

The cashier did as she was told. She didn't know how to operate the CCTV system but Shepherd did, so he sat down at the computer and clicked through the database while the cashier went back to work. There were six cameras covering the forecourt and another four covering the inside of the shop. It didn't take long for Shepherd to locate the camera that was pointing towards the pavement, and he clicked through the timeline to the point where Abbas would be leaving the safe house. He settled back in his chair and folded his arms. The view from the camera covered two pumps at the edge of the forecourt, the near pavement and the road, and two-thirds of the pavement, which is where Abbas would be walking.

Sharpe stood behind his chair and watched the screen. 'I might buy a sandwich,' he said.

'A petrol station sandwich, are you kidding me?'

'I'm hungry. I worked through lunch and then you called. And I missed breakfast.'

'So you're on that five-two diet then. Sort of.'

'You know they're all made in the same place.'

'What are?' asked Shepherd as he stared at the screen.

'Sandwiches. They're made in factories. All the supermarkets get their sandwiches from there, so do the corner shops. A sandwich from here will have come from the same place where Waitrose get theirs.'

'I'm more of a Lidl fan myself,' said Shepherd. 'And I always had you down as a Morrisons customer.'

They stopped talking as a figure appeared in the top right of the screen. But they relaxed immediately when they realised it was a woman. Then a second pair of legs appeared. Another woman, carrying a bag of shopping.

The two women walked across the screen. As they left the field of vision, a man appeared from the opposite direction. They couldn't see above his waist but he was clearly overweight and was walking with a National Health crutch.

Shepherd looked at the time-and-date code across the bottom of the screen. They had been running for six minutes, which is about how long it had taken him and Sharpe to walk to the filling station from the house.

'There you go!' said Sharpe, pointing at the screen. They could only see his trainers, jeans and the bottom of his parka, but it was definitely Abbas.

'Right, so we know he's staying on this road,' said Shepherd. He stood up and headed out of the office. He waited on the garage forecourt while Sharpe bought a sandwich and a bottle of water. Shepherd laughed as he came out of the shop. 'It's not a bloody picnic, Razor,' he said.

'Those biscuits started my stomach rumbling.' He ripped the plastic off the sandwich and held the pack out to Shepherd. 'Go on, you know you want to,' he said. 'Chicken salad. Food of the gods.'

Shepherd laughed and helped himself. The two men crossed

over the road and started walking. There were no turns for five minutes, then they reached a side road. There was no obvious CCTV so they carried on along the main road and came to a row of shops. There was a Santander bank branch with two ATMs. They stopped and Shepherd took out his phone and called Donna Walsh. Footage from bank ATMs was always dealt with centrally, so there was no point in going inside the branch and talking to the manager.

Walsh answered on the second ring. 'Spider, I was just about to call you. No sign of your man at either of the two Tube stations. I had a look at the bus routes that pass through the vicinity and I'm applying for a look-see at buses that were in the area this afternoon. It'll take a bit of time, they're not as efficient as the Tubes CCTV-wise. But I'm on it.'

Shepherd thanked her and gave her the details of the ATMs. She repeated them back to him, promised to get back to him as soon as she could, and ended the call. 'He didn't get the Tube,' Shepherd said to Sharpe.

'Bus, then?'

'They're checking.' He gestured down the road. 'You okay to keep walking or do you want to get the car?'

'I'm good,' said Sharpe. They started walking again. 'This guy, what did you say his name was?'

'Abbas. Abdul Abbas.'

'And what's his story?'

'Syrian asylum seeker. His parents are wealthy and they funded his overland run to France where he was in Calais waiting to get a small boat over the Channel. He fell in with a group of wannabe jihadists who were planning to get to the UK for all the wrong reasons and figured that the intel might have been his ticket to citizenship. He approached the British Embassy and Uthman went to see him. Uthman realised the potential of using Abbas as an agent and persuaded him to stick with the jihadists.'

'So what do you think the bomb was about? The bad guys found out that Abbas was double-crossing them and wanted him dead?'

'They'd want him dead, that's for sure. But how the hell do a group of jihadists in the Midlands go about locating and bombing a safe house in Hampstead?'

'Abbas told them where the safe house was. Or they had a tracking device on him. MI6 thought he was one of their own so they wouldn't have searched him.'

'Except the bomb was inside the house and Abbas didn't take it in with him. So it must have been there when he entered the house. If they knew where the house was, or if they were following the car with Abbas in it, why not just shoot him? Why go to the trouble of a bomb?'

'Maybe they wanted to hit MI6.'

'Yeah, that's what I was thinking. Maybe that's why Abbas got out. Maybe the whole plan was to kill the head of MI6. She's a difficult woman to get to, she rarely leaves the MI6 building unless it's to go home, and her home is supposedly like a fortress.'

'Yeah, I never understood that. Her predecessor was all over social media and was quite happy to be in the papers.'

'Yeah, but Melissa Schofield was different. There were a couple of fatwahs out on her because of anti-terrorism work she was involved with early on in her career and they were never lifted. When she was promoted to head up MI6, various Muslim groups said publicly that they bore her no ill will but the fatwahs are still there. She didn't want to take the risk so she rarely put her head above the parapet.' He sighed. 'It's all conjecture, though. The only way we'll know for sure is to find Abbas and talk to him.'

They reached another crossroads. They stopped and looked around. 'What do you think?' asked Shepherd.

'Straight on is the obvious choice,' said Sharpe. He pointed down one of the side roads. 'The Tube station is that way, but we know he didn't get on the Tube.'

'Straight on it is,' said Shepherd.

They crossed the road and carried on walking. Ahead of them was an apartment block with CCTV cameras on the first floor aimed down at the side of the building and another camera covering the entrance. 'That looks hopeful,' said Shepherd.

They went over to the entrance. There was a keypad and an intercom and a button marked 'PORTER'. Shepherd pressed the button. There was no reply so he pressed again, longer this time.

'Yeah, who is it?' said a laconic voice.

'Are you the porter?' asked Shepherd.

'That's what it says on the button, right? Is it a delivery?'

'No, we're the police,' said Shepherd 'We need to talk to you.'

'Is it about the mugging because I was down at the station two days ago about that.'

'No, this is more recent. Can you come and let us in?'

'Sure.'

The connection clicked and went silent. After a few minutes an overweight balding man wearing a Nike tracksuit and shabby trainers opened the door for them. Sharpe flashed his warrant card. 'Can we take a look at your CCTV footage for today?' he said. 'We're looking for someone.'

'Not a problem,' said the man. 'My name's Noel, I was in the Job myself. Did twenty years, just about, but then retired on a medical.' He headed down a corridor and Sharpe and Shepherd followed him.

'Sorry to hear that,' said Sharpe. 'Are you okay now?'

'PTSD,' said Noel. 'I'm better now, but I'll never be a fan of crowds.' He opened a door to reveal concrete steps leading down. It was well lit but there was a slight smell of damp. He headed down and Shepherd and Sharpe followed him.

'What happened, if you don't mind me asking?' said Shepherd.

'The London riots happened,' said the porter. 'August 2011. I was in Ealing when a mob attacked a pensioner, Richard Bowes. Remember that?'

'I remember the riots but I wasn't in London at the time,' said Shepherd.

There was a short corridor, at the end of which was a fire door with notices saying that an alarm would sound if it was opened. 'You were lucky. They were fucking animals. They stamped him to death when he tried to put out a fire they'd lit in a bin. We saw them do it but we couldn't get to him. The mob held us back.' He shook his head grimly. 'We had to wait for the riot police to push them back before we could get to him with paramedics. The bastards even stole his wallet and phone. I was never the same after that. I still get nightmares. Anyway I'm glad I got out when I did. I've got my pension, this job is easy enough, I get a free one-bedroom flat to stay in and the tenants are all good people. Very generous at Christmas.' To the left of the fire door was a regular door with 'PORTER'S OFFICE' on it. Noel unlocked it and opened it. It was more of a store room than an office, windowless with a metal shelf unit with parcels and mail on it, a double-doored metal cupboard and a desk with a wheeled chair in front of it. 'Nowhere for you to sit, guys,' said Noel. 'I don't get many visitors in here.'

'No problem,' said Shepherd. 'We think the guy we are looking for walked by here at about two-thirty. We're looking for a view of the main entrance.'

The porter clicked onto the mouse and went through to the CCTV server. 'Remember when all this was on tape and you had to get the tapes and physically go through them? Something like this would have taken hours and hours, and now, it's a few clicks of a mouse. There we go.' He sat back to give them a clearer view of the screen. 'So what's he done?'

'We're not sure,' said Shepherd. 'We just need to speak to him. We caught him on tape walking past the filling station up the road, heading this way.'

A woman walked by the door pushing a toddler in a stroller. Then two teenage girls walked past, both with their heads down over their phones. 'That's south, right?' said Shepherd, pointing at the left-hand side of the screen.

'Yup, so if your man was up by the filling station he'll appear from the right side. What is he? IC3?'

The police used identity codes to classify a person's race over the radio. Whites were IC1 and IC2, depending on whether they were north or south European in appearance, and IC3 were blacks.

'IC6,' said Sharpe. Asian.

A man and a girl walked from left to right, his arm around her protectively. 'You said something about a mugging,' said Shepherd.

'Yeah, a resident was robbed at knifepoint outside the building a few weeks ago. IC3, obviously. I had it on tape and he reported it but the cops weren't—'

'There he is,' interrupted Sharpe.

Abbas was walking quickly, his head down and his hands deep in his pockets. Shepherd made a mental note of the time. Five steps and he was gone from view.

'Let me have a look at it again, and if it's okay with you I'll record it on my phone,' said Shepherd.

'No problem,' said the porter. He reran the video and Shepherd captured it on his phone.

'Pity you can't see his face,' said the porter. 'Do you think he's deliberately avoiding the camera?'

'We're not sure,' said Sharpe. 'But it's a bugger, either way.' He patted him on the shoulder. 'Thanks for your help, anyway.'

'Let me know if you need anything else,' said the porter. 'Are you okay to see yourselves out, I've just seen some emails that I have to deal with.'

'Can do,' said Sharpe.

They went back along the corridor, up the concrete stairs, and opened the door to the street. They started walking. Shepherd called Donna Walsh and told her not to bother pursuing the ATM footage. 'I've checked two buses that were in the vicinity and he didn't board them,' she said. 'There are another three possibles that were in the vicinity and I'm getting them checked.'

Shepherd thanked her and put his phone away. Sharpe looked at his watch. 'It's getting late.'

'Have you got somewhere to be?' asked Shepherd.

Sharpe grinned. 'No, I'm good.'

'So long as we can access the camera footage, let's keep going,' said Shepherd.

They started walking down the road. 'You said this guy came over in a small boat?'

'Yeah, you saw the pictures, right, on the TV and in the papers. There were dozens every day, sometimes hundreds,' said Shepherd. 'The French were pretty much helping them when they got to sea, and instead of Border Force turning them back they would bring them ashore, give them a nice cup of tea and take them to a hotel.'

'Weren't they processed?'

'They were fingerprinted, but most of the guys who turn up don't have any paperwork. They give a name and brief statement and that's it. Once they're in a hotel they get interviewed and the asylum process starts.'

'So if they haven't been fingerprinted before, they could say they're from anywhere.'

'Sure,' said Shepherd. 'MI5 has been banging on about this for years but no one listens to them. There are thousands getting in every year, almost all of them men of military age. They all ditch their passports and IDs and spin a story that casts them in the best possible light. According to Uthman's agent, four of them were from Libya, two were Iraqis and the other was a Syrian. They all claimed that they were Christians and that their families had been killed by ISIS. Total bullshit, of course. They were all seasoned ISIS fighters, trained in Afghanistan and who had fought in Iraq and Syria. Between them they'd killed hundreds of people.'

'And Border Force just let them in?'

'That's what they do these days. Innocent until proven guilty.'

'They should put them in camps until they've proved who they are,' said Sharpe. 'Separate the genuine asylum seekers from the terrorists.'

'That's not how it works, Razor.'

'It would be in Razorland.'

'Lots of things would be different in Razorland.'

'You'd love it, you know you would.' He was looking around for CCTV cameras as he talked, his eyes sweeping left and right. 'So these guys came in on small boats and did a runner?'

'They came in on three different boats over two days. Two of the boats crossed without being intercepted and they were collected by the traffickers in Dover. There were two on a boat that Border Force caught, and once they were settled in hotels they were picked up by minibus and driven to Birmingham. If MI6 hadn't been running Abbas they'd have disappeared, but the agent was able to stay in touch with his handler. Uthman.'

'And what did Border Force do when they realised that the men had gone?'

Shepherd shrugged. 'They make a note on their computer and move another migrant into the room. It's a recipe for disaster. And that's what we had today, Razor. Dozens of civilians dead and many many more injured. A total disaster.'

Razor spotted a CCTV camera on the corner of a house, pointing towards the pavement. 'What do you think? Worth a look?'

'Bit close to the apartment block,' said Shepherd. 'Let's keep walking.'

After a couple of minutes they reached a junction controlled by traffic lights. Each traffic light had a CCTV camera mounted on top. 'Perfect,' said Shepherd. He took out his phone, called Donna Walsh and gave her the location of the traffic lights. She promised to call him back.

There was a pub across the road. Sharpe gestured at the building. 'What do you think?'

'CCTV?'

'I was thinking a beer.'

Shepherd chuckled. 'Yeah, why not. There's no point in moving until we know for sure which way he went.'

Shepherd and Sharpe sat at a corner table with their drinks. Shepherd had his regular Jameson and soda with ice, and Sharpe had a glass of Tennent's lager. Sharpe had bought the round and thrown in two packets of crisps. They were halfway through the crisps when Shepherd's phone rang. It was Donna Walsh. 'You're in luck,' she said. 'Two of the four cameras at that junction aren't working but the two that are give us a perfect view of him coming down the road and crossing the junction.'

'Can you send me the video?'

'As soon as I end this call,' she said. 'He's walking from the filling station and the ATMs, he reaches the junction and he crosses to the right. He then stays on that side of the road as he walks away, so he'd be heading west.'

'Brilliant, Donna, you're a star.'

'In view of the fact that he has now changed direction, I'm going to widen the net, bus-wise,' she said. 'If we get anything, I'll tell you right away, obviously.'

Shepherd thanked her again and she ended the call. A few seconds later his phone buzzed and downloaded a five-second video. Shepherd watched it and then showed it to Sharpe. Abbas was still walking with his head down and his hands in his pockets. The camera caught him walking down the pavement, then stopping at the intersection. The light had just turned red and almost immediately he crossed the road. The video clicked to a second view and it showed his back as he walked away.

'This isn't counter-surveillance, is it?' said Sharpe. 'This route isn't to throw pursuers off his trail. He's going somewhere. He's on a mission.'

'It looks that way,' agreed Shepherd. He drained his glass and stood up.

Sharpe took a few last gulps of his beer and followed Shepherd out of the door. They headed down the street, following Abbas's route. There were smaller roads leading off to the right, but Shepherd couldn't see any reason why their quarry would deviate from the main road.

They reached a line of shops – a hairdresser, an off-licence, a charity shop and a cafe. There was a minicab office above the charity shop and there was a CCTV camera mounted above a door with 'HAMPSTEAD PRIME MINICABS' on it. The camera was covering the area around the door but it looked as if it covered most of the pavement. The door that opened onto the stairs was open, so Shepherd and Sharpe went up. There was another door at the top with a small window set into it. Shepherd peered through. It was covered by another CCTV camera. A bearded Asian man was sitting at a desk in front of an old computer, and there were three younger Asians sitting on a plastic sofa playing with their phones. Shepherd tried the door but it was locked. As he raised his hand to knock, the lock buzzed. He pushed open the door and the man behind the counter looked at him over the top of thick-lensed spectacles. 'Cab?'

'Police,' said Sharpe, showing his warrant card. The three men on the sofa immediately stiffened. Sharpe grinned. 'It's okay, guys, nothing to do with your immigration status.'

'How can I help you officers?' asked the man at the computer. His English was good but heavily accented, and Shepherd was pretty sure that he – like his three companions – was from Afghanistan. It was an Afghan who had put a bullet in Shepherd's shoulder many years ago, but he wasn't one to bear grudges.

'We just need a quick look at the footage from the CCTV camera outside,' said Shepherd.

'We wipe it every week,' said the man.

'It's today we're interested in,' said Shepherd.

The man looked pained. 'The quality is not good and it is only black and white.'

'That's okay,' said Shepherd. 'The quality isn't important.'

The three younger Asians had all got to their feet and put their phones away.

'You can tell them it's okay,' said Shepherd. 'We're only here to look at the CCTV footage, we won't be here long.'

The man spoke to them in Pashto but they avoided his look, shook their heads and muttered as they hurried out of the office and down the stairs.

'Sorry about that,' said Sharpe.

The man shook his head. 'They are all here legally,' he said. 'They just don't want any trouble.'

'There's absolutely no trouble,' said Shepherd. 'Just show me the footage from this afternoon and we'll be fine.'

The man nodded and clicked his mouse. He turned his screen

so that they could get a better look. As he had said, the picture was black and white and grainy, but it gave a complete view of the pavement.

'May I?' asked Shepherd, holding out his hand, and the man slid the mouse to him.

Shepherd clicked on the timeline to start the footage from two minutes after the time that Abbas had crossed the road at the traffic light junction. Several people crossed left and right, but no one who looked remotely like Abbas. Cab drivers came and went and two women went in through the door and left with a driver a few minutes later.

Shepherd and Sharpe kept watching but there was no sign of Abbas. Shepherd looked over at Sharpe, who shook his head.

'There is something wrong?' asked the man.

'The guy we're looking for isn't there,' said Shepherd. 'He was Asian, late twenties, bearded, wearing a dark green parka with the hood up.'

'Parka?' repeated the man, frowning.

'A coat. With a hood. And he was wearing jeans. Did you arrange a taxi for anyone at that time?'

'Several. But only two were walk-ins. The girls you saw. And they are regulars.'

'Is it possible that one of your drivers agreed to take him somewhere? He could have spoken to a driver outside the camera range and agreed a fare?'

The man shook his head and threw up his hands. 'Never!' he said. 'They would never do that. Every job has to come through me, they know that.'

'Okay, it looks like we're done,' said Shepherd. 'Thank you for your help and for your time.'

Shepherd and Sharpe went downstairs. The drivers who had been sitting on the sofa were in a huddle outside the hairdresser's, smoking cigarettes and trying to look unconcerned.

'Now what?' asked Sharpe.

Shepherd looked up and down the road. 'I need to talk to Donna Walsh again.'

'We could do that from the pub.'

Shepherd chuckled. 'Yeah, we could.' They walked back in the direction of the pub.

'This guy has never been to London before, right?' asked Sharpe.

'Yeah, he was picked up at sea and taken straight to a hotel. Then a van picked him up and took him to Birmingham. The first time he was in London was today.'

'So he's never been to Hampstead?'

'What are you getting at, Razor?'

'I'm trying to work out where he's going, because from the look of it he's going somewhere. This isn't random, is it?'

'I guess not.'

'And it's not counter-surveillance. Or it hasn't been up until now, anyway.'

'You think that's what's happened? He's cut down one of the side roads to lose us?'

Sharpe shrugged. 'There's a number of possibilities, right? He's kicked into counter-surveillance mode and has cut down a side road. He could have flagged down a taxi. Or he could have crossed the road before he reached the cab office. But if he wants to go somewhere, why not get a mini cab? The office is right there.' Sharpe scratched the back of his head. 'This is making my brain hurt.'

'I'm as confused as you are,' said Shepherd. 'A lot of this just doesn't make sense. For a start, if he was the target of the explosion at the house, you'd expect him to go straight to the cops for protection.'

'Maybe he doesn't trust the cops. Being with MI6 almost got him killed so why would he trust the cops to do a better job of taking care of him?'

'So he's on the run. Okay, but like you said, why didn't he get a cab at the minicab office?'

'Maybe he flagged down a black cab before he got here?'

'I'll get Donna to check that. But then where does he go? He can hardly take a cab back to Birmingham.'

'So the station, then? Trains to Birmingham run from Euston and Marylebone.'

'Plus coaches.'

'Yeah. He's got options.' Sharpe chuckled. 'No one ever said this was going to be easy.'

They went into the pub. The table they had been drinking at was still unoccupied so Shepherd went and sat down while Sharpe went to buy fresh drinks. Shepherd called Donna Walsh. 'We've lost him, within about four hundred yards of the traffic lights,' he said. 'We checked the CCTV of a taxi firm on that side of the road. He could have crossed over the road but if that was his plan, then it would have made more sense to have done it at the traffic lights. So we're thinking that he either went down a side road, or he got into a vehicle. I'm just wondering what our options are?'

'I'm looking at a map now, Spider,' she said. 'These side roads, are they off to the right?'

'Yes. Three of them.'

'They all link up with the same roads, I can check council CCTV. We can assume he'd head south but I can check cameras to the north in case he doubled back.'

'He didn't have a phone with him so he wouldn't have been able to call an Uber, but we were wondering if he might have flagged down a black cab.'

'That would make sense.'

'How would we go about checking that?'

'I can check the CCTV cameras at the junction, and at the next set of cameras down the road. That would show me black cabs moving in both directions.'

'Would you be able to see any passengers?'

'Probably not,' said Walsh. 'But the timings would show me if the cab had stopped between the two cameras and I should be able to get the registration number and maybe even the taxi licence number. Then we could contact the driver for details of his fare.'

'Any idea how long that would take?'

'Checking the footage will only take a few minutes. If there are any cabs I'll know straight away. While I'm doing that I'll get a colleague to start looking at cameras on the other route. Spider, have you considered that his ride might have been waiting for him down one of the side roads.'

Shepherd grimaced. 'No, I hadn't.'

'It's possible that if this was pre-arranged, he went to meet someone down one of the side roads. If that's what happened, it'll get a lot more complicated.'

'Thanks, Donna. Call me when you get something. Anything.'

'I will do,' she said, and she ended the call as Sharpe returned with their drinks and two Scotch eggs.

'A substantial meal,' he said, pushing one of the Scotch eggs over to Shepherd.

He gestured at Shepherd's phone as he sat down. 'What's the plan?'

'Donna's going to do a sweep for cabs.'

'Until then I guess we just stay put,' said Sharpe. He took a sip of his lager.

'We could try checking the other side of the road but my spidey sense tells me he's not heading that way.'

'You weren't bitten by a radioactive spider, were you?'

'Nah, and I can't climb walls. But I've been doing surveillance long enough to know that people don't cross busy roads for no reason. We've lost him.'

The Scotch egg came with a salad and a slice of crusty bread. Shepherd broke off a piece and nibbled it and realised it was actually quite tasty. Sharpe grinned as Shepherd picked up his knife and fork and tucked in. 'You know Fortnum and Mason invented Scotch eggs, back in 1738. They were a luxury snack for wealthy travellers on carriage rides,' he said.

'I did not know that,' said Sharpe. 'But I'm pretty sure that Fortnum and Mason didn't invent the fried Mars Bar.'

Shepherd was eating the final bite of his Scotch egg when his phone rang. He swallowed and grabbed for the phone. 'Not good news, I'm afraid,' said Walsh. 'There were no black cabs travelling along that road at the time Abbas was there,' she said. 'I checked both sides. And I also checked the timings of all the vehicles that passed along the road – either way. None of them appeared to have stopped long enough to pick up a passenger. I also checked the CCTV on the traffic lights further down the road and there's no sign of him on either pavement.'

'Well that's certainly useful,' said Shepherd.

'It means there's a very good chance that he went down one of the side roads,' said Walsh. 'Is it possible that he was meeting someone there?'

'I don't see it,' said Shepherd. 'He doesn't know London and he certainly doesn't know the area. Plus he has no mobile phone.'

'You haven't considered the possibility that he might have taken a phone from the house?'

He groaned. 'No, I hadn't. I was told that he didn't have a phone so I left it at that. But you're right, of course. Can you do a mobile phone sweep, see if any phones left the house at the time Abbas left?'

'I've already started the process,' said Walsh. 'I've marked it as a priority so it shouldn't take too long.'

'Can you start checking for black cabs on the other main road?'

'Of course. And we can check the timing of all the vehicles that passed through the area.'

Shepherd thanked her. 'I think I'll probably head in,' he said. 'I'll see you soon.'

'Head in where?' asked Sharpe as Shepherd put his phone away.

'Thames House,' said Shepherd. 'I think we've done as much as we can here. He didn't catch a cab in this road and he didn't reach the next set of lights, so he must have cut across one of the side roads. That makes six sets of pavements. If we walked them all and found him on CCTV, then all we'd know is that he was heading for the parallel road to this one.'

'We could walk that route.'

'We could, but we wouldn't know if he turned left or right at the end.'

'Right would mean he was doubling back so left is more likely.'

'Do you want to give it a go?'

Sharpe wrinkled his nose. 'I don't know. It's your call. I'm Tonto, you're the Lone Ranger.'

'The problem is that Abbas might have picked up a phone from the house. And if he did, that changes everything. Then he'd know where he was and he'd have a map and he'd be able to call for a lift.' He ran his hand through his hair. 'Walsh is going to check the council CCTV to see if she can spot him on the road. And she can check for black cabs. But if he has a phone . . .' Shepherd shrugged. 'She's going to run a GPS check but that's going to take time.'

'Smart phones are password protected, and I'm pretty sure that the people in that house would all be security conscious. Probably fingerprint or facial recognition access.'

'Sure, but fingerprint access wouldn't be an issue if they were already dead.'

'Except your man left the house before the explosion,' said Sharpe. 'And after the explosion there wouldn't be much left of fingers or faces. Abbas didn't have a gun when he was delivered to the house, so what are you suggesting, that he went Jean-Claude Van Damme on everybody in there, grabbed a phone and left before the explosion? Because that's a hell of a story, Spider.'

Shepherd sighed. 'I know, I know. The only way to find out for sure is to question the guy.' He sipped his drink. 'I guess we've got two choices. We carry on looking for CCTV footage here, or we head back to Thames House.'

'Like I said, it's your call. I'm easy either way.'

Shepherd nodded. 'Let's go back.'

Donna Walsh looked up from her computer screen when Shepherd and Sharpe walked into the operations room. There were two other MI5 officers in the room, sitting in adjacent pods, a turbaned Sikh in his early thirties and a young woman that Shepherd had seen before but never been introduced to. Both were busy tapping away on their keyboards as they looked at their screens.

There was a whiteboard in one corner on which were three photographs of Abbas, a head-and-shoulder shot, a medium shot, and a picture that had obviously been taken from the CCTV camera at the traffic lights.

Underneath the row of photographs was a hand-drawn map of the area, on which the traffic lights and CCTV cameras had been marked.

'Donna, this is Jimmy Sharpe. He's with the NCA and he's been helping me walk the route.' Walsh raised her hand in greeting and Sharpe did the same. Covid had pretty much put paid to handshakes between strangers, though some staffers did occasionally fist-bump or touch elbows. 'Any joy with the phones?' he asked.

'Guntaj has been liaising with the phone companies,' she said.

The Sikh raised his hand, as if there might be some confusion over who was who. 'The phones belonging to Melissa Schofield and Martin Williams haven't been active since the explosion. We've put in a request for Mo Uthman's phone but he was with Vodafone and the person we usually liaise with is on vacation and there seems to be some confusion as to who is handling his work in his absence. There were two other MI6 officers in the house. Their service providers were O2 and I have requests put in for a GPS check. They're usually pretty good at getting back to us so I'm—' He was interrupted by a flashing light on his console. 'Here we go,' he said. He tapped the Bluetooth unit in his ears and began to talk in a hushed voice. He was on the line for less than a minute and then he turned and smiled at Shepherd. 'Both O2 phones were active up until the time of the explosion and have been uncontactable since,' he said.

'So we've only got Uthman's phone to check,' said Shepherd. 'Let me know as soon as you get anything concrete.'

Guntaj went back to looking at his screens.

'We checked for black cabs on both roads,' said Walsh. 'There were only two, and neither stopped. So, what we are doing now is checking every vehicle that passes through the traffic lights to the north and south of the three roads. We're checking the times to see if any of them were delayed long enough to pick up a passenger. It's time consuming, obviously, but it's necessary. And we're also looking for any vehicles that left the area without driving into it – just in case he went to a car that was parked there. Or stole a car.'

'Good thinking,' said Shepherd. 'How difficult a job is it?'

'The inputting takes time,' she said. 'We have to input the registration number of the vehicle entering and leaving the area. Then we have a program that compares the two times. Or flags a vehicle that leaves without entering, i.e. which was presumably parked there.' She looked at her watch. 'Guntaj and Jessica are inputting the numbers, I think we should have them all in within an hour or so.'

'I had another thought on the way over here,' said Shepherd. 'It's possible that he's gone to ground. He could have broken into an empty house or even done a home invasion, planning to lie low for a few days.'

'That makes sense.'

'I'll pop along to see Pritchard and run it by him,' he said. 'Can I leave Jimmy here with you? He doesn't bite.'

'Grab any pod, Jimmy,' said Walsh.

'I wouldn't mind a coffee,' said Sharpe.

'Even better, I was just about to do a caffeine run,' said Walsh. 'You can come with me.'

Shepherd went along to Pritchard's office. Amy Miller was at her desk and she smiled brightly when she saw him. 'He's expecting you,' she said. Shepherd smiled and thanked her, wondering how exactly Pritchard knew he was in the building.

Pritchard was peering at one of the two computer screens on his desk. He waved a hand at one of the two chairs opposite his desk. 'Sit, Dan, please,' he said.

Shepherd sat down, knowing that he wouldn't be in the office for long. There was a sofa by the window and when Pritchard wanted a longer conversation he would sit there. Generally he preferred visitors to perch on one of the two wooden chairs, which were definitely not designed for comfort.

Pritchard took off his wire-framed spectacles and rubbed the bridge of his nose. He was about ten years older than Shepherd and five kilos heavier. He had taken off his suit jacket and loosened his White's tie. 'Bloody nightmare,' he said. 'I've been summoned to Number Ten. But at the moment there isn't much to tell them. I gather Donna's still running registration numbers?'

Shepherd nodded. 'We followed him for about a mile and then the trail went cold. So he's either mobile or holed up.'

'Holed up?'

'He doesn't know the area and as far as we know he doesn't have a phone. If it was me and I was being hunted, I'd find a place to lie up for a while. There are three side roads connecting the two main roads so it's possible he broke into a house, either occupied or unoccupied. At the moment that's just a hunch, but we'll have a better idea once Donna has finished running the numbers.'

'No, that's a good hunch,' said Pritchard. 'I'll get moving on that now. Three roads, so I can send three vans in British Gas livery and six people in overalls, checking for a gas leak. They can check on all the occupants and check the empty properties.' He rubbed the bridge of his nose again. 'Be a lot easier if he has gone to ground, obviously.'

'Here's what I don't understand,' said Shepherd. 'You had the eight guys with guns plus the drivers and mates, all good to go in Birmingham. If you'd moved in then, you could have maybe taken some of them alive. And you could have done that without putting civilians at risk.'

'I did suggest that, but MI6 wanted to let them run to see if any other groups were involved.'

'Who at MI6?'

'It came from the top, obviously.'

'Melissa Schofield?'

Pritchard nodded.

'And what did Uthman have to say?'

'About what?'

'About who else might be involved.'

'From what I was told, he didn't know.'

Shepherd sighed. 'You see, that's not a good enough answer. If you're asked a question like that – is anyone else involved? – there are three acceptable answers. Yes. No. Or, I don't know but I'll find out. It's not good enough just to say you don't have that information. It was his job to go out and get it. Everything that happened today is a direct result of him not knowing if any other groups were involved.'

Pritchard held up his hands. 'I hear what you're saying and I'm not disagreeing,' he said. 'If this had been my operation and Uthman had been reporting to me, yes, I would have told him to put pressure on his agent to beef up the intel. But he wasn't my man and we were only brought in when the jihadists were assembled in Birmingham. And that relationship was soured once you complained about him. At no point did we have access to Uthman or to the agent, not once you were pulled out.' He leaned back in his chair, picked up his glass of water and drank slowly.

Shepherd figured he wasn't thirsty, he was just getting his thoughts in order. 'Do you think I was wrong in expressing my reservations about Uthman?' he asked quietly.

'No, of course not,' said Pritchard, putting down his glass. 'Lives were at risk. Not just yours, his and the agent's.' He narrowed his eyes. 'You're waiting for me to say that you were right and everyone else was wrong.'

Shepherd couldn't help but smile. 'No. That's not it.'

'And that if we had listened to you, no one would have died today.'

'I'm not gloating, why would I when the blood is still on the street? This isn't about me not being listened to, it's about MI6 allowing an inexperienced officer to get out of his depth. Uthman should never have been allowed to run Abbas solo. I said that in no uncertain terms, and I'm the one who got sidelined.'

'It was an MI6 operation, so it's hardly surprising they went with their man.'

Shepherd raised his eyebrows. 'That's a worrying thing to hear.'

'Is it, though? Suppose Uthman had complained about your behaviour? You would have expected me to have backed you up, wouldn't you?'

'If I'd made a mistake, if I had been doing things wrong, then I should have been called on it. If you make a mistake in under-cover work, people die. The men that Abbas was hanging out with were hardened ISIS fighters. They'd have cut off our balls and slit our throats if they'd even thought we were setting them up. We were there to sell them guns, nothing else. Then he went off script and put all of our lives at risk.'

Pritchard held up his hand. 'If it makes you feel any better, Melissa Schofield has paid the ultimate price for her error of judgement.' He grimaced. 'Forget I said that, I've had a stressful day. Give me a minute to arrange a sweep of those roads. What were they?'

Shepherd told him the names of the roads and Pritchard wrote them down on a pad. He picked up his phone and quickly explained to someone in Operations what was needed. When he'd finished he put down the phone, looked at his watch and grimaced. 'And it's about to get even more stressful.'

'Has ISIS claimed responsibility?'

'There was no chatter beforehand but within minutes of the bombs going off they were saying it was their people. No pre-recorded videos from the perpetrators yet but we're expecting them. What's interesting is that they haven't taken the credit for the bombing of the safe house.'

Shepherd frowned. 'But that's a major coup for them, surely? Killing the head of MI6 and four other officers.'

'Exactly. And the fact that they're not claiming responsibility puts us in a quandary. At the moment all we're saying is that there was a gas explosion with a number of so far unnamed casualties. The house was owned through a shell company and there are no names on the electoral register. We haven't yet announced the names of the dead, and we're planning not to.

But if ISIS claims responsibility, then it all gets blown wide open – no pun intended.'

'Is it possible they don't know who was killed? That they don't realise what a coup it was?'

'It's very possible,' said Pritchard. 'It's also possible that the MI6 personnel were collateral and that the plan was to kill Uthman or Abbas. Or both.'

'The bomb was inside the house,' said Shepherd. 'Abbas couldn't have taken it with him. It wasn't thrown through the window so it must have been in the house when Abbas arrived.'

Pritchard took a deep breath and exhaled through pursed lips. 'That's interesting.'

'Exactly. So how could they have got a bomb in the house in advance of Abbas being taken there? Who would have known about the safe house?'

'The MI6 personnel.'

'Uthman?'

'Possibly. So the issue is how ISIS got the bomb into the house.'

'If it was ISIS, of course. The fact that they haven't claimed credit for it suggests otherwise.'

'So you think we're dealing with two unconnected events? That the bombing of the safe house was totally unconnected to what happened in Trafalgar Square?' He shook his head. 'I'm not a believer in coincidences at the best of times. That's why we need to find Abbas as soon as possible. Only he can tell us what happened in there.' He looked at his watch. 'I really am going to have to go.' He stood up and reached for his jacket.

Shepherd got to his feet. 'As soon as there's any news, I'll tell you.'

'Hopefully I'll still be in my job by then,' said Pritchard as he shrugged on his jacket and tightened his tie.

'Are you serious?'

'Someone's going to have to carry the can for this,' said Pritchard. 'That means they want to see someone fall on their sword, and a dead woman can't do that.'

'It wasn't your fault,' said Shepherd.

'And I'll be sure to point that out,' said Pritchard. 'But I can't afford to look as if I'm trying to shift the blame onto someone who can't defend themselves.'

He nodded for Shepherd to leave first and then followed him out of the room, where Amy Miller was standing with his coat in her hands. 'The car's downstairs,' she said, giving him the coat.

'Break a leg,' said Shepherd, and Pritchard couldn't hold back a smile.

By the time Shepherd got back to the operations room, Jimmy Sharpe was halfway through a sandwich. He'd taken off his coat and jacket and taken up residence in one of the pods at the back of the room. He pointed at a second sandwich on the desk in between the two computer screens. 'I got you one,' he said.

'I'm good, Razor, thanks.' He went over to Walsh's pod and she looked up and smiled. 'Well, so far so good,' she said. 'Of all the vehicles that entered the area, all but three left within the time frame we'd expect. Now that was made a bit complicated as some would have been held at red lights, but the traffic wasn't heavy so we were able to identify all those vehicles, and the CCTV footage is good enough to get a half-decent view of the passengers. So we're sure that a black cab didn't drive there and pick him up. Assuming that he didn't have a phone, he couldn't call an Uber.'

'We visited a minicab office and they were sure they didn't pick him up.'

She nodded. 'So that leaves us with two options. Either he was picked up by a car that was waiting for him, or he stole a car. Either way we should pick him up on one of the CCTV cameras.'

'Excellent,' said Shepherd. 'In the meantime, Giles has author-ised a house to house.'

'I gather he's been summoned to Number Ten.'

'News travels fast.'

'The worry is that he'll take the fall for what happened.'

'He's pretty good at fighting his own corner. Best thing we can do for him is to get Abbas.'

'I've got him!' said Guntaj, raising his hand.

'Are you serious?' asked Walsh. 'Good man!'

She hurried over to his pod and Shepherd joined her. 'It's a white Prius. No sign of it entering the area but it left about fifteen minutes after our target walked past the traffic lights.' He pointed at the frozen image of the vehicle waiting at the lights. 'We were lucky, it was held at a red light for about ten seconds.'

Shepherd peered at the screen. The Prius was behind a blue Ford Mondeo which blocked the number plate but they could make out the two people in the front. They were both Asian. The driver was in his thirties with a thick moustache and dark-framed glasses. The passenger in the front seat was a younger Asian with a goatee and a grey hoodie. Shepherd shook his head. 'That's not him.'

'Back seat,' said Guntaj. He clicked his mouse and the screen was filled with a view of the inside of the car. Sitting in the back was Abbas, the hood of his parka pulled down.

Shepherd patted Guntaj on the shoulder. 'Well spotted. Very well spotted.'

'Can we check the owner of the car, and trace it through ANPR?' he asked Walsh.

The National Automatic Number Plate Recognition Data Centre in Hendon, north London, stored data recorded by a network of more than twenty thousand cameras around the country, covering the nation's motorways, main roads, town centres, filling station forecourts and ports. The cameras noted more than a hundred million registration numbers every day and they were stored on the centre's computer for two years, along with the time, date and present location of the vehicle. The intelligence agencies – and police forces around the country – could access the data and use it as part of their investigations. Anyone driving just a few miles would almost certainly be recorded on the system, and a journey of a hundred miles would mean a vehicle would be noted dozens of times.

'Of course,' said Guntaj. He clicked his mouse and slowly went back frame by frame until the Prius was pulling up behind the Ford and they could get a look at the registration plate.

'I'll check the owner,' said Walsh, dropping down into an empty pod. 'You check the ANPR, Guntaj.'

Walsh accessed the DVLA computer and within seconds had the name and address of the vehicle's keeper. Shepherd peered over her shoulder. 'Mohammed Khan,' he read.

Walsh's fingers were already tapping on her keyboard as she searched through MI5's database. Eventually she nodded. 'He's on our watch list but low priority,' she said.

'Well he's obviously gone up a few ranks,' said Shepherd.

'He seems to be mainly a keyboard warrior,' she said. 'But he's posted some pretty graphic decapitation videos and has expressed several views that could see him getting prison time. I'll see if we can get a phone number for him and get a record of his calls and texts.'

Shepherd thanked her and sat down in one of the pods. He logged into the system. As the MI5 logo came up, he thought about Liam and wondered how he was getting on. He was due to rejoin his unit and hadn't been sure when he would be back in London again. Shepherd smiled to himself as he remembered the way Liam had behaved around Naomi. Like a young puppy, eager for approval. He could understand the attraction, Naomi was smart, funny, and drop dead gorgeous. He went through to the Police National Computer and typed in NAOMI CLARKE. There was nothing, not even a parking ticket. He smiled. Good to know that she wasn't a criminal. He cleared the search box and then typed in KINGSTON CLARKE. His finger hesitated over the 'Enter' button. Generally checking the PNC for personal contacts wasn't allowed, but the rules were slightly different for MI5 and MI6 staffers. But that didn't make him feel any better, knowing that he was snooping on the father of the girl his son had clearly fallen in love with. His finger stayed where it was for several seconds, then he snorted softly and logged out of the PNC.

The high point of many a politician or celebrity's life was to turn up at Number 10 Downing Street and to be photographed entering the famous door. But no MI5 employee was ever interested in being photographed, and certainly not after being summoned by the Prime Minister in the wake of a major terrorist incident. Pritchard's driver parked close to the rear entrance to Downing Street. There was a barred gate set into the wall with armed uniformed police officers standing guard. There was another car already parked there – a black Lexus with two men sitting in the front.

Pritchard climbed out and headed for the gate. He took out his wallet, but before he could show his ID one of the armed guards shook his head. 'That's all right, Mr Pritchard, we know who you are.'

One of the guards opened the gate and Pritchard walked into the garden where there were two more armed police. One of the Prime Minister's secretaries was already out of the house heading in his direction, so they had clearly seen him arrive on CCTV.

They met halfway across the garden and then the secretary turned and walked with him back to the house. 'The PM is in the study,' he said. 'He wanted a quick briefing from you and from Julian Penniston-Hill prior to the COBRA meeting later this evening.'

Pritchard nodded. 'Is Julian acting head of MI6?'

'There hasn't been an official announcement but he is effectively in charge, yes,' said the secretary.

'Good to know,' said Pritchard. 'Thank you.' He had never met Julian Penniston-Hill but he had heard of him. Prior to his appointment he had been Director General for Political Affairs at the Foreign and Commonwealth Office for five years and before that he had a distinguished career as a diplomat, serving as British Ambassador to the United Arab Emirates and Egypt. He didn't have much in the way of operational experience but was a skilled manager and adept at the political games necessary to survive in the civil service arena. Pritchard might well be bigger and stronger and have a better right hook, but Penniston-Hill would be the favourite if and when the gloves came off.

The secretary took Pritchard into the house, and down a

corridor to the main hallway. They went up the sweeping staircase past the framed portraits of previous prime ministers and along another corridor towards an open door. Pritchard had been to Number 10 several times but had always been seen in one of the larger rooms – the Pillared Room with its huge Persian carpet on the floor and the portrait of Elizabeth I over the fireplace, and the Terracotta Room, which had been the Green Room when Mrs Thatcher was in residence and the Blue Room before that. This time he was shown into the study, one of the smallest rooms in Number 10, with four high-backed chairs around a small mahogany table. There was an oil painting of a stern Mrs Thatcher looking down from above the fireplace, and the walls were lined with leather-bound books which from the look of them had never been opened, never mind read.

The Prime Minister was sitting in the chair with his back to the fireplace. His dark blue suit was rumpled and the shoulders flecked with dandruff. To his right was Julian Penniston-Hill. He was wearing a dark blue suit that was almost certainly Savile Row and handmade shoes. There was a Prada briefcase at his feet. He smiled when Pritchard appeared in the doorway. Despite the made-to-measure suit, Penniston-Hill had the look of a nightclub bouncer about to ask an unruly customer to step outside.

Standing by the fireplace was the Prime Minister's Chief of Staff, his most senior political appointee. Behind his back he was known as the Grey Man because of his fondness for grey suits, or as The Undertaker, either because of the number of careers he had ended or because he knew where the bodies were buried, depending on who you asked. He had his head down over his tablet and was tapping away as if his life depended on it.

The secretary closed the door behind Pritchard and he realised that there were only to be the four of them at the meeting. The Prime Minister waved at the two empty chairs. 'Take a pew, Giles,' he said.

There were no civil servants in the room. No one from the Joint Intelligence Committee, or the police, or the Mayor's Office. And no one to take notes of what was said. The lack of a notetaker didn't mean that Pritchard would be any less careful in his choice of words. It was common knowledge that a previous Chicf of Staff, having swept the whole building for listening devices, then installed his own, and it was generally assumed that the bugs were still in place and in use.

He chose the seat that faced Penniston-Hill, sat down and placed his hands on his knees, trying to look as relaxed as possible.

'So, this is by way of an informal briefing prior to a COBRA meeting later this evening,' said the Prime Minister. 'I want to get my ducks in a row before we start speaking on the record.' He forced a grin and flicked his blond fringe away from his eyes. Over the years Pritchard had attended several COBRA meetings, and whereas there had never actually been a snake present, various reptiles had shown their fangs. Government crisis response meetings were held in one of several Cabinet Office Briefing Rooms – usually Room A – in the Cabinet Office main building at 70 Whitehall, which was situated behind Number 10. 'What I don't want at the COBRA meeting is for a lot of dirty laundry to be aired. All right?'

Pritchard and Penniston-Hill smiled, but despite the outward appearance of civility Pritchard felt like a bareknuckle boxer who was about to go ten rounds. 'So, what I know at the moment is that there was an MI5 operation that involved following a jihadist cell heading from Birmingham to London. Said jihadists were intercepted at Trafalgar Square by the SAS and CTSFOs and victory seemed to be ours, but then two massive bombs changed everything. We now have eighty-six people dead . . .'

The Chief of Staff coughed to get their attention and raised a hand. 'Ninety-two,' he said, his eyes still glued to his tablet as he leaned against the mantelpiece.

'I stand corrected,' said the Prime Minister. 'Ninety-two dead and many more injured. One of the jihadists was an MI6 agent who was later taken to a safe house where there was a third explosion, killing everybody.' He forced a smile but his eyes were cold and hard. 'So not a good day, obviously.'

He was clearly waiting for them to speak, but Pritchard had

already made up his mind that he wouldn't be the first to open his mouth. In his experience, in any negotiation it was the weaker person who spoke first.

The PM, like MI6, didn't know that someone had walked away from the safe house explosion. But the fact that the Prime Minister had mentioned the agent meant that by not correcting him, Pritchard was effectively lying. And that would only end badly.

Penniston-Hill crossed his legs, a slight smile on his face. He clearly took the same view as Pritchard – that the strong stayed silent – but the longer the silence stretched out the bigger the lie. If Pritchard didn't tell the PM about Abbas leaving the house, there would be hell to pay down the line. 'Actually there was one survivor at the safe house,' he said quietly.

The PM's jaw dropped but Penniston-Hill practically snarled at Pritchard. 'Who?' he said. 'Who survived?'

'The agent. Abdul Abbas.'

'And why am I being told this now? What the hell is going on, Giles?'

The PM stared at Pritchard with ice-cold eyes, the smile now vanished from his lips. 'Yes, that was the question that occurred to me, Giles,' he said.

'It's all happening very quickly,' said Pritchard. 'Our priority was to initiate a search for the agent because the sooner we question him, the sooner we can find out what went wrong.'

'And at no point did you think to inform MI6 that you were searching for one of its agents?' said Penniston-Hill.

'That information wasn't being withheld from you, I can assure you of that,' said Pritchard. 'But all your people were pulled from Thames House after the bombs went off, there were no clear lines of communication.'

'You could have picked up a phone.'

'I really have been working flat out organising the search. Then I was summoned here. And now I'm updating you.'

'Abdul Abbas is an MI6 agent, we should have been informed immediately.' He folded his arms and stared at him crossly.

Pritchard nodded slowly. 'And the fact that he is an MI6 agent rather begs the question of why he went on the run rather than contacting you.'

'Presumably he's in fear of his life,' said Penniston-Hill.

'So why didn't he contact MI6?'

'Because his only point of contact was Mo Uthman, and he's now dead. Or are you going to tell me that he's alive as well?' He shook his head in disgust.

'Only one person left the house, that was Abbas. The explosion occurred shortly after he left.'

'I'm sorry, I'm hearing all this for the first time,' said the PM. 'Abbas? Uthman? Can someone please bring me up to speed?'

'Mohammed Uthman is one of our officers, he recruited Abdul Abbas in Calais and ran him as he travelled to the UK and planned today's attack.'

'And this Abbas is now on the run?' asked the PM.

'He's not a suspect, he's an agent,' said Penniston-Hill.

'Well, that might have changed,' said Pritchard quietly.

Penniston-Hill opened his mouth to say something but then thought better of it.

The PM had folded his arms and there were deep frown lines cutting across his forehead. 'So this Abdul Abbas told your man about today's attack?'

He was looking at Pritchard when he phrased the question, and Pritchard immediately shook his head. 'Uthman wasn't my man,' he said. 'He was MI6 and we weren't privy to much of the intelligence he'd gathered.'

'But today's operation was yours, wasn't it?' said the Chief of Staff from his post by the fireplace. 'MI5 was running the surveillance and interception?'

'Yes. We had been provided with the details of where the jihadist group were meeting and we were tasked with following and intercepting them. But we were brought in very late.'

'How late?' asked the Chief of Staff, looking up from his tablet for the first time.

'Three days ago.'

'And prior to that, you had no knowledge that a jihadist group was planning a terrorist attack in Trafalgar Square?'

Penniston-Hill interrupted before Pritchard could answer, which suited him just fine. The Chief of Staff had asked the question, but he addressed his answer to the Prime Minister. 'If I might, Prime Minister,' he said. 'We worked with MI5 to monitor the jihadists as they travelled to the Midlands. And there was some initial surveillance with MI5 involvement but then once the agent was well embedded we relaxed the surveillance.'

'So effectively MI5 was taken off the case?' said the Prime Minister.

'There was nothing for them to do,' said Penniston-Hill. 'We had an agent in place, so until we had intel on where and when they were going to strike, surveillance was unnecessary.'

'I find that hard to believe,' said the Prime Minister.

'It was Melissa Schofield's decision,' said Penniston-Hill. 'Melissa felt that there was nothing to be gained from intense surveillance until we knew they were ready to move.'

Pritchard had to suppress the urge to smile. Penniston-Hill was already distancing himself from his former boss's decision. That was good news for Pritchard. If Penniston-Hill had nailed his colours to Schofield's mast, then it would become a battle between MI6 and MI5. This way the blame could be shifted to Schofield and if the buck did indeed stop with him, then there was a reasonable chance that Penniston-Hill's appointment could be permanent.

Penniston-Hill flashed Pritchard a tight smile. He was looking for him to acknowledge the favour he had done for him, and Pritchard nodded curtly.

'Abbas told Uthman that they were moving today but that he didn't know where the target was or who else was involved,' continued Penniston-Hill. 'Melissa took the view that we should let them run until we knew the target and whether or not there were other groups.'

'And what about the bombs?'

Penniston-Hill grimaced. 'We had no idea that explosives were in the mix,' he said. 'So far as we knew, we were looking at a Marauding Terrorist Firearms Attack which we had reasonable expectations of managing. As indeed we did. Giles's team did a magnificent job in neutralising the threat when it became clear that Trafalgar Square was the target.' He flashed Pritchard another quick look to check that he was acknowledging his support. He gave him another curt nod. Suddenly they were best of friends. It was unexpected but he wasn't about to look a gift horse in the mouth.

'Except this wasn't about the firearms, was it?' said the Prime Minister. 'With the benefit of twenty-twenty hindsight, it's clear that the guns were to get the crowds stampeding into the path of the bombs.'

Pritchard and Penniston-Hill nodded.

'Which means that there has been a colossal failure of intelligence,' said the Prime Minister. 'Either this agent wasn't aware that bombs were being placed in Trafalgar Square, or he did know and didn't pass that knowledge on to his handler. Either way someone has dropped the ball here.'

Under normal circumstances that would be the point that Pritchard would repeat that MI6 had deliberately kept MI5 out of the loop, but Penniston-Hill had played with a straight bat so he figured the least he could do was to return the favour. 'I think the key is locating Abdul Abbas and questioning him,' said Pritchard. 'Until we question him, everything is supposition.'

'How close are you to finding him?'

'We're tracking him from the safe house via CCTV,' said Pritchard. 'I'm confident we are closing in on him.'

'We have the identities of the jihadists who were killed?'

'We do,' said Pritchard. 'We have had those for some time.'

'Abbas was able to pass on the names and details of all the jihadists to Uthman before they crossed the Channel,' said Penniston-Hill. 'And we were able to track them across the Channel to Kent and then up to Birmingham.'

'We need to show that this was a well-planned operation by a vicious terrorist group,' said the PM. 'We can let Border Force take some of the hit for letting them into the country so easily. We are obviously going to have to sit on the fact that we had an inside man. That must not get out, under any circumstances, and I don't want Abbas's disappearance mentioned at the COBRA meeting. There will be MPs there, the Mayor is insisting that he be allowed in, the Army and the police will be there. It will leak like a sieve so mum's the word. We discuss what happened operationally, and we discuss how we move forward.'

'I'm not sure we can sit on the fact that we had an agent in place,' said Penniston-Hill. 'I don't see how we can explain how we tracked the jihadists from Calais otherwise.'

Pritchard wasn't in the least bit surprised at the way he contradicted the Prime Minister. The PM tended to shoot from the hip and make snap decisions, but those decisions could just as quickly be reversed if he was faced with evidence to the contrary. He had never been afraid of a U-turn, but since his brush with the Covid virus he had if anything become even more likely to change his mind. His decisions also depended on who he had been speaking to. It wasn't unusual for him to come down after breakfast with his fiancée and announce a policy, only to modify it beyond all recognition after a chat with his Chief of Staff or one of the other advisers packed into one of Number 10's offices.

The Prime Minister nodded. 'You could say that you were acting on intelligence received without saying where that intelligence originated.'

'There is every possibility we will be asked about the jihadist who was taken alive,' said Pritchard, taking the opportunity to support him. 'Questions are going to be asked about who he was and what has happened to him.'

The Prime Minister rubbed his chin as he processed what he had been told.

'My advice would be to tell the media that we have a jihadist in custody but to tell the COBRA meeting that said jihadist was an MI6 agent,' said Penniston-Hill.

'If we do that, it opens the door to this being a failed intelligence operation,' said the Prime Minister.

'That's going to happen at some point anyway, Prime Minister,' said Penniston-Hill. 'And if it comes out later rather than sooner, those at the COBRA meeting might feel that we had been less than truthful.'

'But it wouldn't be a lie, so much as a lie by omission,' said the Prime Minister with a sly grin, like a public schoolboy who was playing to get away with a late-night feast.

'I have to agree with Julian,' said Pritchard. 'We can tell the media whatever we want but I'd be reluctant to lie to COBRA, by omission or otherwise.'

The Prime Minister flicked his hair away from his eyes, then slowly nodded. 'We can discuss Uthman running Abbas but I don't want anyone knowing that he is now AWOL. You say that MI5 had the jihadists under surveillance, which was true. And that we had an agent in place. But we don't tell the media about the agent. The jihadists were followed to London and intercepted. Then the bombs went off. ISIS has already claimed credit for what happened, we will be pushing the line that we took out the armed jihadists before they managed to kill anybody. The bombs were the work of cowards and they will never defeat the Great British public etcetera etcetera.' The Prime Minister looked at his watch. He obviously had somewhere to go.

'What about the safe house?' asked Pritchard.

'We are waiting to see if ISIS claims credit for it,' said the Prime Minister. 'If they do, they will surely know that they murdered the head of MI6, and that has to be a major propaganda coup for them.'

'When will we be going public about Melissa's death, and the others in the house?' asked Penniston-Hill.

'We're keeping it under wraps at the moment,' said the Prime Minister. 'Luckily Melissa wasn't a fan of social media and TV appearances, unlike her predecessor, so her absence won't be immediately noticed.'

'There were four other MI6 people in the house,' said Penniston-Hill.

'Indeed, but I've been told that identifying the bodies is going to be problematical.'

'They'll have families. Wives. Kids. People can't just disappear.'

'No, but we can buy ourselves a few days by saying that they're working away from London.'

'And if ISIS do claim responsibility?' asked Penniston-Hill.

'Then we immediately confirm the deaths. But until then . . .' He shrugged and left the sentence unfinished. He smiled but his eyes stayed hard. 'I don't want the safe house explosion to be brought up at the COBRA meeting,' he said. 'We need to deal with the explosions in Trafalgar Square, and obviously we will be raising the threat level and we will discuss the extra security arrangements we will be bringing in, but I don't want to muddy the waters by raising what happened at the safe house. I intend the meeting to focus on what happened in Trafalgar Square, how we react to it and what we will be doing to track down the men responsible.'

Penniston-Hill shifted uncomfortably in his seat. 'What do I say if I'm asked where Melissa is and why she isn't at the COBRA meeting?'

'You can say that she's otherwise engaged.'

'Yes, I could stay that. But if you announce in a day or two or three that she was killed, the people at the meeting are going to know that I – he was going to say lied, obviously, but Pritchard saw his eyes narrow a fraction – 'was less than honest,' he finished. 'By omission.'

The Prime Minister muttered something under his breath, and then turned to look at his Chief of Staff. 'It's a valid point,' said the Chief of Staff, letting his tablet swing by his side. 'Lies by omission are still lies and the last thing we want is a *Guardian* journalist getting his hand on the COBRA minutes and seeing that we claimed the head of MI6 was indisposed and not dead.'

The Prime Minister grunted and settled back in his chair. 'It's as if the more I try to keep a lid on this, the more it tries to blow up in my face,' he said.

The Chief of Staff walked to the empty chair, sat down and

balanced his tablet on his lap. 'The problem is that this has been such a colossal failure of intelligence . . .' He looked at Pritchard and Penniston-Hill in turn. 'No offence intended,' he said. 'But if we are seen to be trying to cover it up in any way, it makes it even worse. It seems to me that we need to be completely honest with the COBRA meeting, about the agent and what happened at the safe house. That Melissa is dead and we are currently hunting for the agent. We make it clear that the information is for their ears only and that under no circumstances is it to become public knowledge.'

'Honesty is the best policy?' said the Prime Minister. 'That's not like you.'

The Chief of Staff flashed the PM a tight smile. 'I propose that we be frank, forthright and honest at the COBRA meeting, but I will go through the list of attendees and whittle out anyone with loose lips, or with close contacts with hostile media. You'll be surrounded by friends so nothing will leak.'

'And what will you tell those that you exclude?' asked the Prime Minister.

'The truth, that sensitive security matters are being discussed and their security clearance isn't high enough.'

'They won't be happy to hear that.'

The Chief of Staff smiled slyly. 'They've all got skeletons in their closet of one form or another, so they won't protest too much.'

The Prime Minister nodded enthusiastically. 'Excellent,' he said. He rubbed his hands together and looked at Pritchard. 'Good to go, Giles?'

'Yes. Sure.'

The Prime Minister beamed at him, and then turned his attention to Penniston-Hill. 'And you, Julian? We're good?'

Penniston-Hill smiled but Pritchard could see that his heart wasn't in it. 'Absolutely, Prime Minister,' he said.

The Prime Minister obviously didn't hear the hesitation in his voice because he made a fist with his right hand and punched the air in front of him. 'Excellent,' he said. 'I've another meeting here so if you guys could show yourself out, that would be great. And we'll see you in the Cabinet Office at seven.'

Pritchard and Penniston-Hill stood up. Pritchard reached the door first, opened it and allowed him to go out first. They went downstairs, where the Mayor of London was waiting, shifting his weight from foot to foot as if he needed to go to the bathroom. They went by him without acknowledging his presence. The Mayor wasn't a fan of the intelligence agencies, or the police, and they regarded him with suspicion. Pritchard would have bet everything he owned on the Mayor not being at that evening's COBRA meeting.

'I've managed to get a pretty good timeline for the Prius,' said Guntaj. Walsh and Shepherd hurried over to his pod. He had a map of the UK on one of the screens. 'It headed north and was clocked on the M40 and the M42 and then on the M6 tollway, up onto the M56 and then on the A34 to Levenshulme. It was last seen near Manchester Central Mosque in Victoria Park.'

'Maybe they went to pray,' said Walsh.

'Maybe, but Khan's house isn't far from there,' said Guntaj.'

'Can we check that Abbas is still in the car at that point?' asked Shepherd.

'You think they dropped him off?' asked Walsh.

'I'd rather know for sure he's in the house before we send in the heavy mob,' said Shepherd.

'There were no detours,' said Guntaj.

'And you'd know if they'd stopped at the airport?'

'Absolutely,' said Guntaj. 'There are ANPR cameras all around the airport. They drove right by.' He studied the data on his screen. 'They did stop at the Moto Knutsford service station,' said Guntaj. 'They stopped there for just under fifteen minutes.'

'Enough time for a coffee,' said Walsh.

'And for him to change cars,' said Shepherd. 'What do you think, Guntaj? Can you get eyes on them at the service station?'

'Sure, no problem. There are ANPR cameras all over the place and we can access the CCTV covering the inside areas,' he said. 'The service stations along the M6 have been used as a meeting place on and off for years. Let me see what's available.'

Shepherd went over to Sharpe, who had started on his second sandwich. 'You okay for a run up to Manchester if necessary?' asked Shepherd.

'I hate Manchester,' said Sharpe. 'It's a shithole.'

'Steady, that's my home town you're talking about.'

'Aye, and you were the best thing to come out of it,' said Sharpe. 'I prefer Liverpool to Manchester, and that's saying something.'

'It looks like that's where Abbas is headed, so we might have to go up there.'

'You want me to drive?'

'That would be nice.'

'Mileage?'

'Standard rate.'

Sharpe grinned. 'I'm your man.'

Walsh came over and ran a hand through her hair. 'This might take some time, we can clock the car arriving but we're going to have to find the right cameras and there are dozens to choose from.'

'That's okay, we're making good progress,' said Shepherd.

'You know what's weird?' she said. 'The internet's on fire about the Trafalgar Square bombs and there is so much ISIS chatter that it's deafening. Everyone's talking about it and the various ISIS factions are all rushing to take credit for it. But there's nothing about the safe house. Absolutely nothing.'

'Maybe they're holding back on that?'

Walsh wrinkled her nose. 'But why? There's nothing to be gained by keeping quiet about it. They killed the head of MI6 and several of her top men, that's a major propaganda coup.'

'Maybe they're waiting to make sure that Abbas is in the clear. Then he and ISIS can go public.'

'But there's no chatter at all, Spider. Not a peep. That's unusual.'

'So what do you think, Donna?'

She sighed. 'Maybe ISIS don't know that there was an explosion at the safe house.'

'But they must do. Khan, the guy who drove Abbas up north, normally you can't shut him up, death to the infidels and all that nonsense. He must know what happened.'

'Maybe he was just sent to pick him up. Just transport. Maybe he wasn't given the bigger picture. What about the guy in the front passenger seat? Any joy?'

Walsh shook her head. 'The quality isn't great and facial recognition hasn't thrown anything up. We might have better luck when we get the service station footage.'

'And what about seeing if Khan has a mobile we can track? I know he's probably using a burner phone but he might have a contract somewhere.'

'I'm on it,' she said. 'I'm running the name and address by the phone companies as we speak.' She looked at her watch. 'I wonder how Giles is getting on. Hopefully he still has his job.'

'He'll be fine,' said Shepherd. 'He's a survivor.'

'Well, that could have gone a lot worse,' said Penniston-Hill as they walked across the garden to the rear entrance, where two armed police officers stood with their carbines across their Kevlar vests.

'He's biding his time,' said Pritchard.

'You think so?'

'Someone has to carry the can.' He turned to look at the MI6 head. 'I did appreciate your support in there.'

'Right back at you,' he said. 'I did wonder when I got the summons if he wanted the two of us to slog it out in front of him. He did seem a tad disappointed that we didn't come out swinging.'

Pritchard chuckled. 'I don't see that having our two agencies duking it out helps anyone,' he said. 'What matters is where we go from here.'

'But as you said, someone has to carry the can.'

'It seems to me that it was Mo Uthman who was at fault,' said

Pritchard. 'The jihadists should never have been allowed to leave Birmingham. Either the agent was lying, or he was being lied to. Uthman should have spotted that. Maybe a more experienced handler would have realised that something was wrong.'

'Do you think the PM will leave it at that? Or will he want a bigger scalp?'

'A lot of people died today,' said Pritchard. 'The Media will be looking for someone to blame. And it was our operation. Our men were on the ground.'

'Is that the Royal "we" you're using?'

'I think the Media will be blaming Five. And I think it would be easier for the PM to go along with that.'

'And the only way to defend yourself and your agency is to attack me and mine?'

'I really don't want to go down that route,' said Pritchard.

The two armed officers moved apart. One of them opened the gate and they walked through. They stopped as the gate closed behind them. Their drivers were both waiting outside their vehicles. There was also an armed plainclothes officer standing by Penniston-Hill's car. 'Are you expecting trouble?' Pritchard asked.

'Just a precaution,' he said. 'We don't know if the attack on the safe house was an attack on Abbas or the agency.'

'What did you make of Uthman?' asked Pritchard.

'That's a very good question.'

'And that's a very evasive response.'

They smiled at each other. They were both veterans of the interrogation game. 'Off the record, Giles?'

'Of course.'

'I trusted Mohammed Uthman about as far as I could throw him. I thought he was arrogant, cocksure, loud, he was everything an MI6 officer shouldn't be. I only met him once but it was obvious he had zero respect for Melissa.'

'Because she was a woman?'

He shook his head. 'I don't think it was misogyny, I think he doesn't respect anyone. I think Melissa had a blind spot for him. In her eyes, Uthman was the future of MI6. Multicultural, fluent in several languages, Asian but British to the core. I tried to express my reservations but Melissa wouldn't listen. Uthman could do no wrong. He was fast-tracked from the moment he joined. Usually our entrants are greenhoused for a year or so, monitored and given help and instruction and training where needed. But Uthman pretty much hit the ground running. We had all those Channel crossings in the summer of 2020 and Melissa needed bodies over in France to keep an eye on who was coming over. She pushed for Uthman to go, and to be fair he did a good job. He lived in the woods outside Calais, infiltrating himself into the different groups there, and then he was given Abbas to run. My advice was that we hand Abbas over to a more experienced handler but Melissa said she wanted Uthman to run him. I was fairly forceful but so was she, so having made my reservations known I dropped it.'

'So how did the DV go?'

Developed Vetting security clearance was the highest form of background checking for anyone who worked for MI6, MI5, GCHQ and other government departments that had access to top secret material. In addition to standard security checks – known in the trade as the Baseline Personnel Security Standard – the applicant's criminal record, spent and unseen, was checked, along with a detailed look at their credit and financial history and interviews with referees. Anyone in MI5 and MI6 – including Pritchard – had to obtain a DV security clearance at least every seven years.

Penniston-Hill shrugged. 'Let's just say Melissa was satisfied, but me, not so much.'

'What weren't you happy with?'

'Look, I'm not saying he wasn't MI6 material. In many ways he was. He was keen to help his country, he was enthusiastic, he was fluent in English, Arabic and Kurdish and was almost fluent in Pashto, he sailed through the drug tests, the one he had notice of and the unannounced one a month later. He was fine in all his interviews, always said the right thing. But his background was . . .' He grimaced as he tried to find the right words. 'Let's just say his family situation was a bit nebulous. A bit difficult to substantiate.'

'How so? He's British, obviously.'

'He satisfies the nationality requirement. He's British and his mother was Iraqi-British and had a British passport. His parents sent him to boarding school when he was eight and he studied at Westminster University and did a Masters at Manchester Metropolitan University so he spent most of the ten years prior to his application in the UK, which satisfied the residency requirements.'

'So his parents got him out of the country just before Iraq was invaded?'

'Exactly,' he said. 'They obviously saw it coming and wanted him in a safe place.'

'Why didn't they leave?'

'Money, I think. The family were asset rich but cash poor. The father owned land and factories and was fairly close to Saddam Hussein. Not friends, exactly, but trusted, and presumably paid enough backhanders to the Hussein family to stay in favour. They sat out the invasion on one of their estates outside Baghdad and the father ingratiated himself into the new regime. Then just as Uthman was about to graduate from university, the parents were killed in a car bomb.'

'Aimed at them specifically?'

'Apparently not. They were just in the wrong place at the wrong time. It was 2016, there was a series of ISIS bomb attacks across Baghdad that killed 340 civilians.'

'I remember,' said Pritchard.

'Well they were caught up in that.'

'Any siblings?'

Penniston-Hill shook his head. 'If you're asking if he inherited everything, the answer is yes. But the new regime was a lot less profitable for Uthman's father than the Hussein years so there wasn't much money to inherit. In fact Uthman hasn't been back to Iraq since they died, not even to attend the funeral.'

'And no family here?'

'None. And no real family back in Iraq. He was an only child, his father had a brother but he died not long after Uthman was born.'

'How come the mother had a British passport?'

'She was born in Britain to Iraqi parents. They were Kurds and they were granted asylum and citizenship back in the Seventies. She went back there to teach and met her husband. Her parents are dead. Anyway, the fact there was no family to look at meant it was difficult to get a handle on who exactly Uthman was. For most of his life he was either at school here or at university. All the vetting officers really had to go on was how he handled himself during the interviews, and he didn't put a foot wrong.' He shrugged again. 'Anyway, Melissa said his lack of family was an advantage. He could never be got at or compromised. He was our man. Or Melissa's man, anyway.' He looked at his watch. 'I'm going to have to go,' he said. 'Look, Giles, I have no right to ask this but I would appreciate it if you'd keep me in the loop with regard to Abbas. I don't want any nasty surprises.'

'I'll stay in touch,' said Pritchard. 'And can you maybe have a look at Abbas's file, see if there's anything that would suggest what he's up to.'

He nodded grimly and then walked towards his car. His driver already had the rear door open for him and the protection officer was scanning the area for threats. The protection officer waited until he and the driver were seated before climbing in the back. The car sped off.

Pritchard watched the car go. If Penniston-Hill was playing fair with him, then this wasn't going to be a battle between the two agencies. Abbas had been Uthman's agent and Uthman had been Schofield's man and so long as everyone appreciated that, then the failure of the operation and the attack on the safe house could all be blamed on Schofield. Sure, neither MI5 nor MI6 would come out of any inquiry smelling anything like roses, but Penniston-Hill would in all likelihood be confirmed as the permanent head of his agency and Pritchard would be allowed to stay in his post. But he knew the dangers of counting chickens before they were hatched and crossing bridges before they were reached and all the other clichés that basically said that no matter what he did, there was still a good chance that a lot of shit could hit a very large fan.

Sharpe looked at his watch. He was leaning back in his chair and had his feet up on the pod's desk, in-between the two computer displays. 'How much longer do you think this is going to be?' he asked.

Shepherd was sitting in the neighbouring pod, but unlike Sharpe he was working. Guntaj had patched in the feeds from cameras covering the BP filling station at Knutsford Services and Shepherd was working through them, checking to see if the Prius had refuelled. The picture quality was good but it wasn't always possible to catch the registration plate so he had to check the drivers when they got out to fill the tank and pay. There were a lot of white Priuses around and a lot of them were driven by Asians, but so far he hadn't seen Khan. 'How long's a piece of string, Razor?' asked Shepherd.

'We know where this Khan character lives, right? We go up there and question him, I presume we're not following PACE, right? So we make him talk and Robert's your father's brother.'

'We need to know for sure that Abbas is still with Khan,' said Shepherd. 'If we go up there kicking in doors and he's not there, they'll know we're onto him. At the moment they probably think they're free and clear.'

'And when we get this Abbas, who does the questioning?'

'There's people here who are good at that sort of thing,' said Shepherd. 'But yeah, I don't think they'll be following PACE.'

A white Prius drove into view and he tensed. He clicked the mouse to freeze the image and almost immediately saw that the car had a personalised number plate.

'It all seems well organised, doesn't it?' said Sharpe. 'That car must have been waiting for him, down the road from the safe house. It looks like he went straight to it.'

'Certainly seems that way.'

'So it was planned. Which means that they knew where the safe house was.'

'Or Abbas had a phone that we don't know about.'

'One of those Beat The BOSS phones, shoved up where the sun don't shine?'

Shepherd flashed him a tight smile. 'Maybe,' he said. Most British prisons had installed Body Orifice Security Scanners – basically a metal detector fitted into a chair that would allow the authorities to spot phones and other objects being smuggled in. The BOSS chair was apparently so sensitive that it would pick up a SIM card, but there were some phones that were so small and had so little metal in them that they were said to Beat The BOSS. A miniature phone might well solve the riddle of how Abbas had been able to contact Khan, because there was no way he could have known in advance where he was going.

Another Prius drove up to the petrol pumps but it was red.

'And why Manchester? Why take him there?'

'Because it's such a shithole, you mean? Says the man from Glasgow.'

Sharpe held up a hand. 'I'll not hear a word said against the Dear Green Place.'

'The what now?'

Sharpe chuckled. 'What, have I finally beaten that trick memory of yours?' he said. 'The Gaelic word for Glasgow translates as Dear Green Place. More green spaces per capita than any other city in Europe. And probably more pubs.'

Shepherd laughed and shook his head. 'I'm sorry to burst your bubble but while the name is Celtic, it comes from Glas which means green and Cau which means hollow. So Glas-cau. Green hollow. The experts reckon that refers to a ravine to the east of Glasgow Cathedral, but the jury is out on that.'

Sharpe frowned. 'Are you sure about that?'

Shepherd grinned and tapped the side of his head. 'Never wrong,' he said.

The driver of the red Prius finished pumping fuel and went inside to pay.

'The point I was trying to make before you insisted on giving me a linguistics lesson was that they are taking him to Manchester but he was in Birmingham before,' said Sharpe. He held up a hand. 'And before you offer to tell me what Birmingham means, I really couldn't give a shit.'

'I hear you, and I'd been thinking the same myself,' said Shepherd. 'But if these guys are pros, then they won't be confined to Birmingham. Having said that, when I was involved with the guns thing, the impression I got was that they were all from the Midlands. But now it looks as if he's plugged into a bigger network.'

The red Prius drove off and was replaced by a BMW.

'So that's all you're doing? Watching cars filling up?'

'There's no short cut on this one, Razor,' said Shepherd. 'It's the equivalent of knocking on doors, good old police work.'

They both looked around as the office door opened. It was Giles Pritchard. From the way he smiled, Shepherd figured he was still in a job. He went over to Donna Walsh and she quickly brought him up to speed.

'So at the moment we're confirming that they left the service station together?'

Walsh nodded.

'Okay, in the meantime can we get a surveillance team on Khan's house?'

'Already done,' she said. 'I have two units covering the house front and back. Infrared suggests that there are six people inside but we haven't identified them yet. I took the view that we should confirm that Abbas was in the car all the way back to Manchester before we think about entering the house.'

Pritchard smiled. 'That makes sense. But you need to be thinking about going home and getting some rest. You've been up since first thing this morning.'

'I'm fine,' said Walsh, but there were dark patches under her eyes and there was a vein twitching in her temple.

'We're going to be on this all day tomorrow,' said Pritchard. 'Grab some rest while you can. We can get a couple of reliefs to check the video feeds and they can call you if they see anything.' He waved over at Shepherd. 'You too, Dan. You might as well knock off and get yourself fresh for tomorrow, which I'm sure will be a long day.'

Shepherd waved his arm in acknowledgement, but his eyes were still on the screen. His eyes narrowed as he saw a white Prius at the far side of the forecourt. He leaned closer to the screen. The driver's side door opened and an Asian man in a dark jacket climbed out. As he walked around to the fuel cap, Shepherd's breath caught in his throat. It was Khan. He looked at the time code on the bottom of the screen. It was about fifteen minutes after the car had been clocked arriving at the service station. They had taken a break and were about to resume their journey. Sharpe saw his reaction, swung his feet down and walked around to Shepherd's pod. 'Is that him?'

'Yeah.' Shepherd could see the man in the front passenger seat but the pumps blocked the view of the rear of the Prius. Khan leaned against the car as he pumped petrol and twice he looked at his watch. He finished pumping and went inside to pay. He returned a couple of minutes later carrying a couple of cans of Coke which he passed over to the front passenger before climbing in and pulling the door closed.

The Prius drove away and Shepherd clicked to freeze the image. They had a pretty good view of the rear of the vehicle.

'What do you think, Razor?' Shepherd asked.

'He's not there, is he?'

'Doesn't look like it. Not unless he's lying down on the back seat. What a scamp.'

Shepherd looked up at Pritchard and waved him over. Walsh followed and he showed them the video and again paused as the Prius drove away. 'So he's swapped vehicles,' said Pritchard.

'Looks like it,' said Shepherd.

Pritchard rubbed his chin thoughtfully. 'This makes it a bit more complicated, obviously. We need to find out when they made the switch and the vehicle he switched to.' He turned to look at Walsh. 'Do we know for a fact that Abbas was in the car when it arrived in Knutsford?'

'No, we tracked the car with ANPR.'

'Then we need to be looking back along the route they took, as well as checking all vehicles arriving and leaving Knutsford.'

'I'll get that started,' said Walsh.

'Bring in some of the night staff to do the donkey work,' said Pritchard. 'As I said, tomorrow is going to be a long day and I'll need you all fresh.'

'Okay, as soon as I've briefed the night team,' said Walsh.

Pritchard patted Shepherd on the shoulder as he headed to the door. 'You too, Dan.'

He let himself out and closed the door. 'Looks like he still has a job,' said Walsh.

Shepherd nodded. 'For the moment.'

There was a chill in the air but Shepherd decided to walk from Thames House to his flat in Battersea. It was a little over three miles and after sitting in a pod for most of the afternoon he needed to stretch his legs. He took out his mobile as he walked along Millbank, the Thames on his left. Liam had phoned three times and left a short message saying that he was now back at the flat. Shepherd returned the call. 'Sorry about leaving like that,' said Shepherd. 'I bet Naomi was a bit freaked out.'

'I think she was a bit nervous meeting you for the first time, you being plucked from the boat by a helicopter didn't make it any less stressful. I'm not sure she's going to buy the "I have a boring job in the Home Office" line.'

'Did she say anything?'

'She asked what was going on and I could honestly tell her that I had absolutely no idea. Where are you?'

'Heading back now. Have you eaten?'

'I was waiting for you.'

'Cool, why don't you order a Deliveroo curry or something?'

'Or why don't I cook something? There's loads of stuff in the fridge.'

'I'll need something more substantial than cheesy scrambled eggs,' laughed Shepherd.

'Dad, we share the cooking in our unit. I know my way around a kitchen. There's lamb chops in the freezer and enough veg for a half-decent ratatouille.'

'Okay, but go easy on the rat.'

'Enough with the dad jokes,' said Liam. 'I'll see you when I see you.'

Shepherd chuckled and put the phone away. He kept up a brisk pace as he walked along Millbank, crossed the Thames on Chelsea Bridge and headed through Battersea Park. By the time he reached the apartment, Liam had cooked the chops and true to his word put together a half-decent ratatouille, along with a salad and what looked to be freshly baked baguettes.

'Come on, you baked? Really?'

Liam laughed. 'They were in the freezer, they just needed reheating. Seriously, Dad, you need to start watching what you eat. You're putting on a bit of weight.'

'I'm pretty much the same weight I was five years ago, I'll have you know.' Shepherd went through to the kitchen, opened the fridge door and dithered for a few seconds as to whether he should drink beer or wine. He decided on beer and took two bottles back to the dining room table.

'Maybe a bit less muscle and a bit more fat since then,' said Liam, sitting down.

Shepherd picked up a knife and wagged it at his son. 'I can still give you a run for your money.'

Liam grinned. 'Challenge accepted.'

Shepherd looked at his son's lean, firm body and realised that it was probably a challenge that he'd lose. Liam wasn't a kid any more and his years in the military had filled him out and toughened him up. 'Sadly I'm really busy at the moment.'

Liam laughed and tucked into his meal. 'Remember when I was a kid, you were always running with that old rucksack, full of bricks wrapped up in newspaper. My friends thought you were mad.'

'It was good exercise, good for cardio and it trains your body to carry heavy loads over long distances.' He shrugged. 'That was okay for the fields around Hereford,' he said. 'These days people don't take kindly to men running around with rucksacks on their backs.' He put down his knife and fork and drank some of his beer from the bottle.

'Speaking of which, I guess they pulled you in because of the Trafalgar Square thing?'

'Yeah.' He took another drink from the bottle. MI5 preferred its employees to tell as few people as possible about their jobs, but families were also a difficult area. It would be impossible to live with a family member and to continually lie to them. Friends and acquaintances could be fobbed off with a story about working for an obscure Home Office department, but Liam knew who his father worked for and had done since he was a teenager. 'It's a bloody mess.'

'Can you tell me anything?' He cut into a perfectly cooked lamb chop.

While MI5 was happy enough for family members to know who their employees worked for, they were less keen on operational matters being discussed with outsiders. 'At this stage you probably know as much as I do,' he said, putting down his beer and picking up his knife and fork. 'It's been all over the TV.'

'It looks like an almighty cock-up,' said Liam. 'They clearly knew there was going to be an attack by armed jihadists but they were then blindsided by the car bombs.'

'That's pretty much the way it went down, yes.'

'I was worried that they had hauled you back for some sort of bollocking.'

Shepherd smiled. 'It wasn't my operation. I had a very small role in it early on but then I was pulled out.'

'So they're not blaming you?'

'No. They want me to find out what went wrong.'

'That's a relief.'

Shepherd nodded. 'I'll say.'

'And the guys doing the shooting, they were your old mob?'

'Some, yes, and some were counter terrorism firearms officers.'

'And they had no idea there were car bombs in the square?'

'No one did,' said Shepherd.

'Wow, that's heavy.'

'You're telling me.'

'So someone screwed up and they want you to find out who that someone was?'

'It's more about catching the people responsible. The bombers.'

'According to the TV, the bombers died when the cars went up.'

'Trucks,' said Shepherd. 'They were trucks. The TV got it wrong, the drivers weren't killed in the blasts. They probably detonated the bombs by phone. A lot of planning went into this.'

'ISIS, right?'

'ISIS are claiming responsibility. But we need to know specifically who was behind it.'

'So you can kill them?'

Shepherd grinned. 'So they can feel the full weight of the law,' he said.

'Be easier to just kill them,' said Liam. 'Send in a drone.'

'We can hardly do that if they're in Birmingham, can we?'

Liam looked up from his plate. 'Is that what you think, they were homegrown jihadists?'

Shepherd picked up a chunk of bread and dipped it in his ratatouille. 'Actually, we know for a fact that they weren't. They came in from France. But they were holed up in Birmingham for a while and whoever planned it must have had local knowledge.' He grinned. 'Anyway, the last thing I want right now is to be talking about work. Tell me how you got on with the boat. And tell me more about the lovely Naomi. We're going to have to work out what we're going to tell her about my sudden departure.'

'We can't just tell her that you work for MI5?'

Shepherd shook his head. 'It doesn't work that way,' he said.

'But you've met her. You've seen what she's like.'

'She's lovely. I can definitely see the attraction.'

'No, I mean you can see the sort of person she is. She's not the sort to go blabbing to anyone what you do. You can trust her.'

'I'm sure I can, but that's not the point. Protocol is that we only tell close family.'

'So you're telling me that none of your SAS pals know who you work for now?'

'That's different. The SAS is as tight-lipped as MI5.'

'What about your police friends?'

Shepherd smiled at his son's persistence. He was right, of course. Friends like Jimmy Sharpe knew who Shepherd worked for, but he'd known him for almost twenty years. He had no doubt that Naomi was totally trustworthy, but rules were rules. And as part of those rules he was duty bound to put her name in his contacts log, detailing who she was, where they had met, and what they had discussed. 'I hear what you're saying, Liam. Let's put it this way – if you marry her, we can tell her. So long as she's just a girlfriend, we keep it vague. I get that she realises I'm not your average Home Office desk jockey, but you can tell her that I'm involved in crime scene investigation and they wanted me at Trafalgar Square as soon as possible.' Liam opened his mouth to argue but Shepherd shook his head and continued to talk. 'The thing is, civilians aren't used to keeping secrets. I am, because it's my job. You are because it's been drummed into you over the years not to talk about my work. But Naomi isn't used to that level of deception and it's not fair to dump the responsibility on her. If we told her, she'd have to promise not to tell anyone else. That means we'd be expecting her to lie to her parents, her friends, to everyone she knows. Most people find lying stressful, do you want her to be stressed every time your name comes up?'

Liam sighed despondently. 'I guess not.'

'You can tell her something close to the truth. I'm involved in the Trafalgar Square investigation and they needed me there quickly. If she presses you, then you just say you don't know exactly what I do.'

'So I have to lie to her?'

Shepherd grimaced. 'I'm sorry. It's protocol.'

'Well it's a shit protocol,' said Liam.

'To be honest, if we were at war you'd be subject to the same sort of restrictions. You wouldn't be able to tell anyone where your unit was going or what it was doing. Loose lips sink ships and all that.'

'But we're not at war, Dad.'

Shepherd waved his knife in the air. 'But we are, that's the point. The war against terror is as real as any conflict between countries, so the rules of war apply.' He cut into one of his lamb chops. 'This is bloody good scoff. Sure you're not in the catering corps?'

'Nice change of subject, Dad.'

Shepherd grinned. 'I'm a professional, remember?' They continued to chat as they ate, mainly about Liam's job, though Shepherd wasn't able to relax as he was sure that his phone would ring at any moment.

He went to bed early. Soldiers all over the world would always grab food and sleep whenever they could and it was a hard habit to break. He slept a dreamless sleep until he was woken at just after five o'clock by a call from Donna Walsh. 'Spider, sorry to wake you but I thought you should know they've spotted a hand-over at Knutsford. I'm on my way in.'

Shepherd sat up, blinking the sleep from his eyes. 'Okay, I'll see you there.'

'You don't have to rush, we don't have the vehicle yet.'

Shepherd ran his hand through his hair. 'What do you mean?'

'I've just had a call from the night team. They found footage of Abbas in the restaurant sitting at a table with Khan and another man. Then Khan leaves a few minutes before you caught him at the filling station. So it looks as if Abbas left with the new guy. They're now looking to see what vehicle he arrived in, and that'll take time.'

'That's okay, Donna, I'll come in now.'

He ended the call and rolled out of bed. He shaved and showered and dressed and left a note for Liam saying that he'd probably be out all day, and then called an Uber. He was in the operations room less than half an hour after Walsh had called, but she had still beaten him to it. Walsh was sitting in one of the front pods. There was a young blonde girl sitting in a pod by the wall, sipping Diet Coke through a straw as she stared at her screens, and behind her was a young black man in an Oxford University sweatshirt with the sleeves pulled up. Like the girl, he was staring at his screens with a look of fierce determination.

There was a view of the service station's restaurant area on one of the large wall-mounted screens. Shepherd walked over to get a better look. There were eight tables in view and Abbas was sitting at the one in the right-hand corner. He had his back to the camera and his parka hood up, but there was no mistaking the distinctive jacket. He was sitting next to Khan and they had cups of tea or coffee in front of them. The Prius front passenger was sitting opposite Abbas with a Coke and some sort of muffin, and next to him was a young Asian wearing a black bomber jacket and a white skullcap. He had round-lensed spectacles and a neatly trimmed beard.

Walsh got out of her pod and joined Shepherd. 'We couldn't find any footage of the Prius arriving,' she said. 'The coverage is pretty comprehensive so we think the view was blocked, by a truck maybe. But we did find footage of Abbas, Khan and the other guy walking into the centre and using the bathroom.' She grinned. 'Not actually using the bathroom, obviously, they don't allow cameras in there, but we clocked them going in and out.' She twisted around and called out to the man. 'Dale, would you show us the bathroom footage.'

Dale nodded and tapped on his keyboard. The view on the big screen was replaced with a picture of a corridor. Men were walking back and forth to the entrance to the toilet. Khan appeared, followed by Abbas and the other man. 'That's them going in,' said Dale. He then fast-forwarded the video until Khan reappeared, leaving the men's room. 'And this is them leaving.' After Khan had walked out of the screen Abbas appeared. His hood was up and his head was down. 'He's avoiding the camera,' said Shepherd. 'Either that or he's incredibly lucky.'

'No, it's not luck, he's been well trained in avoiding surveillance,' said Walsh.

Abbas left the screen and then the third man left the toilets. He wasn't so diligent about hiding his face. 'Freeze it there, Dale,' said Walsh.

Dale did as he was told.

'And zoom in, will you?'

The face of the man filled the screen.

'Facial recognition hasn't been much help so far,' said Walsh. 'So far we don't know who this guy is. But Dale then did a search for him across the service station cameras and he found him again in the restaurant area. Dale, please?'

Dale's fingers played on his keyboard again. The image on the big screen showed the three men walk into the restaurant area. As usual, Abbas had his head down.

The image changed to a view midway down the restaurant area. The three men came into view and walked across the screen.

'They walked over to a table where the new arrival was sitting.'

The view that had been on the screen when Shepherd walked in reappeared. Then Dale played the video in reverse. Khan took away the tray of drinks and then reappeared, the men got up and hugged and then the three men from the Prius walked backwards out of vision. Dale stopped the footage and replayed it. Abbas, Khan and the third man walked across the restaurant area to the table where the fourth man was sitting. He got up when he saw them and they took it in turns to embrace. Then they sat down except for Khan who moved out of shot, presumably to get their drinks. Dale waited for Khan to return and sit down before freezing the image again.

'They sat here for five minutes and then Khan and the Prius passenger left,' said Walsh. 'That was about three minutes before the footage you had of them fuelling the Prius. So it's reasonable to assume that Abbas left the service station with the man who was waiting for them.' She waved over at Dale and the young woman. 'Dale and Tessa are looking for his vehicle as we speak. We have footage of him arriving at the restaurant area about half an hour before Abbas et al arrived and now Tessa is searching the car park footage. Unfortunately, the car park cameras don't cover every parking bay. Dale is following Abbas and the new arrival. He's followed them to the exit but no sign of them yet in the car park. We can get the registration number of every vehicle that left the service station through ANPR and we can watch video of all the traffic rejoining the motorway. But without knowing what vehicle they are in, it's a waste of time.'

'At least we know for sure that he didn't go back to Manchester with Khan,' said Shepherd. 'Have you told Giles?'

'I'd thought I'd let him have a few more hours' sleep,' she said. 'He was still here when I left last night. And to be honest, until we ID the vehicle there isn't much we can do. We still have surveillance on Khan's house and everybody is there, so at the moment it's all down to checking the Knutsford footage.'

Shepherd grinned. 'You've obviously got it all in hand,' said Shepherd. 'Why don't I do a coffee run?'

'And a Danish pastry?'

'On me,' said Shepherd. 'Dale, Tessa, what do you want from the canteen?'

It was just after eight o'clock in the morning when Dale spotted footage of Abbas and the man who had been waiting for him at Knutsford Services. The man had parked in an area not covered by CCTV, but they had to walk past two cameras to get to it. Dale called Walsh over and showed her the footage of the two men. They had their backs to the camera but the distinctive skullcap and parka left no doubt. Dale caught them again on a second camera. There was no more footage of them walking but he managed to find them in a car heading for the exit. It was a blue Ford Fiesta. He froze the image and transferred it to the main screen. The driver was clearly the man wearing the skullcap.

Abbas had his hooded head down and his arms folded across his chest. The front registration plate was slightly blurry but readable.

'Well done, Dale,' said Walsh. 'Now let's get started on the ANPR and find out where they went.' She took out her mobile. 'Time to call Giles.'

While she phoned Pritchard, Shepherd sat down in a pod and accessed the DVLA computer. The Fiesta's registered keeper was Hamid Ibrahim with an address in Salford, west of Manchester city centre. It wasn't much more than a mile from where Shepherd had lived as a child. He pulled up a copy of Ibrahim's driving licence and then input the details into MI5's database. He wasn't known to MI5, which made him a cleanskin. He then logged into the Police National Computer, where he was most definitely known with a series of convictions for cannabis dealing and half a dozen motoring offences, including several dangerous driving convictions.

It took Dale just a few minutes to track the progress of the Ford Fiesta. It continued north on the M6 and then turned onto the M56. Shepherd had already realised where the car was going but didn't interrupt Dale as he outlined the car's progress, ending up with it turning into Manchester Airport. The car spent just five minutes at the airport before driving to Salford.

'What flights were leaving at that time of night?' asked Shepherd.

Walsh dropped into her pod and tapped away at the keyboard. 'Aberdeen, Inverness, Belfast . . . and Dubai,' she said. 'I don't think he'll be travelling local.'

'Dubai makes a lot of sense,' said Shepherd. 'Except for the fact that Abbas doesn't have a passport, so far as we know.'

'It's possible he was given one, either by Khan or Ibrahim.'

'Can we check the flight manifest?'

'We can, but it has to be done through Dubai. The London office were less than helpful.'

The door opened and Pritchard walked in. Shepherd realised he must have been somewhere in the building, probably napping on the sofa in his office. He was wearing the same clothes he'd had on yesterday, which also suggested he hadn't been home.

Walsh brought him quickly up to speed.

'What time did the Dubai flight depart?' he asked. 'Emirates, right?'

'It was scheduled for 8.40 p.m. and left at 8.50 p.m.'

'And the flight time is what, eight hours?'

'Landed just after five in the morning, our time.'

'We've got people in the embassy in Dubai, I'll get them on the case. Obviously we need to know if he's still in Dubai or if he's moved on.'

Shepherd was going to point out that there would also be MI6 officers based at the embassy but immediately realised that Pritchard would know that, so he just nodded.

'Right, first things first. We know that the car went to the airport but obviously we need CCTV footage to confirm that Abbas was in the car and that he entered the terminal and checked in for the flight. We can get direct feeds from Manchester Airport, right?'

'Definitely,' said Walsh. 'Live feeds and historical footage.'

'It's a lot of cameras, right?'

'It is, but we know what time he drove into the car park so we have a pretty tight timeline.'

'Okay, but if you need more bodies, let me know.' He looked over at Shepherd. 'I guess the question is whether we lift Khan now or later.'

'Looks as if he carried out his role by delivering Abbas to Knutsford. We need to lift Ibrahim at some point, obviously.'

'Do we know where he is?' Pritchard asked Walsh.

'ANPR puts the vehicle within a mile of his house,' she said. 'Salford.'

'Right, let's get two teams out there – confirm that he's at home and then keep him under observation. When we do lift them, probably best to lift them together.' He looked at his watch. 'I'll be in my office, let me know as soon as we have confirmation that Abbas was on the Dubai flight.'

Pritchard left the operations room and Walsh asked Tessa and Dale to start checking the footage from the cameras inside and outside Manchester Airport as she hit the phones and organised surveillance on Hamid Ibrahim.

Shepherd's mobile vibrated in his pocket. It was Jimmy Sharpe. 'What's the story?' asked Sharpe.

'Things are moving but we're pretty much office-based at the moment. Not much point in you coming in. I know how bored you get stuck inside.'

'I'd rather be with you than have the NCA find something for me to do,' said Sharpe.

'Come on in, then,' he said. 'Things might get more interesting this afternoon.' He ended the call and went to offer his services to Walsh. She waved to a pod and asked Dale to pass over some of the CCTV feeds to Shepherd. There were three passenger terminals at Manchester Airport linked by walkways. Emirates used Terminal One. There were four cameras covering the departures area and they took one each. There was a steady stream of cars and taxis unloading passengers, but not too many to make surveillance difficult.

It was Walsh who spotted the Ford Fiesta. They all went over to watch over her shoulder. The car pulled up, the passenger door opened and Abbas climbed out. He bent down, said something to the driver, then shut the door and turned and went into the terminal. The Fiesta drove off.

'How many cameras are there inside?' asked Walsh.

'In the departures area?' asked Dale. He called up a map of the terminal building and did a quick count. 'Twenty-four,' he said.

'Let's go straight to the Emirates check-in area,' said Walsh.

Dale looked at the map and then tapped on his keyboard.

'On the main screen, please, Dale,' said Walsh.

They all looked up at the main screen. The camera was aimed down above the check-in desks. It showed three check-in desks and the queuing area. 'There he is,' said Walsh. Abbas appeared in the top right of the screen and walked towards the check-in desks. There was a queue of half a dozen people waiting and Abbas joined it. He kept his head down and turned away from the camera. He barely moved, other than to shuffle forward as one by one the waiting passengers moved forward. When it came to his turn, he stepped forward, removing a passport from his pocket.

'That's a British passport, right?' said Dale.

'Freeze it and get close on it,' said Walsh.

Dale did as he was told. It was definitely a British passport he was holding. 'Now how the hell did he get that?'

Dale clicked his mouse and the picture started moving again. Abbas handed over his passport. The check-in officer busied herself on her terminal as Abbas stood with head down. He shook his head, she had obviously asked him a question, probably asking him if he had any bags. He shook his head and then nodded, then reached up with his right hand and tugged nervously at his right ear. Shepherd frowned. The tugging went on for several seconds and then he held out his hand for his passport and boarding pass. Once he had them he turned and walked away.

'Dale, let me see some footage of him walking across the terminal,' said Shepherd.

'What's wrong?' asked Walsh.

'Just give me a minute, Donna,' he said.

Dale consulted his map again, then tapped on his keyboard. A view of the terminal appeared on the big screen, obviously up in the roof showing a large area of the floor. Dale speeded up the footage and then slowed it again as Abbas appeared at the terminal entrance. Shepherd sat back in his chair and watched as the man walked across the terminal. He had his head down and as always the hood was up so his face remained hidden, but Shepherd wasn't looking for facial details, he was watching the man's gait, the way his weight shifted from side to side, the way his shoulders moved, the way the feet turned as they touched the ground. It took the man more than twenty paces to move from one side of the screen to the other, but by the time he was at the halfway point Shepherd knew that he was right. 'That's not Abbas,' he said quietly. 'That's Mo Uthman.'

'Are you sure, Dan?' asked Pritchard. 'Are you absolutely sure?' Pritchard had arrived in the office within minutes of Walsh phoning him and he had watched the man in the parka walk over to the check-in desks. 'You can't see his face.'

'I don't need to see his face. Surveillance is often about recognising the way the target carries himself more than his facial features. Up to now the CCTV has only given us brief looks at him but there's enough footage here to get a read on the way he moves.'

'And that guy moved like Mohammed Uthman?'

'Yes. I'm sure of it. And he has the same nervous tic, he pulls at his ear when he's under stress.'

Pritchard rubbed his chin. 'This is a bit of a game changer, isn't it?'

'I'd say so.'

'And it raises a whole lot of questions.' He took a deep breath and exhaled slowly. 'If that is Mo Uthman, then what the hell is he playing at?'

'How well did MI6 vet him before he was hired?'

'I asked Julian Penniston-Hill the same thing. He gave me the impression that his vetting was rushed because Melissa Schofield wanted him fast-tracked.'

'Maybe they missed something.'

Pritchard laughed dryly. 'Do you think so?'

He began to pace slowly up and down the room. 'Right, first things first. We need to check that he got on the flight and that he arrived in Dubai. Then we need to know if he stayed in Dubai or moved on. The airline can tell us what name he travelled under. I'll talk to Six and find out what passports he was issued with.'

'What about Khan and Ibrahim?' asked Walsh.

'We should pick them up now, yes,' said Pritchard. 'But let me arrange that. No police, that's for sure. I want it all done off the books at this stage.'

It was about three quarters of a mile from Thames House in Millbank to the MI6 building at Albert Embankment, usually a sixteen-minute walk. The Park Plaza London Riverbank was about halfway, on the south side of the river, a concrete tower with almost five hundred rooms and an anonymous coffee shop which was perfect for a meeting as they were unlikely to bump into anyone they knew. Julian Penniston-Hill had arrived first and taken a table where he could sit with his back to a wall and watch the entrance. He had a latte and a bottle of Evian water in front of him. He made eye contact and then looked away, scanning the room for anyone who might be reacting to Pritchard's arrival. He walked slowly, giving Penniston-Hill time to check that no one was watching him, then as he reached the table Julian stood up and fist-bumped him, two friends meeting for a coffee. 'All good,' he said, letting him know that there didn't appear to be any surveillance in place.

Pritchard sat down to his left, so that he also had a view of the entrance. 'I'm assuming this is bad news, which is why you couldn't – or wouldn't – give it to me over the phone,' said Penniston-Hill.

'It's not good,' he said. 'But then nothing good has happened over the past twenty-four hours, has it?'

A waitress in a black suit came over and Pritchard asked for a coffee. He waited until she was out of earshot before telling Penniston-Hill what had happened in short, clipped sentences.

Penniston-Hill sat and listened, the only sign of his discomfort being a tightening of his jaw. He finished just as the waitress returned with his coffee. He thanked her with a bright smile.

'Fuck,' said Penniston-Hill as the waitress walked away. 'Fuckety, fuckety, fuck.'

'Well, yes, my sentiments exactly.'

'You were quite clear at Number Ten that it was Abbas who was seen leaving the safe house.'

'Yes, that was the information I had been given, in good faith. But it now appears that the witness only saw an Asian man wearing Abbas's parka and we are now satisfied that it was Uthman.'

'Who is now in Dubai?'

'Who flew to Dubai and may or may not be en route to pastures new.'

Penniston-Hill shook his head as if he were trying to clear his thoughts. He sighed, then took a sip of water. He shook his head again as he placed his glass back on the table. 'This is a lot to process, Giles.'

'I'm having trouble myself,' he said.

'There is no valid reason for Uthman behaving like this, is there? He left before the explosion so it's not as if he's shell-shocked?'

Pritchard shook his head.

'Is it at all possible that Uthman has somehow orchestrated all this, the bombings and the explosion in the safe house?'

'I'm afraid it's starting to look that way, yes.'

Penniston-Hill swallowed and forced a smile. 'I do hope you have some way of getting us out of the hole we appear to find ourselves in.'

Pritchard noted the 'us' and the 'we' but this was no time to be playing the blame game. 'We're tracking Uthman as we speak. We have two drivers who took him from Hampstead to the airport under observation and we'll be picking them up for interrogation shortly. What I'd like to do is to start going over Uthman's back-ground. His vetting.' He saw the look of concern flash across Penniston-Hill's face and he held up a hand to placate him. 'Not to apportion blame, I can assure you of that. It's just that it would be helpful to know why Uthman has suddenly gone rogue. You're not aware of anything in his background that would lead him down this path?'

Penniston-Hill shook his head. 'As I told you outside Number Ten, I wasn't involved with his vetting. He was very much Melissa's man. And as I told you then, I did have reservations about the way Uthman was fast-tracked.'

'Did you have any reason to think that he would go rogue?'

'Of course not!' he snapped. 'What are you suggesting?'

'I'm just trying to ascertain what your reservations were.'

'I just thought he was arrogant and cocksure. I didn't think for one moment that he was going to turn against us.'

'And you're not aware of anything in his background that would give him cause to hate the West?'

He stared at Pritchard in astonishment. 'Giles? Seriously?'

'I have to ask, Julian,' he said. 'Your loyalty is one of your strongest virtues, but there's no sense in trying to protect Melissa's memory at this point. There has been a God almighty cock-up and if you have any idea at all what went wrong, best to get it out in the open now.'

'Giles, I felt that Mo Uthman was being fast-tracked too soon, but I never thought for a second that he would go full-blown jihad. He was arrogant, he was full of himself, but it was the arrogance of youth. I felt that he needed a firm hand, he needed to be moulded, to be given a mentor, perhaps. Someone who could shape him.'

'And you don't think Melissa was mentoring him?'

'Melissa gave him free rein. She sent him to Calais and pretty much let him do what he wanted. He was rarely at the embassy, and I told you for part of the time he was living rough in the woodland around Calais. And then when he identified the jihadists through Abbas, Melissa saw that as justification.' He shuddered. 'What do you think, Giles? Uthman was playing us right from the get-go?'

'Either that or he was radicalised after joining Six. If he was left on his own without support and he was spending all his time with committed jihadists . . .' He shrugged. 'Who knows? Stockholm Syndrome?'

'He became radicalised after just a few months? Is that likely?'

'The alternative is that he was radicalised before he joined Six. And if that was the case, how come it didn't get picked up during the vetting? It's a fairly basic question, isn't it? How do you feel about killing non-believers, is it a good thing or a bad thing?'

'It's good to see that you've retained your sense of humour, Giles.'

He shrugged. 'Joking apart, I really need to see Uthman's vetting file. The clue to when he went rogue should be in there somewhere.'

Penniston-Hill opened his mouth and Pritchard could see from the look in his eyes that he was going to object, but then the fight went out of him and he sat back in his chair. 'I'd need to do some redaction, I can't go bandying around names of officers still in their posts.'

'That's okay, I'm not interested in who did the vetting, just what was said.'

'I'll get something biked around as soon as I get back to the office.' He sipped his water. 'Do you think we'll come through this Giles?'

'I think if we can nail the people responsible we'll stand a better chance of keeping our jobs,' said Pritchard. 'What we mustn't do is take our eyes off the ball. There's no point in trying to play the politics, we have to focus on getting hold of Uthman and finding out who he was working for.'

Penniston-Hill took a deep breath and exhaled slowly. 'Okay,' he said.

'One question I'd like answering is where was Uthman before he went to the safe house?'

Penniston-Hill frowned but didn't answer.

'He was in Thames House, in the operations room, with Martin Williams,' said Pritchard. 'He even took a bow when the jihadists were taken down. But then the bombs went off and he ran like a bat out of hell. Williams left some time later. Do you know where Uthman was between the bombs going off and him appearing at the safe house?'

'I wasn't involved in the operation. It was very much Melissa and Martin's project. I didn't see Uthman that day at all, before or after the explosions. But it's a big building and he was nothing to do with me. He could have been there. Or he could have gone home. Or the nearest mosque.' He shrugged. 'I really don't know.'

Pritchard had to force himself not to smile at the man's trans-
parent attempt to keep distancing himself from the debacle that
the operation had become. 'What about Martin Williams? Did
you see him in the building?'

'I was in my office. I hadn't even been told that there was any
operation, the first I heard about it was when the internet went
into overdrive. First Twitter and then Facebook and then of course
everybody was running around like headless chickens.'

'It would be helpful if I could have a list of his phone numbers
so that we can run GPS checks. Unless you've already tracked
him?'

'We haven't, no. And yes, I'll get his numbers.'

'And his address? We might pop around and give that a going-
over. And any phones he has used.'

'Yes. Sure.'

'And seeing that he is now overseas, a list of passports available
to him would also be helpful.'

Penniston-Hill gritted his teeth, but then forced a smile.
'Absolutely.'

'He's the enemy, Julian. You're not throwing an officer to the
wolves, you're helping to track an enemy of the state and bring
him to justice.'

'I know,' he said. 'Force of habit. You spend all your time
guarding secrets and eventually it becomes a habit. I'll bike around
everything you need.' He leaned towards him. 'I do appreciate
everything you're doing, Giles,' he said. 'Anything you need, I'm
here for you. I want to give this fucker his just deserts as much
as you do.'

Shepherd and Sharpe took the lift down to the ground floor. Two
men were waiting for them in reception. The younger of the two
was Rob Miller, a gangly Geordie who was one of MI5's top
locks and alarms specialists. They had the key to Uthman's apartment but that didn't mean that there wasn't an alarm to be dealt
with. The older man was John Weston, overweight and with a
comb-over that almost managed to conceal his baldness. Weston

was a search expert whose ability to find things concealed in a room bordered on the psychic.

Shepherd introduced them to Sharpe and there were fist bumps all round.

They went out to Sharpe's car and climbed in. Uthman's flat was in Brixton Hill, not far from Brockwell Park. Sharpe looked around anxiously as Shepherd told him where to park. 'I don't want to leave the Jag on the street,' he said.

'Why not?' asked Shepherd.

'You know why not,' said Sharpe. 'We'll come back and she'll be on bricks.'

'Razor, the Brixton cop shop is half a mile away.'

'You think they care about stolen cars? Hug your granny without a mask and they'll send out a van load of woodentops to hassle you, but lose a forty-grand motor and an emailed crime report number is as good as you'll get.'

'I thought you were a cop,' said Weston.

'National Crime Agency,' said Sharpe. 'But that doesn't mean they'll cut me any slack.'

'Razor, it's the middle of the day. No one's going to steal your motor.'

'I'll hold you to that,' said Sharpe. They climbed out. Sharpe looked up and down the road as if he expected to see carjackers at every corner, but all they saw were housewives and elderly people heading home with carrier bags.

Uthman's flat was in a three-storey brick house that had once been a family home but had been converted into three apartments. Miller looked up at the second-floor flat. There was a white alarm box with 'BANHAMS' on it, a well-known London alarm company. He grinned. 'Well that looks fake,' he said. 'But we'll know when we get inside.' He was carrying a holdall that contained all the equipment he needed to deal with pretty much any lock and alarm on the market.

There was an intercom box to the left of the door with three buttons. Shepherd took out Uthman's keys and opened the door. There was a narrow staircase and he led the way up to the second floor. Miller put down his holdall and opened it, taking out a notebook in which he had the emergency codes for all the major alarm systems. Most alarms systems had an override code that technicians could use to deactivate rogue alarms, but as a fallback position he had a powerful microwave transmitter that could fry the electrics before the alarm could sound. He slipped the microwave unit into his pocket and flashed a thumbs-up at Shepherd. Shepherd unlocked the door and went in.

There was no alarm console on the wall in the hall and no telltale beeping to say that an alarm had been activated, but all four men moved quickly through the flat checking that the console wasn't hidden away. After ten seconds of fruitless searching, Miller told them to relax. 'Told you it looked like a fake,' he said. He put his notebook and microwave unit back into his holdall and placed it by the door. 'Do you want me to help you or shall I make us all a coffee?'

'Coffee sounds good,' said Shepherd.

'Tea for me,' said Weston. 'Two sugars.' There was a sitting room with a small open-plan kitchen at one end, a door leading to a bathroom and another opening onto a bedroom. While Miller busied himself in the kitchen, Shepherd and Weston went into the bedroom. There was a window overlooking the rear garden and Weston pulled the curtains open to let in more light. Usually the aim was to search a place without leaving a trace, so they would take photographs and video before they searched. But now that Uthman had already bolted, there was no need for secrecy. They went through the wardrobe checking all the clothes on hangers and in the drawers, then they upended the mattress and checked the bed. There was a rolled-up yoga mat by the side of the bed and a set of weights. Weston examined the weights – they were plastic-coated and didn't appear to have been interfered with.

Underneath the bed were two suitcases. They pulled them out and opened them. One contained pullovers and cardigans, the other had four Gap shirts, still in the bag with a receipt. Weston tapped on the walls and the floor, and then worked his way around the skirting board. When they left the room, Sharpe had joined Miller in the kitchen and was searching the fridge-freezer. Miller handed a mug of tea to Weston and a coffee to Shepherd. 'I went through the cupboards, nothing untoward,' he said.

'Fridge and freezer are clear,' said Sharpe. 'The milk is only three days old and nothing is past its sell-by date.' There was a fusebox on the wall above the fridge. Weston pulled over a chair and stood on it to open the metal lid to check inside.

Shepherd went back into the living area. There was a sofa and an armchair in the same dark blue material facing a small television on a pine table. There were piles of newspapers and magazines under the table and he knelt down and pulled them out. There were copies of the *Economist*, the *New Statesman* and the *Spectator*, along with back issues of the *Guardian*, the *Daily Telegraph* and the *Times*.

Weston brought the chair back into the living room and put it by the small table by the window. Then he carefully checked the sofa and the armchair, lifted a rug in front of the TV, and then methodically went through a desk by the bathroom door. When he'd finished with the desk he checked every light fitting, light switch and electrical socket, then walked around tapping the skirting board and the floor, stopping every now and again to sip his tea. Sharpe and Miller watched from the kitchen area. After about an hour, Weston admitted defeat. He looked at Shepherd and shrugged. 'If he's hiding anything, he's beaten me.'

'I think it's clean,' said Shepherd. 'I think he's too well organised to have hidden anything here. But the place feels wrong, doesn't it? It feels off.'

'It isn't what he's hiding, it's what isn't here,' said Weston. 'There's nothing of a personal nature. No photographs of family or friends.'

'His parents are dead,' said Shepherd.

'Which is more of a reason for him to have their pictures around. There are no pictures. Of anyone. That's not normal. Even prisoners plaster photographs and pictures on their cell walls. You're former military, right? Soldiers always have photographs of their loved ones somewhere, don't they?'

Shepherd nodded.

'This is just not normal,' continued Weston. 'Then there's the jihad thing. He's a Muslim terrorist but there's no prayer mat and no copy of the Koran. There's a yoga mat to go with his exercise weights, but no sports equipment. No squash or tennis racket, no football boots, nothing that suggests he takes part in any sports at all. No hobbies, no interests, no nothing.'

'So what are you suggesting, that he doesn't live here? That he's got another place?'

'No, he lives here. The toothbrush is well used, he's halfway through his toothpaste and deodorant, and his hair is in the shower plughole. Or at least black hair that looks like his. There's food in the fridge, opened coffee and tea in the cupboards. No, he lives here. But he doesn't appear to have a life. No computer or iPad. Okay, there's a TV so maybe he watches that, but there's no dip in the sofa to suggest that he spends hours sitting there. And there are no books. Plenty of newspapers and magazines but this isn't a man who reads for pleasure, he reads for information.'

'So you think he's pretending to be something he isn't?'

'No, the opposite. I think this is really him. If he was pretending, he'd have dressed the flat to throw us off the track. We have people who do that, as you know, dress a home to fit in with a legend. Choosing items that go with the story that we're trying to sell. But Uthman isn't trying to sell anything. He's a complete blank canvas.' He rubbed his chin. 'You know what this makes me think of? An astronaut.'

'An astronaut?' repeated Shepherd.

'Yeah,' said Weston, looking around the room. 'Everyone is geared up to the mission. There's nothing here that isn't mission essential.'

'Which is why when he left, he didn't take anything with him,' said Shepherd. 'There are only a few empty hangers in the wardrobe and they're accounted for by the items of clothing in the washing hamper in the bathroom. The mission was over and he left.'

Weston nodded. 'That's exactly how I read it.'

'So this has been a waste of time?' said Sharpe.

'Far from it,' said Shepherd. 'This lets us know that there's a lot more to Mo Uthman than we thought. And it shows a high degree of organisation and planning. This isn't something that suddenly happened, this guy has been living a lie for years.'

'A sleeper,' said Weston.

'And a committed one. He's been living a lie, twenty-four-seven, since the day he joined MI6. Probably even before that. A hell of a lot of dedication has gone into this.'

Mohammed Khan sipped his orange juice and tried to concentrate on the Bollywood movie that his parents were watching. It involved a teacher who really wanted to be a rockstar so that he could win back the love of his life who had dumped him to go out with a factory owner who drove a green Lamborghini. The plot made no sense and as the story was interrupted every ten minutes with a frantic dance scene, Khan had lost track of what was happening. He wasn't a fan of Bollywood movies, partly because their treatment of Muslim characters often bordered on racism, but his parents loved them and it was their house so they got to control the remote.

The doorbell rang and Khan looked over at his parents. 'You expecting anyone?'

The elderly couple shook their heads.

Khan stood up and walked to the kitchen where his two sisters were chopping vegetables as two pans bubbled on the stove. 'Aisha, Layla, you expecting anyone?'

'Mrs Shakoor is coming around with her Avon stuff,' said Layla. She looked at her watch. 'But if that's her, she's early.'

Khan went back into the hallway and headed to the front door. There were two frosted glass panels set into the wood and he could see the blurred figure of a woman in a black burka. She was standing with her back to the door but she turned as

Khan opened it. 'Put your hands in the air,' growled the figure, pointing a gun at his face. It was a man, Khan realised, but before he could react a hand grabbed his throat and pushed him back against the wall. 'I said put your fucking hands in the air!'

As Khan raised his hands, four men pushed their way through the doorway. They were wearing bomber jackets and black ski masks and carrying guns. Two of the men thudded up the stairs. The other two went into the living room.

'Who are you?' spluttered Khan, but the ma⟩ ⟨ding him didn't reply. Instead he swept Khan's feet from unde⟩⟨ ⟨im and he hit the floor hard. The man rolled him over onto his ⟩⟨ and Khan felt his wrists being zip-tied behind his back.

Two more men in ski masks pushed their way through the door and went down the hallway to the kitchen. Khan heard his sisters scream and then go quiet.

'This is a mistake!' shouted Khan, but he fell silent when the gun was jammed against the back of his neck.

Khan heard a thudding footfall on the stairs and his brother protesting that he hadn't done anything wrong. Khan was grabbed by the scruff of his neck, pulled to his feet and thrown against the wall. Then he was roughly turned around. Two masked men were holding his brother Asim by the arms. They slammed Asim against the wall and one of them pulled out a sheet of paper with two photographs on it. He held the paper up between the two men, then gestured with his gun at Khan's face. 'This is Mohammed Khan.' He gestured at Asim. 'But this isn't the fucker who was with him.' The man stuck his gun under Asim's chin. 'Who the fuck are you, mate?'

A wet patch spread around Asim's groin and he began to sob.

'He's Asim, he's my b-b-brother,' Khan stuttered.

'Where's the guy you were driving with? The one you went to London with?'

Khan shook his head. 'I don't know what you—'

The man stopped him short with a slap across the face. 'Don't fucking lie to me.'

'Leave it,' said one of the other men.

The two men who had gone into the kitchen returned, dragging Khan's sisters with them. Both girls were crying and trying to cover their faces with their hands. The men took them into the sitting room. 'Right, all of you, down on your knees!' a man shouted.

'Please d-d-don't hurt my f-f-family,' stammered Khan.

'You brought this on yourself,' said the man with his gun pressed under Khan's chin. 'This is all down to you.'

The man in the sitting room continued to shout at Khan's parents and sisters. 'We're taking the boys to ask them a few questions. I suggest you keep what has happened to yourselves. No talking to the Press, no calling your MP, don't call your imam, don't even talk to your neighbours. If any of you tell anybody about what has happened, we'll be back. And when we come back we'll be here to cancel your British citizenship and send you back to Bangladesh or whatever shithole you are from. We'll close down any businesses you own and confiscate any property you have, and we'll put you on a plane with nothing other than the clothes you're wearing. Do you fucking understand me?' There was no reply. 'That's not good enough!' shouted the man. 'I want you all to say "Yes, sir, I understand, sir." Right?'

Khan heard his father say 'I understand, sir,' and then his mother repeat it, then one by one his sisters said it between sobs.

'Excellent,' said the man. 'Now I want you to all lie down and count to a hundred. When you get to a hundred you can get up and carry on with your lives. When we have finished questioning your boys we will return them to you. Or put them behind bars. That depends on what they tell us. Now start counting!'

The masked men filed out of the sitting room. Khan was grabbed by the arms and a black hood was pulled over his head. He heard his brother protest and then there was a thud and a yelp and he went silent.

He heard the front door open and then he was half pushed,

half carried outside and then thrown into the back of a vehicle. He could feel his brother lying next to him. Then doors slammed and they drove off.

'Who are you? Are you cops? I have the right to a solicitor! I want to see—' His shouts were cut short by a blow to the head that turned everything black.

Pritchard looked up from his twin computer screens as Shepherd walked into his office. 'How did it go?' he asked.

'Nothing of any use, no computer, nothing hidden. John Weston was there and as you know, nothing gets by him.'

'So he'd cleaned up before he left?'

Shepherd shook his head. 'I don't think so. John and I felt the same, Uthman was living like a monk. No interests outside work. And you know yourself, he had nothing with him at the airport. He just walked away.' Pritchard hadn't waved at the sofa or the two chairs so Shepherd figured he wouldn't be in the office for long.

'You'll be glad to know we've just apprehended Khan and Ibrahim.'

'Have they been charged?'

'No, they're not in the system. I took the decision to outsource their capture.'

Shepherd frowned in confusion. 'Outsource?'

'If they are arrested then they have the right to legal representation and said representation is just going to tell them to say nothing. And what do we charge them with? They drove a terrorist suspect from London to Manchester, but I don't see that we can prove they knew that he had anything to do with what happened in Trafalgar Square. They could simply claim that they were giving a pal a lift. Unless they've left an email or phone trail, we'd be stumped. And even if we could prove that they knew what Uthman had done, what's the charge? It's not conspiracy, not if it was after the event. What are we looking at? Aiding and abetting, maybe? Five years? Ten? They'd laugh in our faces. And we'd have zero leverage.

So I thought it best to keep them outside the system, for the time being anyway.'

'The Increment?' The Increment was an ad-hoc group of special forces operatives who were brought together to do missions that MI5 and MI6 couldn't do with their own staff.

Pritchard shook his head. 'I went with the private sector,' he said quietly.

'Ballsy,' said Shepherd.

Pritchard shrugged. 'I don't see that I have any choice, Dan. If these guys are put into the system, then we'll never find out who was behind the bombings. The system will take care of them, as it always does, down to the Halal food they'll be getting in Belmarsh. And if we don't get the people responsible for this outrage, I'll be out of a job. I'm lucky that they didn't sack me within an hour of those bombs going off. I've been given a second chance, but I'm still a dead man walking.' He shrugged again. 'If I have to bend a few rules to get the men responsible, so be it.'

'I hear you,' said Shepherd. 'I've bent a few in my time.'

Pritchard smiled. 'Yes, I know.' He looked down at his desk and picked up a sheet of paper. 'So, I've been looking at Uthman's vetting file and it's pretty light. One of the few referees was his tutor at Manchester University. A Professor Fitzgerald. Can you go and talk to her?'

'Sure.' He took the sheet of paper from him. 'Is it okay if I take Jimmy Sharpe with me. He's good at this sort of thing.'

'No problem. But then I need you to go and help with the interrogation of Khan and Ibrahim.' He pointed at the sheet of paper. 'That number at the bottom is our point of contact. He'll give you directions. How reliable is this Sharpe?'

'I'd trust him with my life. We were undercover cops together many years ago, and he's done more than his fair share of anti-terrorism work.'

'How will he be when he learns that we're using contractors?'

Shepherd grinned. 'Oh, he'll probably be in favour. He reckons regular law enforcement is pretty useless these days. Always better to use professionals. He'll be helpful, we've got a decent good-cop-bad-cop thing going.'

'No need to ask which one you are, Dan,' said Pritchard. 'Soon as you get anything, call me.'

The drive from Thames House to Manchester took a little over four hours, with a short break at a motorway service station near Birmingham to refuel on coffee and bacon rolls. 'It's like Vietnam,' said Sharpe as they sat at a table overlooking the car park.

Shepherd frowned. 'Run that by me again, Razor?'

Sharpe gestured at the tables around them. Half were occupied by Asians and most of the women were wearing headscarves. 'The Americans lost in Vietnam because they couldn't tell the good guys from the bad guys. The only way to be sure was to catch them carrying a weapon. Then you knew. But if a Viet Cong dropped his AK-47 in a ditch and picked up a hoe, he became a farmer. How did you tell a farmer from a VC? You couldn't. They never knew who the enemy was. It's the same out in the Middle East. If they're carrying a gun and waving an ISIS flag, then you know they're a threat. If they're walking down the road with a stick and a herd of goats, they're civilians. You can't win battles against people like that.'

'You're talking about insurgents.'

'Yeah? I guess I am. Well that's what we've got here in the UK. It's impossible to tell the good guys from the bad guys unless we catch them in the act.' He gestured at a table where two young Asian men were tucking into fish and chips. 'See those two? They could be a couple of emergency room doctors just off their shift. Or care home workers on their day off. Or they could be a couple of jihadists who have been trained in an ISIS camp in Afghanistan on their way to blow themselves up in the Bull Ring. There's no way of knowing – until they shout *Allahu Akbar* and blow themselves up.' He took a bite of his roll and washed it down with coffee.

'That's why we put so much effort into surveillance,' said Shepherd. 'We watch them and we listen to them and we read their emails and then we catch them.'

'Except sometimes we don't, and when we get it wrong people die. It's what the IRA said when they almost killed Margaret Thatcher in the Brighton bombing. She was lucky and she would always have to be lucky, but the IRA would only have to be lucky once. Here's the thing, Spider. We need to be more vigilant than ever, but at the same time we're dropping our recruitment standards left, right and centre. Remember GCHQ announcing that they were only accepting job applications from women or our beloved BAME community? How does that make any sense, basically banning white men from joining the fight against terrorism? And you've heard our beloved mayor, saying that he wants forty per cent of the Met to be from ethnic minorities sooner rather than later. And the Met has lowered its standards to meet diversity quotas so much that half of the new recruits can barely walk, never mind run.'

Shepherd raised an eyebrow at Sharpe's expanding waistline and the Scotsman laughed. 'My days of chasing after neds are long gone,' he said. 'But when I joined the cops I was as fit as a butcher's dog. We all were.'

'Is there going to be a point to all this,' said Shepherd. 'Or is it just a rant?'

'My point is that this guy Uthman was clearly fast-tracked because he ticked the right boxes. MI6 wants more Asians, in particular Muslim Asians, so when a guy like Uthman puts himself forward they jump at the chance of hiring him.'

'To be fair, MI5 is also taking on more Asians. It makes sense, when most terrorist acts are committed by Asians.'

'And I bet the standards are being lowered by your mob just as they have been by the cops. You've seen the direct vetting file? There were two interviews. Everything else was done via data searches. The only people interviewed were the woman we're going to see and his tutor at Westminster University. How is that in any way enough for someone who's going to be fast-tracked through the Secret Intelligence Service?'

'He doesn't have family, his parents were killed, remember? And he has no living siblings.'

'So talk to people he knew at university. Did he share a house with other students? Part-time jobs? He was in London for fuck's sake, he'd be crossing paths with hundreds of people.' He grimaced. 'It looks to me that corners were cut to get this guy hired as quickly as possible.'

'Well, let's see what Professor Fitzgerald has to say.'

'And how was someone so inexperienced allowed to be running an operation like this? You told me yourself you didn't think he was up to it. If he'd had to answer to someone like you this would never have happened.'

'I can't argue with that,' said Shepherd. 'But there's no use crying over spilled milk.'

'There is if it stops it happening in the future,' said Sharpe.

'The problem with that is that the woman who fast-tracked Uthman is now dead.'

They finished their food and went back to the car.

They arrived at Manchester Metropolitan University at just after five o'clock. Professor Fitzgerald was at her desk reading through a stack of papers and scribbling comments in the margins. She didn't have a secretary and her door was open, but Shepherd knocked and waited until she said 'come in' before heading inside. He had called from Thames House and explained what they wanted, so she was expecting them and didn't ask for any identification.

She waved them to a table and two chairs and they sat down. She was in her late forties with curly black hair and a round face with cat-like eyes. She was clearly a fan of cats as there was a ceramic one on her desk and several posters featuring cats on the walls. She had a pair of round-lensed spectacles perched on her nose but she took them off and let them hang around her neck on a gilt chain. 'So, gentlemen, you want to pick my brains about Mo Uthman – again?'

Shepherd took out a notebook and pen. His faultless memory meant that he didn't need to take notes, but writing things down made it look more official. 'It's something we do on a regular basis, Professor,' he said. 'Sometimes people think of things they didn't mention the first time, but it's also a way of us fine-tuning the vetting process.'

'Is he doing well?'

'Actually, Professor, I wouldn't know about that,' said Shepherd. 'The vetting team are totally separate from the Human Resources team. We really have no idea what happens to the people that we vet. Though the fact that we are here to see you obviously means that Mr Uthman is still employed by the government.' He faked a look at his notebook as if he was checking what was written there. 'So Mr Uthman studied with you for one year?'

Professor Fitzgerald smiled. 'Yes, Mo studied for an MA in International Relations and Global Communications,' she said. She smiled at the look of confusion on Sharpe's face. 'In layman's terms, how the internet has transformed political behaviour, be it campaigning or voting. We cover hashtag activism, social media campaigning, internet censorship around the world. Basically looking at how new communication technologies shape societies, politics and individual lives.'

'And he was a good student?' asked Shepherd.

'First class. Diligent, hardworking, he produced an absolutely smashing dissertation on the use of social media in the Arab Spring uprisings. Obviously his background and language skills helped, but he did put a huge amount of work into it.'

'And negatives?' said Shepherd.

'Well, as I said the last time your chaps interviewed me, he was sometimes a little arrogant.'

'Arrogant?' repeated Shepherd.

'Mo didn't suffer fools gladly,' she said. 'He would tell you something and expect you to get it immediately. If he thought that you'd missed his point he'd be quick to tell you.' She put up her hands. 'He was young and enthusiastic and obviously in a hurry.'

'In what way?' asked Shepherd.

'To get on with life. To contribute. To make a difference.'

'Did he say that in so many words?'

The professor shrugged. 'He didn't have to. He was studying

as a means to an end. Some people come to university to enjoy the university lifestyle, to make friends and widen their social circle. And to consume large amounts of alcohol.'

'Did Mo?'

'Did Mo what?'

'Did he consume large amounts of alcohol?'

'Oh no, he was a Muslim. So no alcohol, of course.'

'Some Muslims drink,' said Sharpe. 'I was once on a training course with a group of cops from Algiers and you couldn't keep them away from the red wine.'

'Well Mo definitely wasn't a drinker.'

'And friends?' asked Shepherd. 'Did he have many?'

'He wasn't exactly popular and I don't think he had any particularly close friends, but he wasn't a loner. He was a member of several groups and societies and I'd see him chatting to students in the cafeteria.'

'What groups?'

'He was involved with the student paper, mainly on the marketing side. And the astronomy club.'

'Any sports?'

She frowned and then shook her head. 'I don't think so. Can I ask you a question?'

'Of course.'

'Has something happened? To Mo.'

'No, this is just something we do from time to time. Everyone who undergoes this vetting has to have it repeated every seven years, but we also do spot checks every now and again. Sort of quality control.'

'You see, I always thought he would be an asset to the government. The man who came to do the last interview wouldn't say specifically who he would be working for but I assumed . . .' She shrugged and didn't finish the sentence.

'That's usually what happens,' said Shepherd.

'Obviously I assumed that with his language skills and background it would be the security service or something within the Foreign Office, but that's none of my business. But I can tell you what I told the man then – Mo was a hard worker with a good brain and an excellent work ethic. I would have had no hesitation in offering him a post here if he'd expressed interest in academia.'

'And he didn't?' said Shepherd.

'I actually thought he'd pursue a career in journalism, with his interest in the school newspaper. They're all going online these days and he was very internet savvy.'

Shepherd closed his notebook. He'd made the occasional scribbled note but that was for her benefit and not his. 'Well, thank you for your time and your patience,' he said, getting to his feet.

She smiled up at him. 'So will I see you in another seven years?'

Shepherd chuckled. 'No, I think by then there'll be less interest in his university life.'

'Did he ever say why he chose Manchester for his MA?' asked Sharpe. Shepherd threw him a withering look but Sharpe smiled amiably.

'I think he was attracted to the course,' said the professor.

'Sure, yes, it sounds like a fascinating course, but it's a course offered by lots of other institutions. And this is a guy who spent three years getting his degree in London. Westminster University. I just wonder why after three years in London he decided to make the trek up north.'

She laughed. 'We're not some desolate wasteland, this is the UK's second city. What about you? You're from Scotland, right?'

'Glasgow,' he said. 'The Dear Green Place.'

'But you didn't spend your entire career there, clearly. That's what people do. They move to acquire knowledge and skills.'

'But why Manchester? Was it a question you ever asked him?'

She narrowed her eyes as she tried to remember. 'Yes, I think I did, at his interview,' she said. 'At least I asked him if he had any local family connections and he said he didn't. He made some joke about being a fan of Manchester United.'

'Maybe that's it, he followed the Reds,' said Sharpe.

'He didn't say he was unhappy with London, did he?' asked Shepherd. 'It can be a tough city and he was quite young when he went there. Prior to that he was at boarding school, so he'd have had a fairly cosseted existence.'

'It depends on the school,' said the professor. 'Some boarding schools can be a tough experience.'

'Did you discuss that with him?'

She shook her head. 'Our vetting procedure is very different from yours,' she said. 'For a regular degree we might look into their background, but for an MA we're much more interested in their academic performance.'

'And his was good?' asked Shepherd.

'It was certainly adequate for our purposes,' said the professor. 'He gained a 2-1 and I saw a dissertation that he had done. I have to say that he blossomed while he was here. That often happens, of course, a three-year degree can sometimes be a grind and students find they are able to express themselves much more while studying for their Masters.'

She showed them out and they headed for the car park. 'What do you think?' asked Shepherd as they walked towards the Jaguar.

'Yeah, I'd definitely give her one,' said Sharpe.

Shepherd sighed. 'About what she said, you daft bastard.'

'She seems solid enough. And he was a perfect student.' He shrugged. 'I'm not sure that I buy the coming to Manchester because he rated United. Is it a coincidence that he flew out of Manchester? And that the guys who drove him both live here? Maybe he came to Manchester to join a cell here?'

'Or came here and was radicalised.'

Sharpe nodded. 'The Prof said he was a good Muslim but there was no prayer mat or copy of the Koran in his flat. That doesn't seem right, does it?'

They reached the Jaguar. 'Where now?'

'Yeah, I need to talk to you about that,' said Shepherd.

'That's it,' said Shepherd. 'On the left.' They were driving through a small industrial estate in Swinton, four miles to the north-west of Manchester. Shepherd had phoned the number that Pritchard had given him and a man with a Liverpool accent had barked out curt directions. He had also told Shepherd to flash his lights three times and then twice as they approached the unit. Shepherd relayed the instructions as Sharpe turned off the road and headed towards the buildings.

'What are we, the Secret Seven or the Famous Five?' said Sharpe.

'Just do it, Razor, these guys don't mess around.'

Sharpe flashed his lights. There were four black SUVs parked in front of the two-storey unit which had the name of a shopfitting company on a sign above the office area. There were two metal-shuttered doors and a loading bay to the left.

The unit had its own parking area and was on the edge of the estate so it wasn't overlooked. Sharpe slowed the Jaguar. 'I don't see anyone. Shall I beep the horn?'

'Just stop here and wait.'

'Who are these guys?'

'They won't be formally introducing themselves,' said Shepherd. 'They work for what they call the Pool. No one knows if that's because there's a group of them, or because a lot of them seem to come from Liverpool. Some of them are former special forces who went over to the dark side, some of them are criminals who preferred to sign up for the Pool than go to prison, and some of them are common or garden psychopaths.'

'But they're working for MI5?'

'They do occasional jobs for Five. The sort of jobs they can't be seen doing themselves. Dirty jobs.'

'Bloody hell, Spider. The company you keep.'

'This wasn't my idea. Pritchard made the call. And under the circumstances it's probably the right one. We can hold Khan and Ibrahim under anti-terrorism laws but they'll get lawyered up and say nothing. They probably won't get bail but they'll be nice and safe in Belmarsh where every move is recorded on CCTV and our people won't even be allowed to raise their voices. Guys like Khan and Ibrahim aren't scared of our cops, they know it's a completely different system from the countries they're from. In Iraq or Syria or Pakistan the cops can hang them upside down and beat the soles of their feet or attach jumpstart cables to their bollocks or do pretty much whatever they want with impunity.' He gestured at the building. 'But these guys can make up their own rules.'

The door to the office opened and a man dressed from head to toe in black appeared. He pointed for them to park next to the SUVs.

'He's wearing a ski mask,' said Sharpe.

'It's cold out,' said Shepherd. 'Just do as he said.'

Sharpe grunted and drove slowly across the car park to the SUVs. They got out and walked towards the man, who held the door open for them. Inside was a corridor with a green carpet and marks on the walls where there had once been framed posters or photographs. There was a water cooler and a fake rubber plant and two doors leading off to the right. The masked man walked by them. He was wearing a black jacket and from the way it was hanging, Shepherd was sure he had a gun in a holster in the small of his back.

The man knocked on the door and then held it open. Shepherd led the way and Sharpe followed. Shepherd's jaw dropped when he saw the woman sitting at a cheap oak-veneer desk. Her hair was still chestnut brown, a darker shade than when he'd last seen her, but there was the same sparkle in her eyes as she smiled at him. Charlotte Button had been his boss at MI5 before she had left under a cloud, the cloud being that she had used government resources – including the Pool – to take revenge on the Islamic terrorists responsible for the murder of her husband.

'You look surprised, Spider,' said Button.

Shepherd fought to recover his composure and smiled. 'Giles didn't mention you were on the case, but obviously you'd be the best man for the job.'

'And you brought the lovely Razor with you. How nice.'

'Charlotte,' said Sharpe. 'Always a pleasure.'

'He's riding shotgun for me on this,' said Shepherd. 'Fist bump, elbow touch, foot kick, how do we greet each other these days?'

'A simple "nice to see you" works for me,' said Button.

'Nice to see you, Charlie,' said Shepherd.

'Nice to see you, too, Dan.'

The masked man left the room and closed the door. Button waved for Shepherd and Sharpe to sit. 'So how far have you got with them?' asked Shepherd.

'At the moment we're letting them sweat,' said Button. 'We had them unconscious for a while so they've lost all sense of time, and as you'll see from the set-up, they've no idea where there are. They've not been physically hurt. Shaken a bit. We're already pretty sure that Mohammed Khan's brother had no idea what was going on.'

'And presumably torture is an option?'

'They call it enhanced interrogation these days,' she said. 'And yes, it's an option. But not one that we need to pursue. Leaving Asim aside, the other two aren't hardened jihadists. They haven't even had ISIS training, so they're soft. Plus we've looked at their family situation and between them they have four relatives who are being considered for asylum as we speak. Between the carrot and the stick we'll get them to talk.'

'Tell me, will it be the carrot or the stick that gets thrust into their arses?' asked Shepherd.

Button opened her mouth to reply but Shepherd put up a hand. 'I'm joking,' he said. 'How about you let us conduct the initial interrogation. We can do the preliminary questioning and if it looks like they need more, we'll step back and your guys can do what they do.'

'That's absolutely fine by me,' said Button. 'In fact I was fairly sure that you'd suggest that, which is why we're keeping them on ice.' She smiled slyly. 'Not real ice, obviously.' She stood up, still smiling. She was wearing a dark overcoat over a dark suit and there was a pair of black leather gloves on the table next to a black Chanel bag. Sharpe opened the door. The man in the ski mask was standing there with his back to the wall, arms folded across his barrel-like chest. 'Gerry here can take you through to see them. I'll wait here.'

'Keeping your distance?' asked Sharpe.

'I have to confess I've always been a bit squeamish when it comes to violence, but in this case it's more about not giving them the opportunity to tell their captors apart.' She smiled at the masked man. 'Gerry, can you get them kitted out?'

'Yes, ma'am.' As Button closed the door, Gerry took them down the corridor to a set of double doors on the left. He pushed them open to reveal the interior of the main building, two storeys high with a vaulted roof from which hung banks of fluorescent lights. There were three blood-red shipping containers standing ten feet apart, the doors closed. At the far end of the building were two men in dark pullovers and jeans, also wearing ski masks. They were sitting at a table studying their phones. There was a handgun on the table, and what looked like an Uzi.

'Are they expecting a war?' whispered Sharpe.

'We're like the boy scouts,' said Gerry. 'Always prepared.' He had a slight Liverpool accent but Shepherd didn't think he was the man he'd spoken to on the phone. He took them over to a plastic sofa next to a coffee table on which there were half a dozen opened cans of soft drinks and two pizza boxes. By the side of the sofa were two kitbags. Gerry pointed at the bags. 'Get yourself overalls and a mask,' he said.

'We're only going to talk to them,' said Sharpe.

'It's part of the psychology,' said Gerry. 'We don't want them to be able to tell us apart.'

He folded his arms and waited while they zipped overalls on over their suits and pulled on ski masks. 'Does my arse look big in this?' Sharpe asked Shepherd.

Shepherd laughed. 'Your arse looks big in everything,' he said.

'That's harsh,' said Sharpe.

Gerry flashed them a thumbs up. 'Which one do you want to see first?' he asked.

'Khan,' said Shepherd.

'We've got two Khans. Mohammed and his brother Asim. But we're already sure that Asim had no idea what was going on.'

'Mohammed it is,' said Shepherd.

'He's in this one,' said Gerry, taking them to the nearest

container. 'They don't know where they are or who we are. They were unconscious when they were brought here so all they are aware of are the containers. The plan is to tell them they're being shipped to Morocco where they can be tortured at leisure. That's the story so far. Do you want me to go in there with you?'

'I think we'll be okay,' said Shepherd.

'I'll be closing the door behind you, just bang on it when you want out.' He opened the door just wide enough for them to slip through. There was an electric lantern in one corner that emitted barely enough light for them to see. There was a naked Asian man standing with his back to them, his arms up in the air. As Shepherd blinked his eyes, they became accustomed to the gloom and he saw that there were ropes running from straps around the man's wrists up to hooks in the top of the container. He wrinkled at the stench of urine and faeces. The man had soiled himself.

'Well this isn't good,' said Sharpe.

The door closed behind them with a metallic thud.

'Please let me go home, I haven't done anything,' said the man. He coughed and spat on the floor.

In the far corner of the container was a pack of six bottles of drinking water. Shepherd went over to the pack and pulled out one of the bottles and unscrewed the top. He held it to the man's mouth and tilted it up. The man drank greedily. He was in his thirties, bearded with a pot belly that hung over his genitals. Shepherd waited until he had stopped sucking on the bottle before taking it away.

'Please, let me go, there has been some mistake. I am a good man. I have done nothing wrong.'

Shepherd turned his back on the man and put the bottle down next to the pack.

Sharpe walked around and stared at the man. 'There's been no mistake. We know exactly what you did.'

Khan shook his head. 'I did nothing.'

'All those people who died in Trafalgar Square, you were part of that.'

'What? No!'

'Don't fucking lie to me!' spat Sharpe, prodding him in the chest. 'You're fucking ISIS. We know you are and lying is just going to make it worse.'

Khan's eyes filled with tears. 'I am not a terrorist,' he cried. 'I've never fired a gun, I've never killed anyone. You've got the wrong man. I am a good person.'

'Where were you yesterday?'

'Nowhere. I was home.'

Sharpe grabbed Khan's throat and squeezed. 'Do not lie to me. Do you understand? Do not fucking lie to me.'

He let go of Khan's throat and he coughed and spluttered. 'I am not a terrorist,' he gasped.

Sharpe waved his hand around the container. 'You know where you are, right?'

Khan shook his head, tears running down his face.

'You're in a shipping container and the plan is to ship you to Morocco where there are some very nasty people waiting to question you. We can't put you on a plane because well-meaning *Guardian* readers will kick up a fuss, but no one can see you here and after a few days at sea you'll be in your new home. They can do all sorts of things we can't do. Pulling off your fingernails, breaking your fingers and toes. Driving nails into your balls. All the good stuff. And Asim can go with you. You can watch as the interrogators work on him.'

'You can't do this to me, I'm a British citizen.'

Sharpe put his face up close to Khan's. 'Most of the people who died in Trafalgar Square were British,' he hissed. 'It didn't do them any good.'

'I wasn't in Trafalgar Square.'

'No? Where were you?'

Tears were running down Khan's face. He sniffed. 'Hampstead,' he said. 'North London. I never went near Trafalgar Square.'

'No? But your pals did, didn't they? And they killed a lot of people. You know what, I'm going to ask the Moroccans to video what they do to you so that I can watch them pulling out your fingernails.'

'I didn't do anything!' shouted Khan. He began to cough and splutter.

Shepherd picked up the water bottle and walked over to Khan. 'Why the fuck are you giving him water?' said Sharpe. 'He's a fucking terrorist. He deserves everything that's going to happen.'

'He's still a human being,' said Shepherd. 'You can't treat him like an animal.'

Sharpe moved behind Khan and grinned as he made an obscene gesture. Shepherd ignored him and gave Khan another go at the water bottle. Khan gulped it down and he gasped his thanks as Shepherd eventually took the bottle away.

'Why were you in Hampstead, Mohammed?'

'I was sent to pick someone up.'

'Who?'

'I don't know. I was told it was a brother and he would get in the car and I was to drive him to Knutsford, to the service station.'

Shepherd smiled encouragingly. 'And you weren't told who he was? Or what he had done?'

'I was just told that a brother needed driving from Hampstead to the service station and that we were to meet another brother and that we were to hand him over.'

'Who was this other brother?'

'I don't know his name. I had never seen him before, I was told to look for a brother wearing a white kufi.'

'And who was with you, Mohammed? Who drove with you to Hampstead?'

'I don't want to get anyone into trouble,' said Khan. 'I just want to go home.'

'You were seen on CCTV, Mohammed. All we need is his name. If you don't give me a name we'll assume it was Asim.'

'It wasn't Asim. Asim is a good boy. He wouldn't say boo to a goose.'

'Then give us a fucking name!' shouted Sharpe. 'You want me to start slapping Asim around? Because I will. And worse.'

Khan groaned as if he was in pain. 'Okay, okay. Faraz Javeed.

But he was just to keep me company. He did nothing wrong. I did nothing wrong.'

'Were you paid to drive the brother from Hampstead?'

'The imam gave me money for petrol.'

'The imam told you to go and collect the brother?'

Khan nodded.

'And who is this imam, Mohammed? Who gave you the petrol money?'

Khan sniffed. Shepherd gave him more water and he took several rapid gulps.

'What is his name?'

'Abu al-Alwani.'

'He is the imam at your mosque?'

'It is the mosque where I worship. In Salford.'

'And why did he ask you to collect the brother?'

'He needed someone with a car.'

'Had you done tasks like that before?'

'What do you mean?'

'Does the imam ask you to do a lot of jobs for him?'

Khan frowned. 'I do what I can.'

Sharpe walked around Khan and prodded him in the chest. 'You know what we want to know!' he shouted. 'This imam is a fucking terrorist and you know it. He's the one behind the bombs in Trafalgar Square and you were helping him!'

'No!' shouted Khan.

'Yes! Don't you lie to us, we know exactly what you did.' He drew back his hand to slap Khan but Shepherd grabbed it.

'Leave him alone,' said Shepherd.

'He's not going to tell you anything!' shouted Sharpe. 'Just send him to Morocco and let them deal with him. I've had enough of his bullshit. He needs to have the truth beaten out of him.'

Shepherd pushed him away. Sharpe moved behind the man and began pulling faces.

'I don't want to go to Morocco,' said Khan, his voice shaking.

'Then you have to tell us what you know now,' said Shepherd. 'If you help us, we can help you.'

'I didn't know about the bombs,' said Khan. 'I was just sent to pick up the brother.'

'But this imam. This Abu al-Alwani. He is a jihadist? He preaches jihad?'

'Not in the mosque.'

'But privately? When he is among friends. He is a jihadist?'

Khan closed his eyes and nodded. 'Yes,' he whispered.

'Is that why you wanted to help him?' asked Shepherd.

'I wanted to be a good Muslim,' said Khan, opening his eyes again. 'He said the way to serve Allah was to help those who were fighting the good fight. I asked him, two years ago, if I should go to be trained to fight but he said no, my place was to stay and help. Facilitate, he said. I was to facilitate but my role was no less important than the men who were fighting in the desert.' The words had come tumbling out so quickly that he had spoken without thinking and he stopped when he realised what he had said. 'I am not a terrorist, I just want to help my religion.'

'I understand,' said Shepherd. 'So when did the imam send you to Hampstead?'

'Four days ago,' said Khan.

'To Hampstead? He sent you to Hampstead four days ago?'

Khan shook his head. 'He told us to go to London. We stayed in a hotel in Bayswater. It was run by brothers who would let us stay without a credit card. In fact we didn't have to pay at all. Then yesterday the imam called me and told me to park in a road in Hampstead and wait.'

'What time?'

'Time?' Khan frowned, not understanding the question.

'What time did the imam call you and tell you to go to Hampstead?'

'About one o'clock.'

'You're sure?'

'I am sure. Please let me go now. I am not a terrorist, I was just a driver.'

'Where was this hotel exactly? What was it called?'

Khan told him and Shepherd gave him another drink of water.

He put the bottle down next to the pack. 'Can I go now?' asked Khan.

'We have to check what you've told us,' said Shepherd.

'So I have to stay here?'

'I'm afraid so.'

'Can I call my lawyer?'

'Do you have a lawyer?'

Khan shook his head.

'You watch too much TV,' snarled Sharpe. 'This isn't the TV, it's the real world. You'll stay here until we're finished with you.'

Khan began to sob as Shepherd and Sharpe walked to the door and banged on it. Gerry opened it and they stepped out.

'Well, he folded like a cheap deckchair, didn't he?' said Sharpe as they walked away from the container. Gerry slammed the door shut with a dull clang.

'Yeah, he clearly hadn't been given any interrogation resistance training.' Shepherd looked at Sharpe and shook his head. 'How did that go again? "Driving nails into your balls. All the good stuff." Where did you get that from?'

'I was riffing. It worked, didn't it? Scared the beejaysus out of him.'

'I had to bite my tongue to stop myself from laughing.'

Sharpe shrugged. 'How about you play bad cop this time and I'll be good cop?'

Shepherd chuckled. 'Razor, I'd be happy if you were mediocre cop.'

'I just don't like being the heavy every time.'

'No problem, I'll make the threats. You can give him water.'

'How did it go?' asked Gerry, coming up behind them.

'He shat himself, literally,' said Sharpe.

Gerry took them over to the second container. 'You know the drill,' he said as he pulled open the door.

Shepherd and Sharpe stepped inside. Hamid Ibrahim was also naked and his arms were tied to the roof with ropes. Gerry slammed the door closed. There was a single electric lamp in the far corner next to a pack of water bottles. Ibrahim's legs had collapsed and his arms were taking all his weight. Sharpe went over to the pack of water and picked up a bottle. He unscrewed the cap and poured the contents over Ibrahim's head. The man began to cough and splutter.

'Have we switched roles again?' hissed Shepherd. 'I thought you were good cop.'

'I'm just waking him up,' said Sharpe. He finished emptying the bottle, then tossed it away and picked up another.

Ibrahim started to moan. Sharpe stood in front of him and gently slapped his face. 'Wake up, sunshine,' he said. He saw the look of concern on Shepherd's face and shook his head. 'He's just tired. They haven't touched him. Shock and exhaustion is all.'

Ibrahim stood up and blinked at Sharpe. 'Are you the police?' he whispered. 'I want a lawyer. I have my rights. My human rights.'

Sharpe unscrewed the top of the bottle he was holding and let Ibrahim drink from it.

'I want a lawyer,' said Ibrahim when he had finished drinking.

'That's not going to happen,' said Shepherd, walking into view. Sharpe moved away. 'You're in a lot of trouble and so are your family.'

Ibrahim frowned at Shepherd. 'My family?'

'We strip British citizenship from anyone involved in terrorism. That means you, and your parents, and those relatives of yours currently seeking asylum in the United Kingdom, will be sent back to where they came from.'

Ibrahim shook his head. 'You can't do that. I'm British.'

'You were born here but you also have a Syrian passport. So your British citizenship will be taken from you and you will be sent to Syria. Your parents weren't born here and they will be deported with you. And those relatives who are trying to get asylum will be on the plane with you. Your life here is over. You've abused our hospitality and now we're going to send you back to the shithole of a country that you came from.'

'You can't do this,' said Ibrahim, but Shepherd could hear the uncertainty in the man's voice.

'We can and we will,' said Shepherd. 'Who was the man you took to Manchester Airport yesterday?'

'I don't know. I promise you, I do not know.'

'So why were you driving him? You're not an Uber driver, are you?'

'I was asked to pick up a brother and take him to the airport. That's all.'

'That man was responsible for the bombings in London yesterday,' said Shepherd. He prodded Ibrahim in the chest. 'You're a terrorist! You are with ISIS!'

Ibrahim shook his head. 'No, sir, I am not.'

'Do you know how many people died yesterday?'

'Sir, I have never been to London. In my whole life. I swear. I have never been.'

'But yesterday you were at Knutsford Services to collect your friend.'

'Not my friend, sir. He wasn't my friend. I don't even know his name, I was just told to collect him and take him to the airport.'

'You expect me to believe that?' shouted Shepherd. 'You think you can lie to me?' He prodded him in the chest so hard that Ibrahim winced. 'You lie to me and I'll beat you to within an inch of your life. Scum like you, you think you can do what you want in this country. I'll show you . . .'

'Hey, come on,' said Sharpe, appearing at Shepherd's shoulder. 'Give the guy a break. He's trying to help us here. You are trying to help us, Hamid? Right?'

'Yes, sir. Yes I am.'

Shepherd muttered under his breath and walked behind Ibrahim. Sharpe smiled at Ibrahim and patted him on the shoulder. 'Listen to me, Hamid. I believe you when you say you didn't know who that man was. But we do know. He was responsible for the bombs in Trafalgar Square. And you helped him get out of the country. You took him to the airport and he got on a plane. That makes you an accessory to terrorism.'

Ibrahim opened his mouth to protest but Sharpe raised a warning finger to silence him. 'That's what happened, Hamid. We know that for a fact. Now if you want me to help you and your family, you need to be honest with me. You need to help me so that I can help you. Do you understand?'

Ibrahim nodded fearfully. 'I understand, sir.'

'Who told you to go to Knutsford Services?'

'If I tell you, I'll get him in trouble.'

'If you don't tell us, you'll be the one in trouble!' shouted Shepherd. 'And trouble means beating you until you piss blood!'

Ibrahim winced.

'Don't listen to him, Hamid, listen to me,' said Sharpe. 'You need to be honest with me. That's the only way you are going to get through this. Now who told you to pick up the man?'

'My imam,' whispered Ibrahim.

'And what is the imam's name?'

Ibrahim closed his eyes. 'Abu al-Alwani.'

'He's based at your mosque, is he?'

Ibrahim shook his head. 'No, I worship at the Manchester Central Mosque. The big one. I can walk there from my house.'

'And where is Abu al-Alwani's mosque?' asked Sharpe.

'Salford.'

'So how do you know him? You said he was your imam.'

Tears were welling up in Ibrahim's eyes. 'I don't want to say.'

'Why not?'

Ibrahim took a long slow breath before answering. 'Because I will be in trouble and the imam will be in trouble.'

'But if you don't tell us, it will be much worse. You have to trust me on that, Hamid. Yes, you are in trouble but if you co-operate, we can help you.'

'Tell him about Morocco!' shouted Shepherd.

'Morocco?' repeated Ibrahim, twisting around trying to look at him. 'What about Morocco?'

'They want to take you in this container to Morocco and torture you there,' said Sharpe. 'Or Guantanamo Bay. Where there are no laws and you can be tortured and beaten. That's their plan. But if you co-operate now, maybe they'll let you stay in the UK.'

Ibrahim began to sob. Sharpe put a hand on his shoulder. 'You have to be strong, Hamid. You have to tell me everything. How did you know the imam?'

Shepherd and Sharpe walked out of the container. Charlotte Button was waiting for them. 'Everything okay?' she asked as Gerry locked the container door.

'All good, I suppose,' said Shepherd, taking off his ski mask and dropping it into the holdall. 'They're talking, it's just I don't think they have much information to give us. Did Giles say what he wants done with them?'

'I think he's waiting to hear from you.'

'And all options are open?' He unzipped his overalls and shrugged them off.

She tilted her head on one side and looked at him with amused eyes. 'What do you mean?'

'You know what I mean. If Giles wants rid, they end up in a hole somewhere in the Pennines?'

'I don't think it'll come to that.'

'But if that's what he wants, it'll happen?' Sharpe was struggling to remove his overalls so Shepherd went over to help him.

'We do the jobs the government can't or won't do themselves,' she said. 'You know that. Things sometimes have to be done at arm's length. Plausible deniability.'

'Those guys aren't hardened terrorists. If anything, they're idiots.'

'Then tell Giles that.' She flashed him a tight smile. 'A lot of innocent people died yesterday, Dan.' She gestured at the containers. 'Those guys played a part in it. Even if it was a small part, they were still players.'

Shepherd took out his phone. He walked away until Button was out of earshot and called Pritchard, who answered almost immediately. 'Khan and Ibrahim both gave up the same name,' said Shepherd. 'An imam at a small mosque in West Manchester. Abu al-Alwani.'

'Do they have any idea where Uthman went?'

'Khan didn't even know that he went to the airport. Ibrahim was told to drop him at Departures.'

'Do you think they've got any helpful information at all?'

'Not really, no. I think they were just hired hands.'

'Let me run the imam through the system. Can you head back to London?'

'Will do,' said Shepherd. 'What about the Khans and Ibrahim? What happens to them?'

'Let them stay put for the moment, we can't charge them yet because then the imam will know we're onto him. Back to London, Dan, soon as you can.' Pritchard ended the call and Shepherd put his phone back into his pocket. He walked back to Button. 'I'm heading back to Thames House.'

'Give Giles my best.'

'He said to leave the Khans and Ibrahim where they are for the moment until we follow up on the information they gave us.'

'Anything I should know?'

'Not really, just a name. Abu al-Alwani. He's an imam at a mosque in West Manchester. Giles is checking him out.'

'How is Giles at the moment? Under pressure?'

'How much did he tell you?'

She sighed and rolled her eyes. 'Dan, I have signed the Official Secrets Act.'

'I know that, but you're not on staff any more, so I have to be careful what I say.'

'Right, fine.' She tossed her hair and Shepherd fought back the urge to smile. He'd never seen her petulant before. 'Giles said that an MI6 agent might have betrayed them and was involved in the bombs in Trafalgar Square yesterday. He said these two men got the agent from London to Manchester Airport and he wanted them questioned.'

'Yeah, that's pretty much it,' said Shepherd.

'So I'm guessing that MI5 was running the operation against the armed jihadists in Trafalgar Square, and that somehow the bombs were missed. Which means that at the moment Giles and

Melissa Schofield are playing pass the shit parcel as fast as they can. Am I right?'

She looked into his eyes with a slight smile on her face. He would have hated to play poker with her as he had absolutely no idea what she was thinking. Did she know what had happened at the safe house and that Schofield was dead? Was that why she had mentioned her name, to test him? If so, it was a ridiculous test because as much as he liked her, his first loyalty had to be to MI5. 'There's been a bit of a turf war, yes,' he said. 'But it looks as if Giles will come out on top. Not necessarily smelling of roses, but if we can track down this agent and find out who was pulling his strings, he should be okay.'

'Well, he knows he can depend on me,' said Button.

She was still looking into his eyes and he still had no idea if she was playing with him or not. 'I'll be sure to tell him,' he said. He waved over at Sharpe. 'Let's go, Razor,' he said.

'Drive carefully,' said Button.

'I always do, Charlotte,' said Sharpe.

Jimmy Sharpe brought the Jaguar to a halt outside Shepherd's apartment block. It was just after midnight and they had driven back from Manchester without a break. 'You want a quick drink?' asked Shepherd.

'Nah, I'll head home. The missus has barely seen me over the past week as it is.' He tapped his steering wheel.' I thought I might go and see Uthman's tutor at Westminster University tomorrow. He's a Dr Thomas Cohen. He was Uthman's personal tutor during his three years at the University of Westminster.'

'Seriously? Why?'

'Call it a copper's hunch. I still don't understand why Uthman turned down the chance to do an MA in London and switched to Manchester instead.'

'You're continuing with your "Manchester is a shithole" theme, are you?'

Sharpe grinned. 'Sorry about that. But I have to scratch this itch, Spider, it won't go away. There's something not right, I can feel it in my water. He's based at the Harrow Campus. It'll take me forty minutes or so to get there, so write me off for the morning and I'll see you at lunch.'

Shepherd nodded. He had worked with Sharpe long enough to trust the man's judgement. His copper's hunches came from more than thirty years of experience and had stood him in good stead in the past. 'Go for it,' he said. He climbed out of the car and walked into his apartment block as Sharpe drove away.

Liam was still up, drinking a beer and watching a Netflix movie. Shepherd grabbed a beer from the fridge and joined him on the sofa. 'Tough day?' asked Liam.

'Just busy,' said Shepherd.

'So I'm heading back to Yeovilton tomorrow.'

'That's a pity. I've enjoyed having you around. But I think I'm going to be rushed off my feet over the next few days.'

'Yeah, it's been fun. And good that you got to meet Naomi.'

'So you are serious about her?'

Liam grinned. 'You're going all Jane Austen again.'

'It's not easy having a relationship when you're in the Army.'

'She's cool. She sees how it is with her brother so she understands.'

'I know, but you'll be away a lot and it can be hard for wives to deal with that.'

Liam snorted. 'Bloody hell, Dad, we're not married. We're not even engaged.'

'I'm just saying, you have to work at long-distance relationships.'

'She's in London. I'm in Yeovilton. It's a two-and-a-half-hour drive.'

'But if they send you to Belize?'

'Dad, you're overthinking this. It's not like when you were with Mum. Back then if you were off soldiering you couldn't call or anything. These days we've got Facebook and Facetime and Instagram and all that social media stuff.'

'Yeah, that would have helped during my SAS days. Your mum used to be worried stiff when she didn't hear from me, sometimes for weeks at a time. And when you came along, that just made it worse.' He sipped his beer.

'That's why you left the SAS, right? Because Mum wanted to see more of you?'

Shepherd laughed. 'Yeah, that was the plan. The idea was that I'd be a beat bobby and be home every evening. But instead I got thrown into undercover work and I ended up being away more than when I was with the Sass. Best-laid plans . . .'

'The world is different now,' said Liam.

'You mean I'm an old fart and I should stop worrying about your romantic life?'

Liam laughed. 'You got it in one, Dad.' He leaned over and clinked his bottle against Shepherd's. 'I'm doing fine.'

Shepherd took another drink and then tilted his head back and looked at the ceiling. 'Shit,' he said.

'What?'

'If this works out, I'll be a grandfather.'

Liam laughed and shook his head. 'One step at a time, Dad.'

Next morning Shepherd and Liam had breakfast together, with Liam cooking his old favourite cheesy scrambled eggs. They chatted mainly about Liam's work, with Shepherd making a determined effort not to mention Naomi. Shepherd left Liam to do the washing-up and walked to Thames House. A police helicopter was buzzing overhead. Shepherd didn't know if it was crime related or because the Joint Terrorism Analysis Centre had raised the nation's threat level to critical. That meant the JTAC considered that a terrorist attack was highly likely in the near future, though considering what had already happened it was clearly a case of locking the stable door long after the horse had bolted.

Shepherd went straight up to Pritchard's office and was waved through by his secretary. Pritchard was standing at his window, staring out at the river. He had rolled his sleeves up and his club tie was loose around his neck. He turned to look at Shepherd and forced a smile. He had dark patches under his eyes and there was a greyish tinge to his skin. He obviously hadn't slept well, if at all. 'Welcome back,' he said. He waved for Shepherd to sit on the sofa, which meant that he had time to talk. Shepherd sat. He expected Pritchard to join him but instead the man began to pace up and down. 'So. The imam. Abu al-Alwani. He's not on our watch list but he was looked at five years ago after a couple of anonymous calls were made to the anti-terrorism hotline. He's got two wives and two families, all on benefits, and he travels between the two council houses and the mosque on a battered old bike. No assets, no property, no money in the bank.'

'How did he manage to get two families on benefits?' asked Shepherd.

'He fled Iraq in 2003 with his wife and two kids and managed to get to the UK. He had distant family in Manchester who helped him. Ten years and three more kids later he gets citizenship and then he produces a second family who are still in Baghdad. The Home Office in its infinite wisdom allows the second family in. Now he has two wives and nine kids. But when he was looked at, there were no links to terrorism and no inflammatory comments online or during his sermons. We had a couple of agents in the mosque and they confirmed he was clean. It was assumed that the calls to the hotline were malicious.' He stopped pacing, dropped down onto the sofa and stretched out his legs.

'But Khan and Ibrahim both named him,' said Shepherd. 'He contacted both men separately and told Khan to go to Hampstead and pick up Uthman. Khan went with a friend, Faraz Javeed, but I doubt he'll be able to add anything to what Khan said. The imam told Khan to deliver Uthman to Knutsford Services and told Ibrahim to meet Khan there and collect Uthman and to take him to the airport. Both men say they didn't know each other.'

'But they went to the same mosque?'

'No. Khan went to the same mosque as al-Alwani, but Ibrahim worshipped at the main Manchester mosque. They both say that the first time they met was at Knutsford Services. They claim to know nothing about each other and I believe them.'

'So how did this al-Alwani know Ibrahim if he went to a different mosque?' asked Pritchard.

'Ibrahim says that the imam was running jihad lessons in his home. One of his homes, anyway. Small groups of like-minded individuals who wanted to learn more about the more extreme views in the Koran and how they could play a part in global jihad.'

Pritchard sighed. 'What were our agents playing at? They gave him a clean bill of health?'

'I guess the agents had no idea what he was doing at home,' said Shepherd. 'He never put a foot wrong in the mosque or on social media. But according to Ibrahim he was very different behind closed doors. A real "death to infidels" firebrand. But he only ever had small groups around, three or four at most, so he never appeared on our radar. According to Ibrahim, the imam has sent dozens of his acolytes to Pakistan and Afghanistan for training. Ibrahim wanted to go but the imam said that not every jihadist had to fire a gun, that there were other tasks that needed doing that were just as valuable. Then two days ago he got the call. The imam wanted him to wait at the service station, pick up the man who would be delivered to him, and take him to Manchester Airport. The white skullcap he was wearing was so that Khan would recognise him in a crowd.'

'And what about Khan?' asked Pritchard. 'When did he get the call from the imam?'

'Five days ago. He was told to get to London the following day and to stay in a cheap hotel in Bayswater. He was told to be on standby the day before yesterday and that at some point he would go to a street where he would be met by Uthman. He didn't know him as Uthman, he was just referred to as "the brother" throughout.'

'And when was he told to go to Hampstead?'

'About an hour before Uthman got there.'

'So Uthman is told where to go for the debrief and he calls the imam and the imam tells Khan where to go to pick him up?'

Shepherd nodded. 'If you can get Uthman's phone records, we should be able to prove that.'

'Except that Uthman would be canny enough to use a burner phone. The imam too. But yes, I'll get their phones checked. So this imam is a wily bastard. But is he the mastermind behind this?'

'It's possible,' said Shepherd. 'If he was smart enough to fool the agents on his case, he might be hiding a lot more. This whole "poor imam on benefits" could be a sham.'

'Well let me get things rolling on that front,' said Pritchard. 'We'll put him under the microscope this time.'

'You're not pulling him in?'

'That's problematical,' said Pritchard. 'You can't start getting rough with an imam without repercussions.'

'And what about the guys your contractors brought in? What happens to them?'

Pritchard stood up and began pacing again, rubbing his chin. Eventually he stopped and looked out through the window. 'They can sit on them for a while. Then we might consider turning them and using them as agents. Given the choice between prison or helping us, we might convert them. Let's see how we get on with the imam.'

'Do you want to tell Charlotte Button that, or shall I pass on the message?'

Pritchard turned to look at him. 'Ah, she was there, was she?'

'Why didn't you tell me she was handling it?'

'When I discussed the job with her, she was in two minds about turning up herself, considering your previous history.'

'By history you mean I worked for her, for a while?' said Shepherd. 'Why would that be a problem? She was a good boss. And our paths have crossed several times after she left Five.'

'Yes, I know that, but she did leave under something of a cloud and I think there might have been an embarrassment factor in play.'

Shepherd couldn't help but laugh out loud. 'Charlotte Button? Embarrassed? I really don't think so.'

'Then maybe I misunderstood,' said Pritchard. 'I got the

impression she might not be personally involved, so didn't feel it necessary to use her name. There was nothing devious going on, Dan. Charlotte runs one of the private contractor companies that we use and she has access to the Pool. We often use her company. That was part of her deal when she left.'

'Yes, I remember,' said Shepherd.

'I wonder why she decided to get personally involved? Maybe she wanted to catch up.'

'It didn't seem like that. We barely spoke.'

Pritchard sat down on the sofa again. 'I'm sure she'd love to have you in the Pool. Your special forces background plus your intelligence experience makes you a very valuable commodity.'

'Maybe, if I wanted to work for the highest bidder.'

'And you don't?'

Shepherd smiled thinly. 'It's never been about the money. You don't join the SAS for the salary, you join because you want to be the best of the best. And because you want to be challenged.'

'And the excitement?'

'Of course. But it's not just about the adrenaline rush you get in combat. It's about knowing that you are fighting for the right cause.'

'Good against evil?'

'I don't think I could have done what I did over the years if I didn't think I was in the right. It's the same with the job I do now. We keep this country safe. Or at least we try to. Our enemies are the people who want to do harm to our country and its citizens and I'll do whatever I can to stop them. But if you work for the Pool, you don't know what you're fighting for. Other than the money.' He shrugged. 'I know a few ex-SAS guys who work for the Pool and they have no problems doing what they're asked to do, but I don't think I'd be as sanguine.'

'You've got a conscience, is that it?'

'No, it's not a conscience. I'll happily do bad things to bad people and not think twice about it. Charlie knows that. But she also knows that I have my standards and values and I stay true to them. This job you've given her, I get it absolutely. Those guys needed to be taken off the street and questioned and PACE would stop that dead in the water. And if they end up dead in a grave out in the Pennines, I wouldn't shed any tears, not after all the civilians who died in Trafalgar Square. But Charlie doesn't only do your dirty work, she takes contracts from anyone, pretty much.'

'Well, not anyone,' said Pritchard. 'It's true that she is allowed to take contracts and jobs within the private sector, but she has to be careful.'

'Well, that's why I could never work for her. I'd have to be able to justify every job she gave me, and that would end in tears. Anyway, she didn't offer me a job and we didn't really have time for a catch up. Razor and I were in and out.'

'What sort of boss was she, when she was here?'

Shepherd shrugged. 'She was quick on her feet, she was always good at making decisions and she trusted her own judgement. You knew that if she gave you a task, she'd thought it through and considered all the options. I trusted her, I really did. I've had bosses before that I didn't trust and it never ends well, but I trusted Charlie with my life. Literally.'

'I hope you know that you can trust me, Dan. I'd never ask you to do something that I wouldn't do myself.'

Shepherd smiled. 'So far, so good,' he said.

'Good man.' Pritchard stood up and looked at his watch. 'So it's now 1 p.m. in Dubai. I haven't heard back from our embassy staff yet and I'm assuming that no news is no news, so I'll wait until this afternoon before I start rattling their cages. In the meantime, I'll get things moving on the imam. I'm not sure there's much for you to do here at the moment. I'm tempted to put you on a plane to Dubai right now but we'll look a bit silly if he's already boarded another flight. So just hang tight and be ready to head out when we know where Uthman has gone.'

He walked to his desk and sat down, leaving Shepherd in no doubt that the meeting was over.

The traffic was heavy and it took Jimmy Sharpe almost an hour to drive to the University of Westminster's Harrow Campus, which housed the university's school of arts and its school of media and communication, where Uthman had studied. On the way he phoned ahead and let Dr Cohen know that he needed a half-hour of his time.

Sharpe parked the Jaguar and walked into the main building, where a bored receptionist told him the way to Dr Cohen's office.

Dr Cohen was in his late forties with a receding hairline and blue-framed glasses. He was wearing a collarless white shirt and dark green corduroy trousers that whispered as he walked behind his desk and sat down. There was a circular table with five chairs around it by the window and he gestured at Sharpe. 'Pull up a pew,' he said.

Sharpe took a chair and sat down. Dr Cohen's computer was at the side of his desk and was switched off. 'So I didn't quite understand from your phone call why we have to do this again,' he said. On the wall to his right were dozens of framed photographs of Dr Cohen standing with different groups of students.

Sharpe took out a small black notebook and a pen. 'It's mainly to review the vetting procedure,' he said. 'It's constantly being fine-tuned.'

'It's a growth industry, apparently,' said Dr Cohen.

'What is?' said Sharpe.

'This whole vetting business. I think Mo was only my third or fourth interview in my entire career, but in the last year or so I've done about another twenty. Post Covid, the government is just about the only employer that seems to be hiring.'

'It can't be an easy time for your graduates these days. Things were very different when Mo was hired.'

'The man who came to see me back then wouldn't say exactly which department was thinking of hiring him but I assumed it was something to do with sensitive material. GCHQ maybe?'

'They tend not to broadcast who the potential employer is,' said Sharpe.

'But it would obviously be for the government, right?' said Dr Cohen.

'To be honest, I don't think they are even able to confirm that,' said Sharpe.

'Well, it did surprise me that Mo wanted to work for the government in any capacity,' said Dr Cohen. 'He was always anti-government.'

'So not a Tory?' said Sharpe. 'Nothing wrong with that. Plenty of lefties work for the civil service.'

'No, I mean he was against all government. I think in his mind utopia would be a stateless society.'

'So he was an anarchist?' said Sharpe. 'Did you tell the vetting officer that?'

Dr Cohen laughed and held up his hands. 'Oh no, Mo wasn't an anarchist. He just didn't like governments. Any governments. There's a world of difference between that and anarchy. He just felt that decisions were always better taken at a local level. He thought that governments tended to act in their own interests and not in the interests of their people. I think because of what he'd seen happen to his own country. His argument was always that central governments did more harm than good and that we would be better off without them. But he certainly didn't suggest anarchy as an alternative. He was just a typical student, you know? Ready to protest about anything.'

'Did he do that? Protest?'

'No, he never got involved like that. Don't get me wrong, please. He was a good student, well balanced and eager to please, maybe not the brightest or the most articulate, but these days half of all kids go to university so you tend to get a mixed bag of abilities. He was average. Just average. But his language abilities would make him an asset in the sort of job I'm assuming he had applied for. All I was saying is that with hindsight, after the vetting interview, that's when it struck me that it was a strange choice of career. I didn't mention it at the previous interview and frankly I'm starting to wish I hadn't mentioned it this time.'

'It's not a problem,' said Sharpe. He flashed the man a reassuring smile. 'That's one of the reasons we do these follow-up interviews, to see if your views had changed over time.'

Dr Cohen nodded thoughtfully. 'Yes, that makes sense,' he

said. 'But my views haven't changed. He'd be a good employee, I'm sure.'

Sharpe tilted his head on one side. 'Dr Cohen, are you Jewish?' he asked.

'Guilty as charged,' said Dr Cohen. He frowned. 'But why would you ask that question?'

'You seem to like Mo, and I wondered if him being a Muslim had ever caused any issues between you?'

Dr Cohen shook his head. 'This is one of the most diverse universities in the country, in one of the most diverse cities. It was never an issue. I was Mo's personal tutor for three years – if at any point he'd wanted to change that, all he had to do was to ask. But the short answer is no, there were no issues.'

'What sort of person was he?' asked Sharpe. 'Popular? Loner? Extrovert? Introvert?'

'If I had to choose a word to describe him, it would be average. He was average academically. His time-keeping was as good as most and better than some, he met pretty much all of his deadlines and he contributed reasonably well in class, though he was a bit shy and had to be prodded sometimes. He wasn't the most popular kid on campus, but he wasn't a wallflower. I saw him several times in the Undercroft with different groups.'

'The Undercroft?' repeated Sharpe.

'The student union bar. Mo was a regular.'

'He drank alcohol?' asked Sharpe.

'Beer. Bottled beer, usually. Sol, the Spanish one. I know what you're thinking, why was a Muslim drinking? I don't think his religion was a big thing to him. It's like all those Church of England people who only ever go into a church for christenings, weddings and funerals. And I'm a Jew but I'm comfortable working on the Sabbath and – but don't tell the wife this – I'm actually partial to lobster.' He shrugged. 'Mo was a Muslim but he didn't really live like one. There's a Muslim Society at the university but he didn't move in those circles. Don't get me wrong, he had Muslim friends and I'd often see him talking to girls in headscarves, but he had more non-Muslim friends, it seemed to me.'

'Girlfriends?'

'No one special but I saw him holding hands with girls from time to time. He had a bit of a thing with a girl on his course in his first year but I don't think anything ever came of it.'

'You said you were surprised that he applied to work for the government,' said Sharpe. 'What did you think he'd do, career-wise?'

'I assumed journalism. He worked on the student newspaper and in his final year he was on the editorial team. I think he was quite keen to work for the BBC. He'd heard that they were very keen to boost their ethnic content, on screen and in the studios, and I had the impression that was what he wanted to do. He was looking at doing a Masters here, that much I do remember.'

'He decided to do his MA in Manchester,' said Sharpe. 'I was wondering why he didn't do it here.'

'Yes, that did come as a surprise,' said Dr Cohen. 'I was certainly under the impression he wanted to do his MA here at Westminster and that he was considering Multimedia Journalism. We had a number of discussions about it.'

'He liked London?' asked Sharpe.

'He was very happy here. Prior to enrolling at Westminster he'd been at quite a restrictive boarding school, out in the middle of nowhere. Somewhere in Devon, not far from Dartmoor. He loved London. And he was very happy with university. He wasn't the brightest student but he was never in the bottom quartile. When he applied himself he could do quite well. But he was attentive in lectures. So many students these days spend more time on their social media than listening to their lecturers, but I did get the impression that Mo was genuinely interested in the subject.'

'So he could have done his MA here?'

'Very easily. As I said, we discussed that possibility several times. And my understanding was that he had been offered a place on the course. Then of course his parents were killed, out in Iraq.'

'How did that affect him?'

'He was distraught, obviously. He had taken his finals, which I suppose was a blessing, and I saw him a couple of days after it happened. He was in shock. I don't think he went to the degree ceremony, I am pretty sure we posted it out to him. And then not long after that I realised he hadn't taken up his MA offer here and was going to Manchester.'

'Did you meet his parents?'

'I did, yes. Twice, I think. They came with him to the university during his first week here and I think I saw them again in the second year. They were a lovely couple, well travelled, intelligent, good company, it was awful what happened. Truly awful.'

'Did you discuss it with him?'

'A little, but he wasn't very talkative. He was in shock, maybe.'

'Did you remain in contact with Mo after he left the university?' asked Sharpe.

'No, but that's par for the course.' He smiled. 'No pun intended. When they leave most of them swear that they'll stay in touch, but they almost never do. I did send him an email when I heard that he'd gone to Manchester, but he never replied.' He shrugged. 'I suppose he just wanted a fresh start. It makes sense, I suppose. He was in London when he heard about the death of his parents, maybe that tainted it for him.' He leaned forward, his eyes narrowing behind his glasses. 'Is everything okay with Mo? I'm getting the feeling this is more than just a review?'

Sharpe flashed his most disarming smile. 'No, nothing's wrong. I've done a dozen of these follow-up interviews this week. It's partly to add to the original vetting interviews but it's also a matter of quality control, to see if there are ways that the interviews can be improved. It's an ongoing process, as you can imagine.' He faked a look at his watch, even though he knew exactly what time it was. 'Well, thank you for your time,' he said. 'You've been very patient with me.' He stood up and went over to look at the framed photographs. They were of Dr Cohen's tutorial groups over the years, with the doctor in the centre and between six and ten students gathered around him.

Underneath the picture was the year and the names of the students. The earliest, on the far left, had been taken in 2006. The latest, on the right, was the previous year. Over the years Dr Cohen had lost his hair and gained his glasses and about twenty pounds.

Sharpe looked at the photographs for the years that Uthman had been at the university. There was an Asian boy in all three of the photographs but it wasn't Uthman. This boy was shorter and stockier, though he had a similar beard and glasses. 'So I don't see Mo here,' said Sharpe.

'No, he's there,' said Dr Cohen. 'Right in front of you.'

Sharpe blinked as he peered at the names at the bottom of one of the pictures. Mohammed Uthman. His eyes widened and he leaned forward to get a better look. 'That's interesting,' Sharpe whispered.

'Is there something wrong?' asked Cohen.

'No, nothing's wrong,' said Sharpe, taking out his phone. 'Do you mind if I take a picture, for the record?'

'Sure, of course.'

Sharpe took photographs of the three pictures and smiled. 'Right, I think that's all I need,' he said. 'Thank you again for your time. You've been very helpful.'

Pritchard had put a head-and-shoulders shot of Uthman's MI5 file picture on one screen on his desk and the three pictures Sharpe had taken in Dr Cohen's office on his second screen. He looked from one to the other, frown lines deepening across his forehead. Shepherd stood next to them, his eyes flicking from screen to screen. 'Oh shit,' said Pritchard.

Sharpe sat on the sofa grinning widely. He had driven back to London as fast as the speed limits would allow, phoning Shepherd on the way telling him only that there was something he needed to see. Shepherd had been waiting for him in reception and had taken him through security. Sharpe had stayed tight-lipped during the ride up in the lift and Shepherd had been tempted to throw him up against the wall and beat it out of him, but he had just smiled and let Sharpe play whatever game he was playing.

The secretary had ushered them into the office and then Sharpe had uploaded the three photographs to Pritchard's computer and suggested he compare them with the photograph he had of Mo Uthman.

Pritchard began to grind his teeth as he stared at the two screens. Eventually he looked over at Sharpe. 'So the man MI6 hired, the man who left the Hampstead safe house before it exploded killing everyone inside, was NOT Mohammed Uthman?'

'That's pretty much definite,' said Sharpe.

Pritchard stood up and began pacing. 'How the hell could the vetting process not pick up the fact that the man they are vetting isn't who he claims to be?'

'I guess because that's not what the vetting process is there for,' said Sharpe. 'Vetting is to check that the person is of good character and has no skeletons in his closet. And if you only ask questions to that end, Uthman comes through with flying colours.'

'And no one thought to look at his photograph? It's clearly not the same person.' He stood with his back to the window and folded his arms. A small vein was pulsing in his temple.

Shepherd had remained behind Pritchard's desk looking at the photographs. He straightened up. 'I hate the fact that I appear to be playing Devil's Advocate here but when a vetting officer turns up and starts asking questions about Mohammed Uthman and you know a guy called Mohammed Uthman, you're not going to ask for a photograph, are you?' he said. 'The vetting officer knows that Uthman went to Westminster University so he goes there to talk to his personal tutor. They both assume they are talking about the same man.' Shepherd walked around the desk and sat on one of the wooden chairs.

'Jimmy here spotted the anomaly,' said Pritchard.

'Yes, but more by luck than judgement,' said Sharpe. 'I was looking at the photographs on the tutor's walls. Up until then I had no idea that we were talking about different people.'

Pritchard walked back to his desk, sat down and rubbed the

back of his neck as he looked at the screens again. 'So what happened to the real Mohammed Uthman?'

'Dead presumably,' said Shepherd, stretching out his legs. 'Dead and buried where no one will ever find the body. It must have happened after his parents were killed in the Iraqi bombings. That's why he didn't go over for the funeral, and shortly afterwards the replacement cancelled plans to do an MA in London and instead applied for a different course in a city far enough away that he was unlikely to come across anyone who knew the real Uthman.'

'And again, no one realised that the man who turned up to study in Manchester wasn't the same man who had done the degree at Westminster?'

'Why would they?' said Shepherd. 'He has the credentials, he has all the paperwork, and he is an Asian guy of about the same age.'

'Before I attended all my diversity classes I might have said they all look alike,' said Sharpe. He grinned mischievously. 'Obviously I wouldn't say that now, but the simple fact is that both men have black hair, brown eyes and brownish skin and with the beard and glasses they do look similar. If you see a bearded Asian guy who says he's Mo Uthman and his paperwork is all in order, is someone going to ask to see his driving licence?'

'What about his passport?' said Pritchard. 'He would have had to submit his passport when he applied for a post with MI6.'

'If the passport was issued when he was eighteen, it would have been four or five years old when he applied to join MI6,' said Shepherd. 'People change a lot over those years. And you're allowed to wear your glasses in your passport photograph, so if the doppelgänger arranged to have a matching pair that would pretty much clinch it.'

'But the doppelgänger couldn't ever use the passport to travel,' said Pritchard. 'Even if he looked similar to the real Uthman, facial recognition computers at the airport would pick it up.'

'Only if he used the eGates,' said Shepherd. 'If he went through a manual check, it would be down to the eyes of the

Border Force officer and we know that they make hundreds of errors like that every year. But he didn't leave the country for the funerals of his parents and once he was operational with MI6 they would have issued him a passport and driving licence to go with his legend. He wouldn't have to use the Uthman passport.'

Pritchard leaned forward and put his palms on his desk, then beat a rapid tattoo. 'This is a bloody nightmare. So we don't even know who this guy is? All we have is his photograph?'

'Well, MI6 would have his DNA and his prints. But that doesn't mean we'll find a match.'

Pritchard frowned. 'So this guy what, three years ago, kills Mo Uthman and takes his place. Moves to Manchester and turns himself into the perfect candidate for joining MI6. And he does that, why? Because he was planning a terrorist incident right from the start? Why not just go full jihad and blow himself up on the Tube?'

'Because he wanted something bigger,' said Shepherd. 'And he certainly achieved that. It's the deadliest terrorist attack ever on British soil and ISIS are taking full credit for it. It's the British 9-11. Three years planning is a small price to pay for a spectacular like they had in Trafalgar Square.'

'I don't know, Dan. It just seems there has to be more to it. He didn't have to join MI6 to get those jihadists into the country and get the guns and explosives.'

'No, but it made it that much easier, didn't it? By involving MI6 right from the start, he knew every step of the way what they were doing. It was a Trojan horse operation and MI6 were too busy staring at the wooden horse to see the bigger picture. It was the perfect distraction.'

'The real Mo Uthman is twenty-four years old,' said Pritchard. 'The fake can't be much older. A twenty-four-year-old couldn't possibly have organised this.'

'ISIS have already claimed responsibility,' said Shepherd.

'The organisation, yes. But no mastermind has stepped forward to say that they put the whole thing together.'

'Because by identifying himself he'd be inviting a drone attack. They know that if they stick their head above the parapet there's likely to be a Hellfire missile heading their way with their name on it.'

'Yes, you're right, of course. But that doesn't explain why they haven't taken credit for the death of Melissa Schofield. On that score, we've just had the preliminary results from the forensics team who are looking at the house. They have found traces of PETN. The two truck bombs appear to be common or garden ANFO. Our people are running their analysis of the explosives residue through the University of Rhode Island's Explosives Database to see if they can come up with a match.'

Shepherd nodded. He knew about the Rhode Island database. It was funded by an anti-terrorism institute and collected data from explosions around the world, which was made available to police and intelligence agencies worldwide. PETN – pentaerythritol tetranitrate – was a major ingredient of Semtex and was similar to nitroglycerine. It was incredibly powerful and four ounces would be more than enough to destroy a vehicle. A pound of the explosive could easily have caused the damage to the Hampstead safe house and killed all the occupants. ANFO on the other hand – ammonium nitrate fertiliser mixed with fuel oil, favourite of the IRA – was a bulk explosive that was only really effective in barrel-sized quantities, and even then to be truly effective it had to be padded out with metal objects such as nails and screws to form devastating shrapnel. 'Do you think there were two different bombmakers?'

'Could be the same bombmaker using different techniques,' said Pritchard.

'Uthman, or whoever is pretending to be Uthman, is a bit young to have those sorts of skills,' said Shepherd.

'True. But whereas the vetting officers would have looked at Uthman's travel history, we've no way of knowing the background of his replacement. For all we know he could have spent years in Syria or Iraq receiving any amount of terrorist training. He's a total unknown. Except as you say, we have his DNA and his fingerprints, so there is a possibility he'll be in the system some-where.'

'Wouldn't the vetting officers have spotted that?' said Sharpe. 'I mean, Uthman wasn't Uthman but he would have had to have given his DNA and fingerprints.'

'He was British, they'd have confined their checks to the UK,' said Pritchard. 'Jimmy, this is amazing work, well done and thank you. It's thrown a spanner into the investigation but at least now we know what's going on. I can get the ball rolling on that, but since we left Europol as part of the Brexit process, it'll take time. But if he was a cleanskin and managed to sneak into the country, then we'll have a devil of a job identifying him.'

'So what do we think, that Uthman – or whoever was passing himself off as Uthman – took the Semtex into the house?' asked Sharpe.

'It's the obvious answer, isn't it? He had the device ready and was just waiting for Schofield to tell him where to go. No one would have searched him. We assumed it was Abbas who was the rotten apple, so we could never work out how the house was bombed. But once you realise that Uthman was bad, then it all makes sense.'

'It explains how it was possible, yes,' said Shepherd. 'But I don't see how it makes any sense at all. The Trafalgar Square bombs had gone off, he was free and clear, he could have just gone to ground. Or played it out as an MI6 officer who screwed up. He'd be thrown out but he wouldn't have faced criminal charges. Why up the ante by blowing up the safe house?'

'To throw us off the trail, maybe?' said Pritchard. 'Like you said, he wanted to go to ground, but if he just vanished then that would raise suspicions. But by blowing up the house and leaving as Abbas, everyone would assume that he was among the dead and no one would be looking for him. If he stayed and tried to bluff it out, there was a chance he would have been discovered. This way he starts a new life overseas safe in the knowledge that no one is hunting him.' Pritchard sighed and scrunched up his face as he considered his options. 'We need to start looking for whoever is behind all this. It's just about possible that the imam in Manchester is the mastermind. He grooms Uthman, or at least the man who took over Uthman's life, and takes him to Manchester and turns him into the perfect MI6 candidate. The imam then arranges for the explosives and has the bombs planted in Trafalgar Square on the day of the firearms attack. Then he arranges for the Uthman doppelgänger to take a bomb into the safe house and destroy everyone there.' He forced a smile. 'Even as I say it, I realise that it doesn't sound in the least bit likely, does it?'

'It's not the imam,' said Shepherd. 'I'm sure of that. I think the imam was used, as was Uthman's doppelgänger.'

'By whom?'

'Well, yes, exactly, that's the big question,' said Shepherd. 'Whoever it is has money, either money of their own or access to ISIS funds. And it seems to me that if this had been ISIS funded, there would have been chatter prior to the event. There always is. So I think we're looking for someone either within Islamic State or someone outside who has money of their own. Did Uthman ever say where the money came from to buy the guns we sold him?'

Pritchard shook his head. 'I asked Melissa at the time and she said Uthman was working on it. Then we were distanced from the operation and I never got an answer to the question.'

'That was a few thousand pounds for the guns, but two truckloads of ANFO took time and money to prepare, plus there's all the money it cost to keep the jihadists housed and fed, then there's the Semtex, that's not cheap and bloody difficult to get your hands on. That's another reason I don't think the imam put it together. I don't see that he'd have the contacts for something like that. And then there's the death of the real Uthman's parents.'

'Yes, that's been worrying me, too,' said Pritchard. 'Was that just fortuitous, or planned?'

'If it happened by chance, it's one hell of a coincidence, isn't it? Mr and Mrs Uthman are killed in a car bombing in Iraq and

ISIS manage to find a doppelgänger for their son, kill him and replace him, all in a matter of weeks.' He shook his head. 'It's too much of a coincidence.'

'So that means that they deliberately arranged to have the parents killed so that they could then get rid of Uthman and put the doppelgänger in place,' said Pritchard. 'There's no way an imam in Manchester could have done that. You remember the 2016 Iraq bombings, right?'

Shepherd nodded. There had been suicide bombings and car bomb attacks in Iraq throughout 2016, with more than a thousand deaths. The deadliest attack had been on July 3 when ISIS jihadists had killed 340 civilians and injured hundreds more in a series of bomb attacks across the Iraqi capital. The main bomb was in a truck in a middle-class suburb of Karrada, detonated by a suicide bomber as locals were breaking their Ramadan fast at local restaurants. Other smaller bombs went off around the city at the same time and ISIS were quick to claim the credit, and more bombs went off during the evening, adding to the death toll. It would have been relatively simple to target Mo Uthman's parents during the carnage. But obviously Pritchard was right – an imam in Manchester couldn't possibly have orchestrated an assassination on the other side of the world. It would have required contracts with senior ISIS officials and large amounts of money. 'So whoever is behind this, they're probably in Iraq?'

'Or they were in Iraq, back in 2016,' said Pritchard. 'They must have known that Mo Uthman was getting to the end of his degree and looked for a replacement. They find the replacement, kill his parents and then kill Uthman. They might have been planning it long before 2016. They'd have to make sure that their doppelgänger bore at least a passing resemblance to Uthman and had the same language skills. Then they'd have to get him into the country, and they would have to smuggle him in because any visa application would require fingerprints. The amount of planning is just mind-blowing. Who the hell could have done that?'

Shepherd shrugged but didn't say anything. It wasn't a question he could answer.

Pritchard sat back in his chair and sighed. 'And what the hell am I going to tell Julian Penniston-Hill?'

Amy appeared in the doorway. 'I'm sorry but Forensics are on the phone and they say it's urgent.'

'Put the call through, Amy.' He smiled apologetically at Shepherd and Sharpe. 'I've got to take this.' His phone buzzed and he picked it up. He listened intently and grunted a few times. 'Can you email that to me? You did? Thank you.' He ended the call and sat down behind his desk. 'Just give me a minute, I need to read this,' he said. He put on his wire-framed spectacles, tapped on his keyboard and peered at the screen on his right. Eventually he sat back and shook his head in annoyance. 'This just gets worse and worse,' he muttered.

'What's happened?' asked Shepherd.

'We've had some preliminary results back from the forensics at the Hampstead house. There wasn't much left in the room but there was enough DNA to identify who was killed. Interestingly there was DNA from Uthman on a set of keys and his phone case, so it looks as if he left them there to muddy the waters. We don't have DNA on file for Abbas but we did for Schofield, Williams and the two MI6 analysts. But they also found bullets in the room. They were badly deformed in the explosion but they all have DNA on them, so it looks as if some of the occupants of the room were shot before the explosion. With 9mm rounds.'

Shepherd's eyes widened. 'What?'

'I know, I know. It means Uthman took in a gun and explosives. Presumably in the backpack he was carrying. He shot them, grabbed Abbas's coat and left the back way before the bomb went off.' He peered at his screen, then sat back and removed his glasses.

'And the gun? Was there any sign of the gun?'

'No. But if it had been a Glock it could easily have been completely destroyed in the explosion. They're mainly plastic.'

'He's more likely to have taken it with him,' said Shepherd. 'In case he encountered any opposition on the way to the car. That being the case, what has he done with it? He couldn't have taken it on the plane.'

'There's a lot of options,' said Pritchard, leaning back in his chair. 'He could have dumped it on the way to his pick-up, thrown it out of the window on the journey, or left it in the car.'

'Be worth getting the cars searched,' said Shepherd. 'After what he'd done, I think he'd feel happier with a gun. If it was me, I'd keep the weapon and lose it at the last moment.'

'I'll get Charlotte to check the vehicles,' said Pritchard. 'The one piece of possible good news is that our experts think they have a lead on the explosive used. Analysis of the residue suggests that it was from the same batch of Semtex that was used in Turkey in 2016.'

'Turkey?'

Pritchard put his glasses on and tapped on his keyboard. 'In Ankara, the capital. There were attacks in 2015 and 2016. More than a hundred died in two bombs outside the railway station in 2015. In February 2016 a bomb killed thirty soldiers and civilians in a convoy leaving the Army HQ. The Kurdistan Freedom Hawks claimed responsibility. Then in March the same group claimed responsibility for a car bomb that killed twenty-seven civilians. Our people have heard back from Rhode Island. The explosive used in the house was Semtex and it was from the same batch that was used in the March attack.'

'Uthman's parents were Kurds. And he spoke Kurdish, right? Do you think that's significant?'

Pritchard took off his glasses again. 'Except that there's no record of him ever visiting Turkey. And let's not forget that this isn't the real Uthman we're dealing with. It's his doppelgänger. We've no idea what his background is.' He got up and began to pace around the room. 'Our Forensics people got in touch with the Explosia Company in the Czech Republic and they were told that batch was delivered to the Turkish Army in 2015. It's Semtex 1H and is widely used in demolition work. As you probably know, of all the varieties that the company makes, it has the highest detonation velocity, which is why it's the explosive of choice for terrorists. It was used by Kurdish extremists in the two car bombings in Ankara in 2016 and explosives from the same batch have been used by criminals in Ankara. Once to blow open a safe and once to knock over an armoured car in a robbery.'

'So either the Kurdish group stole the explosives and sold some on to criminals. Or the criminals stole it and sold it on to the Kurds. I met an arms dealer when I was in Ankara last year. Small time, but then Ankara is a small city.'

'That's exactly what I was thinking. You should go and see him, see what he knows. The Semtex is the key to this. You were with Michael Warren-Madden on that jihadi bride business, right?'

'Yeah. He ended up coming with us all the way from the refugee camp to Bulgaria. He's the one who put me in touch with the Turkish arms dealer.'

'Are you okay to work with him again?'

Shepherd nodded. 'He might well be helpful. He obviously knows the criminal community out there. But he's Six's man. So anything we find will be fed straight back to Julian Penniston-Hill.'

'We're still on the same side, Dan.'

'They're not going to try to dump this on us?'

'I think that ship has sailed,' said Pritchard, folding his arms. 'Pretty much everything that has happened is a direct result of Melissa Schofield fast-tracking Mo Uthman and his Calais operation. Your reservations about Uthman and Abbas are on file, and Schofield took the decision to run the operation without MI5 involvement. Julian Penniston-Hill has managed to distance himself from what happened, so the way things stand, all this will be put on Schofield.'

'Who isn't in a position to defend herself.'

'You make it sound as if that's a bad thing,' said Pritchard. 'No one gets sacked, no one gets publicly censured, there'll be an inquiry but at the end of the day the woman responsible is dead.'

'Along with three members of her team and an agent.' Shepherd shrugged. 'Every cloud has a silver lining, right?' He didn't bother trying to hide his sarcasm.

'And the best way to honour the dead is to nail the man who killed them, and the person who planned it all. And for that, I need you in Turkey.'

'What about me?' asked Sharpe.

'You're good, Jimmy,' said Pritchard. 'You did awesome work today but Dan can take it from here.'

Shepherd arrived in Ankara at just after five-thirty in the afternoon after changing planes at Istanbul Airport. He was using the same legend and passport as the last time he'd been in the country – Paul Easton of the Home Office. He only had hand luggage and he was through immigration and in the arrivals area less than half an hour after the Turkish Airlines jet had touched down. The arrivals area was busy and Shepherd looked left and right but couldn't spot Michael Warren-Madden. He gritted his teeth in frustration and took out his phone but it started to ring before he had a chance to dial. The caller's number was being withheld but Shepherd recognised the laconic voice immediately. 'Welcome back to Ankara, squire,' said Warren-Madden. 'I knew we wouldn't be able to keep you away.' Shepherd opened his mouth to reply but Warren-Madden continued to talk. 'There's a gift shop to your left, could you stroll over and I'll check you're not being followed. Two minutes there, then if you could go out of the terminal via the left entrance, then pull a U-turn and if we're all clear I'll take you over to the car.'

Before Shepherd could say anything the phone went dead. He scowled as he scanned the terminal again, looking for the elusive MI6 officer. There was no sign of him so Shepherd did as he'd been told and headed to the gift shop. He knew this had nothing to do with serious counter-surveillance. The first time that Warren-Madden had met him at the airport, Shepherd had admonished him for walking straight over and using his name and then saying in public that he had come from the embassy. Warren-Madden was clearly now making him suffer for the embarrassment he'd caused him. But counter-surveillance was protocol for meetings at airports, so he had no choice other than to honour the man. He wandered around the gift shop for the required two minutes, left via the appropriate exit, pulled a U-turn and walked back along the outside of the terminal. He looked around and realised that Warren-Madden was on the other side of the road, smoking a cigarette with an amused smile on his face.

Shepherd walked over, swinging his black holdall. Warren-Madden was in his early fifties, with the wrinkled skin, lank hair and nicotine-stained fingers of a heavy smoker. When he grinned at Shepherd he revealed stained teeth and a crop of amalgam fillings. Warren-Madden transferred his cigarette to his left hand and offered to shake, but Shepherd went for a fist bump. One of the few benefits of the Covid pandemic was that it gave Shepherd the chance to avoid shaking hands with people he didn't like the look of. Warren-Madden was wearing a grey suit that had gone baggy around the knees and a brown tie that looked as if it might have been knitted by an aged aunt.

'So, a whole different world since we last met,' said the MI6 officer as he turned to walk towards a multi-storey car park. 'Must have made your job easier with everyone locked up at home for months on end. And I'm told that your lot took the opportunity to take DNA swabs from people that you'd never normally get near with a cotton bud. Now they're queuing up to give samples.'

Shepherd just grunted in reply. In fact he was absolutely right. Crime and terrorism levels had tumbled during the pandemic and MI5 officers had indeed been trained to take Covid samples and had used NHS credentials to take DNA samples from criminals and suspected terrorists throughout the country. But it wasn't the sort of conversation to be having in public, even if there was no one within earshot.

'And this latest bombing. That came out of nowhere, right? I'm told that it took everyone by surprise. No chatter, no nothing, right?'

'It was a surprise, yes,' said Shepherd. 'But terrorism never went away, even during the pandemic. The terrorists just used the time to plan and prepare and train.'

Warren-Madden took a final drag on his cigarette and flicked it away before walking into the multi-storey car park. They headed up the stairs to the second floor. 'I caught it, you know?' said the MI6 officer. 'The Covid.'

'Really?'

'Yeah, that first summer. It was quite bad here but even so, the death rate was a third of what it was in the UK. I was as sick as a dog for a week but to be honest I've had flu worse.'

'And no after effects?'

'No. I went in to see my doc when I first fell ill and he just told me to stay home, take paracetamol and drink lots of water. Now I'm as fit as a fiddle.' He laughed. 'Well I would be if I didn't smoke so many cigarettes. They said early on that cigarette smokers had some sort of immunity, but that turned out to be bollocks.' He pointed at the white Nissan Qashqai ahead of them. 'You remember the old girl, of course. You can't imagine the trouble I had with the accounts department in London trying to claim back expenses for that jaunt of ours to Bulgaria. I showed them a receipt for the Merc we rented and receipts for all the fuel but they didn't want to pay the mileage allowance. You'd think it was their own bloody money they were paying out.'

He unlocked the car and they climbed in. Shepherd dropped his bag on the rear seat. 'So, I wasn't sure from your email how you were fixed time-wise,' said Warren-Madden. 'Is this a flying visit or is it open-ended?'

'A lot will depend on how forthcoming Metin is,' said Shepherd.

'Do you want me to go with you to see Metin?'

'I think that would be better. Is he still in that bar in Ulus?'

'Angelique's? Sure.'

'My brief is to find out how that Semtex got to the UK and I'll be here as long as that takes.'

'Perfect,' said Warren-Madden, starting the engine. 'Metin usually gets to Angelique's about eight and he plays from nine. We could check you into the Mövenpick Hotel again and have a quick drink and a chat in the bar before we head out.' He drove out of the parking structure.

'How well do you know him?'

Warren-Madden shrugged. 'He's an intel source. I put payments through the Reptile Fund for him from time to time.' He drove onto the road and headed towards the Mövenpick. 'You know it was John le Carré who coined that phrase? No one in Six ever used it before he put it in his books. Now everyone uses it. And he came up with Lamplighters and Pavement Artists for the surveillance teams, though those names never caught on. He died, you know.'

'Yeah, I know. But I think you'll find he borrowed the Reptile Fund from Otto von Bismarck who used it in the late nineteenth century.'

'Are you serious?'

'I read it somewhere.'

'Well I loved his books when I was a kid. That's why I joined MI6. I mean, you read Ian Fleming and you know you can never be James Bond, but you read Le Carré and you think, yeah, I could do that job.' He looked across at Shepherd. 'What about you? Why did you join?'

'I just fell into it, I guess,' said Shepherd. 'I was doing under-cover work for SOCA, and MI5 offered me a job.'

'SOCA, that was a bloody joke, wasn't it? Put cops, customs officers and taxmen together and expect them to fight crime. And the name? Serious Organised Crime Agency. I mean, what organised crime isn't serious, for fuck's sake. You know the crime-solving rate fell during the SOCA years? Everyone was too busy fighting over their turf to actually go out and fight crime. I hear good things about the NCA, though.'

'So, what do you pay Metin for?' asked Shepherd, eager to change the subject.

'Like I said, intelligence. The sort of intel I can't get from traditional sources. I'm running a girl in the Turkish Defence Ministry for instance, who is a goldmine for information on forthcoming procurement and recruitment levels, but Metin can give me stuff about the criminal community that she would never turn up in a million years. The girl gives me intel because she doesn't like what the Turkish government are doing and would love to have a British passport. Metin already has three passports and doesn't give a shit about politics, but if you put five grand in his pocket he'll talk until the cows come home.'

'Do you see him a lot?'

'We're not buddies, but I try to check in with him every month or so. I actually like his club. There's never any trouble there. They keep out the riff-raff.'

'Yeah, I had a run-in with his bouncers. Apparently being a friend of yours wasn't enough to get me in.'

Warren-Madden grinned. 'As I said, they do try to keep out the riff-raff.'

'Did he mention me the next time you saw him?'

'I think he asked if you were happy with the guns, and I said I hadn't heard any complaints.' He shrugged. 'He wasn't especially curious.'

'So he didn't ask any questions about who I was or what I did?'

'Not that I recall. You were just a guy wanting to buy a couple of guns.'

'Good to know I'm not memorable.'

'In our line of work, that's an asset.'

They chatted about Metin as Warren-Madden drove to the hotel. They parked and walked inside. 'Why don't you check in, freshen up and I'll wait for you in the lobby bar,' said Warren-Madden. He pointed off to the right. 'It's over there, I've got a few calls to make, so take your time.'

Shepherd checked in using his Paul Easton passport and went up to his room on the ninth floor. He sat down on the queen-size bed and called Pritchard to let him know that he had arrived in Ankara and met up with Warren-Madden. 'We'll be seeing the arms dealer in a few hours,' said Shepherd. 'Any news on the Uthman doppelgänger?'

'We've confirmed that he was on the Dubai flight, using an

MI6 passport he was issued with before the Calais assignment. The name was Salim Raheef. We've run the name by most of the hotels in Dubai and he hasn't checked in under that name. But he could easily have different documents now. He could actually be using his real identity, of course. We've got him flagged now so we'll know if he flies out using that passport, but I would think it's very unlikely he'll do that. I'm pretty sure he'll have disposed of the Salim Raheef passport by now.'

'He could have landed and flown out within hours, of course.'

'If he did, he would have had to change passports,' said Pritchard. 'But yes, that's a possibility. If he did, I'm not sure that we'll be able to find him because Dubai is a major hub and there are thousands of passengers flying through it.'

'Can we check CCTV?'

'It's Dubai, not Heathrow, so the simple answer is no. Down the line we might get approval but there are several layers of bureaucracy to go through. I've got people at the airport with his picture, but it's a needle in a haystack. We're looking for a bearded Asian man, that's probably half the passengers passing through there.'

'We mustn't lose him,' said Shepherd.

'We won't,' said Pritchard. 'We have his photograph, his fingerprints and his DNA. We don't have a name, but that's just a matter of time.'

'I was thinking, the Uthman I met spoke very good English. Pretty much fluent. He must have spent time in an English-speaking country to get that good. The real Uthman went to school in the UK, but what about the doppelgänger?'

'He hasn't been to the UK as a student, we checked,' said Pritchard.

'How?'

'Fingerprints,' said Pritchard. 'Since 2008 anyone who applies for a student visa, or any visa, has to provide their fingerprints in the country of application. They are kept on file and can be checked on-line. As soon as we realised that Uthman wasn't Uthman we ran his prints and there were no matches.'

'So he could have had a British passport, same as Uthman.'

'Yes, that's possible. But the doppelgänger spoke Kurdish. And Arabic. Fluently, by all accounts. That suggests he was born out in the Middle East. Though he could have been born in Britain to Kurdish parents.'

'Is it possible to check that?' asked Shepherd.

'In theory, yes.'

'When the doppelgänger applied to join MI6 he used Uthman's passport. The genuine passport. What we need to do is to run the doppelgänger's photograph through the Passport Office and DVLA databases. That way we'll know if he was ever issued a UK passport or a driving licence. We already know he didn't come in on a visa.'

Pritchard grunted. 'Let's not forget that he could have done what the jihadists did and taken a boat over from Calais or hidden in a truck.'

'The Uthman I met was arrogant and over-confident. I don't think he would want to be smuggled into the country, I think he'd walk in with his head held high. And I think he's British.'

'Okay, I can run a check through the Passport Office database, but from experience it's unlikely we'll get a match.'

Shepherd frowned. 'I don't get that. That's how the eGates work, right? You put your passport on the reader and it checks the photo against your face. If it matches, the gates open.'

'The system is fine for one on one. You show the system two pictures and ask if it's a match. It will tell you to a high probability that there is. Or isn't. But it's not as accurate when you try to get a match from the whole database. The accuracy certainly is well below one in a million. In fact early on, the facial recognition system was only good for about 1 in 350, which means that in a pool of a million pictures, you might get a match with almost three thousand. Now the technology gets better with every year that goes by but also five million passports are issued each year and there are what, fifty million in circulation.'

'So the system comes up with too many possibilities?'

'Well, yes. But we can input parameters that would narrow the search. The fact that we are looking for a guy halves it at a stroke, obviously. And we know his age to give or take a few years, right? Uthman was twenty-four and his doppelgänger was about the same, maybe between twenty-one and twenty-seven. That'll cut it down. Let me see what I can do.' He sighed. 'Of course he could have come in on an EU ID card, and if he did then we'll probably never find him.'

'How so?'

'Pre-Brexit any EU citizen only had to show his or her national ID card to get into the UK. They couldn't be read by the eGates so they had to be physically checked by a Border Force officer and the details hand-typed into the system. So the photograph was never recorded, just the name and date and place of birth.'

'That's not good.'

'It gets worse. The EU was awash with fakes and at one point you could buy a good enough counterfeit to get you into the country for just fifty euros. There were so many varieties that they weren't swipeable, it was all done manually. Security-wise that was one of the benefits of Brexit, everybody has to use a passport. But that doesn't help us. If he came in at any time on an EU ID card, real or fake, he won't be in the system.'

'But we could check the ID card databases?'

'Of seven hundred and fifty million people? No, and even if we could we're not in Europol any more, the red tape would take forever. If we're lucky he'll be in the UK passport database, if he isn't then we're not going to be able to identify him from his photograph. I'll get on it and let you know if we get any matches. What's your plan?'

'Warren-Madden is waiting for me downstairs. We'll head out to see the arms dealer.'

'Just make sure Warren-Madden doesn't know what the Semtex was used for. I don't want him on the phone to London telling them that Melissa is no more.'

'And no one has claimed responsibility for the safe house bombing?'

'Nothing public and absolutely zero chatter. It's as if it never happened, though I doubt it'll stay that way for long.'

Pritchard ended the call and Shepherd lay on the bed staring up at the ceiling. It didn't make any sense that ISIS hadn't publicised the fact that they had killed four senior members of MI6 and the undercover agent who had tried to betray them. It was a major publicity coup that would energise their foot soldiers around the world. They had been quick to take the credit for the bombs in Trafalgar Square, so why the reticence when it came to the house in Hampstead?

After Shepherd had showered and changed into a clean shirt, he took the lift down to the lobby bar. Warren-Madden had commandeered a table in the corner that gave him a view of the bar and the hotel entrance. He was sprawled on a purple sofa with two red winged armchairs facing him. He was drinking a gin and tonic and working his way through a bowl of mixed nuts. Shepherd dropped down into one of the armchairs and almost immediately a waitress appeared at his side. Shepherd ordered a Jameson with ice and soda water.

The waitress slid away and Shepherd reached for a handful of nuts. 'You wouldn't happen to know what's happening about Melissa Schofield, would you?' asked Warren-Madden.

'In what way?'

'She's pretty much disappeared since the bombings. Julian Penniston-Hill has been running the show. Martin Williams has also gone missing. There seem to be two schools of thought.'

He fell silent, a standard interrogator's trick – leave a silence and hope the other person would feel the urge to fill it. It wasn't a technique that ever worked with Shepherd. He continued to pop nuts into his mouth and waited for Warren-Madden to continue.

'Right,' said Warren-Madden eventually, as if he realised that Shepherd wasn't going to be bullied into talking. 'So it could be that Schofield and Williams have been hauled off to the Tower of London prior to being tried for incompetence following what was clearly an almighty intelligence cock-up. Or they're heading up some super-secret investigation into what happened. Either way they've not been seen since the bombs went off.'

'What does Penniston-Hill say?'

'I'm just a small cog in the machine, I can hardly give him a call and ask him what's happened to his boss.'

'While I work for a different organisation entirely,' said Shepherd. 'I've never met Schofield or Penniston-Hill, though I have crossed paths with Martin Williams on a couple of joint MI5–MI6 operations.'

'But you're involved in the bombings investigation?'

'I was just told to pin down where a stock of Semtex had originated. It matches a sample that was used here in Ankara.'

'And this Semtex was used in the Trafalgar Square bombs?'

'I'm just tasked with identifying the Semtex,' said Shepherd, avoiding the question. He didn't want to lie to Warren-Madden, but there was a limit to how much he could tell the man.

'Because I would have thought that bombs that size would be more the Paddy's favourite, ANFO.'

'I think the forensic boys are still working on it,' said Shepherd.

'So was the Semtex an initiator?'

'That's really not my field,' said Shepherd. 'So, last time we spoke about Metin you said he thought you worked for Europol?'

'Yeah. I use the name Andy Dunham. Ankara is a small place and there's a very good chance that he'd find out I worked at the embassy, so I needed some role to explain that. Also the sort of questions I ask are a bit of a give-away that I'm in law enforcement.'

'But we're out of Europol post-Brexit.'

'If it comes up I'll say I'm Europol liaison now. He'll be fine. To be honest, if he knew I was with Six I don't think he'd mind.'

'Because of the money?'

'That's right.'

'From the Reptile Fund?'

Warren-Madden frowned. 'You sound dubious.'

'I don't quite understand why a people-trafficking drug-dealing arms dealer would get so excited about a few grand now and again.' He smiled at Warren-Madden and let the silence grow. Warren-Madden smiled back, swirling his ice cubes around his glass.

They smiled at each other for almost thirty seconds before Warren-Madden took a deep breath and sighed. 'Right, fine, yes, I do from time to time pass him information.' He held up a hand. 'Nothing sensitive, just titbits that he might find interesting.'

They were interrupted by the return of the waitress, who put down Shepherd's drink in front of him along with a fresh bowl of nuts. They stayed silent until she was out of earshot.

'That's a very dangerous game to be playing,' said Shepherd, picking up his glass.

'Everything I tell him goes into the diary. There's nothing untoward. And the little I give him pales into insignificance compared with the intel and leads I get from him.' He could see the look of disbelief on Shepherd's face and he shook his head. 'My boss in London cleared it in principle and checks my diary.'

'If you say so. But you want to be careful that it doesn't come back to bite you in the arse.'

'Metin has given me two guys who have gone on to become very productive agents,' said Warren-Madden.

'Does he know that?'

'Of course not. One runs a people-smuggling ring out of Iraq, the other is a junior official in the Ministry of Energy and Natural Resources who is a functioning heroin addict. The names came from Metin and I made the approaches some time afterwards. I've had gold from both of them. So if I give Metin the odd tip-off, it's worth it.'

Shepherd thought about it for several seconds and then nodded. 'Okay, you've convinced me.'

'That's good to know,' said Warren-Madden, raising his glass in salute. 'Now the question is, how do we run the questions by Metin?'

'What do you mean?'

'The last time you were here, you wanted to buy a couple of

guns off him. Now you're proposing to go back and ask him about stolen Semtex. It might be better if I asked him.'

'I need to be there. This is an MI5 operation, I can't leave it up to you.'

'I wasn't suggesting I steal your glory, I just meant that it would be better if I did the talking. But either way, we're going to need a reason for you being here.'

Shepherd nodded. He was right, of course. Metin was Warren-Madden's contact. Shepherd couldn't expect to simply push him out of the way and deal with Metin direct. And he had no right to jeopardise the relationship that Warren-Madden had put so much time and effort into. 'Do you have any thoughts?' he asked.

'To be honest, I'd prefer to do it myself. It's the sort of conversation I would generally have with him. It wouldn't raise any red flags. But with you there . . .' He shrugged. 'But I get it, you've been assigned a task and you can't be seen to be getting someone from another agency to do it for you.'

'It's really not that. It's about me seeing how he reacts, his body language, whether he knows more than he's saying.'

'This isn't my first rodeo, squire. I'm sure I'd be able to tell if he was lying.'

Shepherd laughed. 'You need to stop being so defensive,' he said. 'I understand what you're saying, and if the roles were reversed I'd be saying the same to you. But I need to be there. How about this? I'm your mate and I'm just passing through. He did me a favour last time. I never really told him why I wanted the guns, we'll just say I had a personal problem that's over and done with. We're swinging by just to say thanks and to have a drink. We chat. You bring up the Semtex. I just nod and smile.'

Warren-Madden nodded thoughtfully. 'Okay, that should work. Did you ever tell him why you wanted the guns?'

'No. He figured I wasn't a cop because I'd have my own gun, and he made a joke about me wanting to kill my wife. I changed the subject and he didn't raise it again. All he knows is that I'm a friend of yours.'

'How long have we known each other?'

'Let's say ten years or so. I live in Spain. Marbella. I'm a drug dealer who's a useful contact.'

'Did you tell him your name?'

'Just Paul. No surname.'

'You're sure?'

'My memory's pretty much infallible. I just said I was Paul and that I was a friend.'

'Why are you in Ankara?'

'To see you?'

'It's a long way to come for a chat.'

'Business here?'

Warren-Madden looked pained. 'Metin knows pretty much everyone in the city. He'd ask who you were seeing and you couldn't give him a name because he'd have you checked out and if you didn't tell him, that would be a red flag.'

'Okay. So I was in Cyprus doing some banking stuff and flew over to see you. It's what, an hour's flight?'

'Just over. Okay, that'll work. But if he asks, you were doing business in Southern Cyprus. The Greek part. He's less likely to have contacts there.'

'It's about money so I'd obviously be vague anyway.'

'Okay, that works. Give me a few more details.'

'Divorced, no kids, I travel between Marbella and London, we met in London ten years ago, we're friends but I give you info on dealers in Spain. You've stayed in my villa a few times.'

He nodded. 'Okay, that should do. If there's a problem and you think we need to get out of there, you say you're expecting a call back at your hotel. If I think we need to bail I'll just say we arranged to meet someone else in a club on the other side of the city.' He drained his glass. 'Okay, let's go. We can put the drinks on your room, right?'

'My pleasure,' said Shepherd.

Warren-Madden parked in a road close to Ulus Square. They climbed out and walked through the square, past the four bronze statues that made up the Victory Monument that celebrated the end of the Turkish War of Independence in 1923. They reached a nondescript office block. There were two big men standing by black railings at the top of the stairs leading down to the basement club and they both fist-bumped Warren-Madden. The two men hadn't been there the last time Shepherd had visited but they were a similar type – shaved heads and tattoos, wearing black bomber jackets, black jeans and black lace-up boots. They nodded at Shepherd and stepped to the side to allow them to go down.

They went down the steps and through another door where a pretty blonde girl sat in a booth with a dozen or so coats hanging behind her. Shepherd did recognise her. She had been there last time he visited. She smiled brightly at Warren-Madden and ignored him. They could hear a guitar being played and as they walked into the club Shepherd saw Metin on a podium at the far end of the room. To their right was a bar of polished mahogany that ran the length of the club with a couple of dozen wooden stools, many of which were occupied by men in leather jackets or sharp suits and women in short skirts.

There was a cluster of round tables in front of a small dance floor, most of them occupied by tough-looking men with expensively dressed girlfriends or wives. The drink of choice seemed to be Cristal champagne, favoured by gangsters and rap stars around the world. There was a single empty table and Warren-Madden took Shepherd over to it and they sat down. A dark-haired waitress in a low-cut black T-shirt asked them what they wanted. Shepherd had drunk the local beer, Efes, the last time he was in the club so he ordered the same again. 'Yeah, go on, I'll have a beer,' said Warren-Madden.

'You're okay with the local brew?' asked Warren-Madden as the waitress walked away.

'It's what I drank when I was here before so I wanted to stay consistent,' said Shepherd. 'But yeah, it's a nice beer.'

They looked over at the podium. Metin was sitting on a stool playing 'Hotel California' on an acoustic guitar. He was tall with steel-grey hair and a neatly trimmed goatee beard that hadn't been there the last time Shepherd had seen him. He was wearing a brightly coloured Versace shirt loose over tight Versace jeans and he had on lizard-skin cowboy boots with pointed toes. He sang with a slight American accent and was surprisingly good. It seemed that they had arrived midway through his set, so they were halfway through their second beers when he finished and put his guitar onto a metal stand to enthusiastic applause from the audience.

He made his way across the dance floor, shook hands with several of the men sitting at the tables and air kissed a couple of the women.

He reached their table and his face broke into a wide grin. 'Andy, good to see you again, my friend.' His English was perfect, but now that he wasn't singing he had a slight Turkish accent. Warren-Madden stood up and the two men hugged enthusiastically. When they broke apart, Metin held out his hand to shake with Shepherd. 'And your friend, Paul. Good to see you again, Paul. Are you here for more Glocks?'

Shepherd went to fist-bump him but Metin took back his hand in mock horror. 'What, you won't shake hands with me?'

'Covid,' said Shepherd.

'Fuck Covid,' said Metin. 'Real men shake hands. Nancy boys bump fists. Are you a real man or a Nancy boy?'

Shepherd grinned and held out his hand. 'I'm not a Nancy boy.'

'Neither am I,' said Metin. He shook his hand firmly, then sat down. A waitress appeared with a large glass of red wine and he took it from her with a smile. He raised the glass in salute. '*Şerefe!*' he said. 'Cheers.'

'*Şerefe!*' said Shepherd and Warren-Madden and they all drank.

Warren-Madden gestured at the full tables. 'Business is good, obviously.'

'It is now, but the Covid shut us down.'

'It shut everywhere down,' said Warren-Madden. He looked over at Shepherd. 'They clamped down pretty hard. They had a curfew for kids, they could only go out between one and three.

The elders could also only go out at set times. And the young and old weren't allowed on trains and buses.'

'Did it work?' asked Shepherd.

'They did a lot better than the UK, not that that means anything,' said Warren-Madden. 'About twenty-five thousand died in all.'

Metin leaned forward and grinned at Shepherd. 'You remember Omer? The security guy you gave a hard time to? The one you threatened to shoot in the balls?'

'Yes, I remember.'

'He died of the Covid. His mother got it and he was taking care of her. She recovered but he caught it and he died after about three weeks on a ventilator.'

'I'm sorry to hear that,' said Shepherd.

Metin grinned. 'Really?'

Shepherd shrugged. 'Actually, no, I couldn't give a fuck.'

The grin vanished and Metin stared at him for several seconds, but then he began to laugh and pound the table with his free hand. 'That's what I thought!' he said. 'He was a bastard, wasn't he? He was always having problems on the door. I told him, he needed to be nicer to people. You catch more flies with honey than vinegar, isn't that what they say?'

'They do, but you catch even more flies with shit,' said Warren-Madden.

Metin laughed even louder and hit the table so hard that several heads turned their way. Metin drained his glass and waved the waitress over, then motioned with his finger that he wanted drinks for all three of them.

'The Glocks, they were okay?' Metin asked Shepherd.

'They were fine, thank you. I had a bit of a problem but it sorted itself out and it was useful to have the firepower if I needed it.'

'Well if you ever need more, you know where I am.' He reached out with his glass and clinked it against Shepherd's beer. 'Any friend of Andy's is a friend of mine.'

Their fresh drinks arrived, along with a plate of pastries that looked like a cross between cigars and spring rolls. Shepherd picked one up and looked at it quizzically.

Metin laughed at his reaction. 'Sigara böreği,' he said. 'They are stuffed with cheese and parsley. Try one.'

Shepherd bit into it, chewed, and nodded his approval. 'Good.'

'Just don't eat too many, my friend, they will make you fat.' He popped one into his mouth and chewed happily.

Warren-Madden took a sip of his beer. 'So, Metin, do you remember that armoured car robbery last year? The villains put a bomb under a manhole and blew the truck on its side.'

'That was a laugh, wasn't it?' said Metin. 'They used too much explosives, blew the thing six feet in the air. Almost killed the guards inside.'

'What did they get away with?'

'Ten million lira, the bank said. But word on the street is it was only half that and the bank was lying to the insurance company.'

'Ten million lira is about a million quid,' Warren-Madden said to Shepherd.

'Nice earner,' said Shepherd.

'They never caught the guys who did it,' said Warren-Madden. 'Any idea who it was?'

Metin grinned and reached for another pastry. 'I heard it was the Yavuz brothers. The younger brother bought a new Porsche not long after.'

Warren-Madden took a sip of his beer. 'Did you ever hear where they got the explosives from?'

Metin's eyes narrowed. 'You think I sold it to them?'

'Did you?'

Metin chuckled and shook his head. 'What would I do with explosives? It's dangerous stuff. Treat it badly and it'll blow up in your face.'

'It was stolen from an Army base, is what I heard,' said Warren-Madden. 'I'm just wondering how it ended up in the hands of the Yavuz brothers.'

'Why are you so interested, my friend?' asked Metin. He was smiling but his eyes had gone hard.

Shepherd knew instinctively that to lie to Metin at this point would be a mistake. He wanted to warn Warren-Madden but also knew it would be as big a mistake if he were to interrupt. He sipped his beer and said a silent prayer that the MI6 officer would read Metin's body language.

'I'll be honest with you, it's my bosses back in England who want to know,' said Warren-Madden. 'They found some Semtex there and it's a match to the Semtex that was used in that armoured truck robbery here. They want to know how it got from here to there.'

'How could they know that?' asked Metin.

'There's a university in America that collates samples from explosives around the world and keeps them in a database,' said Warren-Madden. 'If you send them a swab of the residue of an explosion or the explosive itself, they can tell you if there's a match.'

Metin nodded thoughtfully. 'So they think the Yavuz brothers are planning something in England?' He shook his head and grimaced. 'Those boys never travel. They don't speak English, they're just thugs. They were lucky on that job because they had a cousin working in the company's control room.'

'It's the explosives they're worried about. I think they believe that whoever sold the Semtex to the Yavuz brothers sold it to someone in the UK. Is that at all possible?'

Metin shrugged. 'Anything's possible,' he said. 'I heard that it was Faruk Sazak who sold it to them.'

'Really?' said Warren-Madden. 'Now that is interesting.'

'Who's he?' asked Shepherd, figuring that it was a valid question for him to ask under the circumstances.

'My competitor,' said Metin with a grin.

'Chalk and cheese,' said Warren-Madden.

Metin frowned, not understanding the reference. 'Chalk and cheese?'

'It means you're very different, Metin. Totally different. I wouldn't think of sitting down and having a drink with Sazak.' He looked at Shepherd. 'Sazak is a nasty piece of work. He's involved in the heroin trade and he supplies weapons to the likes of the Kurdistan Freedom Hawks.'

'The what now?' said Shepherd, feigning ignorance.

'Terrorists who want a Kurdish homeland,' said Warren-Madden. 'They plant bombs and murder government officials. Sazak sells to anybody and doesn't care what they do with his product.'

'He is a maniac,' said Metin, nodding in agreement. 'He killed his own nephew a few years ago because he thought he was informing on him. Turns out he wasn't but it was too late then.'

'Do you have any idea how Sazak would have got his hands on Semtex?' Warren-Madden asked.

'I heard that he stole it from an Army base outside the city,' said Metin. 'Rolled up in an Army truck and stole a whole load of weapons and explosives at gunpoint.' He leaned forward. 'The Army were so embarrassed that they never went public about what had happened. They took surface-to-air missiles, anti-tank weapons, RPGs . . .'

'And Semtex?'

'That's what I heard,' said Metin. 'They're sure it was the same Semtex?'

'I think the science is pretty definite,' said Warren-Madden. 'It's to do with the chemicals in the explosive. It's a bit like DNA or snowflakes, no two are exactly the same.'

'And it's nothing to do with the bombs that went off in Trafalgar Square?' asked Metin quietly.

Shepherd sipped his drink. Metin was watching Warren-Madden carefully to judge his reaction, as was Shepherd. Shepherd was starting to realise that behind Metin's easy smile and casual manner was a razor-sharp mind.

Warren-Madden's shrug was relaxed, and he maintained eye contact with Metin as he prepared to answer. 'I don't think so, but then they don't tell me everything. I'm pretty sure the bombs in Trafalgar Square were ANFO – fertiliser and fuel oil. Big bombs like that usually are.'

'Really?' said Metin. 'I thought that the car bombs we had here in Ankara in 2016 used Semtex.'

'I wasn't far from the first one when it went off,' said Warren-Madden. 'I was in a cafe with a colleague. The explosion rattled the cups and then you could hear the screams in the distance. Fucking animals. What can you do?'

It was a clever deflection to avoid answering Metin's question and it seemed to have worked. Metin scowled and shrugged. 'They're animals. They didn't care who they killed. Women, children . . .'

'I've never understood the whole Kurdish problem,' said Shepherd, trying to distract Metin even more from thinking about the Semtex. 'What is a Kurd? Is it a religion thing?'

'The problem is that they want a big piece of Turkey to create their own country,' said Metin. 'Most of them are Sunni Muslims but it's not about religion. They're troublemakers. Bit like your Scottish people, always saying they want their own country.'

'Well at least the Scots don't set off car bombs,' said Shepherd.

'No, but the Irish do,' said Warren-Madden. 'You know your history, right? About the Kurds?'

'Not a clue,' said Shepherd, shaking his head. Actually he knew quite a lot about the Kurds but the important thing was to stop Metin thinking about the Semtex.

Warren-Madden looked over at Metin. 'Correct me if I get any of this wrong, but I did study history at university.'

Metin waved his glass. 'Go ahead, my friend, I always enjoy being lectured about my own country.'

Warren-Madden either ignored the sarcasm or didn't notice it. 'So, the Kurdish people are mainly from what would have been the Mesopotamian plains and highlands that now form part of northern Iraq, north-western Iran, north-eastern Syria, south-western Armenia and south-eastern Turkey. When that part of the world was divided up by the Allies after the end of the First World War, the Kurds were promised their own homeland but they never got it. They've been fighting for it ever since. They make up about twenty per cent of the Turkish population, and the Turkish government hates them. Once the Kurds realised they weren't going to get their homeland, they started protesting and the government cracked down by banning Kurdish names and costumes and destroying villages and resettling people. Hundreds of thousands of Kurds were displaced and some forty thousand were killed.'

'You say that like it was a bad thing,' said Metin. It was hard to tell if he was joking or not.

'You don't like the Kurds?' asked Shepherd.

'They are troublemakers,' said Metin. 'And they are terrorists.'

Shepherd nodded. While it was certainly true that Kurdish militants had been behind a number of atrocities in their quest for independence, including hundreds of civilian deaths, they had also been at the forefront of the fight against ISIS in the region. Kurdish units had fought against ISIS in Syria and Iraq, often supported by American firepower. He sipped his beer, not wanting to show Metin how much he knew about the subject.

'I guess your bouncers won't let them in,' said Warren-Madden with a sly smile.

Metin laughed. 'Actually, I have Kurdish friends,' he said. 'When I say they are troublemakers, I don't mean all of them. Of course. That would be racist. Most Kurds want what we all want. A quiet life. Good food. Good music. A warm body to sleep next to at night. A good education for our children. And Netflix.'

Shepherd laughed. 'Netflix?'

'Sure,' said Metin. 'How boring would life be without Netflix? Have you seen Turkish television? It's shit.'

The three men laughed and the conversation turned to the merits of the various streaming platforms and which VPNs were best. It looked as if Metin had forgotten all about the Semtex questions. At one point while Metin was waving at the waitress for fresh drinks and snacks, Shepherd caught Warren-Madden's eye and gave him a slight nod and a smile. He'd done a good job. Warren-Madden grinned back and raised his glass. Yes, he knew.

Shepherd and Warren-Madden left the club just after one o'clock in the morning. They had stayed to watch Metin perform another set of ten songs, including two duets with the waitress who had been serving them. She had a deep, earthy voice and the two of them sang well together. Metin had hugged them both and made Shepherd promise to visit the club next time he was in Ankara.

'He really does seem like a nice guy,' said Shepherd as they walked into Ulus Square.

'He is,' said Warren-Madden.

'Not your normal people-trafficking drug-dealing arms dealer.'

Warren-Madden chuckled. 'That is an accurate description, but it makes him sound worse than he is, I suppose. The arms dealing is small time, like the Glocks he sold you. He's not supplying terrorists with RPGs or armies with tanks. Handguns and shotguns, mainly. And yes, he's a drug dealer but he only sells hashish. Large quantities, to be fair, but it is legal for medicinal reasons in Turkey so it's a grey area.'

'And people trafficking?'

'Metin would probably say it was more refugee facilitation,' said Warren-Madden. He took out a pack of cigarettes and lit one with a disposable lighter. 'He supplies boats, lifejackets and guides to get refugees from Turkey into Greece, crossing the Med. Most of the refugees are from Syria but he's an equal-opportunity trafficker, if you can pay his fee he'll get you into Greece. Or at least on to one of the Greek islands.'

'So he's a villain with a heart of gold?'

Warren-Madden chuckled. 'I wouldn't go that far. He's broken a few heads in his time, but so far as I know he's never killed anybody. Or had anyone killed.'

'And what about this Faruk Sazak?'

'Ah. A totally different kettle of gangster.' He blew smoke up at the night sky. 'There's no way we can pop around for a chat with him. He ships heroin to Europe, big time. I didn't realise he dealt with the Hawks, I'll get that checked out. Like I told Metin, I was here in 2016 when the bomb went off,' said Warren-Madden. 'A student set off a massive car bomb, killed thirty-seven and injured a hundred and twenty-five. It was aimed at civilians. It was detonated at a place where there were several bus stops so there were loads of people waiting on the pavement. The Ministry of the Interior said that the student was a Kurdish militant and a few days later the Kurdistan Freedom Hawks claimed responsibility. Then in December the same group was behind two more explosions in Istanbul that killed forty-eight people, mainly cops.'

'The Semtex wasn't used in the Istanbul bombings,' said Shepherd. 'Only in the bombing and robberies here in Ankara. What do you know about the Kurdistan Freedom Hawks?'

'They're a Kurdish nationalist militant group. They want an independent Kurdish state in the east of the country. They used to be part of the Kurdistan Workers' Party but broke away because they didn't think they were militant enough. The Hawks have been labelled a terrorist organisation by the US, the UK and the EU. They're like a Turkish IRA, pretty much. They've been quiet for the last few years.'

'Covid?'

'Maybe, but they didn't do much in 2018 or 2019 either.' They reached Warren-Madden's car and he stood by the driver's door smoking the last of his cigarette. 'I suppose the question is, did Sazak give the Semtex to whoever took it to the UK, or did Sazak give it to the Hawks and they passed it on?'

'Who do you think is more likely to tell us?'

'If this was Belfast, it would be the choice between an IRA terrorist or a murdering Shankhill Road drug dealer. The devil and the deep blue sea comes to mind.'

'Do you know where this Sazak lives?'

'I can find out. But I don't think you'll be able to just knock on his door.'

'Message received and understood,' he said. 'Get me the address and let me worry about who goes a-knocking. What about the Hawks? Do you have any contacts there?'

Warren-Madden flicked the remains of his cigarette away and it skidded across the tarmac in a shower of sparks. 'Please tell me you're not serious.'

'I need to know how that Semtex got to London,' said Shepherd.

'It would be like turning up in Belfast and asking to speak to someone in the IRA. Can you imagine how that would turn out?'

'Actually I've done exactly that,' said Shepherd. 'And I'm still here.'

Warren-Madden opened the door. 'In the words of the Spice Girls, if that's what you want, what you really really want, I'll get the intel for you. It's not something I've worked on but there are names on our database.'

He climbed into the SUV and Shepherd got into the front seat. 'Just be aware that the Hawks are a dangerous bunch,' said Warren-Madden. 'The foot soldiers are recruited from the slums of Istanbul and Ankara. The majority of their parents would have fled the Kurdish villages destroyed by the Turks in the 1990s. They're born into poverty and have got nothing to lose. You'd be taking your life into your own hands if you tried to talk to them. If they even got a sniff that you were connected to law enforcement, they'd gut you like a fish.'

'People always want something,' said Shepherd. 'All you have to do is find out what that is and offer it to them.'

'The Kurdistan Workers' Party have pretty much given up their calls for independence and are trying now to get autonomy within Turkey, but the Hawks want nothing less than their own nation state and they're not going to get it. They're terrorists, pure and simple. I don't see that there's anything you can offer them that will get them to talk to you.'

He started the car and pulled away from the kerb.

Shepherd showered and pulled on a hotel robe before he phoned Pritchard and went through what Metin had told them. 'So how do you want to play this?' asked Pritchard when Shepherd had finished.

'I don't really have an answer, I wanted to see what your thoughts were. I could probably come up with a good reason to approach Sazak. I'm a drug importer based in Spain looking for a new heroin supplier. I've got a legend that will check out, I'd just need the funds to show that I was serious. But there's no

way I can bring up the subject of Semtex without him getting
suspicious. And when this guy gets suspicious he has a tendency
to kill people.'

'Would Warren-Madden be able to help?'

'With intel. But he doesn't have an in with the guy. The only
way I can think of doing it is a smash and grab followed by a
hard interrogation, but we're not equipped to do that.'

'But you think that would work?'

'If the interrogation was hard enough. But assuming that it
was Sazak who stole the Semtex and gave it to the robbers, that
doesn't mean he gave it to whoever sent it to the UK. He could
have given it to the Kurdish terrorists and they could have passed
it on. If that's the case, then we'd still have to find some way of
getting the intel from the Hawks. And Warren-Madden says
they're dangerous.' He sighed and ran his hand through his hair.
'I keep coming back to the point that Uthman's mum was a
Kurd. And he spoke Kurdish.'

'But we're not looking for Mo Uthman. We're looking for his
replacement.'

'Yes, I get that, but it can't be a coincidence, can it? Both
Uthman and the replacement spoke Kurdish.'

'Coincidences happen.'

'And then there's the fact that the Kurds hate ISIS. They've
been fighting for years out in Iraq and Syria. They hate each
other with a vengeance and have committed countless atrocities
against each other. Why would a Kurdish group help ISIS with
a bombing in London?'

'We don't know that they did. It could have been Sazak.'

'So Sazak is helping Kurds in Turkey and ISIS in London?'

'He sells to anyone. He wouldn't be the first arms dealer to
sell to both sides in a conflict. And anyway, it's not the motivation
we need, it's finding out who rather than why. So my question
still stands, how do you want to play this?'

'I'm going to have to talk to Sazak first. And if that doesn't
work, then I'll go the Hawks route. But I'll need back-up.'

'Is Warren-Madden useful?'

'He was fine with Metin, but Metin's a pussycat compared with Sazak. And he'd run a mile if I asked him to approach the Hawks. He's not geared up for action man stuff.'

'But you are?'

Shepherd chuckled. 'Not without back-up.'

'Is that what you're asking for? Back-up?'

'I don't see any other way. Like I said, if I got an introduction to Sazak then I could talk to him, but it would take weeks or months to get to the stage where I could bring up the Semtex. A hard interrogation would be a lot quicker. And if we go the Hawk route, force is the only thing that will work.'

'It'll have to be off the books, obviously.'

'Yes, I figured that.'

'So the choice would be Major Gannon putting together a team from the Increment, or using Charlotte Button and the Pool. What are your thoughts?'

'I'd be happier with the Increment,' said Shepherd.

'I thought you'd say that,' said Pritchard. 'What time is it there?'

'Coming up for two o'clock in the morning.'

'Okay, sleep on it and I'll have something arranged by the time you wake up.'

Shepherd woke at a quarter to eight as the first rays of the dawn sun cut through the gap between the curtains. He rolled over and looked at the phone on his bedside table. There was a text message from Pritchard. 'BACK-UP EN ROUTE, DETAILS TO FOLLOW'. He hoped that Pritchard had followed up on his promise to draw on the Increment rather than to subcontract out the job. The problem with the Pool was that you never knew what you were going to get. Some were special forces, many were criminals of one form or another, and there was a sprinkling of psychopaths. He trusted Charlotte Button but at short notice he didn't know what resources she would have available. The Increment was made up of SAS and SBS, some retired but most active, and so could all be relied on. As he remembered his previous run-ins with the Pool, a thought occurred to him and he sat up. He tapped out the Thai number from memory and it was answered on the fifth ring by Lex Harper, who was breathing heavily.

'Please don't tell me this is coitus interruptus,' said Shepherd.

Harper laughed. 'I'm jogging, mate. Well, jogging now, I was running when you called.' He had a strong Liverpool accent, even though it had been almost two decades since he had lived in the city.

'You're in Thailand?'

'Pattaya. Between jobs. What's wrong?'

'Why would something be wrong?'

'Because you only ever call me when you want something, Spider. That's your style.'

Shepherd had known Harper since his SAS days, when as a young paratrooper Harper had been on attachment to the Regiment. It had been clear from the start that Harper wasn't SAS material, he didn't have the mental toughness to be a special forces soldier, but he was a more than competent paratrooper and the two men had always got on. Harper had left the Paras and was now based in Thailand from where he ran a number of shady operations and did the occasional job for the Pool. 'Have you ever crossed paths with a guy called Faruk Sazak?' asked Shepherd.

'You'll have to give more than a name, mate, I don't have your trick memory.'

'He's a Turkish gangster out of Ankara. He traffics Afghan heroin into Europe.'

'Ah, yeah, I've heard the name. He ships to Spain but no one likes dealing with him because he's a nutter with a temper.'

'You've never met him?'

'I'm not a big fan of heroin, as you know. If the DEA get on your case they'll put you away for life. I tend not to hang out with those guys because I don't want to get caught in any surveillance photos that might come back and haunt me.'

'Could you get a meeting with Sazak? Friend of a friend?'

'Probably. Yeah. But he's dangerous. Look at him wrong and he'll cut off your knackers.'

'We'll have back-up.'

Harper laughed. 'Your secret squirrel mates are all well and good for steaming open envelopes and listening in to phones, but I've never met one yet who could punch his way out of a wet paper bag. Other than you, of course.'

'It won't be Five backing us up, it'll be the Regiment.'

'That's more like it. This is official, right? So I'll be paid?'

'You won't do it as a favour?'

'Are you working for free?'

Shepherd laughed. 'I'll see about getting you on the books. Five a day?'

'I'd prefer ten.'

'I'll ask for eight but don't be surprised if they stick at six.'

'And First Class tickets.'

Shepherd sighed.

'Mate, it's a nine-hour flight, plus I'll probably have to change at Istanbul. I'll need my beauty sleep.'

'Okay, consider it done. Can you come right away?'

'I'll run home and shower and head out to the airport. If all goes well, I should get there first thing tomorrow.'

'Text me your flight and I'll have you met at the airport.'

'Always a pleasure, Spider.'

Shepherd ended the call and phoned Pritchard. 'I was just about to call you,' said Pritchard. 'There are six men in the air as we speak. They're changing planes at Istanbul and should be arriving at Ankara at 10.05 tonight your time, but the connection in Istanbul is tight so if they miss it they'll get there after midnight.'

'I'll be waiting for them,' said Shepherd.

'Major Gannon says you'll know three of them. Mutton, Paddy and Mustard, if that means anything to you.'

'It does,' said Shepherd. 'Familiar faces.'

'Major Gannon can't make it himself, he's got to be at Number Ten later today. The others in the team were at Trafalgar Square so they're keen to get involved. Obviously as they're flying commercial they won't have much in the way of equipment so the Major asks if you can get something fixed up.'

'No problem, Metin will have what we need. I'll need funds, ideally cash.'

'I'll Western Union cash to you under the Paul Easton name. I'll text you the details.'

'And I could do with the help of a particular guy who works for the Pool. Lex Harper. He can give me an in to Sazak. We might be able to swerve the smash and grab, if it comes off.'

'I'll talk to Charlotte and get him on your team.'

'No, I can deal direct with Lex. We go back a long way. It's just at some point he'll want paying.'

'That's not a problem, send me details when you're ready and I'll have him paid out of the Reptile Fund.'

'You really do call it that?'

'What? The Reptile Fund? Sure. Everyone here did once *Tinker, Tailor* came out. Before my time, obviously, but yes, that's what we call the accounts we use for AOTBPs.'

'Run that by me again.'

Pritchard laughed. 'Authorised Off The Books Payments. You can see why everyone prefers Reptile Fund. Just let me know what this Harper wants and I'll put the money through. Don't worry about the cost of this, Dan, I'll keep the accountants at bay.'

Shepherd ended the call and rang Warren-Madden. The phone rang out and then went through to voicemail. Shepherd didn't leave a message. He headed for the shower and when he returned, wrapped in a towel, he had three missed calls. He phoned back and this time Warren-Madden answered. 'The early bird,' said Warren-Madden. 'What's up?'

'We need to visit Metin again,' said Shepherd.

Western Union had a $2,500 limit on overseas transfers so Pritchard sent four lots of money from an offshore account to four separate Western Union offices. There were more than fifty in the city to choose from, but the ones that Pritchard used were all a short walk from Ulus Square. Warren-Madden parked in a side road close to the square and walked around with Shepherd as he produced his Paul Easton passport and collected the money. By the time they had finished they had more than seventy thousand Turkish lira. They walked to Metin's club. The lights were off and there was a single leather-jacketed doorman in the street who had obviously been told to expect them as he opened the gate and waved them to go down without a word.

Angelique's was a lot less salubrious in the daytime. There were no windows but all the lights were on, revealing that the podium was painted plywood and the carpet stained and threadbare in places. Metin was wearing Versace jeans and a white cotton shirt open to the waist revealing a large gold medallion. He was sitting at one of the circular tables with a pot of Turkish coffee, a sugar bowl and three small cups in front of him. He stood up and waited with arms outstretched as they walked over, then shook hands with Warren-Madden and hugged him. When he'd finished greeting Warren-Madden, he raised an eyebrow and looked at Shepherd with a sly grin. 'So are you a man today, Paul, or a Nancy boy?'

Shepherd faked a sheepish grin and shook hands with him, then allowed Metin to give him a bearhug. As they sat down, a young girl in a T-shirt and cut-off jeans came over with a plate of Turkish pastries. She put the plate down as Metin poured thick black coffee into the cups. 'My chef makes the best baklava,' said Metin. 'Filo pastry with chopped nuts and honey. Try, please.'

Shepherd and Warren-Madden took one each. It was too sweet for Shepherd's taste but he made the appropriate noises as he chewed and swallowed.

'So now you are here as a customer?' Metin said.

'You have what I want?' asked Shepherd.

Metin waved a languid hand at three grey cases stacked by the podium. Next to them was a black nylon holdall. 'Of course, but I would like a little chat first.' He sipped his coffee and studied Shepherd over the top of his cup.'

'Always happy to chat,' said Shepherd. 'Chatting is good.'

Metin smiled. 'You asked for eight handguns, and I have them. And sixteen magazines, which I also have. You wanted two Uzis or similar and I have two MAC-11s which as I am sure you know is a subcompact version of the MAC-10. Easy to use, but not accurate beyond twenty feet or so.'

'That will be fine, I'm familiar with the MAC-11,' said Shepherd. 'It's a perfectly acceptable substitute for the Uzi.'

'That's what I thought,' said Metin. 'And I have plenty of holsters. You also wanted ballistic vests and they were harder to source at short notice. I had two and I managed to get another one. They are all second-hand, but none have been tested in combat, shall we say?'

'Three will be fine, Metin. As you say, it is very short notice.'

'And that is what worries me, my friend. Last night we talked about Faruk Sazak. This morning you are preparing to go to war. You can see how I might suspect that those two events are connected.' He sipped his coffee.

Shepherd sighed. 'What is it you want me to say, Metin? Is there some sort of arms dealer's code that says I have to tell you what I'll be using the guns for?'

'If you were taking them to another city or another country it wouldn't be an issue. But if my guns were used to hurt a competitor, said competitor might well think that retribution was in order.'

'A gun is a gun, Metin. A bullet is a bullet. No one will know where the guns or the bullets came from. And I certainly wouldn't be telling anyone where I bought them.'

Metin looked over at Warren-Madden, who immediately grimaced and put his hands in the air. 'Nothing to do with me,' he said. 'I'm just his driver.'

Metin chuckled. He looked back at Shepherd. 'I am guessing this is something to do with drugs, but in truth I don't want to know. I will sell you the guns and the ammunition but you must never tell anyone where you got them from.'

'Absolutely,' said Shepherd.

Metin stared at him for several seconds, then looked over at the bar. There was a barman there in a black T-shirt and jeans who was polishing glasses and setting them in a wooden gantry.

Metin clicked his fingers to get the man's attention. The man nodded, bent down under the bar and for a wild moment Shepherd thought that he was going to return with a weapon and start shooting, but almost immediately he reappeared holding a brown A4 envelope. He walked around the bar and Metin waved for him to give it to Shepherd. Shepherd took it and opened it as the barman walked away. Inside were several printed sheets. There was a copy of a map with a house outlined in blue, and several photographs of the house and of cars leaving it with the registration plates clearly visible. The final sheet had two photographs on it, one a head-and-shoulders shot of a tough-looking man with a shaved head and a broken nose and another of the same man standing by a Mercedes SUV. There was another map, and clipped to it a photograph of a car dealership. Metin pointed at it. 'Most days he is in the office, upstairs. With a lot of heavies. Downstairs they sell upmarket cars and at the back they strip down stolen cars for the parts. What do you call it? A chip shop?'

'A chop shop.' Shepherd handed the sheets of paper to Warren-Madden, who was equally surprised by the contents.

'I don't know what to say, Metin,' said Shepherd. 'I was not expecting this.'

Metin shrugged and raised his coffee cup in salute. 'A thankyou will suffice. There's no charge.'

Warren-Madden gave the sheets back to Shepherd. 'So I suppose this means there's no love lost between you and Sazak?'

'He is an animal,' said Metin. 'He has no soul. He doesn't bother with me because he sees me as small time. But in the past he has put friends of mine out of business. Sometimes permanently. If you are really going to try to take him down, then I think you should have every possible advantage. Because if you fail . . .' He shrugged, then he smiled and gestured at the papers. 'Like the guns and the ammunition, you did not get that from me, of course.'

Shepherd put the sheets of paper back in the envelope, folded it, and slid it into his pocket. 'Get what from you?' he asked.

Metin laughed and slapped his hand down on the table hard enough to rattle the cups. 'I like you,' he said. He looked over at Warren-Madden. 'I like your friend, Andy.' He finished his coffee, then stood up and walked over to the three cases. He opened the first to reveal four Glock 17s, eight loaded magazines and four nylon underarm holsters. Shepherd joined him. He knelt down and quickly checked each gun. 'Nice,' he said.

Metin opened the second case. Inside were two Glock 19s and two Berettas. They were the 92FS model, favoured by the US military and police forces across the country.

'I couldn't get eight Glocks, I trust the Beretta is satisfactory,' said Metin.

'It's fine,' said Shepherd. 'It's a nice gun. Even an amateur can put a ten-shot group in three inches at fifty yards.'

'You know a lot about guns?'

Shepherd shrugged. 'It's a hobby.' He checked the guns and the eight magazines. There were also four holsters designed to be tucked into the back of trousers. 'The guns are all brand new,' he said, an observation rather than a question.

'Never been fired,' said Metin.

'Have they been out on sale and return?' asked Shepherd. Sometimes gun dealers would sell a gun and then buy it back, usually for half the price, if it was returned unfired. It was a way that criminals could cut their costs by effectively renting their firepower.

'Two of the Glock 17s and one of the Berettas, but I know the guys who had them and they can be trusted.'

Metin opened the third case to reveal two MAC-11s and two extra magazines for each. As Metin has said, they weren't accurate at any distance but they were visually threatening, and generally waving a MAC-11 around gained more respect than a Glock or Beretta.

He checked them over and nodded his approval. 'And again, not fired?' he asked.

'You have my word,' said Metin. He pulled over the holdall and unzipped it to show Shepherd the three bulletproof vests.

Shepherd pulled one. Three would probably be enough. In fact if it went well, they wouldn't be needed. He put it back in the holdall and took out the envelope of money. 'This should cover it,' he said.

Metin took it and ran his thumb down the notes. 'Last time you paid me in euros,' he said.

'This was all a bit of a rush,' said Shepherd.

'Money is money,' said Metin with a shrug. He folded the envelope and shoved it into the back pocket of his jeans.

'I think I should drive around with the car,' said Warren-Madden. 'Better than us walking through the square with all that ordnance.'

'Makes sense,' said Shepherd.

As Warren-Madden headed out, Shepherd sat down at the table with Metin. The Turk poured them more coffee. 'So, you are in the drugs business?' he asked casually, but his eyes were clearly reading Shepherd's body language.

'I dabble,' said Shepherd.

'And Andy is a good friend?'

'Yeah, I'd say so. We don't see each other that often.'

'Do you know him well enough to know that his name is not Andy?' Again Metin was measuring him up over his coffee cup.

Shepherd had only seconds to decide how to play it. Metin might well be bluffing, but the look in his eyes suggested otherwise. Ankara was a small city and Shepherd had always thought it unlikely that Metin wouldn't find out who Warren-Madden was. This could well be a final test – Shepherd hadn't left with the guns yet and there was still time for the Turk to back out of the deal. But the fact that he had come up with the intel on Sazak was a good sign. Shepherd smiled and shrugged. 'I think he's wary of giving people his real name.'

'And what about you? Is your name really Paul?'

'It was my father's name,' said Shepherd.

'And you are scared of giving me your real name? After all I've done for you? Only Nancy boys use fake names.'

Shepherd laughed. 'My name is Dan.'

Metin clinked his coffee cup against Shepherd's and they both drank. 'Good to meet you, Dan.'

Metin smiled slyly. 'I knew you weren't a Paul. I could tell. And do you live in Spain?'

'I move around.'

'And are you a drug dealer?'

Shepherd shook his head. 'Metin, please. I'm just a guy who has a job to do, and I'll do whatever it takes to get that job done. Everything is being rushed at the moment and things are being done on the fly. I need your guns, and I'm grateful for the intel you've given us. But there is a limit to how much I can tell you.'

'You have ten guns here. So you have a crew?'

Shepherd nodded. 'Yes, I have a crew.'

'You will need one,' said Metin. 'I won't ask you any more questions, Dan,' he said. 'But I will ask you to do me one favour. If this goes wrong, and it might well do, I would not want Sazak to know that I've helped you.'

'You have my word, Metin.'

'And I believe you, Dan. Only Nancy boys do not keep their word.' He poured more coffee for them.

'Have you ever been to London?' Shepherd asked.

'A few times. I don't like the place.' He grinned. 'Too many Turks.'

Shepherd laughed. 'There is a big Turkish community there, that's true.'

'I read there are more than six hundred thousand Turks in London,' said Metin. 'Though most are Turkish Cypriots.'

'They're mainly in Wood Green, Stoke Newington, Enfield, north London mostly. But there was a very vicious Turkish Cypriot gang in South London a while back.'

'The Arifs?' said Metin.

'You know them?'

Metin shrugged. 'I used to drink with a couple of the Arif boys, but that was a long time ago. Twenty years maybe.'

Shepherd sipped his coffee. The Arif crime family were one of several gangs that had moved into the vacuum created by the removal of the Kray brothers in the late Sixties. They were involved in drugs, armed robberies and contract killings across the city. Most of the senior members of the family were now behind bars, but even in prison they kept a close eye on their empires. Arif family members in Turkey were still behind multi-million-dollar heroin shipments to Europe.

Shepherd wanted to talk more about the Arifs, but they were interrupted by the return of Warren-Madden. He sat down at their table and Metin poured coffee for him. 'Good to go?' Warren-Madden asked Shepherd.

'I think so,' said Shepherd. He grinned at Metin. 'But I think I might manage one of these amazing baklavas.'

'So what's the plan?' asked Warren-Madden as they walked to his car, which he had parked opposite the club.

'I'd like to be brought up to speed on the whole Hawks thing now, before we talk to Sazak.'

'No problem, I can let you look at our files. You'll have to be in the embassy's secure room to look at them, but you're cleared for all that sort of thing.'

'And we'll need to arrange transport for the guys. Two SUVs, sturdy rather than flashy.'

'They'll be staying in the country this time?'

'You're worried about the expenses? Don't worry, we can use one of my credit cards.'

They climbed into Warren-Madden's car and he drove them to the embassy, which was between two of the city's larger parks, a nondescript white-walled three-storey building with a red roof and rectangular chimneys. Warren-Madden guided the car between concrete bollards to a white metal gate set into a rail-ing-topped stone wall that was overlooked by a concrete sentry box with a large bullet-proof window. A uniformed guard walked out, nodded at Warren-Madden and checked Shepherd's passport and Home Office ID. He went back to the sentry box and a few seconds later a black and yellow metal barrier slid into the ground and the gate rattled back to reveal the embassy building. They parked behind the embassy and Warren-Madden and Shepherd went over to a rear entrance that opened with a swipe card and a pin code. 'I'm sorry about having to bring you here but the terrorism intel can't leave the embassy. Criminal information is okay but terrorism is a big no-no.'

'I understand,' said Shepherd.

'I'm not even allowed to access the files in my own office, I have to use the skiff.'

Shepherd nodded. All British embassies were equipped with a skiff – a Sensitive Compartmented Information Facility, a windowless room that could be used to process and transmit classified information. The rooms were usually lined with lead and copper and had extra soundproofing, which blocked any electronic surveillance.

The Ankara embassy's secure room was three doors along from Warren-Madden's office with a sign reading 'SCIF – AUTHORISED PERSONNEL ONLY'. To the right of the door was another keypad but this one had a fingerprint reader on the top. Warren-Madden swiped his card through the reader, tapped in his pin code and pressed his index finger on the scanner before the lock clicked and he pushed the door open. After all the security, the room itself was quite boring. Two tables, each with a computer on it, a large safe marked 'TOP SECRET' and two grey filing cabinets. There was a small CCTV camera in one corner of the room. Warren-Madden gestured at it. 'It records twenty-four-seven. There's no one watching but it records everything on a hard drive and can be accessed in real time if necessary. Phones and cameras are prohibited. You can make notes, that's all.'

He pulled open one of the filing cabinets, looked through the files and pulled one out. He sat down at one of the tables and opened it. Inside were several dozen head-and-shoulder shots and a thick pile of printed sheets. 'Some of this is on the computers, but not all, and I prefer old school,' he said. 'Most of it is from the Turkish military and the MIT.

MIT was Millî İstihbarat Teşkilatı, known in English as the

National Intelligence Organisation, and was responsible for counter-intelligence activities in Turkey.

'What about Europol and the CIA?'

'Europol has never really been interested in the Kurds because they tend not to get busy in Europe, beyond the odd demonstration. Europol are more worried about what the Turks are up to because that whole Turkey–Greece thing is going on. The Americans are in a difficult position because generally they are very anti-terrorism but they needed the Kurds to do their fighting against ISIS. So up until a few years ago the US security forces were running training camps in Syria for the Kurdish People's Protection Units in northern Syria. They were training ethnic Kurds but there were also Arabs and foreign volunteers. The Kurdish People's Protection Units were part of the Syrian Democratic Forces who were fighting to bring down the Syrian government any way that they could. Then in 2018 the Syrian National Army and the Turkish armed forces acted together in Operation Olive Branch to attack the camps, killing close to a thousand people, mainly civilians. It was nasty, as it usually is when the Turkish and Syrian armies get involved. They were using chemical gas and shooting refugees trying to flee into Turkey.' He grinned. 'So the short answer is no, very little intel from Europol or the Yanks.' He pointed at the file. 'But lots from MIT and the Army. And they're always happy to get any titbits I might have on what the Kurds are up to.'

'You share intel with the Turks?'

'Quid pro quo,' said Warren-Madden. 'I play poker with a group of their intelligence guys once a month and we chew the fat. Nothing sensitive, obviously. But it works as a clearing house for intelligence. Plus they've all got terrible tics. I always walk away with money.'

Shepherd flicked through the file. The photographs were mainly of middle-aged men with hard eyes and sullen faces. On the back of each photograph was a printed sheet with biographical details. Most of them were in the Kurdistan Workers' Party. Two of the photographs were members of the Kurdistan Freedom Hawks, one a man in his fifties with a scarred cheek and an eyepatch, the other a man in his twenties staring at the camera with undisguised hatred.

'So these people are all out on the streets?' asked Shepherd.

'It's not against the law to be a member of the Kurdistan Workers' Party. And because the Hawks have been quiet lately, they're on a loose leash. There's some surveillance going on but it's half-hearted.'

'How up to date is the file?'

Warren-Madden shrugged. 'Not very, to be honest. The Kurds aren't really of interest to us. Like I said, they hold the odd demonstration in London but that's as far as it goes.'

'Anyone strike you as the sort who would buy Semtex off Sazak?'

Warren-Madden went back to the filing cabinet and returned with another file. 'These are the details of the 2016 explosion. The Hawks claimed responsibility for the bombings but no one was ever arrested. Half a dozen Hawks were shot and killed in the months after the bombings, which may or may not have been the work of the MIT.'

'So MIT had suspects?'

'I think they just assumed that anyone in the organisation was fair game.'

Shepherd flicked through the files. There were more photographs, mainly of hard-faced young men, many bearded and wearing skullcaps. Several had DECEASED stamped across them.

'The Hawks are all underground but there are some addresses. There's more information available on the Kurdistan Workers' Party people, obviously. If you read the file you'll see that one of the names is a banker for the organisation. It's possible that if they did buy the Semtex from Sazak, that he came up with the money.'

Shepherd flicked through the photographs, checking the information on the back. He found the banker's picture and quickly scanned the details. 'He's a possibility,' he said. 'We'll have to see what Sazak has to say.'

'Those guys who are flying in, they're all SAS?'

'The ones coming in tonight, yes.'

'And I guess you are. Or were.'

'It's not something we talk about.'

Warren-Madden tapped his nose. 'Message received and understood.'

'I won't be involving you in the heavy stuff, if that's what you're worried about.'

Warren-Madden smiled. 'I'm not worried,' he said. 'What you're planning seems to be way beyond my skill set. But happy to help where I can.'

'You're helping me by getting me in here,' said Shepherd. 'I'd like to work my way through as many files as I can, if that's okay with you. That way I'll be fully prepared for when I meet Sazak.'

'Be my guest,' said Warren-Madden. 'While you're doing that I can rustle up a half-decent cup of coffee.'

Shepherd grinned when he saw Jeff Taylor walk into the arrivals area with a dark blue nylon holdall over his shoulder. He was wearing a leather bomber jacket and black jeans and his trademark Timberland boots. He was with three men he didn't recognise, but the way they carried themselves alone was enough to identify them as SAS. 'Mutton, great to see you again,' said Shepherd.

'You putting on weight, Spider?'

'Fuck you too,' said Shepherd.

The two men hugged and patted each other on the back. Taylor had done more than twenty years in the SAS and he and Shepherd had been on operations together several times before Shepherd had left the Regiment. He was a couple of inches shorter than Shepherd and considerably wider. So far as Shepherd knew, Taylor still held the Regimental record for press-ups.

'I don't think you know these guys,' said Taylor. 'They all joined well after you left.' He gestured at the man next to him. 'This is Alan Sage. He's not long back from Syria and will probably be there again after this.'

Sage fist-bumped Spider. He was in his late twenties, sunburnt with a neatly trimmed beard. He was wearing a blue Patagonia Fleece and cargo pants. 'Good to finally meet you,' Sage said. 'Your name comes up a lot at Stirling Lines.'

'All good, I hope,' said Shepherd.

'Fifty-fifty,' said Taylor with a grin. 'Now these two reprobates are Thing One and Thing Two. Jack and Joe Ellis. Fucked if I can ever tell which is which.'

It was only then that Shepherd realised that the two men were twins. They were dressed differently – one in a baseball hat and reefer jacket and the other in a leather jacket and tight jeans – but physically they were identical with brown eyes, wide chins and matching drooping moustaches. Both were carrying sports bags.

'I'm Jack,' said the one in the baseball cap. 'I'm the good-looking one.'

Shepherd fist-bumped him.

The second twin offered his fist. 'I'm Joe. The one with the brains.' Shepherd laughed and fist-bumped him.

Shepherd looked around. 'They said there were six of you.'

'Yeah, Mustard and Paddy had check-in luggage,' said Taylor. 'They shouldn't be long.'

'Great,' said Shepherd. 'I've worked with them both before.'

'Really? They're both fairly recent recruits.'

'Last year, in London,' said Shepherd. 'We had a jihadist group planning mayhem on New Year's Eve.' He smiled when he saw Terry 'Paddy' Ireland and Ricky 'Mustard' Coleman walk into the arrivals area pulling wheeled suitcases behind them. He went over to greet them.

Ireland was the taller of the two, broad-shouldered and wearing a quilted jacket and jeans. He had several days growth of beard, presumably in anticipation of a mission out in the Middle East. He fist-bumped Shepherd. 'Good to see you again, Spider,' he said in his strong Norfolk accent.

'You too, mate.'

Shepherd fist-bumped Coleman. He had done almost four

years with the Regiment but had put in ten years with the Paras and was in his mid-thirties. His hair was receding and he had cut it short.

'So what's the story?' asked Coleman. 'It's all been kick, bollock, scramble. We had our feet up in Wellington Barracks and the next we know we're on a plane to Turkey.'

'I'll brief you at the hotel,' said Shepherd. They went over to join the rest of the group and Shepherd took them over to the car park where Warren-Madden was waiting with two Peugeot SUVs they had rented, one black, one white. He was smoking a cigarette and he tossed it away as they walked up to him.

'This is Michael, he's with Six,' said Shepherd.

'He doesn't look like James Bond,' said Coleman.

'More like his uglier older brother,' said Ireland and they all laughed.

'Thanks for the vote of confidence, guys,' said Warren-Madden.

'Be nice, guys,' said Shepherd. 'He's on our side.'

'Until the shit hits the fan, at which point in my experience we won't see him for dust,' said Taylor.

'Right, I've booked three rooms for you at the Mövenpick,' said Shepherd. 'Hope you don't mind bunking together, but we shouldn't be in the rooms much.'

The Ellis twins and Sage went with Warren-Madden in the white Peugeot and Taylor, Coleman and Ireland rode with Shepherd.

Shepherd didn't want to talk about the operation until they were all together so he spent the short journey to the hotel catching up on Regimental gossip. As always there were funny stories to share, but there was also bad news, two troopers had been killed in Syria and their names added to the bottom of the clock tower in Stirling Lines. Shepherd didn't know the men but that didn't make any difference, the loss of one member of the Regiment hurt them all.

'So how long have you been out of the Regiment, Spider?' asked Taylor.

'Going on twenty years.'

'Miss it?'

'I miss some of it. It has its ups and downs, as you know.'

'Too right,' said Taylor. 'I'm planning on getting out before I get too old to do anything else.'

'I thought they were desperate to keep people these days,' said Shepherd.

'They are. They just let a fifty-one-year-old grandfather rejoin because they're so stretched. But if I'm ever going to earn any real money, I'll have to get started sooner rather than later.'

'Got any plans?'

'A few irons in the fire but nothing definite.' Taylor shrugged. 'That bloody Covid fucked it up for everybody. There's not much hiring going on at the moment.'

'You could try the cops,' said Shepherd.

'I put out some feelers but the pay isn't great and apparently I don't tick the right boxes, if you get my drift.'

They reached the hotel and parked close to Warren-Madden's SUV. Shepherd checked them in using a Paul Easton credit card. The rooms were all on the sixth floor. One was a suite with two queen-size beds and an adjoining door to one of the other rooms. Taylor and Jack Ellis took that one and Shepherd suggested that they use it as the briefing room. The troopers dumped the bags on the floor, then raided the minibars in all the rooms before gathering around one of the beds which Shepherd used as an impromptu whiteboard.

Before he started, he gave Warren-Madden his keycard and asked him to bring the gear they had bought from Metin.

'Okay, big picture,' said Shepherd, after Warren-Madden had left. 'Semtex explosives have been used in London, and they match a batch used by a couple of criminal groups here in Ankara. We have intel that the explosives were stolen from an Army base outside the city.' He placed the photographs of Sazak on the bed. 'Faruk Sazak, local gangster and hard man. He is believed to be behind the theft of the Semtex, along with a stack of weapons. He then sold the Semtex to criminals who used them, and to a Kurdish terrorist group. The mission is to get Sazak to tell us if he sold the Semtex to someone who used it in the UK.'

He dropped the map of Sazak's car dealership onto the bed. 'He has an office here with plenty of heavies around.' He put the photographs and map of Sazak's house on the pillow. 'This is where he lives. Now, I might have a way of getting a meeting with him, in which I'll be going in with one other, a former Para who went over to the dark side. Lex Harper. He's flying in first thing tomorrow. If we're lucky, we can persuade Sazak to give us the information.'

'And if we're not lucky?' asked Taylor.

Right on cue, Warren-Madden returned with the cases and holdall. Shepherd pointed at the cases. 'Then we take it to the next level.'

Warren-Madden put the cases on the floor. 'I think this is probably the point where I should make my excuses and leave,' he said. He tossed the SUV keys to Shepherd, who caught them one-handed.

'Are you okay to take me to the airport tomorrow to pick up the last member of the team?'

'Sure,' said Warren-Madden. 'Is he SAS?'

'Not exactly,' said Shepherd. 'If you could collect me at nine, that would be perfect. Earlier if you want to grab breakfast here.' He smiled. 'On me, obviously.'

As Warren-Madden left, the troopers opened the cases and began checking the handguns. Taylor laughed when he saw the MAC-11s. 'Are you serious?' he said. 'Have you ever fired one of these?'

'They're more for show than anything,' said Shepherd. 'Shock and awe.'

Taylor laughed as he showed the weapon to Sage. 'Spray and pray, more like.'

Shepherd pointed at the holdall. 'I've got three ballistic vests. It's all I could get, I'm afraid.'

'We've brought two with us,' said Coleman.

'Excellent,' said Shepherd. 'I've got holsters, but so far as comms go we're going to have to use our phones.'

'I brought six radio sets as well,' said Coleman. 'We had a bit of a stores raid before we left. I've got some night vision gear, climbing gear and a couple of first-aid kits. I would have brought some flash bangs but it being a commercial flight and all . . .'

'Great,' said Shepherd. 'Lex arrives first thing tomorrow. I don't think we'll do anything before then.'

Taylor waved at the guns. 'That's a lot of firepower for one gangster,' he said. 'You said something about a Kurdish terrorist group?'

'That's a bridge we can cross when we get to it,' said Shepherd. 'Sazak may or may not have sold the Semtex to Kurdish terrorists and they in turn may or may not have sent it to London. I'm hoping that Sazak will have the answers but if not . . .'

'Then we'll need the firepower?'

'Bridges, chickens, eggs,' said Shepherd. He looked at his watch. 'Okay, it's late, you guys can grab a meal or drink in the restaurant, then get some shut-eye. While I'm picking up Lex, you guys can get started on a recce of Sazak's house and the dealership. Entrances, exits, escape routes. The works. Once you've done the recce we'll decide whether we go into the house or the dealership.'

'Sounds like a plan,' said Taylor. He grinned. 'The bit about the drink, I mean.'

Shepherd had been standing in the arrivals area for about an hour before Lex Harper strolled out, swinging a red Liverpool sports bag. His sandy hair was pretty much hidden under a Singha Beer baseball cap. He was wearing tight blue jeans and gleaming white Nikes. He grinned when he saw Shepherd. 'You're a sight for sore eyes, Spider,' he said, giving him a one-armed hug. 'Long time no see.' He was about the same height as Shepherd, thinner and with a slightly crooked nose that suggested he had been hit in the face at least once.

'How was the flight?'

'Fucking nightmare. I ended up flying through Qatar and changing at Istanbul. Business Class, couldn't get First. And the food was shit.' He looked around. 'Just you and me?'

'The Sass team are back at the hotel so we'll have a full briefing there. The local MI6 guy is waiting with the car.'

'What's he like?'

'He's okay. I was with him on a job last year and he didn't let me down. And he's a smoker so you'll get on.'

They headed towards the exit. 'Anything you need to tell me?' asked Harper. 'Before we get to the car.'

'What do you mean?'

'You left him with the car, just thought you wanted to say something out of earshot of the spook.'

'I think he just wanted a cigarette while he was waiting.'

'Really?'

'Really. You're always so suspicious.'

Harper grinned. 'When you're dealing with MI5 and MI6 and all those other initials, you have to be. What does he know about me?'

'I told him you were a former Para who's now a bit dodgy but has a heart of gold.'

Harper laughed. 'I'll use you next time I need a reference. He's Six so he'll know about the Pool, but does he know I'm a part of it?'

'No, so best not mention it. You're just a pal helping me out. You've got an in with Sazak and I'm taking advantage of that.' They walked out of the terminal and headed for the multi-storey car park. 'You have got an in with him, right?'

'Like I said, I've never met the man or done business with him. But I know a couple of guys out in Spain who have. Sazak has been running migrants from Turkey into Greece for years and often he'll put heroin on the same boats. He has the heroin collected in Greece and driven overland to Spain. The guys I know are Irish, based in Fuengirola on the Costa del Crime. They take Sazak's heroin and get it into the UK and Ireland. Covid and Brexit have made their lives harder so Sazak will be looking for alternative routes, which means he'll be open to offers. The guys will get in touch with Sazak and vouch for me. Then it's up to us.'

'Who are these guys?'

Harper grimaced. 'I'd rather not say too much about them.'

'Honour among thieves?'

'More like snitches get stitches. They're mates but they wouldn't want their names bandied about. Let's just leave it at Mick and Ant. Mick said he'd make the call, but basically all he'll do is say that a guy called Lex will be in touch with a business proposal. He doesn't want to say any more than that in case it goes tits up. This Sazak is a vicious bastard.'

They reached the car park. Warren-Madden was just finishing a cigarette and he fist-bumped Harper. 'Good flight?'

'Shit,' said Harper. 'But I'm here now.'

Harper climbed into the back. 'Okay to smoke in here?' he asked.

'Go ahead,' said Warren-Madden. 'Though strictly speaking my car is classed as a workplace so it's not allowed.'

'I thought the Turks were big smokers.'

'They used to be, but as in the rest of the world we're pariahs now.'

Harper lit a cigarette, took a deep pull and sighed contentedly. 'So what's the plan?' he asked.

'That depends on what the guys came up with on the recce,' said Shepherd. He opened the window to let in some fresh air. 'So far we've two options, his house and a car dealership he owns.'

'And we've got guns?'

Shepherd laughed. 'Yes, we've got guns.'

'Because we'll need them.'

Warren-Madden flashed Shepherd a worried look but Shepherd just smiled.

The SAS team were sitting around drinking coffee and eating room service sandwiches when Shepherd and Harper walked in. They had checked Harper into a room on Shepherd's floor and dropped off his bag. Warren-Madden had gone home, he didn't want to be involved in what was obviously an off-the-books operation. Shepherd hadn't tried to persuade him otherwise. Besides, there wasn't much the MI6 officer could add other than intel, and Shepherd had memorised everything he had read in the secure room. Shepherd introduced Harper and he fist-bumped them one by one. 'Where are Mustard and Thing One?' asked Shepherd.

'They've got eyes on Sazak,' said Taylor. 'He's in his office and they're parked up outside. They'll call when he moves.' He looked over at Sage. 'Get the curtains, Sagey.'

Shepherd looked at Taylor in confusion. 'What's happening?'

Terry Ireland held up a small white box with a lens on the side. 'We brought a projector with us,' he said. 'Makes briefings easier.'

'Nice,' said Shepherd.

Sage pulled the curtains shut. Shepherd and Harper sat on one of the beds as Ireland connected his smartphone to the projector and switched it on. A beam of light flashed onto the wall by the television, then there was a blurry picture which came into focus as Ireland adjusted the lens. It was a grey stone villa with a red tiled roof behind a high wall.

'This is where Sazak lives,' said Taylor. 'On the outskirts of the city, nice neighbourhood.'

Ireland clicked through a succession of pictures, of the house, the large metal gate that led to the driveway, the security wire on top of the walls.

'The villa is on the side of the hill and we managed to get into a garden higher up that gave us a decent view of the plot,' said Taylor.

Ireland flashed up half a dozen photographs of the house and its grounds. There was a patio at the back with a barbecue area, an indoor swimming pool in a separate glass-roofed building, and a garage that looked big enough for four cars. There were two black vehicles parked in a circular driveway directly in front of the building.

'No CCTV that we could see, I'm guessing that everyone knows who he is so there's not much chance of being burgled.

The wire is mainly for show, it's not electrified, a pair of wire-cutters and you're through.'

'Was he at home?' asked Shepherd.

'No, he was in his office the whole time we were there,' said Ireland. 'The cars are for his security or bodyguards or whatever he calls them. We saw two but there might be more.' He nodded at Ireland who flashed up another series of photographs. The first set were of a bulky bald man in an Adidas tracksuit who walked out of the front door to smoke a cigarette. The second were of a taller, thinner man who left the house to get a bag from the boot of one of the cars. 'These are the two we saw.'

'There were no wife or kids that we could see,' said Taylor.

'He's not married any more,' said Shepherd. 'His wife divorced him five years ago and she died shortly afterwards.'

'Convenient,' said Ellis.

'Not for her,' said Shepherd. 'Drove into a lake and drowned. Allegedly. There were no kids.'

'His office is, as you said, above a car dealership,' said Ireland. 'Some very shady characters going in and out throughout the day. Mainly delivering flash motors. The sort of guys driving them didn't look like they could afford them, so we're thinking stolen.'

'Yeah, he's running a parts chop shop, apparently,' said Shepherd.

Pictures flashed up of a Porsche, a BMW SUV similar to the one Shepherd owned in London, and a Ferrari.

'There are sales staff downstairs and some men who are wearing suits but are carrying concealed guns.'

A dozen photographs flashed onto the wall of various thick-set men walking in and out of the front door of the dealership. Then there was a photograph of a very pretty blonde girl in a short skirt and blazer. 'We're pretty sure that she's with sales, unless those are hand grenades up her shirt,' said Taylor. They all laughed. Shepherd couldn't help but smile. Political correctness had yet to work its way into the SAS. He could only imagine what would happen if he made a crack like that in an MI5 operations room.

'We did manage to get a look at the man himself,' said Taylor.
'He and three of his heavies went to a local cafe for coffee and
raki.'

Raki was the Turkish national drink, a fiery spirit made from
twice-distilled grapes and aniseed. More pictures flashed up of
Sazak and three of the heavies walking across the road. They
were followed by a short video of the same scene. Sazak was
short but powerfully built with a shaved head and rolls of fat
around the back of his neck. There was a thick rope-like scar
above his left ear and he favoured his right leg as if it had been
injured at some point in the past and never healed properly. He
was talking into his phone but the three heavies were all on full
alert, scanning the area for any possible threats. A gust of wind
blew against the back of one of the men and for a second they
could see the outline of a gun. The men crossed the road and
disappeared from view.

'We decided not to risk going into the cafe. They were there
for about half an hour and then went back to the office.'

Another video flashed onto the wall. Sazak walking in the
opposite direction, the phone still glued to his ear. His three
bodyguards were sticking close and constantly on alert. 'His guys
are good,' said Shepherd.

'Yeah, I'm guessing former military,' said Taylor.

The video came to an end and Sage opened the curtains again.

'The big issue with the office is there is only one way in, and
that's through the showroom,' said Taylor. 'You have to go up a
flight of stairs and the stairs are clearly visible from the showroom.
There are always at least two heavies there so you'd have to get
past them. We could do that, of course, but not without causing
a commotion so Sazak and the heavies upstairs would hear us
coming.'

'What about when he leaves the building?' asked Shepherd.

'You saw what the heavies are like, they stick to him like glue.
I'm pretty sure the car would pull up outside and they'd walk
him to it. I don't see that we could snatch him without a hell of
a fight. I mean, we could do it, of course, but not without shots

being fired. Someone would call it in and the nearest police station is only two minutes away by car. Turkish cops are armed, it could all get very messy very quickly.'

Shepherd rubbed his chin. 'The thing is, Lex can get us in for a chat, there's no question of that. We'll be dangling the carrot of a drug deal, so he'll want to hear what we've got to say. But the moment we bring up the Semtex, he'll know we're not there for the drugs so he'll either answer the question or he'll throw us out. With the best will in the world, I don't see a guy like that being in the least bit helpful. That means he'll throw us out and then he knows something's up. He'll be on full alert and we won't get near him again.'

'So his house, then?' said Taylor.

Shepherd nodded. 'I think that's the way to go but I'm open to differing opinions. Lex and I go into the house, we introduce ourselves, and we raise the matter of the explosives. If he talks, we're good. We get the intel and get out. If, as I suspect, he kicks off, you guys move in and we start a hard interrogation.'

'That works for me,' said Taylor. 'Anyone any thoughts?'

'We can climb over the wall easy enough,' said Sage. 'No CCTV to worry about, and if Spider and Lex are inside that's probably where all the security will be. And if we go in after dark we can use the night vision gear that Paddy and Mustard brought with them.'

'It gets dark here about six-thirty, but we're going to have to wait until Sazak gets home,' said Shepherd. 'But we can't leave it too late, he's not going to let us in at some God-awful hour.'

'As soon as he leaves the office, Mustard will let us know,' said Taylor.

'Should we head out to the house first?' asked Shepherd.

'I don't see the point,' said Taylor. 'It's a twenty-minute drive away and if we do park up we risk being seen.'

'What about vehicles? We'll need one for me and Lex to visit the house.'

'You could taxi it. Or we could drop you close by and you walk up.'

'We'll get no respect turning up in an Uber,' said Harper. 'A man like Sazak isn't even going to open the gate.'

'Lex is right,' said Shepherd. 'I'll call Michael, last time I was here he rented me a no-questions-asked Mercedes for cash. I'll get him to do the same again. So we just wait now to hear from Mustard?'

Taylor nodded. 'He'll call and he'll follow to check that he's heading home and then he'll pull back.'

'Okay, great. Lex and I'll grab some grub in the lobby.'

Shepherd and Harper were in the lobby bar finishing off their meal when Warren-Madden arrived with the rented Mercedes. Shepherd had ordered a steak sandwich, Harper had gone for the Mövenpick basket – a selection of fish nuggets, chicken nuggets, beef sausages, jalapeño poppers, onion rings and French fries, with three sauces. Harper had polished it off in record time and then ordered a chocolate sundae.

Warren-Madden put a Mercedes keyfob on the table. 'It's in the car park. A white C-Class.'

'Thanks,' said Shepherd. 'Do you want to eat?'

'I'm good,' said Warren-Madden. 'Are things progressing?'

'Just waiting for the call.' As he was speaking his mobile phone rang. 'Speak of the devil.'

'I'll leave you to it,' said the MI6 officer. 'Let me know if you need anything else.'

As he walked away, Shepherd took the call. It was Taylor. 'Mustard says Sazak is on the move,' he said. 'Looks like he's heading straight home.'

'I'll be right up.' Shepherd signed for the bill as Harper bolted down the last of his ice cream. They took the lift up to Taylor's room where the team were adjusting their holsters and checking their weapons. Taylor and Sage were already wearing ballistic vests under their shirts and Joe Ellis was putting one on.

Ireland had taken one of the MAC-11s and Joe Ellis had a Glock.

'Help yourself,' said Taylor, pointing at the remaining guns.

'We can't go in armed, or wearing vests,' said Harper. 'It'll show a lack of faith.'

Shepherd picked up a Beretta and tucked it into his belt. 'We can leave the guns in the car. They'll pat us down but I doubt they'll search the car. And yes, you're right about the vests.'

'I don't think you should be going in without guns or vests,' said Taylor.

Shepherd shook his head. 'Lex is right. We can't go in there as if we're looking for trouble.'

'At least take comms with you so you can call us in if there's a problem.'

'And what do we say when they find the radio?' asked Harper. 'We have to go in clean. First thing they'll do is search us and if we have anything on us that we shouldn't it'll be Goodnight Irene.'

'So what's the signal if you need us?' asked Taylor.

'I'll throw something through the window,' said Harper. 'Ideally one of the heavies.'

'Is he serious?' Taylor asked Shepherd.

'It's always hard to tell with Lex,' said Shepherd. 'How about this? We go in through the front door, you guys move in over the wall. Night vision gear if the gardens aren't floodlit. One of the guys can run surveillance from up the hill. You can watch from the garden. You'll be able to see if there's a problem.'

'I still think throwing something through the window is the best bet,' said Harper.

Taylor put on his jacket and checked his reflection in the mirror over the dressing table. Ellis finished adjusting his vest and pulled on his shirt.

'So, Lex and I will drive in the Merc,' said Shepherd. 'I guess we should follow you. You get there first and drive around the back and then Lex and I will approach the house.'

Taylor nodded. 'Sagey can drop us at the rear of the house and then head up the hill. Coleman and Thing One can park near the house and get over the wall near the main gate later, assuming all the heavies are inside.'

'How many heavies do we think?'

'There are three in the car with Sazak now. One of them is driving. We only saw two when we had the house under surveillance earlier. If we're lucky there are no more in the house and if we're really lucky his three bodyguards will drop him and go. But we can handle five.'

Shepherd looked over at Ireland. 'We can take a comms set in the car.'

The Sass team began assembling their radio kits, clipping the transceivers to their belts and popping in Bluetooth earbuds. They spent several minutes checking that all their units worked, then headed for the door.

'You should call Sazak and let him know you're on the way,' said Shepherd.

Harper went out into the corridor and returned after a couple of minutes. 'Okay, he's expecting us,' said Harper. 'He's not exactly putting out the red carpet, but he'll see us.'

They took the lift downstairs and went to their vehicles. Sage led the way out of the car park in the white SUV, Shepherd and Harper followed in the Mercedes. It was dark and there wasn't much traffic. They reached the outskirts of the city and then took the road that led up a hill to the west. At the base of the hill were dozens of small single-storey cottages each with their own plot of land. The further up the hill they went, the bigger the houses became and the more space there was between them, and the higher the surrounding walls.

Shepherd was driving. He had memorised the route but it was easy enough to follow Sage as he was a careful driver and never went above the speed limit.

Harper had his radio in his lap. He had put his gun in the glove compartment. Shepherd had put his Beretta under his seat. Harper touched his earbud and listened. 'Sazak is back at the house. Mustard and Thing One are outside.'

They drove for a few more minutes, the road winding around the hill.

'Taylor says they're coming up to the house,' said Harper.

'Yeah, it's a couple of hundred yards on the left,' said Shepherd.

'He says they're going to drive around and that we should park up and wait.'

Shepherd indicated and pulled over to the side of the road. There were no streetlights and no other vehicles around.

Harper looked across at Shepherd. 'You okay?'

Shepherd took a deep breath and sighed. 'Yeah. Just getting pre-match jitters.'

'It'll be fine,' said Harper. 'It'd be different if we had a few hundred kilos in the boot or a bag of money. People kill for that, no problem.'

'This guy is a serious gangster. You know that.'

'Yeah, but we're knocking on his door with a business proposal. He'll listen to us. He won't shoot us because we're offering to give him money. Now when you raise the matter of the Semtex, he might kick off. But he won't shoot us because he doesn't like the question. He'll want to know what we're up to so he'll have questions for us. And if it turns to shit, your guys will have plenty of time to intervene. Trust me, I've been to dozens of meetings like this and no one has ever drawn a gun.' He put his hand up to the earbud and listened. 'Okay, they're at the back of the house. Taylor, Ellis and Ireland are going over the wall. They're cutting the wire. Taylor says they're using the night vision goggles but that the lights are on in the house.'

He listened again. 'Coleman says the heavies haven't left. They're still inside with Sazak.'

'That's a pity,' said Shepherd.

Harper put his hand up to his earpiece. 'Okay, Sagey says he's up on the hill and has parked with a view of the garden.' He pointed forward. 'We're good to go.'

Shepherd drove forward. Harper took out his earbud and put it into the glove compartment with the radio.

'There's Mustard and Jack,' said Shepherd, nodding at the SUV parked at the side of the road. They drove by and Jack Ellis threw them a mock salute from the driving seat.

Sazak's villa was surrounded by a ten-foot-high wall which was topped with razor wire. The main gate was black-painted metal with studs in it and spikes on the top. Shepherd drove slowly up to the gate. There was a four-sided metal post set into the ground with a speaker and a white call button. There was a small camera lens above the speaker. Shepherd rolled down the window and leaned out to press the intercom button. He kept his head turned away from the camera. After a few seconds of static, a voice growled something in Turkish.

'Yeah, we're here to see Faruk Sazak,' said Shepherd. 'Anyone there speak English?'

'This is a private house, fuck off,' said a voice with a heavy Turkish accent. There was a click and then silence.

'Well that went well,' said Shepherd. He pressed the buzzer again. When there was no answer he pressed it again. And again.

'Fuck off,' said the Turkish voice eventually.

'Tell Mr Sazak that Lex Harper is here to see him. I spoke to him on the phone earlier. He should be expecting me. Lex Harper. From Spain.'

There was static and then silence. Shepherd was just about to reach out to press the bell again when they heard two loud clicks and the gate rolled to the side to reveal the house and three cars parked in front of it.

'Here we go,' said Shepherd. 'Into the lion's den.' He pressed his foot on the accelerator and drove through the gate, the tyres crunching on the gravelled driveway.

Taylor crouched by the wall, looking at the house through the night vision goggles, which gave everything a soft green glow. Ireland was moving through a clump of orange trees to his left and Joe Ellis was off to the right. The lights were on in the covered swimming pool but there was nobody there. The patio area and barbecue pit were in darkness, as were the upstairs rooms of the house.

'They're driving through the gates,' said Sage in his ear. 'The gates are closing behind them.'

'We're getting out of the vehicle,' said Coleman. 'Let us know when it's safe to go in.'

'Roger that,' said Sage.

Ireland moved through the trees and then dropped to the grass.

Taylor knelt down and began to crawl forward. Most of the lawn was in darkness. There was no moon and enough clouds overhead to blot out most of the stars. The lights were on in the room overlooking the patio, and in the kitchen to the left of the house.

'Two heavies have come out of the house,' said Sage over the radio. 'With guns. Spider and Lex are getting out. They're putting their hands up.'

'That's par for the course,' said Taylor. 'It's the gangster equiv-alent of a fist bump.'

'Another heavy's at the front door, also carrying. Shepherd and Lex are going inside. The front door's closing.'

'Shall we go over the wall?' asked Coleman.

'Give it a few minutes,' said Taylor. 'Paddy, Joe, let's get closer to the house.'

The door slammed shut behind them and Shepherd flinched. He turned to see one of the armed heavies grinning at him and realised that the slam had been deliberate. 'Can we put our hands down?' he said. 'It's tiring.'

'Shut the fuck up,' growled the heavy, grabbing him by the shoulder and pushing him against the wall. 'Open your fucking legs wide.'

'You're not going to rape me, are you, because you're really not my type?'

The heavy sneered at Shepherd and slapped the back of his head.

Harper turned to face the wall without being asked and put his hands up. 'His dick is so small you won't even notice it,' he said to Shepherd.

The heavy raised his hand to slap him but Harper turned and sneered at him. 'You might want to wait until we've spoken to Faruk before you go laying your hands on us. Just so you know.'

The heavy lowered his hand and began to search Shepherd. One of the other two heavies roughly patted Harper down.

'No cellphone?' said the heavy who was searching Harper.

'It's under my cock, sweetie. Why, do you want to make a call?'

The heavy said something in Turkish that clearly wasn't complimentary and Harper laughed.

When the two heavies had finished searching Shepherd and Harper they stood back.

The third heavy, the biggest of the three, was standing by a set of double doors. He opened them and motioned for Shepherd and Harper to go through.

They walked into the room. Sazak was sitting behind a massive ornate desk with curved legs. Behind him was a huge oil painting of the man himself sitting astride a white horse and holding a sabre, a plumed hat on his head. There were two sets of French doors leading onto the patio and barbecue area. Most of the garden was in darkness but they could see the swimming pool building illuminated with a yellowish glow. Shepherd couldn't see Taylor and his men but he knew they were out there somewhere.

The heavy who had patted Shepherd down walked up to the desk and said something in Turkish, probably telling him that they weren't carrying guns or phones or wired for sound. Sazak said something back to him and the heavy went over to one of the French windows and stood with his back to it, his arms folded.

'No phones?' said Sazak in a heavy accent.

'Phones make people nervous,' said Harper. 'These days the cops can listen in to anything, even when they're switched off.' He grinned and walked over to the desk. 'I'm Lex Harper.' He held out his hand but Sazak made no move to shake hands. He pointed at a sofa with a hand encrusted with gold rings. 'Sit,' he said.

The two other heavies came in and closed the double doors behind them. They stood impassively, their hands cupped around their groins like footballers preparing to face a free kick.

Harper sat on an overstuffed leather sofa with a coffee table in front of it. Shepherd looked around. To the right was a pool table and beyond it two more sofas in front of a big-screen TV. On the wall beyond the pool table was another oil painting of Sazak, this one life-size and showing him as a Roman gladiator with bulging muscles and a trident, facing a snarling tiger. There were two winged armchairs facing the sofa where Harper was sitting and he took the one with the best view of the garden.

'So how long have you known Mick?' Sazak asked Harper.

Harper shrugged. 'Six years, seven maybe.'

'Good friends?'

'Yeah, we meet socially. And I've done some business with him. My main supplier is having logistics problems and Mick suggested you might be an alternative supplier.'

Sazak nodded thoughtfully. 'And what sort of amounts would you be looking for?'

'Four hundred keys,' said Harper.

'A week?'

'A month. Maybe more down the line.'

'And Micky told you my price?'

'He gave me three prices. Delivery here, delivery in Greece, and delivery in Spain. I'll take delivery in Greece.'

Sazak gestured at one of the heavies. He brought over a phone and gave it to Sazak. He tapped on the screen and it started to ring.

'What's going on?' asked Harper.

Sazak waved for him to be quiet. He smiled at the screen. 'Mick, hello, you are looking well.'

'Ah, that's nice of you to say, Faruk. You're looking pretty spiffy yourself.' It was an Irish voice, Shepherd realised.

'Spiffy?'

'It means elegant. Well turned out.'

Shepherd flashed Harper a worried look but Harper just shrugged.

'Well thank you. Mick, I just want to confirm that this is your friend Lex.' He turned the phone so that the screen was pointing at Harper. The face on the screen frowned. He was in his forties with glistening black hair that was combed back to show off a widow's peak and wearing a thick gold chain around his neck.

Harper lifted his hand to wave but Sazak turned the phone around. 'Well?'

'Never seen him before in my life,' said Mick.

'Mick! For fuck's sake!' shouted Harper.

'I knew it,' said Sazak, ending the call and slamming the phone down. The two heavies by the door both reached inside their jackets and pulled out guns. Shepherd jumped to his feet. 'Don't kill them,' said Sazak. 'Take them down to the basement.'

Harper picked up an ashtray off the coffee table and hurled it at the two heavies. They flinched and Shepherd took the opportunity to jump forward and grab the gun arm of the man nearest him.

The phone began to ring.

Harper was on his feet now. The heavy by the French windows had been slow to react and his hand had only started to reach for the gun.

Shepherd swung the man around, then bent his arm down and around, twisting it behind his back. He jerked the arm up and the gun fell from his nerveless fingers. Shepherd kneed the man in the side and as he bent down he punched him in the side of his head. The man slumped to the floor. Shepherd grabbed the gun, but as he straightened up he saw that the second heavy had his gun pointing directly at his face.

Harper took a step towards the heavy by the window but the man already had his gun out. Harper stopped and raised his hands.

'Everyone needs to calm the fuck down!' shouted Shepherd. 'No one has to get hurt.'

'It's too late for that,' said Sazak. He waved at the heavies by the door. 'Shoot the fuckers.'

'Oh shit,' said Taylor. 'It looks like it's kicking off.' He was close enough to the house to see inside without the night vision goggles so he had taken them off and let them hang around his neck.

He had crawled halfway across the lawn and was about thirty feet from the patio.

'I can't see anything from here,' said Sage.

'They're in the room that backs onto the garden,' said Taylor. 'Paddy, do you have eyes on Sazak?'

'Yeah. He's sitting behind a desk.'

'Armed?'

'I don't see a gun. But the three heavies are all waving their weapons around.'

'I only see three,' said Taylor. 'Joe, how many do you see?'

'Three confirmed,' said Ellis. 'All armed. Two by the door, one with his back to the window.'

'I only see the one by the window,' said Ireland. 'But I have a clean shot.'

'Let's move closer,' said Taylor.

'Roger that,' said Ellis.

'Moving forward,' said Ireland.

'If it looks like their lives are in danger, we do whatever is necessary,' said Taylor.

The heavy closest to Shepherd gritted his teeth and tightened his finger on the trigger of his Glock. 'Don't do it,' said Shepherd.

The phone continued to ring.

Shepherd had his gun trained on the heavy's chest. He was staring at the man's face waiting for the tensing of the man's jaw muscles that would let him know that the man was about to pull the trigger. The second heavy also had his gun out and Shepherd knew that he was on a hiding to nothing. Two guns against one never went well.

The phone was still ringing but Sazak was ignoring it.

'Maybe answer the phone, Sazak,' said Harper.

Sazak ignored him.

'I'm serious, Sazak. Answer the fucking phone.'

Sazak picked up the phone and pressed the green button to accept the incoming video call. 'For fuck's sake, Faruk, I was joking!' shouted Mick.

'What?'

'It was a fucking joke! I thought it would be funny! I didn't think you'd fucking hang up on me!'

Sazak pointed the phone around so that Mick could see Harper, who was standing with his hands in the air, the gun still pointing at his face. Harper glared over at the phone. 'For fuck's sake, Mick!'

'Mate, I'm sorry. Irish humour. What can I say?'

'You almost got us fucking killed!' Harper slowly lowered his hands and turned away from the man with the gun. He pointed at the phone. 'You and I will have a serious fucking talk next time I see you.'

Sazak turned the phone around and looked at the screen. 'So you do know this man?'

'Yeah, yeah, yeah, sorry, Faruk. That's Lex Harper. In the flesh.'

'You think this is a laughing matter?'

'It was a bad joke, Faruk, I'm sorry.'

Sazak ended the call. As he put the phone back on the desk, the window to his left exploded in a shower of glass. The heavy who was pointing his gun at Shepherd turned to look at the window and almost immediately two shots hit him in the face and the throat and he staggered backwards, banged into a side-board and fell to the floor.

The heavy opposite Harper raised his gun, but before he could even aim it he was hit three times, two shots in the chest and once in the face. He took two steps back and collapsed into an armchair, the gun still in his hand.

The heavy next to Shepherd was up on his knees but Shepherd hit him with the butt of his gun and the man slumped to the floor.

The door burst open and two more heavies crashed into the room. The first one saw movement in the garden and raised his gun but before he could pull the trigger was hit twice in the chest. The other heavy roared with anger, bringing his gun to bear on Shepherd. Shepherd dropped into a crouch and put two rounds into the man's heart.

Sazak was sitting at his desk, his mouth wide open in shock.

Taylor appeared at the window. 'You good?' he asked Shepherd.

'I'm good,' said Shepherd, straightening up. 'But I had it under control.'

'Yeah, that's what it looked like.'

Shepherd knew there was no point in arguing. He looked over at Harper. 'Lex, can you open the front door and let them in?'

Harper grinned. 'They're Sass, they can come in through the window.' Shepherd opened his mouth to reply but Harper grinned. 'I'm on it.' He stepped over the dead heavy and went into the hallway.

'All five accounted for?' said Taylor.

'Yeah. You got four and one is out for the count.' He put the gun in his pocket.

Taylor and the rest of the men disappeared around the side of the house. Shepherd knelt down, took the belt from around the unconscious heavy's waist and used it to bind the man's wrists.

Sazak was still sitting behind the desk. 'Can I smoke?' he asked, regaining his composure.

'It's your house,' said Shepherd. He straightened up and took the gun from his pocket.

Sazak slowly reached for a cigar box. Shepherd kept his gun pointed at the man's face as he opened the box and took out a large cigar. He bit off the end and spat it away, then lit a match. Once he had the cigar going he took a long drag on it and blew smoke towards Shepherd. 'Who the fuck are you?' he said.

'That doesn't matter,' said Shepherd.

'I know Mick, and I know that your friend is Lex Harper, but who are you?'

'I'm the guy with the gun, which is all you need to know,' said Shepherd.

'Lex said they were Sass. What is Sass?'

Shepherd's eyes narrowed but he didn't reply.

'This isn't about money, is it? If you think I have money you are mistaken. A few thousand lira, a few thousand euros.

Chickenfeed. There are my watches, they are valuable, but I don't think you killed my men to get watches, did you? So what do you want?'

'You'll find out soon enough,' said Shepherd.

Harper returned with Taylor, Coleman and the two Ellis brothers. 'How do you want to play it?' asked Taylor.

'He mentioned a basement. We can talk to him there. Any reaction outside?'

'We're far enough away from the other houses that I don't think we'll have a problem,' said Taylor. 'The garden is visible from up the hill but not the back of the house. I think we're good.'

'I'll check for a basement,' said Coleman.

Sazak stared at the Ellis brothers, from one to the other. 'Twins?' he said.

'No mate, you're seeing double,' said Joe.

Coleman came back. 'Yeah, there's a basement,' he said.

'Let's get him down there,' said Shepherd.

The Ellis brothers walked over to Sazak. 'What do you want?' he asked.

'We want to talk to you,' said Shepherd.

'We can talk here.'

'You were going to take us down to the basement. Now we're going to take you.'

Sazak held up the cigar. 'Can I take this with me?'

'No, you fucking can't,' said Joe Ellis. He grabbed the cigar and stubbed it out in a large crystal ashtray.

'That's an Arturo Fuente,' said Sazak. 'Do you have any idea what they fucking cost?'

Joe grabbed one arm, Jack seized the other. They pulled him to his feet and dragged him around the desk.

Shepherd went into the hall with Taylor. Ireland was guarding the main entrance. Coleman was standing by an open door. He moved to the side so that Shepherd and Taylor could go down a flight of stairs. The basement was huge, pretty much the size of the house, with a concrete floor and wooden beams running overhead. There was a large boiler in one corner and stacks of cardboard boxes in another. Chains had been fixed to the beams in the middle of the basement and there were several dark red stains where blood had soaked into the concrete. There were a dozen tools including pliers and saws on a metal bench, along with several knives of various shapes and sizes.

'This is a fucking torture chamber,' said Taylor.

'Looks like it,' said Shepherd.

The walls and ceiling had been soundproofed with thick sheets of black rubber. Next to the table was a racked hi-fi system and two large Wharfedale speakers. Sazak was clearly a man who liked music while he worked.

There was a wooden chair by the table and Shepherd pulled it out and gestured for them to put Sazak on it. He picked up a roll of duct tape, and between them they bound his arms and legs to the chair. Sazak stared at Shepherd, hatred pouring from his eyes.

'Guys, you can wait upstairs,' Shepherd said to the Ellis brothers. They looked over at Taylor for confirmation and Taylor nodded.

They went up the stairs and closed the door behind them. Shepherd walked over to look down at Sazak. 'A few years ago your people stole weapons and explosives from an Army base,' he said.

Sazak shrugged. 'So?'

'What did you do with it? The stuff you stole?'

'Why do you care?'

Harper stepped forward and slapped Sazak across the face. The sound was like a pistol shot and blood seeped from between Sazak's lips as he glared up at Harper. 'I will fucking kill you,' he said, then he spat at Harper. Harper had already stepped back and the phlegm missed him and splattered on the floor.

'Yeah, you're not the first person who's said that.'

'Listen, Faruk,' said Shepherd. 'I know what you did with the Semtex, but I need you to confirm it.'

'You think I'm stupid? If you knew, why would you do this to me?'

'Because I need the details.'

'Fuck you. You come into my house and kill my men and you want me to give you details. Who the—'

Harper stepped forward and hit him again, harder this time.

'Don't make this any more difficult than it has to be,' said Shepherd. He pointed at one of the dark patches on the floor. 'You've had people down here and done bad things to them. That's obvious. Now you're the one in the chair, tied up with duct tape. You know what's going to happen.'

'You think I'm scared of you?'

Shepherd shrugged. 'It's not about fear, Faruk. It's about the way this will end. And that's down to you. Do you want to die in this basement? Because that's what will happen if you don't co-operate.'

'What do you want?'

'I told you what I want. The ordnance, who did you sell it to?'

Sazak frowned. 'Ordnance?'

'The weapons. And the explosives.'

Sazak frowned. 'I sell to many people. It's my—'

Again he was cut short by a slap from Harper.

Shepherd pointed his gun at Sazak and pulled the trigger twice. Both shots missed his head by inches and the bullets buried themselves in the cardboard boxes at the far end of the basement. The sound was deafening in the confined space and the cordite stung Shepherd's eyes. Sazak's eyes were wide and his mouth was open. 'You are fucking crazy,' he panted.

'Yeah, that's his nickname,' said Harper. 'Crazy Eric. His forte is shooting people in the balls and letting them bleed to death.'

Shepherd pointed the gun at Sazak's groin. 'It can take up to five minutes.'

Sazak spat bloody phlegm onto the floor.

'The guns. Who did you sell them to?'

Sazak sneered at him. 'They're dangerous people. People you want to stay away from.'

'Let me worry about that. I need a name.'

Sazak laughed harshly. 'You want to talk to them? You are fucking crazy!' Harper stepped forward and raised his hand. Sazak flinched and Harper laughed.

'I need a name,' repeated Shepherd.

'The man I dealt with said he was with HPG. Hêzên Parastina Gel.'

'Who the fuck are the HPG?' said Shepherd. 'Are they Kurds?'

'The armed wing of the Kurdistan Workers' Party.'

'I thought the Hawks were the armed wing?'

'The Hawks are a breakaway group. The HPG is part of the Kurdistan Workers' Party.'

'And the man you dealt with? His name?'

'Abdullah Khanim.'

Shepherd nodded. That had been one of the names in the file that Warren-Madden had shown him in the embassy's secure room. The guy was in his fifties and had an eyepatch. But the notes on the back of the photograph definitely had him down as a member of the Hawks.

'See, now that wasn't too hard, was it? What did you sell him?'

'Guns. RPGs. Grenades. Ammunition. A truckload.'

'And had you sold to him before?'

Sazak shook his head. 'I never had weapons like this before. It wasn't the sort of stuff I could sell to just anybody.'

'It was specialised?'

Sazak nodded. 'Yes. Specialised.'

'And what about the Semtex you stole? You sold some of the Semtex to the Yavuz brothers?'

He nodded again. 'They wanted to blow up an armoured car.' He laughed. 'Crazy bastards.'

'How much did you sell them?'

'They wanted a kilo or two but I couldn't split a pack so they bought it and then they sold some of it to a guy who wanted to break into a safe.'

'And how much Semtex did you steal?'

'Five hundred kilos.'

'That's a lot. That's an awful lot.'

Sazak shrugged. 'I suppose so.'

'So who did you sell the rest to?'

'Why do you want to know?'

Shepherd raised the gun and fired in one smooth movement, the bullet passing so close to Sazak's head that it grazed his ear. Sazak yelped in surprise.

'The next one will be in your balls,' said Shepherd.

'Khanim bought the Semtex, too,' said Sazak hurriedly. 'He bought everything we stole from the base except for a few hand-guns and the one pack of Semtex.'

'How many kilos in one pack?' Shepherd knew that Explosia supplied the explosive in twenty-kilo and twenty-five-kilo packs.

'Twenty,' said Sazak.

'And how many packs did you sell to Khanim?'

'The rest. Twenty-four packs.'

'And how much did he pay? Per kilo?'

'We agreed on a thousand euros per kilo.'

That sounded right to Shepherd. The commercial price of the explosive was about five euros a kilo but prices were obviously much higher on the black market.

'And you know what the Semtex was used for, right?'

Sazak frowned. 'What do you mean?'

'Don't play the innocent with me,' said Shepherd. He pointed the gun at Sazak's groin. 'You know, don't pretend that you don't.'

'Okay, okay. There were some car bombs in Ankara.'

'People died, didn't they? A lot of people?'

'That was nothing to do with me. I'm a businessman. I sold what I had, it's nothing to do with me what happens to it.'

'Okay, but this is what doesn't make sense to me. You're telling me that you sold the Semtex to the HPG. But the car bombs were the work of the Hawks. Two totally different organisations, you said.'

'I'm telling you what Khanim told me. Maybe he lied.'

'The Hawks planted the bombs. They claimed responsibility.'

Sazak's Adam's apple bobbed as he swallowed. 'You're going to blame me for the bombs? Is that what this is about?'

Shepherd shook his head. 'No, this isn't what this is about.' He nodded at Harper. 'Okay, that's what we need.'

'We're done?' asked Taylor.

'We're done here,' said Shepherd. He headed for the stairs.

'Are you going to untie me?' Sazak called after him.

Shepherd ignored him and went up the stairs. Taylor and Harper followed him.

Coleman and Ireland were in the hallway. 'Jack and Joe went out to the cars,' said Coleman. 'Everything is cool outside.'

'We can head off now,' said Taylor. 'We've got the intel we wanted.'

Shepherd nodded. 'Call Sagey, get him to the gate.'

'We can't leave him like that,' said Harper quietly.

'We can't call for an ambulance,' said Shepherd. 'Not with the bodies here.'

'That's not what I meant, Spider. If he's alive, he'll want revenge. And he'll get it.'

'Plenty of people want to get to me, Lex. One more won't make much of a difference.'

Harper put his face close to Shepherd's. 'I don't give a fuck either, but it's not about you or me,' he whispered. 'Mick and Ant have got families. They're not boy scouts but I'd never forgive myself if anything happened to them. And if we leave Sazak alive, he'll kill them. And worse.' Harper shook his head. 'I can't let that happen.' He pointed at the front door. 'You should leave. The Sass guys too. Best you're not in the house when it happens.'

'Plausible deniability?'

'You don't know what happened. You didn't see or hear a thing. It's all on me.'

Shepherd wasn't happy about Sazak being murdered in cold blood, but he knew that Harper was right. If the situation was reversed, Sazak would be doing the killing and he'd be doing it with gusto. And Harper was right about what would happen to his friends in Spain. And their families.'

'Best you wait outside with the guys,' Shepherd said to Taylor. 'You too,' he said to Coleman and Ireland.

The three SAS men headed out of the front door. Shepherd handed the heavy's gun to Harper. Harper took it and winked. 'See no evil, hear no evil,' he said. He turned and walked back down the stairs.

Shepherd parked the Mercedes and climbed out. 'Drink?' asked Harper, nodding at the lobby bar as they walked inside the hotel. They had barely spoken during the drive back from Sazak's house. Shepherd had the Beretta tucked into his belt.

'We need to drop our gear in Taylor's room, and then I have to call the office.'

'Sure. But then we should have a drink. Right?'

Shepherd nodded.

'I didn't have a choice, Spider.'

'I know.'

They rode up in the elevator in silence and walked along to Taylor's room. The Ellis brothers were stripping off their vests. Taylor and Ireland were sitting at a table by the window. They had broken their guns down and were cleaning them. Shepherd put his gun down on the table.

'You're not expecting me to clean that for you?' asked Taylor.

'It's not been fired,' said Shepherd.

'I'll do mine now,' said Harper. He sat on the bed and put the heavy's Glock next to him. He also had the Glock he'd taken from the Mercedes. He ejected the magazines and quickly and efficiently field stripped the guns.

Shepherd left them to it and went back to his room. He sat on the bed and phoned Pritchard, who answered on the third ring. 'We're back at the hotel,' said Shepherd.

'How did it go?'

'Sazak sold the Semtex to the Hawks. He gave me a name and we have a location for him so all good.'

'And Sazak?'

'Not so good.'

'Ah,' said Pritchard.

'And four of his heavies are no longer with us.'

'Messy?'

'Messy but it didn't attract attention.'

'And what about Sazak? Was that you?'

'No, Lex took care of it. The Sass guys did the rest. They had guns on us and Sazak was planning on torturing us.'

'Collateral damage,' said Pritchard. 'Live by the sword and all that jazz. Are you okay?'

'Yeah, I'm fine. In a way it's for the best. Sazak can't tip off the Hawks that we're onto them. The plan is to go see them tomorrow.'

'Keep me in the loop, obviously. And we've got some matches back from the Passport Office.'

'Great.'

'Well, not so great, actually. Just over a thousand matches of ninety-five per cent and better.'

'None at a hundred per cent?'

'As I said before, it doesn't work like that. The facial recognition system just isn't that good, unfortunately.'

'So when can I see them?' He did a quick calculation in his head. If he could look at ten pictures a minute he'd be able to go through them all in under two hours.

'It has to be over secure link, so you'll need to go to the embassy and use the skiff.'

'That's not a problem. I need to check in with Warren-Madden about getting to the Hawk guy. I'll do it then.'

Shepherd ended the call and looked at his watch. He was dog tired and the last thing he wanted was to be drinking in a bar, but he knew that it was important to show his face. They were a team and teams stuck together. He got up off the bed, stretched, then went into the bathroom to splash cold water onto his face.

When he walked into the lobby bar a few minutes later, the SAS guys had commandeered an area of the bar by the window. Harper was carrying over a tray of beers and shorts and he grinned. 'Jameson's and soda?' he said.

'Yeah, why not?' said Shepherd.

Harper nodded at the tray. 'Already got you one,' he said.

Shepherd took his drink and dropped down into an armchair as the SAS guys grabbed at their beers as if there was a shortage.

Harper sat down on a sofa next to Jack Ellis. 'There can't be many twins in the SAS, right?' said Harper. 'I never saw any in the Paras. Plenty of brothers, and I served with a father and son once, but twins is unusual.'

'I think we're only the second set,' said Ellis.

'Did you ever pull the old Fan Dance switcheroo?' asked Shepherd.

Ellis laughed and he and his brother burst out laughing. 'Yeah, we did. How do you know about that?'

'It's a classic,' said Shepherd.

Harper frowned. 'How does it work?'

Shepherd waved at Ellis. 'I'll let Jack tell you.'

Ellis sipped his beer. 'You know the Fan Dance, right? Part of SAS Selection?'

'I did it once when I was a Para,' said Harper. 'It wasn't so bad.'

'A lot depends on the weather,' said Shepherd. The Fan Dance was a twenty-four-kilometre route march up and down the 2,907 feet Pen y Fan peak in the Brecon Beacons. For Selection it had to be done with a packed Bergen and carbine in less than four hours and ten minutes. On a nice spring day it was challenging but doable, but in the middle of winter or in the pouring rain it was a serious test of fitness and resolve.

'We've usually got visitors at Stirling Lines, special forces guys from around the world are always dropping by, and quite often they stay on attachment for a few months,' said Ellis. 'We do a reciprocal thing with our guys spending time overseas. Usually it's Navy SEALs or Delta Force but we get them from all over.'

His brother tapped him with his foot. 'For fuck's sake, Jack, tell the bleeding story.'

'Okay, okay. So we get this guy from Delta Force. What was his name? Bernie, something. Bernie Big Bollocks we called him. Anyway, he keeps going on about the Fan Dance and how it was no big thing, so we said we'd let him have a go against a group of us. Had a little wager. We all put a hundred quid in the pot, winner takes all. There were three others, and me and Joe. So we pulled the old switcheroo. Fuck me, it was funny.'

He saw the look of confusion on Harper's face. 'We got Joe to go up the peak early and set up a hide. Then we start the race and the guys make sure they keep up a fast pace. I hang back. As soon as they cross the summit, Joe comes out of hiding and starts down. Obviously he's as fresh as a daisy so he increases the pace. The guys know what's happening so they throttle back but Bernie Big Bollocks gives it all he's got. They reach the halfway point and then head back up the hill. Joe sprints the last bit of the peak and hides and I start sprinting down the hill. When Bernie Big Bollocks gets to the top he sees me in the distance but no matter how fast he goes there's no way he can get near me. By the time it's over I'm still fresh and he's fucked. I mean seriously fucked. We make sure that he never sees Joe and me together, until the last night. Then the shit hits the fan.' He laughed and slapped the table. 'We kept the hundred quid though. Point of principle.'

They all laughed and drank. 'What about you, Lex?' asked Coleman. 'If you didn't find the Fan Dance a problem, why didn't you put in for Selection?'

'To be honest, I just didn't like being a soldier. I enjoyed the fitness side, and the guns, but I hated being told what to do.'

'Nobody tells us what to do,' said Ireland. 'The Ruperts make suggestions, but if we don't agree we tell them. We have Chinese Parliaments before every op and we all have equal voices.'

'Yeah, I get that. And I know you guys are the business, but I just wanted more freedom.'

'Freedom?' repeated Taylor. 'Freedom to do what?'

Harper laughed. 'This and that,' he said. He got to his feet. 'I'm getting another round in.'

Harper was filling his plate at the breakfast buffet and Shepherd was tucking into a cheese omelette when Warren-Madden walked into the restaurant. He spotted Shepherd and walked over. 'That looks good,' he said, nodding at Shepherd's plate.

Shepherd reached into his pocket and handed over the Mercedes keyfob. 'We're done with the Merc. Thanks.'

'No bullet holes?'

'It's pristine,' said Shepherd. He gestured at the buffet with his knife. 'Help yourself, it's all going on our bill. The omelette guy is a wizard. This is my second.'

'I will, thanks,' said Warren-Madden. He leaned forward and lowered his voice. 'The cops know what happened at Sazak's house.'

Shepherd frowned. 'What do they know?'

'That he and four of his heavies are dead. One of them is alive but he's not saying anything. Said a blow to his head gave him amnesia.'

'That's a shame. What do the cops think?'

'Sazak was duct-taped to a chair in his basement and he was shot execution-style in the face and chest. They reckon it was a business rival.'

Shepherd smiled brightly. 'Well that's good news.'

'And you got what you wanted?'

'I think so. I'll run it by you once you've got your omelette.'

Warren-Madden leaned closer and lowered his voice to a whisper. 'Did you have to kill him?'

Shepherd held his look for several seconds. 'I didn't,' said Shepherd. 'And they started the heavy stuff. Trust me, Michael, the less you know, the better.'

Warren-Madden straightened up and smiled thinly. 'I hope you're right,' he said. His smile widened. 'About the omelette.'

As he left the table, Harper arrived with a plate piled with food. 'Turkey isn't bacon, is it?' said Harper. 'I don't see how they get away with calling it bacon.'

'It's a Muslim country. When in Rome . . .'

'At least in Rome I'd get real bacon,' said Harper, sitting down and reaching for the tomato sauce. He gestured over at Warren-Madden who was standing by the omelette station. 'How's super spook?'

'He's okay. Best we keep him away from the sensitive stuff.'

'You don't trust him?'

'He's career MI6. His loyalty is always going to be to the agency.'

'Whereas you and me, we're mates?'

Shepherd chuckled. 'Yes, Lex. We're mates.'

Harper buttered a slice of toast. 'And how are you going to play this Hawks guy?'

'We talk, and if he's not helpful . . .' He shrugged and left the sentence unfinished.

'Do you need me?'

'It's your call, Lex. You did a great job getting us in to see Sazak, you definitely earned your money. If you want to stay on, that's fine. But no pressure.'

'I'll head off, then,' said Harper. He bit on a sausage and frowned. 'This isn't a real sausage. It's chicken.'

'You gonna go back to Thailand?'

'Thought I might fly to Spain and buy Mick and Ant a few drinks.'

'Yeah, and maybe fix Mick's sense of humour while you're at it. He could've got us killed last night.'

'The bigger problem is that he's going to have to find himself another supplier. That'll wipe the smile off his face.'

'Will you tell him what happened?'

Harper grinned. 'I'll give him a sanitised version, don't worry.'

Warren-Madden came back with an omelette and four hash browns. He nodded at Harper and sat down. Harper pushed the tomato sauce towards him.

'So, one of the faces you showed me at the embassy was Abdullah Khanim,' Shepherd said to Warren-Madden. 'Early fifties, eyepatch, scarred cheek.'

Warren-Madden shrugged and cut into one of his hash browns. 'There are a lot of faces in that file.'

'This guy is with the Hawks. According to the info on the back of the photograph he's one of their financiers, funnelling money to the fighters in Iraq and Syria.'

Warren-Madden raised his eyebrows. 'You really do have a trick memory.'

'It also says that he's in a place called Karapazar?'

'It's a village in Bolu Province, to the west of Ankara. The village itself is tiny but there's a compound outside the village where a lot of Kurds live. Most of them are refugees but it's not a refugee camp. It's not a terrorist training camp, either, so the Turks leave it alone.'

'So we could drive in and talk to him?'

'I doubt he'll want to talk to you.'

Harper laughed. 'Yeah, well Sazak didn't want to talk but Crazy Eric here changed his mind.'

Warren-Madden frowned. 'Crazy Eric?'

'It's his little joke,' said Shepherd. 'Have you been to this compound?'

'No, but I've read about it. I'm not sure where.' He smiled. 'My memory isn't as good as yours.'

'Do you think you could dig out a map or something?'

'I think so. If not, one of my contacts at the NIO can send me something over.'

'Would they be looking to arrest Khanim? If we got him?'

'He's not on their hit list. Of course if you could tie him into the car bombings, that would be a game-changer.'

'I'm not sure we want to be co-operating with the Turks on this.'

'Understood,' he said. He jabbed his fork at his plate. 'You were right. This is a great omelette.'

Warren-Madden parked his SUV and Shepherd followed him over to the rear embassy entrance, where the MI6 officer used his swipe card and pin code to open the door. 'Let's go to my office first, I might have some information on the compound where Khanim is holed up. I can show you my new Nespresso machine, too.'

Warren-Madden took Shepherd to his office. Shepherd sat down on a sofa by one of the two windows that overlooked the gardens at the rear of the embassy as Warren-Madden went over to his desk. There was a large map of Turkey and the surrounding countries on the wall. The MI6 officer pointed at the middle of the map. 'This is Karapazar, where the Kurdish compound is. It's about a two-hour drive from here.' He sat down and turned to a filing cabinet. He pulled out the bottom drawer and ran his finger along a series of manila files, then took one out. He dropped it on his desk and flicked through the papers. 'I got an Interpol report a year or two back about a murder case out there. Turned out to be a domestic and the guy fled to France.' He pulled out several sheets that had been stapled together. 'Here you go. It had quite a lot of detail about the compound and the people there.' He walked back around his desk and handed them to Shepherd. 'Maybe my memory's not so bad after all.'

As Shepherd read through the papers, Warren-Madden busied himself at a coffee machine on top of a fridge in the corner of the room. 'How do you take it?' he asked.

'Splash of milk, no sugar,' said Shepherd.

One of the sheets was a hand-drawn map of the compound. There were almost fifty small boxes, which Shepherd assumed were houses. There were several larger boxes with the words 'MOSQUE', 'SCHOOL' and 'MEDICAL CENTRE' written on them. There were two small crosses in one of the boxes. According to a footnote the crosses represented the bodies of a young woman and her daughter. The police were looking for the woman's husband. On another sheet there were fingerprints and a photograph of the man the police were looking for, a sixty-two-year-old Turkish Kurd. Shepherd wasn't interested in the killer, he only cared about the compound.

'Any photographs of the area and the buildings?' he asked Warren-Madden.

'All I have is what's in the file,' said the MI6 officer, putting a mug of coffee down in front of him.

'What about Google Earth?'

'Sure, I can do that.' He took his coffee over to his desk and sat down in front of two large monitors. He tapped on his keyboard.

'What's it like out there, the terrain?' asked Shepherd.

'It's pretty desolate but there are wooded areas and some farmland,' said Warren-Madden, peering at one of his screens. 'There's one road into the village and then a track that leads to the compound.' He pressed a button and a printer burst into life. It spewed out two sheets and Warren-Madden took them over to Shepherd and sat down next to him. 'The village has a population of fewer than two hundred, and the compound is about the same. They cultivate some crops and raise animals on land outside the compound. Some of them have jobs in the city. Others work locally. If it was in Israel it would be a kibbutz.'

Shepherd looked at the two maps, side by side. One was of the compound, the other was a view of the compound and the surrounding area. There was a single track from the main road to the entrance of the compound so it was a case of driving down it or getting there on foot through the woodland.

'It's not a terrorist training camp, you said? So no guns?'

'No obvious weapons,' said Warren-Madden. 'The Turks wouldn't stand for that. So no armed guards, no Kalashnikovs on show. But there'll be weapons hidden away. The Kurds don't trust the government. Hardly surprising when you see how they've been treated over the years.'

'It looks to me as if we have no choice other than to go in on foot,' said Shepherd. 'But then what do we do with Khanim?'

It was clearly a rhetorical question, so Warren-Madden sipped his coffee and didn't say anything.

Shepherd stood up and walked over to look at the map behind Warren-Madden's desk. Incirlik Air Base was just under five hundred kilometres away. It was close to the Syrian border and had been the base for US operations against ISIS in Iraq and Syria. The US were running down their forces at the base but other NATO members, including Germany, Spain and the UK, still had troops there. He took out his phone and called Taylor. He answered almost immediately. 'Jeff, do you have any guys at Incirlik?'

'I'm sure we do, yeah. We're always running training programmes with the OKK.'

The OKK – Özel Kuvvetler Komutanlığı – was the Turkish Special Forces Command.

'Specifically, a chopper.'

'You want to requisition an SAS heli?'

'The Kurdish guy we're looking for is in a compound a hundred clicks or so from Ankara. I need to be able to fly the guy out, I can't see us making it by road. We just need it for tonight, we can have it back at Incirlik by dawn.'

'I'll have to clear it with the head shed in Hereford.'

'Call the Major. He can do the admin through the Increment. We'd need the heli here just after dusk.'

'I'm on it, Spider.'

Shepherd ended the call and went back to the sofa.

'You can do that, you can just commandeer a helicopter?'

Shepherd grinned as he picked up his coffee. 'I can't, but I know a man who can.' He gestured at the door. 'Can you let me into the secure room?'

Warren-Madden took Shepherd down the corridor and opened the door for him. Shepherd sat down in front of one of the terminals and logged onto the MI5 computer. 'I'm going to need copies of the photograph of Khanim.' He gestured at the CCTV camera. 'Is that a problem?'

'We're not supposed to make copies of anything in here. That's why there's no printer.'

'I need to be able to show the guys what he looks like. Do you have a picture in the office?'

Warren-Madden shook his head.

Shepherd grimaced. 'I need a picture, Michael.'

'Okay, okay,' said Warren-Madden. 'I'll get the file and put it on the desk. I'll block the camera and you snap a picture with your phone.'

'Perfect.'

Pritchard had left Shepherd a link to the Passport Office photographs. He clicked on the first picture and sighed. The man was Asian and about the Uthman doppelgänger's age, but he looked nothing like him. He clicked for the second photograph.

The man was more like him but had a wider chin and narrower eyes.

By the time Warren-Madden had retrieved the file with Khanim's picture from the filing cabinet, Shepherd had done more than a hundred photographs. Warren-Madden put the file on the desk with the photograph on the top, positioning himself between Shepherd and the CCTV camera. Shepherd slipped out his phone, took two quick snaps, and put it away. Warren-Madden stepped to the side. 'That's all you need, right?'

'He's the only one we're interested in.'

'And what's the plan?'

'If we can get a helicopter, we'll go in and get him tonight. Assuming he confirms that he had the Semtex and tells us who he passed it on to, then we'll be out of your hair.'

'You do a lot of stuff like this?'

'Some. I'm not really an office person.'

Warren-Madden laughed out loud. 'Yeah, I got that impression.' He picked up the picture, slotted it back into the file and took it over to the filing cabinet.

'I'm going to be doing this for about two hours,' said Shepherd. 'There's no short cut. I have to look at every photograph.'

'I can leave you here on your own,' said Warren-Madden. 'I'll bring you another coffee in an hour or so.'

'Maybe in half an hour,' said Shepherd. 'I'll need all the caffeine I can get.' He sat back in his chair and began clicking through the photographs.

Warren-Madden drove Shepherd back to the hotel. None of the passport photographs had been of the Uthman doppel-gänger. There had been several very close matches but that was all. That meant that the doppelgänger had never held a British passport and that wasn't good news. 'It's been fun working with you again,' said the MI6 officer as he pulled up at the entrance.

'Fun?' repeated Shepherd.

'Sure. Life around you is never boring.'

'Well it's certainly not going to be boring tonight,' said Shepherd. 'I'd invite you along but I guess you'd rather give it a miss.'

'Thanks for the offer,' said Warren-Madden. 'But I'll leave it to the professionals.'

Shepherd offered his fist. Warren-Madden grinned and fist-bumped him. Shepherd climbed out of the car and waved as the MI6 officer drove off. It was still early in London so he didn't call Pritchard, instead he went up to Taylor's room. Taylor, Sage and Jack Ellis were watching a war movie and munching on crisps from the minibar. 'You know those are like ten euros a pack?' said Shepherd.

Taylor held out the pack. 'Want one?'

Shepherd grabbed a handful of crisps and went to stand by the window.

'So, we have a heli, a Dauphin,' said Taylor.

'Excellent. One of ours?'

Taylor nodded. 'The guys are from 658 Squadron so they're sound.' The 658 Squadron was a secretive unit of the Army Air Corps which was based at Credenhill Barracks and was used exclusively by the SAS.

'Can we get the guys together and I'll brief everybody at the same time?'

'I'll get them,' said Ellis. He headed for the door and returned a couple of minutes later with his brother, Ireland and Coleman.

They stood around the bed as Shepherd dropped the maps of the compound and surrounding area onto the duvet. 'This is where the target is holed up,' said Shepherd. He took out his phone and showed them the picture he'd taken in the security room. 'This is our target. Tango One. He's fifty-three and the eyepatch is a giveaway so I doubt we'll have much trouble finding him. I'll send this to Mutton's phone and he can pass it on. Tango One will be in the compound somewhere but we don't know where. There are about fifty houses and a total of two hundred or so occupants. I figure we move into the compound after dark and try to blend. We ID Tango One and then a heli will pick us up. We fly out with Tango One.' He looked around the group and everyone was nodding.

'The heli is noisy, obviously, so we can't use it for insertion. Five of us can drive up in one of the SUVs. Four of us go into the compound and the driver heads back here.'

'Why don't we take Tango One out in the vehicle?' asked Ireland.

'The track is the only way in and out,' said Shepherd. 'They have vehicles in the compound and guns so there'd be a nasty chase all the way back to Ankara. If they see him fly off in a heli, there's nothing to chase. I need to go in the compound, for the other three I'm thinking Sagey and Paddy because of the facial hair, and either Jack or Joe. Whoever doesn't go in can drive us there and then head back.'

'Bagsy me for going in,' said Jack Ellis.

'Bagsy? How old are you?' said his brother.

'You know exactly how old I am, we're fucking twins remember? I got in first. I go.'

'You two guys could wrestle for it,' said Taylor, and everyone laughed. 'Seriously, Spider, I think I should go in with you,' he said.

'Normally I'd say yes, but you've shaved off your beard and the skin is lighter and it might be noticed. I thought you could be in the chopper with Coleman. You can meet them at the airport and fly with them to the compound. Joe can drive the SUV. He drops us away from the compound and we go in over the wall. The compound doesn't have mains electricity, there are some generators but most illumination will be fires or oil lamps. As soon as we have Tango One, we call for the chopper.'

'How far is the compound from here?' asked Taylor.

'About a hundred and twenty clicks, as the crow flies.'

'So about half an hour flying time? That's not good. A lot can happen in thirty minutes.'

Shepherd tapped the map showing the area around the compound. 'The heli can wait here. We go in and we look for

Tango One. We call you as we grab Tango One and take him out of the main gate. You get the heli to fly to us, we pile on board and we're out of there. From grabbing Tango One to being in the air, three minutes max.'

'What sort of firepower will we be facing?' asked Sage.

'Nothing overt. These guys don't carry Kalashnikovs with them. But there are known terrorists there and there's every chance they will have weapons available. But any guns they have will be well hidden, so if we move quickly we should be out of there before they get a chance to pull them. I can't stress this enough, we really don't want a firefight and we definitely don't want to be leaving casualties. Sazak and his heavies deserved everything they got, but most of these people are civilians and a lot of them are refugees.'

'So we do what, fire above their heads?' said Ireland sarcastically.

'Yes, Paddy. That'll work. We'll take the MAC-11s, because if we do need to fire we're better off with shock and awe. Just try not to kill anyone. Clothing-wise we need to dress down. Baggy shirts and coats, old jeans, cheap shoes. They're Muslims and the women wear headscarves but they tend not to wear the full burkha.'

'That's a pity, it's the best disguise going,' said Jack Ellis. 'We've worn the old burkha a few times in Afghanistan. Gets you up close and personal and then you pull out the short and give them the good news.'

'Unfortunately it's not an option tonight,' said Shepherd. 'We have to blend and we can't do that in brand new Nikes and Diesel jeans. We need cheap Chinese crap that we can pick up at the market or a second-hand shop. Hats would be good to hide our faces and the earbuds. We'll buy the crappiest clothes we can find and change on the way, probably best not to sit in the lobby dressed like tramps.'

'And what about Tango One?' said Taylor. 'You need to interrogate him, right?'

'Absolutely. As quickly as possible.'

'How are you going to do that?'

'I have a plan,' said Shepherd. 'Let me run it by you.'

Joe Ellis arrived in front of the hotel in the black SUV at five o'clock. Shepherd walked out of the lobby with Sage, Ireland and Jack Ellis. They were all wearing their regular clothes but were carrying bags of less salubrious gear they had purchased from a second-hand shop a short walk from the hotel. The radios and guns were in a holdall that Shepherd put between his legs once he had climbed into the front passenger seat. The other three men got into the back.

Taylor and Coleman had left in the other SUV, heading for the airport to meet up with the helicopter which was already en route from Incirlik airbase.

Ellis drove out onto the main road and headed west. They chatted as Ellis drove, mainly reminiscing about past operations with plenty of banter and insults. To an outsider there'd be no sign of any stress, but under the surface they were all thinking ahead, running through possible scenarios and how they'd react.

After about half an hour, Shepherd handed out the radios and they checked that they could all transmit and receive. When they were satisfied that the radios were working, Shepherd called up Taylor.

'Heli's coming in to land as we speak,' said Taylor.

'We're about ninety minutes away,' said Shepherd. 'Our ETA is still nineteen hundred hours.'

'We'll try to get there at the same time,' said Taylor. 'I assume the pilots want to refuel and take a piss. I'll call you when we're setting off.'

'Roger that,' said Shepherd.

The sky darkened as they headed west, and eventually the sun dipped below the horizon. An hour into the journey and Ellis pulled off the road and drove behind a farm building that had fallen into disrepair. The windows were all broken and the roof had collapsed and a tree had grown up through the chimney stack. Ellis switched off the headlights and they sat for a few minutes until their night vision had kicked in, then they climbed out and changed into the old clothing and shoes. Shepherd had a blue denim shirt, a wool coat that had streaks of blue paint down one sleeve, and cargo pants with a repair patch on one of the pockets. Even when the coat was open it hid his holstered Beretta. He pulled a black wool beanie hat low over his ears to cover his earbud receiver.

Jack Ellis had a tartan hat with earflaps and long coat. The MAC-11 was too large to hide under his coat so he put it in a grey canvas knapsack. Sage had also brought a cheap backpack for his MAC-11 and he found an old reefer jacket with a button missing and paired it with jeans that had faded at the knees.

Ireland had a grey hoodie and tracksuit bottoms and scuffed Nikes. The hoodie was baggy enough to conceal his holstered Glock.

They checked each other over, walking up and down to confirm that their weapons were well hidden. Shepherd rubbed some dirt on his face and the others did the same. Then they checked their comms again and took it in turns to talk to Taylor in the helicopter, then they packed up their clothes and put them in the back of the SUV. 'Right, are we good to go?' asked Shepherd.

They all nodded.

'We need to keep conversation to a minimum inside the compound. We look the part but the moment we open our mouths we'll be made. If anyone does speak to you, pull the old deaf and dumb routine, point to your ear and grunt. So far as we can, keep away from other people. You all know who we're looking for, there can't be too many fifty-year-olds with eyepatches in there. Sagey and I will head anti-clockwise, you two move clockwise.'

Jack Ellis and Ireland nodded.

'First one to spot him calls it in. We grab him and take him out to the chopper, ideally on the QT but if the shit hits the fan we can use shock and awe. And I repeat, try not to shoot anybody.'

'We'll do our best,' said Ellis, patting his bag. 'But you know the MAC-11 is not the most accurate of weapons.'

'Not in your hands, anyway,' said Sage.

'Just fire high if you have to fire at all,' said Shepherd. 'There are terrorists in there but most of them are refugees, and there are families with kids. The last thing we want to be doing is hurting kids.'

Joe Ellis pulled the car over. The compound was in the distance. There was a wooded area off to the right and scrubland to the left. If they got any closer they'd be seen by the people in the compound, so they were going to have to walk. 'We'll walk separately, me and Sagey, you two about a hundred feet back, so it doesn't look like we're together,' said Shepherd.

They climbed out of the SUV. 'We'll have the heli drop us back at the place where we changed our clothes,' Shepherd said to Joe. 'A couple of hours, maybe longer. Just make sure you wait for us unless we tell you otherwise.'

The SUV had to do a three-point turn to change direction before speeding off. Shepherd and Sage began walking down the track. Ellis and Ireland followed at a slower pace. Shepherd blinked his eyes as his night vision kicked in. There was enough starlight to see by, though the track was rough and uneven so he had to be careful where he put his feet.

There was no gate at the entrance to the compound, just two stone pillars that had been painted white. The wall was also painted white. It was about a metre high, more to mark the boundary than to stop people getting in.

Shepherd could see a group of men in the woodland, gathering up wood. A horn beeped and he looked around to see a battered Volkswagen bus driving down the track. He and Sage stepped to the side and as it went by he saw half a dozen men sitting inside, probably workers returning to sleep.

Ellis and Ireland had crossed over to the other side of the track and were now about a hundred feet behind them. No one would assume they were together.

'Sagey and I are about to enter the compound,' he said.

'Roger that,' said Taylor, his voice vibrating from the helicopter rotors. 'We'll be landing in a few minutes. We'll wait for your call.'

Shepherd and Sage walked into the compound. There was a house to the left that was being used as a shop. There were fluorescent lights hanging from the ceiling, powered by a humming generator at the side of the building. There were stacks of bottled water on one side of an open door and a table loaded up with loaves of bread on the other. Off to the right was a medical centre and beyond it was the white minaret of the compound's mosque.

He took a look over his shoulder. Ellis and Ireland were walking into the compound, their heads together as if they were talking.

Shepherd heard shouts and tensed but then realised it was only children playing. 'Right, let's see if we can find this guy,' he said to Sage. He headed to the right. There were three old men sitting in rattan chairs against the wall of the medical centre, smoking cigarettes. No eyepatches. As they skirted around the medical centre, a lone voice began to wail. At first Shepherd thought it was someone in pain but then he realised it was wailing in Arabic. He looked at his watch. It was seven-thirty, it must be the call to Isha prayers, the last prayers of the day. The three men in front of the medical centre slowly got to their feet and stubbed out their cigarettes.

Shepherd looked at Sage and Sage nodded back. They had to go into the mosque, to avoid doing so would only draw attention to themselves.

'Paddy, Jack, we need to go in the mosque with everyone else,' he whispered. 'Stay at the back, try not to attract attention.'

'Roger that,' said Ireland in his ear.

Sage moved closer to Shepherd. 'I've not been in a mosque before,' he whispered.

'It'll be fine. Just stay at the back and do what everyone else does. It's all about bowing and kneeling and putting your head on the ground. And muttering in Arabic. All the devout ones will be at the front.'

'What about hats?'

'Hats are fine.'

They joined the crowd of men heading towards the mosque. There were two large doors that had been opened and there was a yellowish glow coming from oil lamps inside. Ireland and Ellis were approaching the mosque behind a group of teenagers. They both had their heads down. Shepherd wasn't happy about walking into the lion's den but it might well make spotting Khanim easier. All the men in the compound would be at prayer, it was just a matter of spotting the one with an eyepatch.

The women were heading for a side entrance, presumably they were praying in a separate part of the building.

Once they got to the door they took off their shoes and left them in a rack. Sage started to take off his socks but Shepherd shook his head. Socks were okay in the mosque.

They went inside into an anteroom with troughs of water where some of the worshippers were washing themselves. Muslims had to make sure they were clean before praying, a process called wudu. Wudu involved washing the hands three times, the mouth three times, the nose three times, the face three times, the arms three times, the head and ears one time, and the feet three times. It was a complicated process, accompanied by spoken phrases, most of which praised Allah. But the thing about wudu was that it didn't have to be performed before every prayer, providing the worshipper remained in a state of purity from the previous prayer. Actions that broke wudu include going to the toilet, breaking wind, falling asleep and bleeding. As this was the last prayer of the day, most of the worshippers were still in a state of wudu so they walked past the troughs and straight into the prayer hall.

'We don't need to wash,' whispered Shepherd. Sage nodded.

They walked into the prayer hall. It was illuminated by oil lamps and the back of the hall was gloomy. Men were already praying, muttering in Arabic and bowing, kneeling and prostrating themselves.

Shepherd went to the right with Sage, Ireland and Ellis to the left. No one gave them a second look. Shepherd had seen Muslims perform their prayers – the rakah – many times and his near-perfect memory meant that he had no problems replicating the actions. He did them slowly so that the others could follow his lead. The bowing, kneeling and prostrating were easy enough but there were lines from the Koran that had to be said out loud. Shepherd just muttered and hoped that those worshippers within earshot would be too busy concentrating on their own rakah.

For the Isha prayers, the rakah had to be performed four times, twice with the words said out loud, and twice silently. The three SAS men did a good job of following Shepherd's example, and although the prayer room gradually filled up, no one came too close to them.

As they went through the fourth and final rakah, three men in the front row finished their prayers and turned to leave. Shepherd's heart pounded as he recognised Khanim. He nudged Sage and gestured in Khanim's direction. Khanim was wearing a light brown shalwar kameez tunic and trousers and a matching brown skullcap. His beard was longer than in the file picture but the eyepatch and scarred cheek meant there was no doubt.

They avoided eye contact as the three men walked by, then they turned and followed them.

'Mutton, we have eyes on Tango One,' Shepherd whispered. 'Fire up the heli.'

'Roger that,' said Taylor in his earpiece.

Khanim walked through the anteroom. His two companions stayed close. Shepherd didn't know if they were friends or body-guards but so far as he could tell they weren't armed.

'Sagey, if the two guys stay with him then we have to knock them out, then show our weapons to Tango One. If he comes quietly all well and good. If not, then he gets knocked on the head and we'll carry him out.'

Sage nodded.

Khanim and his two companions collected their sandals and started walking away from the mosque. Shepherd and the three SAS men hurriedly put on their shoes.

'Cover us,' Shepherd said to Ireland and Ellis. Their MAC-11s were only to be pulled out as a last resort.

The two men nodded.

Shepherd and Sage headed after Khanim. They were walking slowly, deep in conversation. Khanim had his hands clasped behind his back and he was nodding as if agreeing to something. Shepherd's mind raced. It would be much easier if Khanim was on his own, but the longer they left it, the further away they were from the entrance. There weren't many people around, probably as many as half the residents were still in the mosque. But someone would surely see two bodies on the ground and once the alarm was raised then all bets were off.

'We're going to have to do this now,' Shepherd said to Sage. Sage's hand slid inside his coat.

Shepherd put his hand on his own gun. He nodded at Sage and the two men quickened their pace.

Ellis and Ireland were on the path, looking around, their hands on their bags, ready to pull out their MAC-11s if necessary.

Shepherd and Sage went up onto the balls of their feet to minimise any noise and then ran the last three steps. Shepherd had his gun out and he slammed the butt against the temple of the man on Khanim's right. The man slumped to the ground without a sound.

As Khanim turned to look down at the man on the ground, Sage caught the second man on the back of the head. The man grunted and swayed unsteadily and then crumpled.

Khanim was so shocked by what had happened that he froze, his mouth wide open and his hands still clasped behind his back. Shepherd showed him his gun and then shoved it against his ribs. 'Make a sound and you're dead,' he said. He grabbed the man's shoulder and turned him around. Sage grabbed Khanim's left arm and they started walking him towards the compound entrance.

'Mutton, we're heading out.'

'Roger that,' said Taylor. There was a roaring noise behind his voice. The helicopter's turbines and beating rotors. 'ETA three minutes.'

'Faster!' Shepherd hissed to Khanim.

'Who are you?'

Shepherd jabbed his gun into Khanim's side. 'Just do as you're told.'

A woman screamed behind them and shouted something in Kurdish. Then there were more shouts.

Khanim slowed down.

'Hurry up!' said Shepherd.

Khanim shouted at the top of his voice in Kurdish. Shepherd reacted quickly, slamming his gun against his head. As Khanim collapsed, Shepherd and Sage grabbed him and threw his arms over their shoulders. They began to run, their feet slapping on the pathway. Heads turned to look at them but it was several seconds and almost twenty metres before anyone reacted. Worshippers outside the mosque started to point at the three men and began screaming in Kurdish.

'Keep going, Sagey, we're almost there,' grunted Shepherd.

'I wasn't planning on stopping,' said Sage.

There were more shouts behind them and Shepherd took a quick look over his shoulder. There were three bearded men in quilted jackets and baggy trousers running after them waving machetes. 'Shit,' he grunted and tried to run faster, but Khanim's feet were dragging on the ground and that was slowing them down.

'It's okay, Spider, we've got this,' said Ireland in his ear. He took another quick look over his shoulder. Ireland and Ellis stepped onto the path and pulled out their MAC-11s. Ireland fired a quick burst into the air and the three machete-waving men stopped and stood where they were, unsure what to do.

'Come on!' grunted Shepherd. The entrance was about fifty metres ahead of them. Two young men in pullovers and jeans started jogging in their direction but Shepherd fired a shot into the ground in front of them and they both turned and ran.

Shepherd heard another short burst of MAC-11 fire. There were shouts and screams coming from all around the compound now, but there was no returning fire. Shepherd's lungs were burning and his legs were aching but he kept up the pace. In the distance he could hear the whup-whup-whup of the helicopter's main rotor.

They reached the entrance. There was a red pick-up truck parked just outside the gates with half a dozen men sitting in the back. Sage fired a shot over their heads and they all ducked down.

They could see the helicopter now, about a hundred metres away, preparing to land.

There were two more bursts of fire from the MAC-11s, followed by screams and shouts. Shepherd said a silent prayer that Ireland and Ellis hadn't forgotten that there weren't supposed to be any casualties.

The helicopter was hovering about two metres above the ground, its whirling rotor kicking up a dust storm and flattening what little grass there was. Shepherd and Sage were gasping for breath now but they increased the pace. The door slid open and Shepherd saw Taylor cradling a carbine. Taylor jumped out and ran away from the helicopter bent double, then he straightened up and started firing. His shots went in the direction of the entrance, but high.

Coleman also jumped out and he ran towards Shepherd and Sage. 'I'll take him!' shouted Coleman above the noise of the turbines. He grabbed Khanim, threw him over his shoulder and ran towards the helicopter, which had now landed and was resting on its wheels.

Shepherd turned back to look at the entrance. He heard the two MAC-11s firing, and then Ireland and Ellis appeared, looking anxious but not scared. There were angry screams and shouts coming from all over the compound but still no returning gunfire.

Ireland and Ellis ran full pelt for the helicopter. They were followed by at least a dozen screaming men waving machetes and knives. Shepherd and Sage took aim and fired over their heads and Taylor began putting rounds into the compound wall.

Ireland and Ellis ran between Sage and Shepherd and headed for the helicopter. Sage and Shepherd backed away from the mob, firing into the ground just ahead of them. They slowed but were still screaming and brandishing their weapons. Taylor fired half a dozen shots, some so close that dirt kicked up over the legs of the screaming men. The men stopped, staring fearfully at Taylor.

Shepherd took a quick look over his shoulder. Ireland and Ellis were scrambling into the helicopter.

'Go, I'll cover you,' said Taylor in Shepherd's ear.

Shepherd looked over at Taylor, who slapped a fresh magazine into his carbine. 'Thanks.' He tapped Sage on the shoulder and pointed at the helicopter. Sage turned and the two men ran together.

Taylor had something small and metallic in his hand and he threw it. It landed in front of the mob and a second later there were a series of ear-splitting incapacitating bangs and flashes. Several men fell to the ground and others put their hands to their faces. Taylor followed up with a series of short bursts from the carbine, aiming above their heads.

Shepherd and Sage reached the helicopter and Ireland and Ellis helped them in.

Taylor threw another stun grenade and then ran back to the helicopter. Shepherd hauled him in and slammed the door shut. The helicopter sprang into the air and flew away from the compound. Shepherd grinned at Taylor. 'Who gave you the fire-power and the flashbangs?'

Taylor grinned. 'When I told the guys at Incirlik that you had resorted to MAC-11s they said they'd pop a few extras in the heli for me.'

'Excellent,' said Shepherd. The mob was standing at the entrance to the compound. Some were still disorientated by the flashbangs and the covering fire, but dozens more were waving their machetes and knives and screaming angrily at the departing helicopter.

'Anyone hurt?' asked Shepherd.

'We're good,' said Ellis.

'I meant the Kurds,' said Shepherd. He grinned. 'But I'm glad you're okay.'

There were six seats in the cabin, two sets of three facing each other. Ireland and Ellis were sitting either side of Khanim, whose wrists had been bound with zip-ties. A black hood had been pulled down over his head.

'Is he still out for the count?' asked Shepherd.

Ellis grabbed the hood and pulled it up. When he let it go, Khanim's head slumped forward. 'Yeah,' said Ellis. 'Land of nod.'

Shepherd looked out of the window and nodded at Taylor. 'We'll do it here,' he said. He prodded Khanim in the stomach. The man grunted and shifted his feet. 'He's awake,' said Shepherd.

Ellis pulled off the hood. Khanim looked around frantically. The men around him glared back at him and his single eye widened in terror. 'Who are you?' he said, but his voice was lost in the noise of the turbines.

'Give him a headset,' said Shepherd.

Ellis pulled a headset out of a side pocket, pulled it open and rammed it onto Khanim's head.

'Can you hear me?' said Shepherd.

Khanim nodded fearfully.

'I need you to answer some questions. If you answer truthfully you can go home. Do you understand?'

'I am just a—' began Khanim, but Shepherd put up a hand to silence him.

'I will ask the questions, and you will answer them,' said Shepherd. 'Tell me the truth and you can go home. Do you understand?'

'Yes.'

'Good. Now what is your name?'

'Abdullah.'

'Your full name.'

Abdullah Khanim.' He looked around anxiously. 'Where are we going?'

'I'm the one asking the questions, Abdullah.'

Khanim looked at the window to his left. There was just blackness and the stars.

'Look at me, Abdullah. Don't worry about where we're going.'

Khanim looked back at Shepherd. 'I am just—'

Shepherd held up a finger to silence him. 'You bought some Semtex. Five years ago.'

Khanim stared fearfully at Shepherd but didn't say anything.

'That's right, isn't it?'

Khanim nodded.

'You need to say it to me.'

'Yes,' said Khanim.

'How much Semtex?'

'Five hundred kilos.'

'Exactly five hundred?'

'I don't know.'

Shepherd grabbed him by the throat. 'You do know. And if you don't tell me, I'm throwing you out.'

'Almost five hundred kilos,' gasped Khanim. 'The man who sold it said there was five hundred but there was a package missing.'

'Good. That's good. And what did you do with the Semtex? How did you use it?'

The man looked away. He was shaking now and a vein in his forehead was pulsing.

Shepherd poked him in the chest with his gun. 'Look at me. Look at me and answer the question.'

Khanim met Shepherd's gaze with undisguised hatred. 'You know what I did with it.'

'You need to tell me.'

Khanim shook his head.

'Open the door,' shouted Shepherd. 'We're throwing this fucker out.'

Taylor reached for the door handle but Khanim threw up his bound hands. 'No, no, don't. Please. It was used in car bombs. In Ankara. But it wasn't me. The bombs had nothing to do with me.'

Shepherd smiled and patted him on the chest, though he kept the gun pointing at the man's face. 'Good, that's the answer I wanted. But who else did you give the Semtex to?'

The man frowned. 'What?'

'Did all the Semtex go into the car bombs? Or did you sell some?'

'Okay, okay,' said Khanim, nodding frantically. 'Yes, we sold some. Somebody wanted to buy a pack, twenty kilos.'

'Who?'

'I don't know.'

Shepherd gestured at the door with his gun and this time Taylor opened it. The wind blew in, whipping around the compartment like a living thing, tugging at their clothes. Shepherd undid Khanim's harness.

'No, please, no!' shouted Khanim.

'Tell me who you gave the Semtex to.'

'I didn't give. I sold it.'

'Who to?'

'I don't know!'

Shepherd grabbed the man's shirt with his free hand. 'You're going out.'

'I didn't know her name! No one told me her name! I don't know.'

'A woman?'

'A German Kurd. She was Kurdish but she lived in Germany. She had the money but she used a middle man. So the man I dealt with was an Iraqi.'

Shepherd smiled. 'Okay. That's better.' He looked over at Taylor and motioned for him to shut the door.

Taylor slid the door closed and immediately the wind died down.

'Who was the man?' said Shepherd.

'His name was Mohammed, that was the only name he gave me. He said he represented a woman who was in Istanbul. He brought a case containing a hundred thousand euros. He said it was a donation.'

'He gave you a hundred thousand euros?'

Khanim nodded frantically. 'Yes. It was a gift. And then he said he wanted some Semtex.'

'Did he say why?'

'He said he was acting for a woman. In Istanbul. She wanted Semtex and he knew I had some.'

'How?'

'Because of the car bombs.'

'The bombs were in 2016.'

'Yes,' said Khanim.

'And when did this man approach you with the money?'

'Two weeks after the bombs.'

'So in 2016?'

'Yes.'

'And why did she want the Semtex? What was she planning to do?'

'Mohammed didn't say. He said she wanted Semtex and detonators.'

'You gave her detonators?'

'Yes.'

'For a hundred thousand euros?'

'It was a donation. For our expenses.'

Shepherd pushed the gun under the man's chin. 'You need to tell me this woman's name.'

'I don't know.'

'I don't believe you. I think Mohammed knew and I think he told you.'

'No. Maybe he knew but he didn't tell me.'

Shepherd sneered at him. 'I don't believe you.' He looked at Taylor. 'Open the door. He's going out.'

'No! You can't! I have a wife. I have three children. I take care of my mother. You can't do this!'

Taylor pulled the door open and wind whipped through the compartment again. Shepherd ripped the headset off Khanim's head and dropped it onto the floor.

'Please, don't do this!' shouted Khanim.

'Tell me who the woman is?'

'I don't know!'

Shepherd handed his gun to Taylor and grabbed Khanim by the lapels with both hands. 'Tell me!'

'I don't know! Please, believe me, I don't know.'

Shepherd pulled him out of his seat and pushed him backwards to the open door. 'Last chance!' he shouted.

'I don't know! If I knew I would tell you.'

'Liar!' shouted Shepherd. 'Give me her name or you're going out!'

'I don't—'

Shepherd pushed him through the door and let go. Khanim's frantic screams were lost in the roar of the turbines. Taylor shrugged. 'I think he was telling the truth. He didn't know.'

Shepherd grinned. 'Yeah, I think you're right.'

They both leaned through the open door and looked down. Khanim was lying on the grass about ten feet below the helicopter, his hair and clothes whipped around by the downdraught. He was staring up at them glassy-eyed and he had soiled his pants. Shepherd gave him a thumbs up, then pulled the door shut.

The helicopter was already climbing and banking to the east. Ireland and Ellis were laughing out loud and Taylor was shaking his head. 'You're a madman,' said Taylor.

Shepherd grinned. 'It worked, didn't it?'

Taylor called up Joe Ellis on the radio and confirmed that he was parked up behind the derelict building where they had changed their clothes. The helicopter landed in a field close to the building and Shepherd, Sage, Ellis and Taylor jumped out. The plan was for Ireland and Coleman to go back to the airport and pick up the SUV and then the helicopter would head back to Incirlik Air Base.

As the helicopter lifted into the air, the three men stripped off their clothes and shoes and put them in a pile. Taylor went over to the SUV and returned with their bags and a can of lighter fluid. As they pulled on their regular clothes, Taylor poured lighter fluid over the pile and set fire to it.

Taylor collected their guns and put them into a large holdall which he stashed into the back of the SUV, then all the men climbed into the vehicle. Shepherd took the front passenger seat and the three others crammed into the back after a heated argument over who would be in the middle. Sage lost and he sat with a disgusted look on his face and his arms folded.

It was close to eleven when they got back to the hotel. The SAS guys were buzzing and wanted to start drinking in the lobby, but Shepherd had a better idea. He suggested they all freshen up and then head out to Metin's bar.

Shepherd went up to his room and phoned Pritchard and quickly ran through everything he'd learned. Pritchard listened in silence.

'So this woman was looking for Semtex in 2016?' he said after Shepherd had finished. 'After the Ankara car bombs?'

'Exactly. Whoever this woman was, she acquired explosives in 2016 that were used five years later. She had it for five years before using it. The man who signed up for the postgrad course and who joined MI6 wasn't Uthman. Uthman was replaced in 2016, then the doppelgänger applied for the postgrad course in Manchester which he started in 2017. A year later he applies to join MI6. All this was planned a long time ago.'

'By this woman. Then who the hell is she?'

'I don't have a name. She stayed in a hotel in Istanbul in 2016, and she is supposedly a German Kurd.'

'So a German Kurd puts in place a doppelgänger MI6 officer on a four- or five-year mission to betray MI6 and kill their top people?'

'Al-Qaeda planned the World Trade Center bombings for years. They sent their people for pilot training long before they attacked. That's what they do. They sit in their caves and they plot and they plan. This woman, whoever she is, made a donation of a hundred thousand euros to the Kurds in Turkey. Yet she then is involved in a terrorist attack that ISIS have claimed credit for. That makes no sense to me. ISIS hates the Kurds and vice versa.'

'So what do you want to do?'

'I've done everything I can here. I've been thinking about Uthman. As part of this plan, Uthman's parents had to be killed, and then Uthman himself had to be taken out of the picture. How did they find Uthman?'

'What do you mean?'

'He was rarely in Iraq. He was at a boarding school in the UK and at university in London. It's unlikely he could have been targeted in Iraq so maybe he was chosen in London. Maybe somebody was in London looking for someone they could replace. And they were looking for a student, someone who could conceivably be accepted by MI6.'

'A talented Mr Ripley? Hunting for a victim?'

'Yes, but not a psychopath. This was all done for a reason. They wanted someone who could be replaced and used to infiltrate MI6. So maybe the person doing the looking was at the same university. Westminster is huge, there are more than twenty thousand students and a lot of them are from overseas. It's a huge hunting ground. So maybe the doppelgänger was also a student there. Or worked there, maybe.'

'Do you want to check through their student photographs?'

'That's what I was thinking. As soon as I get back.'

'Go for it,' said Pritchard. He ended the call.

Shepherd made a quick call to Jimmy Sharpe and arranged for him to meet him at Heathrow the next day, and then went downstairs to the lobby bar. Taylor had just bought a round and as they raised their glasses, Ireland and Coleman arrived back from the airport. Shepherd told them they were off out, so the two men hurried upstairs to get changed.

There were seven of them so they had to take the two SUVs. Shepherd showed them where to park, close to Ulus Square, and then took them to Metin's club. There were three heavy-set doormen and a line of a dozen people, mainly girls with long hair and short skirts and men in sharp suits. One of the doormen was the guy who had been there when Shepherd called to get the guns, and he said something to his two companions in Turkish. One of them opened the gate and the men filed down into the basement.

The club was busy but there were several empty tables.

Shepherd looked around but Metin spotted him first. He was sitting at the bar and he slid off his stool and waved a greeting. Shepherd waved back. Metin came over, smiling broadly. He was wearing Versace jeans and this time had paired them with a brightly coloured Versace shirt. He threw out his arms and hugged Shepherd and then waved an arm at his companions. 'So this is your crew?'

'Yes it is,' said Shepherd.

'Are they men or Nancy boys?' asked Metin.

Shepherd laughed. 'Oh, they're definitely men,' he said. He introduced them and one by one they shook hands with Metin. Taylor was carrying the holdall containing the weapons and he held it out to Metin. Metin looked at Shepherd with a frown on his face.

'We're heading off tomorrow so I thought we'd give the equipment back to you,' said Shepherd. 'We can't take it with us and it seemed a pity to throw them away. No charge.'

Metin grinned and waved at one of his security team to come over. Metin spoke to him in Turkish and the man took the bag from Taylor and headed to the office.

'The Uzis have been fired but no one was hurt,' said Shepherd. 'The Glocks were used in anger, though.'

'Yes, so I heard,' said Metin. He waved over at a VIP area which was cordoned off with brass poles and red ropes. A heavy in a black suit unclipped one of the ropes to let them through. There were three red sofas around a gilt table and the men dropped down. A waitress appeared. 'What are we drinking, guys?' asked Metin.

'Beer's fine,' said Taylor.

'I'll have a Jameson's, if you've got it,' said Shepherd. 'With ice and soda.'

'Ah, the Irish whiskey. Yes, we have it. And some very old single malts.'

'Jameson's is fine,' said Shepherd.

A waitress with close-cropped dyed-blonde hair with blue streaks appeared. She had piercings in her nose, ears, lips and chin and she looked expectantly at Metin, who ordered in Turkish. As she walked away he dropped down on the sofa next to Shepherd and slapped him on the leg. 'So a little bird tells me you have been busy,' he said.

'You don't want to believe everything you're told, Metin,' said Shepherd.

'But this I do want to believe,' said the Turk. 'My competitor and four of his men have met an untimely end. I had no idea you were such an animal. Definitely not a Nancy boy, hey?'

'The information you gave us was very helpful, thank you for that.'

'The thanks are all mine,' said Metin. 'He was a very dangerous man and I am sure that at some point I would have cropped up on his radar and my life would have changed for the worse.' He patted Shepherd's leg again. 'I have a new respect for you, I really have. When you left here with the guns, I must confess that I had my doubts. But you proved me wrong.' He waved his hand at the SAS guys. 'And this crew, they are all from Spain?'

'No, they're from the UK.'

'They look like good men.'

'Oh they are,' said Shepherd. 'The best.'

The Ellis brothers were sitting on separate sofas and Metin did a double-take as he realised they were identical. 'Twins!' he said. 'Wow, twins!'

'Yeah. Have you only just noticed?'

'Their clothing is different and their hair isn't quite the same. But now I see it. Twins. I had twins, once. Russian girls. Best sex I ever had. Twins are great fun.'

Jack Ellis held up his hand. 'Whoa there, hoss,' he said. 'You are definitely not having sex with us.'

Metin laughed uproariously. 'That is funny,' he said. 'That is very funny.'

The waitress returned with their drinks on a tray. Metin helped her put the drinks down on the table and then clinked his glass against their drinks one by one, accompanied each time by a loud 'Şerefe!' They all drank. Two blonde girls were at the podium, unpacking guitars and getting ready to perform. 'Tonight you are my guests!' Metin shouted. 'You pay for nothing.'

He noticed that the Ellis twins were twisting around in the seats to get a better look at the girls at the bar. A pretty blonde waved at them and they waved back. 'Toss you for it,' said Jack.

'Nah, you're a professional tosser,' said his brother.

Metin laughed. 'Do you like girls?'

Jack laughed. 'Who doesn't?'

'Girls would be good,' said Coleman.

'Definitely,' said Joe.

'We have the prettiest girls in Ankara,' said Metin. He called over in Turkish to the suited heavy by the ropes. The heavy smiled and went over to the bar. Metin grinned at Shepherd. 'You and your crew should think about spending some time here,' he said. 'Men like you could do well in this country. Turkey can be a very profitable place to be, the place where Asia meets Europe. There are many opportunities here.'

'We love the place, Metin, we really do, but this was only ever going to be a flying visit.'

The heavy returned with five young girls in tow, two blondes and three brunettes, all in high heels, short skirts and cropped tops. They were giggling as they eyed up the men and whispering to each other in Turkish. Metin waved at the waitress and said something to her. The only word Shepherd recognised was Cristal, the champagne of choice of gangsters and hookers around the world.

The girls slid onto the laps of the SAS guys and introduced themselves.

'What about you, my friend?' Metin asked Shepherd. 'What sort of girls do you like?'

Shepherd raised his glass. 'The night is young, Metin,' he said. 'I'm sure I'll find something.'

Shepherd walked into the arrivals area at Heathrow Airport and grinned when he saw Sharpe was munching on a sandwich. 'You miss breakfast?' asked Shepherd as they fist-bumped.

'I've been working my arse off,' said Sharpe. 'With you out of the country Pritchard decided I was surplus to requirements and I was sent back to the NCA. They needed help with an immigration scam. I'm due to marry a Nigerian girl, two Chinese girls and a Russian next week.'

'Busy boy.'

'There's a registrar in Chelsea who does a marriage package for ten grand a pop. There are plenty of girls doing the scam but she was short of guys. I have to meet the girls for a chat in case any questions get asked on the big day.'

'But you're okay to hang with me today?'

'Yeah, sure. But I'm spoken for tomorrow.'

'Should be done with this in a few hours.'

They walked to the short-term car park and got into Sharpe's Jaguar. Shepherd dropped his holdall on the back seat. 'How did it go in Turkey?' asked Sharpe.

'It had its high points,' said Shepherd. 'Some useful intel but we're still some way off working out what the hell is going on.'

The admissions office of the University of Westminster was in their Marylebone campus, which was a grand name for a nondescript building on the always busy Marylebone Road, just south of Regent's Park.

There was a 24-hour NCP car park a short walk from the university building. Sharpe drove in and parked. 'No ticket?' asked Shepherd as they climbed out of the Jaguar. 'How do you pay?'

'It's all hi-tech these days,' said Sharpe. 'They use the same number plate recognition system that we use. You don't even pay here. You can prepay online, but if you don't the system clocks you in and out and then waits for you to go online to pay. If you don't pay, they use the number to track you down and send you a parking charge notice. If you don't pay that, it ends up with them sending in the bailiffs. It's all Big Brother, these days. You know their aim is to get us all chipped with our bank account details and as you walk around they'll take money for all the services we use.'

'I heard the chip was in the Covid vaccine.'

Sharpe looked at him, his eyes widening. 'That's what I heard.'

Shepherd shook his head sadly. 'I was joking, Razor.'

'Many a true word said in jest, as my dear old mum used to say.'

They went into the building. Sharpe showed his warrant card to a receptionist and she directed him to the lifts. 'The woman we're here to see is called Stephanie Badger,' said Sharpe as they rode up in the lift. 'Do you think that's really her name?'

'What, Stephanie?'

Sharpe shook his head contemptuously. 'Mrs Badger. It sounds made up. Like something from a Beatrix Potter book.'

'And Mr Sharpe sounds real? And what about me? Shepherd. A man who looks after sheep. Let's not go throwing stones when it comes to names.'

They went up to the Admissions Office and Sharpe showed his warrant card again, this time to a secretary who buzzed through to her boss and showed them into a corner office with a view of the traffic crawling down Marylebone Road.

Mrs Badger was in her twenties, tall and thin with birdlike features and jet-black hair tied back in a ponytail. She smiled brightly as Shepherd and Sharpe sat down opposite her desk. 'So, I've spoken to our Human Resources department and there's no problem with my showing you photographs of the student population, along with personal details they provided on admission, but I'm not allowed to show you any test results or work submitted or any assessments made by the teaching staff.'

'We understand that,' said Shepherd. 'How many students do you have?'

'We have more than twenty-two thousand students across our various campuses. That includes undergraduate, postgraduate and professional qualifications. Do you know in particular what you are looking for?'

'Undergraduate,' said Shepherd.

'That will reduce the number, obviously,' said Mrs Badger.

'We think he might have been here between 2012 and 2016. So I'd like to see the photographs for those four years.'

'Sure, yes, we can do that. What about the course he was on?'

'We don't know.'

'Could we rule some out? Specialised science courses for instance? Computer programming?'

'We know very little about him, unfortunately,' said Shepherd. 'I don't think we can rule out anything.'

'Then you'd be looking at fifteen thousand undergraduates for each year,' said Mrs Badger.

'But we could rule out female undergraduates,' said Sharpe.

'Unfortunately our database doesn't work like that,' said Mrs Badger. 'We can sort by years, and we can sort by course, but we wouldn't be able to sort by gender. And it would be gender, not by sex. These days the students assign their own gender.'

'What about race? The man we're looking for is Asian.'

'Again, we wouldn't be able to do a search based on race.'

'What about searching for international students?'

Her face brightened. 'That we can do, because international students have different funding arrangements.'

'That would bring the number down?' asked Sharpe.

'Probably down to about five thousand students a year,' she said.

'Great,' said Shepherd. 'How can we do this?'

'It'll take some time to check that many photographs,' said Mrs Badger.

'Actually I've done something similar recently and I averaged close to a thousand pictures an hour.'

'You must have been exhausted,' said Mrs Badger sympathetically.

'It wasn't fun, but it was doable,' said Shepherd. 'I'd need somewhere quiet and a terminal.'

'One of my colleagues is off today, I could set you up at her work station.'

'Perfect,' said Shepherd.

'You don't need two terminals?'

'No, I'm the only one who knows what he looks like.' He gestured at Sharpe. 'Jimmy here will be supplying me with coffee.'

'And backrubs,' said Sharpe with a grin. 'He likes backrubs while he's working.'

It was late afternoon and he was on his third cup of coffee when Shepherd found the correct photograph. He had switched hands dozens of times and both were aching but he was still usually able to make a judgement in four seconds or less. He was able to reject women immediately and non-Asians in a second or two but it always took a little longer to reject male Asian students. When he saw the real thing, he stared at it for several seconds to be sure, then he grinned and sat back in his seat. 'Bingo!'

'Bingo?' said Sharpe. He hurried over to peer over Shepherd's shoulder. 'You're sure?' The picture was of a dark-haired man with a beard and glasses, staring at the camera with a half-smile. To the right of the picture were some details. His name. Yousef Rashid. His date of birth, which put him at twenty-five years of age. And his nationality. German. Shepherd pointed at the nationality. 'A Kraut?'

'Probably Iraqi-German. Yeah, I'm sure.'

'I don't get this,' said Sharpe. 'He was at university here. He's Asian. Clearly a smart guy because he fooled everyone. Speaks all the languages. Why didn't he just apply to join MI6? They'd have snapped him up. Why go to all the trouble of pretending to be Uthman?'

Shepherd sat back in his chair. 'Because Rashid isn't British. He's German. Iraqi-German. Pre-Brexit he could come and go as he pleased, he wouldn't even have needed a passport, his German ID card would get him in. He could live in the UK, he could claim benefits, he could attend a British University. The one thing he couldn't do is work for MI6 or MI5. For that you have to be British and have lived for most of the last ten years in the UK. For his plan to work, he had to have British citizenship.'

'How does a kid plan all this?'

'That I don't know,' said Shepherd. He looked at the details on the screen. 'There's nothing for next of kin.'

'Try his school,' said Sharpe. 'It says what school he attended, right?'

'Yeah, a boarding school in Somerset.'

'They'd have the details of his parents or his guardian.'

Shepherd grinned. 'You ought to be a detective.'

'Yeah, I've been told that.'

Shepherd used Google to find a phone number for the school and asked to be put through to the school secretary. A very well-spoken woman by the name of Mrs Gillespie listened to his request and three times told him that it wouldn't be possible to give that information out over the phone. She was polite but firm and there was nothing he could say to get her to change her mind. He passed the phone over to Sharpe, who explained who he was and gave her his name, rank and warrant card number. He gave her the phone numbers of three senior officers at the National Crime Agency, all above the rank of superintendent, and asked her to phone them to confirm his identity. They sipped their coffee as they waited and she called them back within five minutes. 'I've been told that I should offer you every assistance,' she said. 'So how can I help you?'

'I'll pass you back to my colleague,' said Sharpe.

Shepherd gave her Rashid's name and date of birth. 'Oh, I remember Joey, he was a sweet boy.'

'Yousef is the name on his file.'

'Well, Yousef, but the teachers kept calling him Joseph and then he became Joey. Let me see, yes, here we are. His mother is Zahra Rashid. Now she was a lovely lady. Very well spoken. She always used to bring Joey to school at the start of the term when he was little. And pick him up.'

'And the father?'

'Ali Aziz Rashid. I don't think I ever met him. It was always his mother. The father was in finance, I think, he ran a hedge fund or something. Nothing has happened to Joey, has it?'

'We're trying to find him at the moment,' said Shepherd. 'And not having much luck.'

'He went to Westminster University, I think. He was doing media studies, if I remember correctly.'

'Joey had a German passport, right? Do you know why his parents wanted him to go to school in the UK?'

'His mother said she wasn't impressed with the schools in Germany. I remember once she said she wanted him to speak English like an Englishman. I think authenticity was important to her. I know she used to take him to Iraq during his school holidays. She said she didn't want him to lose touch with his roots and wanted him to speak Arabic like an Iraqi. But they lived in Germany, I seem to recall. Yes, here we are, I have an address if that would help.'

'That would be amazing, thank you.'

Mrs Gillespie gave him an address in Frankfurt. 'If you do see Joey, please do give him my best. He always used to bring me back the most delicious Turkish delight.'

Shepherd thanked her and ended the call. He sent Pritchard a text message with the Rashid family details, then looked at his watch. 'Fancy a drink? The Globe is a two-minute walk away.'

Sharpe grinned. 'You read my mind.'

Sharpe parked the Jaguar and walked into Thames House with Shepherd. Shepherd signed him in and they went up to Pritchard's office together. He wasn't there and his secretary pointed them to an operations room. When they opened the door, Pritchard was standing next to a pod where Donna Walsh was peering at one of her screens. A man was talking into his mobile phone just behind him. He was heavy-set with short dark hair, in a double-breasted suit and gleaming brogues. He looked Shepherd up and down as he continued to talk into his phone.

Walsh said something to Pritchard and Pritchard nodded. The Sikh officer, Guntaj, was in the pod next to Walsh's, his fingers playing over his keyboard.

Pritchard patted Walsh on the shoulder and straightened up. The man finished his phone call and looked up expectantly. 'Dan, this is Julian Penniston-Hill, he's running Six at the moment.'

'I'm not sure I like the phrase "at the moment" actually,' said Penniston-Hill. 'I'd prefer Acting Chief.' He smiled at Shepherd. 'I've heard of Mr Shepherd, obviously.' He held out his hand to shake, then smiled awkwardly and changed it into a fist bump. 'Old habits die hard,' he said. 'Good work in Ankara by the way.'

Shepherd smiled back. He was Warren-Madden's boss but he wasn't sure how much he would have told him. 'Good work' covered a multitude of sins. 'Thanks,' he said. 'It was an interesting trip.'

'At least now we know where the Semtex came from,' said Penniston-Hill.

'Well, we know who sold it, but we still need to find out how it got into the UK.'

'And well done on identifying the doppelgänger,' said Pritchard. 'It's blown the case wide open.'

'How so?'

Pritchard gestured at Walsh. 'Donna, can you put Rashid's picture up? And the cuttings?'

A head-and-shoulders shot of a middle-aged Asian with a neat beard and gold-framed spectacles flashed up onto one of the wall-mounted monitors. He was wearing an expensive suit and a tie that oozed quality. 'This is the father of Yousef Rashid, the boy you identified from the university's student database,' said Penniston-Hill. 'His name is Ali Aziz Rashid. Ostensibly a hedge fund manager based in Frankfurt, specialising in business opportunities in the Middle East. Used to hang out with the likes of Angela Merkel and Jean-Claude Juncker, big charity benefactor, featured in *Forbes* magazine, the works. But behind the scenes he was an ISIS financier, sending funds out to fight the good fight and then acting as a broker for anything from stolen antiquities to pillaged oil stocks.'

'Was?' said Shepherd.

Another screen flickered into life showing cuttings from major newspapers in the UK and Europe, reporting Rashid's suicide. 'He fell to his death from the window of his office. Twenty-six storeys.'

'Suicide?' asked Shepherd. 'Or was he pushed?'

'Definitely suicide,' said Penniston-Hill. 'He left more than a dozen handwritten notes. To his wife. To his son. His business partners. His lawyer. His stockbroker. He had updated his will that morning. And he left his wallet on his desk, along with his glasses.' He looked over at Shepherd. 'People who kill themselves always remove their glasses, did you know that?'

'I did, yes.'

'Maybe they don't want to see the ground rushing up to hit them,' said Penniston-Hill. 'Anyway, Rashid's suicide came just twenty-four hours after he had a meeting with . . .' He paused for effect. 'Melissa Schofield.' He grinned when he saw Shepherd's jaw drop.

It was truly the last thing that Shepherd had expected and he shook his head in confusion. 'I'm sorry, what?'

'In 2016 Melissa was working out of our Berlin Embassy and had been collaborating with the CIA in a joint operation investigating ISIS financing. They had identified half a dozen bankers and financiers who were moving money for the terrorists, and Rashid was one of the bigger fishes. They had everything they needed, a money trail that proved his hands were dirty, GCHQ had all his emails and phone calls and MI6 had bugged hotel rooms and limousines around the world. After six months they had an open-and-shut case. The original plan was for him to be arrested in Frankfurt and face trial in London, as a lot of the money came through the City. But at the last minute MI6 got wind that the Americans were going to act unilaterally. They wanted to whisk Rashid over to the States and either lock him away in a Supermax or bury him in Gitmo. That would cut us out of the loop and so Melissa went to talk to him. The idea was to persuade him to voluntarily give evidence against his paymasters, maybe take part in a couple of stings, in return for a reduced sentence in a British prison. One of the letters Rashid left was for Melissa, basically saying thanks but no thanks. Rashid knew that ISIS would come after him and his family if he betrayed them, and his life would be over if he went to a British prison.

He's right, of course. Most British prison officers are scared to death of the Muslim population and they pretty much run their own wings. There was no way Rashid could be promised protection while inside, and there was even less that could be done about his family.'

Penniston-Hill gestured at Walsh. 'Can we see Mrs Rashid, please, Donna?'

A photograph of a dark-haired middle-aged woman wearing a headscarf and Chanel sunglasses flashed up onto a third screen. 'This is the wife, now widow. Zahra Rashid.'

Pritchard flashed Shepherd a tight smile. 'A German Kurd. I'd bet the farm on her being the woman you were told about who wanted the Semtex.'

'Her husband dies and a few months later she's buying Semtex and detonators. And not long after that her son becomes Uthman.' Shepherd ran a hand through his hair. 'This has been five years in the planning?'

'Everything started to happen after Rashid died,' said Pritchard, nodding. 'Everything.'

'So this was all about getting revenge on Schofield? And MI6?'

'Melissa never showed Rashid's letter to anyone,' said Penniston-Hill. 'She always said it was personal. If you ask me, Rashid threatened Melissa from beyond the grave, and she was so scared that she hardly left the building afterwards. And her home was a fortress with CCTV and an alarm connected to the local police station and fitted with an escape room. It was always assumed she was taking precautions because of the fatwahs against her, but with hindsight . . .' Penniston-Hill shrugged.

'Whatever Melissa said to Rashid, he must have taken it personally.'

'I think we can assume that she was fairly forceful,' said Penniston-Hill. 'She probably tried persuasion and when that didn't work she could well have used threats. Rashid felt trapped and came to the conclusion that suicide was the only way out. And before he did it he made sure that his family were financially secure and probably told them about Melissa. Maybe even asked them to get his revenge after his death.'

'Rashid wasn't a Kurd, right?'

'No, he was from central Iraq,' said Penniston-Hill. 'A Sunni Muslim. But very relaxed about his religion. In Germany he would drink wine and he wasn't a regular visitor to the mosque.'

'But Mrs Rashid is a Kurd. And Joey spoke Kurdish. Why would they get involved with ISIS? Islamic State and the Kurds hate each other.'

'She's a Kurd, but not political,' said Penniston-Hill. 'She married Ali Aziz when she was eighteen, Joey was born when she was nineteen. Ali Aziz was twice her age and she was almost certainly pregnant when they married. Ali Aziz wasn't really political or fundamentalist. With him it was all about the money. That's probably why Melissa thought she could talk him around.'

'But she misjudged it, right? She read it wrong.'

'I think she misjudged Rashid's fear of ISIS and what they would do to his family. He'd always been true to them in the past but the moment they learned that he had betrayed them, all bets would be off.'

'Did you ever talk to Melissa about what happened?'

Penniston-Hill shook his head. 'We were never that close. Her boss at the time was Melissa's mentor and he helped smooth things over. And to be fair it was only one blip on a stellar career.'

'A blip that killed her,' said Shepherd sourly. 'And a lot of innocents.'

'Well yes, there is that.' Penniston-Hill looked away uncomfortably.

'On a more positive note, our forensic team have discovered traces of Semtex residue in the truck wreckage,' said Pritchard. 'It looks as if Semtex was used to help detonate the ANFO.'

'The same Semtex that was used in the safe house?'

'We're running it through the Rhode Island database as we speak. But I'd say the chances are good. Now we're doing a reverse trace of the trucks. We got their number plates on camera and we've tracked them back to Bristol.'

'Bristol? The truck bombs came from Bristol?'

'Yeah. So we've got groups in Birmingham, Manchester and now Bristol. A lot of planning went into this. A hell of a lot. Hopefully if we keep back-tracking, eventually we'll spot the bombmaker.'

'Joey Rashid couldn't have organised the bombmaking in Bristol,' said Shepherd. 'He wouldn't have had the time or the opportunity.'

Pritchard nodded. 'Somebody else must have done that. If we're lucky, the ANPR will tell us.'

'My money is on the wife,' said Penniston-Hill. 'I think she's been running the whole thing. She was the one who got the Semtex, I've no doubt she took care of Uthman's family in Iraq, and she pushed her son to take Uthman's place.'

'Joey was good,' said Shepherd. 'He played the part to perfection.'

'Oh, he's definitely hot to trot,' said Penniston-Hill. 'But his mother was pulling the strings.'

'It also makes sense that Joey would run to Dubai,' said Pritchard. 'His father had property there. A very large villa by the sea and a duplex in the Burj Khalifa, the tallest building in the world and probably the most luxurious. Either would be the perfect place to hide.'

'So the family kept Rashid's money, even though he had links with ISIS?' said Shepherd.

'Some assets were in his wife's name and others were held in trust. The Americans seized his US accounts, his private jet, his yachts, and all his US property. We confiscated what was left in his UK accounts but he had been pretty thorough in emptying them before killing himself.'

'Anything in Manchester or Birmingham?' asked Shepherd. 'Or Bristol?'

'We had the same thought,' said Pritchard. 'Unfortunately, no. But the Dubai properties are in the wife's name and she also has homes in Frankfurt and Paris. I think they're lying low to see how it pans out. They must be figuring that we don't know that they're behind the bombs and that we think that Uthman was killed in the Hampstead bombing. They must be assuming that they've gotten away with it.'

'Do we know if Joey is still in Dubai?'

'We're checking. Obviously it'll be a lot easier now we have his real name.'

'And assuming we find him, then what?'

'The decision about what steps we take will be made at senior level, more senior than Julian and I. But our voices will hopefully be heard and listened to.'

'Does the UK have an extradition treaty with the UAE?' asked Shepherd.

'Yes, since 2008,' said Pritchard. 'So in theory we can issue an extradition request and the Dubai police will move in and arrest them and put them on a plane. But of course life is never perfect, as you know. We don't know what connections they have in Dubai and the moment we raise the issue of extradition they might just cut and run. Plenty of countries they could hide in.'

'At the moment they are lying low,' said Penniston-Hill. 'The Rashids haven't gone public with what they've done, presumably because they realise that to do so will reveal their involvement. Nor have they made ISIS aware of what happened to the Hampstead house, otherwise Islamic State would be taking the credit for killing Melissa and her colleagues.'

'Wouldn't that make more sense?' said Shepherd. 'For the Rashids to give ISIS the credit for killing Melissa Schofield?'

'I think they're waiting to see if they are in the clear,' said Penniston-Hill. 'Also I think they are waiting to see what we announce. So far we haven't even admitted that there was a bomb, we're sticking to the gas explosion story. I think they want to see how that plays out, whether or not we announce that it was a bomb and that it killed Melissa and her team. Once they are sure we're not looking for them, then they'll probably tell ISIS and ISIS can take credit for it. That would be a major publicity coup for Islamic State, obviously. And we are very keen to avoid that. If we do issue a warrant for the Rashids, everything will become public. We will have to explain what Yousef Rashid did. He was able to infiltrate MI6, brought in Islamic jihadists, equipped them to take part in an MTFA, organised two massive car bombs in the centre of London and killed the head of MI6 and a senior colleague while all the time being on the fast track to the higher echelons of the organisation.' He shuddered. 'The Press will have a field day. And heads will roll. The PM will have no choice other than to clean house. Personally I can see this being used as an excuse to combine the two agencies, overseen by a more political appointee. Various people have wanted to rein in the intelligence agencies for some time and this would give them the perfect excuse. They have pretty much emasculated the police and they would love to do the same to us.'

Pritchard nodded in agreement. 'Obviously we don't want that to happen,' he said. 'What we are hoping is that back-tracking the Trafalgar Square trucks will lead us to the bombmaker and his team. Hopefully that will lead to arrests and charges. The men behind the MTFA all died at the scene, so we can draw a line under that.'

'Except Rashid was taken away,' said Shepherd. 'He was almost certainly seen. Maybe even caught on a phone.'

'We can say that he was injured and later died of his injuries,' said Penniston-Hill. 'Once we have the bombmaker we can also charge him with the Hampstead bombing and go public with that. The fact that it's the same Semtex will make that open and shut. So the only loose ends will be the Rashids.' He paused to see if Pritchard was going to add anything but Pritchard just flashed him a tight smile so he continued. 'There is a time element involved, as well. The Rashids clearly want to hurt the UK, for whatever reason, and we don't know if they have anything else planned. Joey Rashid was fast-tracked through MI6, heaven knows what sensitive data he's picked up that can be used against us. He knows names, he knows our protocols, he knows about ongoing operations, he's had full access to the MI6 database during that time. There's no way of knowing the extent of the damage he could do. They need to be stopped. The sooner the better.'

'The first thing we need to do is to establish that they are still in Dubai,' said Pritchard. 'Then we can decide what to do. And at the end of the day it'll be the PM's call.'

'I guess the fact that they're in Dubai is the issue,' said Shepherd. 'If they were in Iraq, Syria or Afghanistan we could just paint their location with lasers and send in a drone with Hellfires.'

'Indeed,' said Penniston-Hill. 'Or send in an SAS hit team.' He smiled thinly. 'That would be so much easier all round.'

Shepherd's mobile burst into life, waking him from a dreamless sleep. He sat up, rubbed his eyes and looked over at the five phones on his bedside table. Four of them were four undercover jobs he had been running but it was his office phone ringing and it was Pritchard calling. It was just after six. 'Dan, sorry about the early call but we've located and identified the Bristol bomb-maker,' said Pritchard. 'The CCTV tracking paid off. The trucks were prepared in a warehouse in Staple Hill, to the east of the city. We were lucky, there's a CCTV camera on a set of traffic lights that gives us partial coverage of the road outside the ware-house, so we can see the vans enter and leave. We went back until we found the vans arriving, two weeks previously, with different number plates. And we spotted a motorbike arriving and leaving every day, owned by a Syrian refugee who was granted asylum ten years ago. His name is Salim Al-Qassab. Came in on the Calais route back in the days when they hid in trucks rather than using rubber dinghies. Spun the old "Gaddafi hates me and wants me dead" story and was granted asylum, then leave to remain and is on his way to citizenship. His wife joined him a couple of years ago and they have a son, born here. He's always kept his nose clean, works as an electrician for the NHS, butter wouldn't melt. But we've checked his browsing history and his phone records and he's the leader of a cell of another four homegrown cleanskins, two of whom drove the vans down to London. We're sure now that they left the vehicles and detonated by phone. We don't have them behind bars yet but it won't be long. Al-Qassab is already in custody. We're going to let the anti-terrorism boys take the credit so SO15 will be picking him up later today. I've cleared it with the Bristol cops for you to have a preliminary interview. I doubt that he'll be saying anything, but obviously we'd like to confirm that Mrs Rashid supplied him with the Semtex that they used. Also we need to know if he gave Joey Rashid the bomb that killed Schofield. Can you head to Bristol ASAP? I'll text you a contact name.'

'What if this Al-Qassab does implicate the Rashids? Does that mean we might look at extraditing them for trial?'

'Everything is up in the air at the moment,' said Pritchard. 'The PM is waiting to hear how you get on before making his final decision.'

It took Shepherd just under three hours to drive to Bristol. Bridewell Police Station was a six-storey modern building in the centre of the city that could easily have been mistaken for a shopping centre. The reception area went up the full height of the building, and beyond was a large seating area with green and blue chairs and IKEA-style coffee tables.

The reception desk reminded Shepherd of the check-in area at the Mövenpick Hotel in Ankara but the woman who dealt with him was a lot less friendly. He smiled and explained who he was and gave her the name of the Avon and Somerset Counter Terrorism officer he was supposed to meet. Her face remained impassive as she tapped on her computer, then she nodded at the waiting area. 'DI Opperman will be out to see you,' she said.

Detective Inspector Linda Opperman was a good deal friend-lier. She was tall and had a confident walk as she crossed the reception area, and she initiated the fist bump. 'So I'm told you want a one-on-one interview,' she said, as she took him over to security gates.

'Just a preliminary chat before the Met's anti-terrorism boys come and collect him.'

'Not a problem. We've been holding him in a custody suite but I've had him put in an interview room.'

She used a keycard on a lanyard around her neck to open a security gate.

'How has he been?' Shepherd asked as she took him down a corridor.

'He's not said a word. Wc explained that he was being held on a pre-charge detention order under the Terrorism Act and he just shrugged. He hasn't asked for a lawyer or a telephone call. He's prayed a few times and when we gave him lunch he asked if it was Halal, but other than that he's stayed quiet.'

Shepherd was surprised at how helpful the detective was being. Often police officers became quite defensive when dealing with MI5 personnel and he had run into several turf wars with belligerent officers who considered it a personal affront that MI5 were taking over one of their cases. DI Opperman seemed more than happy to get Al-Qassab off her hands.

She had to use her keycard to get them into the custody centre, then had a quick word with a grey-haired sergeant behind a chest-high counter before taking Shepherd down a corridor where there were three rooms each with 'INTERVIEW ROOM' on them. A uniformed constable was standing next to the middle door. 'Do you want me to sit in?' she asked.

'No need,' he said. 'And if possible, I'd prefer there to be no recording of the interview. Nothing he says will be used in evidence and I won't be cautioning him.'

'Just a chat?'

'Exactly.'

She smiled brightly. 'Be my guest,' she said. She gave him a business card. 'I'll be in my office, my mobile number is there, give me a call if you need anything.'

As she walked away, her high heels clicking on the tiled floor, the PC stepped to the side and Shepherd opened the door.

Salim Al-Qassab was sitting on a plastic chair, staring down at the table in front of him. There were two more white plastic chairs facing him and Shepherd sat down on one. He waited, but Al-Qassab didn't look up.

There were two small black domes on opposite corners of the ceiling but neither had the red light to show that the CCTV was working. There was a voice recorder on a shelf above the table, but this wasn't a conversation that Shepherd wanted a copy of. He was looking for information, not evidence to be put before a court.

Al-Qassab was wearing a white paper forensic suit and blue plastic shoe covers on his feet. Shepherd presumed his clothing had been taken away for forensic analysis.

'So, you work for the NHS?'

Shepherd wasn't expecting an answer, he was surprised when Al-Qassab nodded and lifted his head. He was in his forties with a greying beard and watery eyes. His hair was greasy and flecked with grey. 'I am an electrician at the Bristol Royal Infirmary.' He spoke slowly with a thick accent.

'I clapped for you. During the pandemic.'

'A lot of people did.'

'How did you feel, when people clapped?'

'It felt good to be appreciated.' He smiled. One of his upper front teeth was gold and it glinted.

Shepherd smiled and held the man's look for several seconds. 'That must be a good feeling,' he said. 'You realise that a lot of those people who died in Trafalgar Square probably clapped for the NHS?'

Al-Qassab's jaw tightened but he didn't say anything.

'Was it your idea? The two bombs going off at different times? Putting them where the crowds would be moving?'

Al-Qassab's Adam's apple wobbled. 'I just did what I was asked. For Allah.'

'But Allah didn't tell you where to put the trucks, did he? Or do you have a direct line to the almighty?'

Again the man's jaw tightened.

'It was clever, there's no getting away from that. A master stroke. Did you study military techniques?'

'I am an electrician.'

'And a bombmaker. A very good bombmaker, it has to be said.'

Al-Qassab shrugged.

'The small one, that was clever. Very powerful. The truck bombs, they were easy enough, right? Lots of ANFO, a bit of Semtex to get the thing going, and a detonator linked to a phone. Anyone could do that. But the small one, that was the work of an expert. It had to be carried so it had to be robust, and it had to take out an entire room. But it had to be small enough to fit in a backpack. Where did you learn to make a device like that?'

Al-Qassab shrugged again but didn't answer.

'You don't want to say anything?'

'What is the point? Is there anything I can say that will mean I can go home?'

'That's a good question.'

Al-Qassab held his look. The man wasn't scared or fearful, he was simply resigned to his fate. 'Can you answer it for me?'

Shepherd looked at him for several seconds before answering. 'We know what you did, Salim. We know where you built the bombs, we know how long it took you, we know who you built them for. Those bombs killed a lot of people. So no, there is nothing that you can say that will allow you to go home.'

'Then I shall be quiet. Until I have a lawyer here. And then the lawyer will tell you that I have nothing to say.'

'If I was you, that's probably what I would do. Except that I'm British.'

Al-Qassab frowned. 'What does that mean?'

'Well, we're different, you and I. You'll be in prison for ever, pretty much. Your wife isn't British and she hasn't been here long enough to get leave to remain so she'll be sent back to Libya. And your son, well, he has absolutely no rights to be in this country.'

'My son was born here, he's British.'

'No, neither you nor your wife are British citizens so it makes no difference where he was born. He isn't British so he will be sent back to Libya with your wife.'

Al-Qassab stared at him with his watery eyes but didn't say anything.

'You know you were used, right? They always expected you to be caught. They wanted you as a martyr.'

Al-Qassab frowned. 'Who? Who used me?'

'They betrayed you, Salim. And they always meant to betray you. The same as they betrayed the men who drove the trucks. Did they intend to be shahid, Salim? Did you plan to kill them from the start?'

'What do you mean?'

'The men died in their trucks, Salim.'

Al-Qassab shook his head. 'No, that's not true. They were detonated by phone. They weren't there when they exploded.'

'But they were. They might have thought they had time to get away, but they were lied to. They're dead. They were betrayed and now you've been betrayed.'

'How? How have I been betrayed?'

'Your bosses betrayed you, because they want to show the world that they were responsible. They want you on trial so that the world can see what they did. They'll proclaim you to be a hero, but they won't care that you will spend the rest of your life in prison and that your wife and son will be sent back to Libya.' He leaned forward across the table. 'What did they tell you, Salim? That afterwards you could go back to your normal life? That nobody would know? And the men who died? Did they tell them they were going to be shahid?'

Al-Qassab was frowning as he tried to process what he'd been told.

'And the smaller Semtex bomb. That also killed the man who used it. Was that your plan, too? That he would die when the bomb exploded. Another shahid?'

'No, that bomb had a timer. There was time for him to get away.'

'Then you made a mistake. Because your man died in the explosion.'

'That is not possible, I do not make mistakes.'

'Exactly. So this was planned from the start. Maybe they altered the timer after you gave them the bomb.'

Al-Qassab shook his head. 'She would not do that. She would not lie to me like that.'

'No, Salim. Everybody has been lying to you, right from the start.' He reached into his pocket and took out two photographs. He put the first one down on the table in front of Al-Qassab. It was Yousef Rashid, MI6's file picture. 'This is the man who died, Salim. You gave him the bomb and it killed him.'

'I do not know him,' said Al-Qassab.

Shepherd put down the second picture. Zahra Rashid. Shepherd saw Al-Qassab's eyes widen and he knew that his hunch had been right. He knew her. 'She betrayed you, Salim,' said Shepherd as Al-Qassab continued to stare at the photograph. 'She was using you. She paid for the bombs and she gave you the Semtex but all the time she planned for you to be blamed for this. For everything. Everyone else is dead, Salim. The men in the trucks. The men with the guns in Trafalgar Square. The man who used the smaller bomb. They're all dead. You know what that makes you, Salim?'

Al-Qassab shook his head as he stared at the photograph of Zahra Rashid.

'You're what we call a fall guy,' said Shepherd. 'You are the one who has to take the fall. The blame. ISIS will call you a hero and a great Muslim, but you were the fall guy. You will spend the rest of your life in a prison cell and you will never see your family again.' He tapped the photograph of Zahra Rashid. 'She used you, Salim. And now she has left the country. She is safe. And all she wants now is for you to stand up in a court and praise Islamic State and say that the West deserves these attacks for all the wrongs that have been committed against Muslims and then she will have no more use for you.' Shepherd paused to let it all sink in. 'Are you happy with that, Salim? Are you happy to be the fall guy?'

Tears were welling up in Al-Qassab's eyes and he blinked them away. Shepherd sat back and waited. The seconds ticked by. Eventually Salim swallowed, and then he took a deep breath.

'Nothing happens unless it is decreed by Allah,' he said. He folded his arms. 'I have nothing more to say. I want a lawyer now.'

As he drove out of Bristol towards London, Shepherd called Pritchard on hands-free. 'Zahra Rashid was in the UK and she gave the Semtex to Al-Qassab.'

'He told you that?'

'As good as. His reaction when I showed him her photograph was enough. And he referred to her as "she". And when I accused her of betraying him, he didn't deny it. I could see it in his face. He met her.'

'Unfortunately there's no way of confirming that with Border Force. She would have used her German ID card to enter and leave the country.'

'Well yes, except she clearly brought the Semtex with her. You said that the Americans took away their private plane, but she's got money. She could have flown in on a private jet to a West Country airport where checks would be minimal.'

'I'll get someone on that,' said Pritchard. 'Do you think he'll now co-operate?'

'No. He shut down. The will of Allah and all that. I told him that the guys who were in the trucks died in the explosion and that Joey died when the small bomb went off and that Rashid was just using them all. That still didn't persuade him.'

'He met Joey?'

'No, he didn't recognise his picture. I just made it seem that Zahra Rashid was betraying everyone and I think he believed me. But at the end of the interview he made it clear he's not going to say anything else. He's accepted his fate.'

'Well he was never going to cut a deal even if he had told us everything. Good work.'

'So what happens now?'

'I'll run that intel by the PM's office. Then it's his call as to how we proceed. Drive safely.' Pritchard ended the call.

Shepherd felt no guilt at all in lying to the bomber. He smiled to himself as he remembered the toast he'd given on the boat with Liam and Naomi. 'Here's to lying, cheating, stealing and drinking. If you're going to lie, lie to save the life of a friend.' Perhaps he should amend the toast for future use. 'Here's to lying, cheating, stealing and drinking. If you're going to lie, lie to save the life of a friend. Or to get a murdering jihadist bomb-maker to tell you what he's been up to.' He chuckled and shook his head as he imagined how Liam and Naomi would have reacted to that. Some things were best not said out loud.

Shepherd was just outside Swindon when Pritchard phoned him back. 'For once the PM has made a snap decision,' said Pritchard. 'He wants us to go to Dubai and bring the Rashids back, for questioning and possible trial.'

'So extradition, then?'

'No. I think kidnapping would be a more accurate description of what he has in mind. He doesn't want to get bogged down in legal issues and we've made him aware that once they know we're onto them they will probably bolt. So he wants us to go at the earliest possible opportunity.'

'And by "us" you mean who exactly?'

'Major Gannon is putting together a plan as we speak. I've sent him the preliminary intel from our people in Dubai. Can you divert to Hereford and liaise with him?'

'Sure,' said Shepherd.

'Obviously you know Rashid, so you should be on the team that goes in.'

'That's fine,' said Shepherd. 'How does Julian feel about this? I got the feeling he'd prefer to send in the SAS with guns blazing.'

'He's not happy at all, obviously. He knows the damage it'll do if the Rashids appear in court. But at the end of the day it's not his call. Or mine. It's the PM's.'

'Let's just hope he doesn't make one of his famous U-turns while we're in the air,' said Shepherd, just before Pritchard ended the call.

Shepherd phoned Major Gannon when he was half an hour away from the Stirling Lines camp, and when Shepherd drove up to the main admin building he was waiting for him. The Major was wearing a white Aran pullover and brown cargo pants and carrying a plastic expandable file. He waved as Shepherd climbed out of his BMW SUV. 'Hungry?'

'I haven't eaten since breakfast, so yes,' said Shepherd.

'Let's hit the officers' mess,' said the Major. 'They've just had some excellent T-bone steaks in, a gift from our colleagues in Virginia Beach.'

Virginia Beach was where Navy SEAL Team Six was based. They were the closest equivalent the US had to the SAS and they often trained together.

'Steak sounds good, boss.'

They walked to the mess. There were only two tables occupied and Shepherd didn't recognise any of the men eating. Officers came and went in the SAS, generally for just two or three years; for them it was generally a stepping stone to greater things.

The Major gestured at a table by the window and they sat down. In the distance was the clock tower, which had been moved to the current Credenhill base after the old HQ had been shut down. It was where the Regiment remembered its dead, the names of men who died in action immortalised on metal plaques at the base of the tower. Shepherd had been at the official opening ceremony on September 30, 2000, when the clock tower had been re-erected by the side of the parade ground. By then he had already left the Regiment and had started his undercover career but it had still been an emotional experience.

The Major ordered steaks and all the trimmings and a bottle of red wine. 'So, your boss wants the Rashids picked up ASAP,' said the Major as the waiter walked away. He put the file on the table and opened it. 'Though frankly that's easier said than done.'

He took three photographs from the file. They were different views of the Burj Khalifa tower in Dubai, including a close-up of a terrace outside one of the apartments. 'This is where they're holed up,' he said. 'Four bedrooms, it's one of the most expensive apartments in the building, on the ninety-ninth floor. Food has been delivered to the apartment and there have been several outgoing calls, all with a middle-aged woman speaking Kurdish. Just chit chat, but it's definitely her. Dubai airspace is very tightly controlled but the guys managed to get a helicopter fly-by last night, ostensibly on a sightseeing flight, and they were able to get these.'

He took out several more photographs and spread them out. They had clearly been taken with a long lens from a helicopter. They were shots of a wall of glass and behind it a woman sitting on a sofa. 'The quality isn't great but everyone is pretty sure that's Mrs Rashid,' he said.

There was a man standing on the terrace in front of the window. He was broad-shouldered and wearing a black suit. He was either bald or had shaved his head. 'That's not Joey, is it?' said Shepherd.

'Security,' said the Major. He showed Shepherd a surveillance picture taken in the lobby. There were three men in dark suits, all in their thirties and looking as if they would be more at home in fatigues and carrying big guns. 'These men headed up to the apartment earlier today. Russian speakers. A few minutes later three other men came down. Also Russian speakers.' Another photograph showed three different men leaving an elevator. 'We've identified two of them as former Spetsnaz, now working in the private sector.'

Shepherd nodded. Spetsnaz – Russian special forces – weren't as well trained as their UK equivalent but they were as hard as nails.

'So, the flat is on the ninety-ninth floor. Getting into the lobby is easy enough, tourists pass through there all the time, and there are dozens of offices and two hotels in the tower. But entry to the residential floors is tightly controlled and you need a keycard to operate the lift. All the common areas are covered by CCTV, as are the lifts. That pretty much rules out a frontal assault. Even if we were successful, everything would be recorded.'

'So the terrace?' said Shepherd.

'I think so. But we can't use a helicopter to access it, Dubai air traffic control monitor and direct all flights over the city. There are several public access points above the ninety-ninth floor, including a hotel and a viewing platform, but there's no way anyone could go over the side without being seen. Best bet is to gain access to one of the flats above the terrace and abseil down. Pritchard's Dubai people have looked into it and there's one available above the target flat. They're in the process of signing a lease as we speak.'

'Directly above?'

'Two floors above. Thirty feet or so. So you can take your equipment up in the lift, shielding your face from the cameras. Maybe use suitcases rather than holdalls. No one ever looks at a wheeled suitcase.'

'But afterwards, they'll know which apartment we came from.'

'Of course. But Pritchard has arranged for the flat to be leased from a shell company in the Cayman Islands that is itself owned by an off-the-shelf company in Tel Aviv. The payment for the lease was also made from a bank in the Cayman Islands but a minimal amount of digging will reveal that the ultimate owner of the bank account also resided in Tel Aviv.'

Shepherd laughed. 'He wants to blame the Israelis?'

'I think he's just trying to muddy the waters.'

'And how do we get the Rashids out if the lifts are covered by CCTV?'

'Tandem base-jumping.'

Shepherd's jaw dropped. 'You are kidding?'

The Major shook his head. 'You do it in the small hours, you knock the Rashids out with sedatives and you strap them to two of the guys using extra-large chutes. Into a van and off to the airport.' He grinned. 'Sadly I won't be there myself, but I'm sure it'll be fine.'

'What about the bodyguards? They're armed so we'll have to be armed, too. I wouldn't want to be shooting them, they're only earning a living.'

The Major grinned. 'I'm ahead of you there,' he said. 'As soon as the steaks arrive I'll explain everything.'

After they had finished their steaks, the Major walked Shepherd back to the admin building and took him along to the briefing room which had been assigned to the operation. 'You've got the same team that you had in Ankara, with the exception of the Ellis brothers who are needed down at Wellington Barracks. So Mutton, Sagey, Mustard and Paddy. To be honest, five is a good number, any more than that and you'll be tripping over each other on that terrace.'

'Cheers, boss. They're all good guys, it'll be fine.'

The Major pushed open the door and Shepherd followed him into a room with a white Formica table in the middle and two large whiteboards dotted with photographs, maps and Google Earth pictures. The four troopers were already there, lounging in chairs and drinking mugs of tea. They all stood up and fist-bumped Shepherd. 'Thought you'd got rid of us, I bet,' said Taylor.

'Yeah, the ultimate bad pennies, us lot,' said Coleman.

'Let's dive straight in,' said the Major. He went over to the whiteboards and tapped two photographs. 'So, our targets are this woman, Zahra Rashid, and her son, Yousef. Tango One and Tango Two. They are presently holed up on the ninety-ninth floor of this building.' He pointed at a photograph of the Burj Khalifa. 'It's eight hundred and twenty-eight metres high, twice as tall as the Empire State Building and three times as high as the Eiffel Tower.'

'So it's tall then, boss?' asked Taylor with a grin.

'Yes, Mutton. It's what architects refer to as really tall,' said the Major. 'The two Tangoes do not leave the building and are protected by three bodyguards in their apartment and another two down in the lobby. They are on an eight-hour rotation and the ones we know about all appear to be former Spetsnaz. The tower is very security conscious and all lifts are key controlled so we can't get to their floor that way. The stairs are all covered by CCTV and the fire doors only open inwards.'

'We can do what Tom Cruise did,' said Sage.

'Say what?' said Shepherd.

'Tom Cruise,' Sage repeated. 'In that *Mission Impossible* movie. The second one or the third one. He had to climb up ten floors outside that building so he had these Spider-Man-type gloves that meant he could climb glass. "Blue for stick like glue, red for dead," they said. It was that guy from *Shaun of the Dead* who gave them to him.'

'You've lost me, Sagey,' said Shepherd.

'We ask if we can borrow those gloves and we climb up. Easy peasy.'

Shepherd couldn't tell if the man was joking or not, but knowing how SAS troopers loved to take the piss he assumed Sage was trying to be funny.

'Sadly that's just a movie,' said the Major. 'We've rented a flat above the one the Tangoes are in. The plan is to go through the window and abseil down to the terrace of the target flat. You'll do it at night. Hopefully the Tangoes will be asleep and security will be relaxed.'

'So you're not coming, boss?' said Taylor.

'Sadly I have to hold the PM's hand over the next few days, so Spider will be running the show. He's seen one of the Tangoes up close and personal.'

'You know the windows in buildings like that can't be opened,' said Sage.

'How did Tom Cruise open his?' asked Shepherd.

'That *Shaun of the Dead* guy used this really neat laser to cut it out.'

'We'll definitely try and get one of those, Sagey,' said the Major. 'Anyway, you'll abseil down and move through the flat using night vision goggles. You neutralise security and isolate the Tangoes.'

'We're extracting them?' asked Coleman.

'That's the plan,' said the Major. 'They can't be taken down in the lifts so you'll be base jumping off the terrace. Paddy and Mustard have the most jumping experience so they'll take the Tangoes down in tandem. They'll have double-size chutes and extra harnesses.'

'With the Tangoes kicking and screaming all the way?' said Ireland.

'No, they'll be sedated. Mutton's a medic, he'll administer a sedative before the jump. They'll be out cold.' He pointed at a floor plan of the apartment. 'Now the apartment they're in has four bedrooms, two en suite, so we're assuming the Tangoes will be in the en-suites. The apartment is just over four thousand square feet and the terrace is another two thousand. It was on the market for a few years with every estate agent in Dubai so we have all the maps and photos we need. As we speak we've got carpenters building a mock-up in one of the sheds so first thing in the morning we can start practising. We'll spend all day on it and then we're flying out the following morning, zero four hundred hours.'

'Emirates First Class?' said Taylor.

'It'll be a Hercules, so no,' said the Major. 'Any other sensible questions? If not, maybe an early night and we can hit the mock-up at sparrow's farts?'

'Maybe a drink first,' said Taylor.

'Yeah, just to relax us,' said Ireland. 'All this planning makes me a bit tense.'

Shepherd laughed. 'I guess a drink or two wouldn't hurt.'

Shepherd was in the canteen at six o'clock in the morning, dressed in fatigues and rubber-soled boots. Coleman, Ireland and Taylor were already at a table, munching on bacon rolls and washing them down with coffee. As Shepherd was helping himself to coffee, Sage arrived. They grabbed bacon rolls and sat down.

'So is it true that you ate a tarantula while you were on the jungle phase?' asked Taylor.

'What can I say? I was hungry.'

'I'm told that if you burn the hairs off, it doesn't taste bad,' said Coleman.

'I'll be sure to try that if there's ever a next time,' said Shepherd. He held up his bacon roll. 'But until then, I'll stick with the bacon butties.'

'Jungle phase is a bitch,' said Sage. 'That was the only time I ever thought of bailing. Six weeks of non-stop rain.'

'And the insects,' said Taylor.

'And the fucking snakes,' said Coleman.

They all shook their heads at the memories of their time in the Belize jungle.

'And the crazy thing is, the hardest part of selection, yet have any of you ever been in the jungle since?' said Sage.

Taylor raised his hand. 'Yeah. Colombia.'

'Colombia? Drugs?'

'Yeah. Training their special forces to take on the cartels. But the Colombian jungle is a hell of a lot more pleasant than Belize.'

'See that's what I don't get,' said Sage. 'They test us in a bloody jungle and when we're working, most of the time it's in the desert. That's where they should be testing us, in the desert.'

'I don't mind the desert,' said Coleman. 'Heat is fine, it's the rain I can't take.'

'I think they know that,' said Taylor. 'It's not really about teaching us jungle survival skills, it's about testing our stamina and resolve. The jungle does that. The desert wouldn't.'

They finished their breakfast and Shepherd walked them over to the outdoor firing range. A red flag was flying to show that the range was being used. There were ten life-size targets with a wall of earth behind them, facing the roofed area where the weapons were prepared. Usually there was a range-master in attendance but today the Major was filling that role. He was wearing a fleece over a black Adidas tracksuit.

'Right, this is what we'll be using,' said the Major, taking them over to a table on which he had lined up six Mossberg pump-action shotguns. He picked one up. 'As you know, five rounds in the magazine, one in the chamber.'

'Shotguns?' said Taylor. 'Are you kidding me?'

The Major handed him the shotgun, then picked up a box of shells. He took one out and showed it to them. 'With a very special type of ammunition,' he said. 'We're going in with Taser rounds.'

'Are you serious?' said Taylor, taking the round from him. 'We go to all this trouble and we shoot them with toy guns?' The exterior of the shell was clear plastic; inside was a mass of electronics with four metal prongs at the end.

'The shotguns are standard, they're not toys,' said the Major. 'The shells are self-contained Taser units that will drop a full-grown man in less than a second. They'll rip right through clothing, but not vests. But you can hit the target anywhere on the body and they'll go down.'

He handed a shell to Ireland who looked at it with disdain on his face. The Major held out the box and Sage and Coleman took out shells and examined them. 'I'm confused,' said Taylor. 'These will just stun them, right?'

The Major nodded. 'The decision has been taken that we're not to kill the bodyguards. They're hired hands, they're not terrorists, they're not jihadists, they're being paid a salary to protect their clients. There but for the grace of God could be any one of our mates who have left the Regiment. A fair few have gone into the personal protection business. How would you feel if we went in there and saw someone you knew?'

'I don't know many Russians,' said Sage.

'No, but you must know plenty of Sass guys who could quite easily end up being in that flat earning a crust to support their families. Would you slot them for doing their job?'

Sage shrugged. 'They knew the risks. The job is to protect the client and if necessary take a bullet for him.'

'My worry is that Tasers can be unreliable,' said Coleman. 'And the guys we're going up against will have the real thing. I'm going to be standing there with a Taser while the guy I'm trying to bring down has a Glock aimed at my head.'

'Against gangbangers fired up on meth or coke, Tasers can sometimes be less than effective,' said Shepherd. 'And they're not great against body armour. But these guys won't be fired up on drugs and we'll be going in at night so they won't be wearing body armour. And these aren't regular Tasers. They're self-contained units. You'll have six shots so if the first doesn't take, you can fire immediately afterwards. There's no recharging time, each shell has its own power supply. Look, I understand your reservations, but it'll be night and we'll have the element of surprise.'

The Major gestured at the shells they were holding. 'Those little beauties are Taser XREP FL shells. They have finned rounds, small fins pop out as soon as they leave the barrel, giving added accuracy. The firm calls them 12-gauge less-lethal munitions. Basically they do exactly the same thing as a regular Taser. The prongs embed themselves in the target and discharge enough electricity to incapacitate the target. They definitely work, but if anyone is in any doubt we can rig up a demonstration and I'll fire one at you. They say non-lethal but they do pack a punch.'

'What's the range?' asked Ireland.

'A hundred feet in theory but you're better off at half that. But we'll be inside an apartment so it'll all be close range.'

'And it can go in any shotgun?' asked Taylor.

'Any smooth-bored shotgun, yes,' said the Major. 'If you want to use another model, that's fine, I've just always been a fan of the Mossberg. The plan is to go in with the Taser shells but we'll carry regular 12-gauge shells with us just in case things take a turn for the worse. You can take whatever you feel comfortable with. Birdshot, buckshot, slugs. Your choice. The Taser shells use a much-reduced charge so they make a loud pop rather than a bang and there's almost no recoil.'

'What about sidearms?' asked Ireland.

'Just the shotguns,' said Shepherd. 'Body armour is optional.'

'Flashbangs?' asked Taylor.

Shepherd grinned. 'You do like your flashbangs, don't you, Mutton? Yes, we can take a few with us if that'll make you happier.' He looked at his watch. 'Why don't we fire off a few rounds here to get the feel for them, then we'll try them for size in the mock-up.'

Shepherd and the Major led the team from the firing range to one of the massive brown hangars that dotted the Stirling Lines base. They were carrying the shotguns and boxes of the Taser shells. The huge buildings were little more than metal shells and had a multitude of uses, from storing supplies and vehicles to indoor training areas. There were no signs on the buildings to say what was inside and no way of guessing their function from the outside.

'So, because of the equipment, scheduled flights are obviously out of the question, so we'll put your team on a Hercules C-130,' said the Major as he walked with Shepherd. 'Dubai is not far off six thousand kilometres so you'll need to refuel halfway which is Istanbul. Cruising speed of the Hercules is five hundred and forty kilometres an hour, give or take, so we're looking at twelve hours in the air. Arriving at Dubai isn't a problem, we've got people out there training the UAE special forces so we're coming and going with men and equipment all the time. The plane will refuel and wait for you. Seems to me that you'll attract less attention going into the building in the evening rather than the small hours. So how about we aim to get you to Dubai at twenty hundred hours?'

'Sounds good,' said Shepherd.

'That'll mean wheels up at zero four hundred hours. The early bird.'

'We can sleep on the plane,' said Shepherd. 'It won't be the first time.'

They went inside. The cavernous hangar had been used to store motorbikes and off-road vehicles but most had been shipped to Syria and the few dozen that were left had been stacked against the far wall. A team of local carpenters had been brought in to build the mock-up, driven onto the base inside a windowless van and not allowed to leave the hangar until the job had been completed. The finished product was functional – they had used plywood for the walls, installed metal frames for doors and windows, and had painted everything white. The terrace was marked out with pieces of wood and there was a metal-roofed frame representing a cabana big enough to shield a dozen people from the sun.

A scaffolding platform some twenty feet high had been erected next to the terrace, offering a bird's-eye view of the structure.

The team were standing in the terrace area, looking at the cabana. 'Where will we come down?' asked Ireland.

'On top of the cabana,' said Shepherd. 'It's steel so it should take our weight.' He walked over to the metal frames that represented the floor-to-ceiling windows that looked out over the terrace. 'These are sliding glass panels. There's no reason for them to be locked, so I'm assuming we just slide them back to gain entry. We need to check that there is no one out here obviously. It's possible that one of the guards might pop out for a smoke. If there is anyone outside, we Taser them from the window or the cabana. Anyone Tasered is then gagged and zip-tied.'

He stepped through the frame into the main area. It ran the length of the flat and was the main entertaining area. 'There will be sofas, coffee tables, a dining table, all sorts of furniture,' said Shepherd. 'We don't know how it's furnished but we'll have the night vision gear so hopefully we won't be bumping into things.' He took them across the room to a door at the far end. Before they reached it, there was a door to the right. Shepherd opened it. 'This is a bathroom. It'll need to be cleared before going to the kitchen.' He pushed open the kitchen door and they all filed in. An oblong box had been built in the middle of the room, six feet wide, twelve feet long and four feet high. 'In all of the estate agent brochures the kitchen has this island in the middle so we're assuming it's still here. I think it's reasonable to assume that at least one of the security detail will be here. I'm proposing that Paddy and Coleman break left and come straight here.' He pointed at another door at the end of the room. 'That's a pantry, it'll need checking. Once you've cleared the kitchen, call it in and move back to the main room.'

Ireland and Coleman nodded.

Shepherd walked them back to the main area. There was a hallway leading off it that went left and right. Shepherd pointed to the right. 'At the end of this hall there are two master suites, each with their own dressing room and bathroom. They are far enough away that I'm sure they won't hear anything that happens here. You've heard what the shotguns sound like, there's less noise than a bursting balloon.' He pointed to the left. 'This leads to the front door, and two more bedrooms and a common bathroom. You have to pass the bedrooms to get to the front door so it's a bit complicated. I'll show you.'

He took them down the hallway. There were three makeshift doors which had helpfully been labelled 'BEDROOM 4', 'BATHROOM', and 'BEDROOM 3'. The hallway then took a turn to the right where there was a lobby area about twelve feet by twelve feet with two doors, one labelled 'FRONT DOOR' and the other 'CLOAKROOM'. 'This area is big enough for a sofa or a couple of chairs, so it might be that one of the guards will be stationed here. The hallway getting here is quite narrow so I suggest that as Paddy and Mustard clear the kitchen, Sagey comes straight here. You'll pass the three doors if they're closed. If they're open then you need to hang fire and call us. We'll join you here and we can take out the bedrooms as you move to the lobby. We're going to have to run that a few times to see how it pans out.'

He took them back to the hallway adjoining the main area. 'Right, so me and Mutton will stay here as Paddy and Mustard clear the kitchen, and Sagey checks out the lobby. If the bedroom doors are open, Mutton and I will join Sagey. If not, he moves back to cover the hallway outside the bedrooms.'

All members of the team nodded. Shepherd hadn't expected any comments, they would wait until he had finished before chipping in.

'So assuming the kitchen is clear and the lobby is clear, I'm thinking that I'll stay here and cover the entrance to the master suites while Mutton, Paddy and Mustard join Sagey and clear the bedrooms, two apiece. If there's a lot of noise, I'll move immediately into the master bedroom area. Hopefully there won't be, and once the two bedrooms and bathroom have been cleared, you all come back here and we move into the master bedroom area together.' He grinned. 'Well, best-laid plans of mice and men and all that,' he said. 'Any questions?'

'I'd be happier tossing flashbangs into the bedrooms,' said Taylor. 'But I'm guessing you're going to veto that.'

Shepherd grinned. 'Yeah, the whole apartment is fitted up with smoke detectors. Plus the noise will wake everyone up, in this flat and the others on the same floor. We're going to have to keep the noise to a minimum.'

'When do I carry out the sedation?' asked Taylor.

'As soon as the first Tango is Tasered, you sedate them and then Mustard or Paddy can fit the harness. Then you move to the second Tango. We'll have to play it by ear because we don't know which Tango is in which room. What sedative were you thinking of using?'

'Probably Midazolam,' said Taylor. 'It's a fast-acting benzodi-azepine, they use it to knock out mental patients having psychotic episodes. Ideally you'd administer it through an IV but an injection into muscle mass will work.'

'So the arse, then?' said Coleman.

'Exactly,' said Taylor. 'Just flip them over, needle in the bum, job done.'

'What if, say, two of the bodyguards are in the bedroom?' said Ireland. 'The other one is outside, or in the kitchen. You take out the one on the terrace, easy enough. Why don't you then just move to the master bedroom and get the Tangoes? Leave the bodyguards on the other side of the flat none the wiser.'

'The worry would be that if there's anyone not in the bedroom, they'll hear us and raise the alarm,' said Shepherd. 'I do like the sneaky scenario, but that will depend on them being in the bedrooms with the door shut and if they're pros that's unlikely.' He looked over at the Major, who was standing in the area marked off as the terrace. 'What do you think, boss?'

'If I was running the security and there was a high threat level then I'd have a four-man team. One inside the front door, one on the terrace, and one in the master bedrooms area. All standing, not sitting. The fourth one on a break. Then I'd rotate them every thirty minutes to keep them on their toes. If I only had three men then the same positions but with no breaks. I'm thinking that on the ninety-ninth floor with full security downstairs and the lifts keycard operated, they're not going to think there's a serious threat. My gut feeling is that they'll be pretty relaxed. But they are former Spetsnaz, which means they'll be as tough as old boots. I think the chance of getting to the Tangoes without going through the bodyguards is slim.'

'What are the odds the lights are going to be off?' asked Coleman. 'I'm thinking in terms of the night vision gear. If one's in the kitchen, he's not going to be in the dark, is he? Same with the guy at the front door. Why turn the lights off, especially when you're trying to stay awake all night?'

'Good point, Mustard,' said Shepherd. 'But it's a possibility so we need to train for that. Hopefully by the time we're done we'll be able to go through the apartment with our eyes closed. Anything else?' He was faced with shaking heads. 'Right, let's get started.'

Ricky Coleman led the way down the corridor, with Terry Ireland tucked in behind him, their shotguns up high. The bathroom door to their right was ajar. Coleman peered inside, then headed to the kitchen. There was a cut-out terrorist figure with a bullseye on its chest standing behind the makeshift island. Coleman pulled the trigger and the Taser hit the top of the bullseye. The Taser was designed to bite into flesh or clothing but it made no impression on the cardboard target and it fell to the floor.

'Hostile in kitchen neutralised,' said Coleman in the Major's ear. 'Returning to main room.'

The two men moved silently along the hall.

Sage was moving along the hallway that led to the front door. He shuffled to the left and trained his shotgun to the right, and as he moved a cut-out terrorist came into view and he pulled the trigger. The Taser went high and hit the target's throat before tumbling to the floor.

'Hostile at front door neutralised,' said Sage in the Major's ear, then he began moving back towards the main room.

As Sage, Ireland and Coleman got back to the main room,

Shepherd and Taylor moved down the corridor towards the bedrooms.

Sage, Ireland and Coleman followed them. Taylor opened the door to the first bedroom and went in, crouching to make himself a smaller target. 'Bedroom three clear,' he said over the radio.

Shepherd pointed for Sage to check the bathroom and then he opened the door to the remaining bedroom. He ducked inside and swung the barrel of the shotgun around. He saw a target standing at the far side of the room. He fired and hit the bullseye, just off the centre. 'Hostile down in bedroom four,' he said.

They went back along the hall and headed towards the master bedrooms. There was a door at the end of the hallway and it opened onto a lobby area. There were two doors leading off the lobby, left and right. Shepherd, Sage and Coleman went right, the other two went left. Shepherd seized one door handle, Ireland the other. They opened them at the same time and piled in.

There was a cardboard terrorist cut-out lying on the bed in the room that Shepherd had entered and he fired quickly, hitting the bullseye dead centre. 'Bedroom one, Tango down,' said Shepherd in the Major's ear.

There was no cut-out in the bed in the other room and the troopers fanned out. Ireland and Taylor moved into a dressing area beyond which was a door leading to a bathroom. Ireland opened the door and immediately stepped to the side to allow Taylor in. There was a terrorist cut-out in the corner and Taylor fired, hitting the centre of the bullseye.

'Bedroom two, Tango down,' said Taylor over the radio.

'End exercise,' said Shepherd. 'Well done, guys.'

The Major carefully climbed down the ladder at the side of the scaffolding tower and walked over to the mock-up. The five men were standing with their shotguns resting on their shoulders, looking pleased with themselves. 'I thought that went well,' said Shepherd. 'Best yet.'

'Do you, now?' said the Major. 'Come with me, my fine feathered friends. As in sitting ducks.' He led them down the corridor towards the kitchen and stopped at the door leading to the bath-room. He pushed open the door and motioned for them to go inside. They filed in and groaned when they saw the terrorist cut-out behind the door.

'Fuck,' said Coleman.

'Yeah, not everyone who uses the bathroom shuts the door,' said the Major. 'He'd have shot you in the back.'

'Sorry, boss,' said Coleman.

'To be fair, you said three targets, boss, not four,' said Taylor.

'Sure, and if there's an extra guy in the flat when you go in, I'm sure he'll play by the rules and not get involved.' He grinned. 'Anyway, we live and learn. That's what these exercises are for. Train hard and fight easy. Right, everyone outside and I'll replace the targets and we'll do it again.'

The loadmaster came over to Shepherd and handed him a cup of tea from a tray. There was no galley on the Hercules so Shepherd had no idea how the man had rustled up a brew but he took it gratefully. 'We'll be landing in twenty minutes,' he said. He was wearing green fatigues and had a strong West Country accent. He looked as if he was barely out of his teens.

Shepherd was in a bulkhead seat with a shoulder harness and seat belt that limited movement but meant that he could sleep sitting up. He'd napped most of the way to Istanbul where they had been given the opportunity to grab a bite to eat and to use the toilet. Toilet facilities on the Hercules consisted of a Portaloo behind a curtain and it was generally accepted that it was only to be used in emergencies.

Once the plane had taken off for the second leg of its twelve-hour flight, Shepherd had slept again, as had the rest of the team. Taylor and Sage were sitting to his left and Ireland and Coleman were opposite. They were all dozing and one by one the load-master woke them up and gave them tea.

They were all casually dressed in polo shirts and jeans and had baseball caps and were carrying sunglasses against the fierce Emirates sun. They were wearing jackets because Dubai could get chilly at night. The clothing was camouflage, they were trying to look like regular tourists.

Their equipment had been packed into three wheeled suitcases and three holdalls, secured to the floor by nylon straps. They were bringing everything they needed with them, including the shotguns and Taser ammunition, Kevlar vests, coveralls, ropes, night vision goggles and parachutes.

After the loadmaster collected their empty mugs, he told them to prepare for landing. Their ears popped as the Hercules descended, did a couple of gentle right turns and then the nose came up and the wheels hit the runway and there was a squeal of brakes. They taxied for several minutes and then the plane came to a halt.

The loadmaster unfastened the straps that were holding the cases and holdalls in place. Shepherd and the troopers undid their harnesses and stood up and stretched.

The rear ramp of the Hercules lowered with a grinding sound of metal against metal and bumped onto the tarmac. The five men grabbed the cases and holdalls, thanked the loadmaster, and headed down the metal ramp. Off to the left was a grey minibus with the logo of a tour company on the side and Arabic and English writing including a Dubai address and phone number.

The driver climbed out and stood waiting with his hands on his hips. He was in his early thirties, balding and wearing a denim shirt and jeans.

Shepherd walked down the ramp, pulling one of the wheeled suitcases with him. Ireland and Taylor followed with two more suitcases while Sage and Coleman dealt with the holdalls.

Shepherd headed over to the driver. 'Dan Shepherd?' said the man. He had a strong Geordie accent. Shepherd nodded and fist-bumped him. 'Chris Fallows,' he said. 'At your service.' He gestured at the van with his thumb. 'Your chariot awaits.' He opened the rear doors and helped Shepherd lift the suitcase in, then helped Ireland and Taylor load theirs.

'Who do you work for?' asked Shepherd.

'For the next day or two, that would be you,' said Fallows,

though Shepherd suspected it wasn't his real name. The fact that he wasn't upfront about who he worked for almost certainly meant he was with Six.

'And you're up to speed on what needs to be done?'

'The flat is ready and my colleague Adi is waiting for you there. I'm to get you into the flat and then collect you once the operation is complete and drive you and two passengers back here to RV with the plane.'

'Excellent.'

Sage and Coleman came down the ramp carrying three hold-alls between them, Fallows helped put them into the back of the van. 'I suggest you ride up front with me, while your colleagues sit in the back,' said Fallows. 'I'll show you what I think is a suitable drop zone on the way to the Burj Khalifa.'

Shepherd nodded. No matter who Fallows worked for, he seemed to have everything under control.

He sat in the passenger seat while the SAS troopers took the seats behind. They were at the General Aviation terminal and nobody came to check their passports or their luggage.

'You're classed as a military flight,' explained Fallows, as if reading his mind. 'You were pre-cleared with a military designation when you entered Dubai airspace.' He showed his ID at the exit but the guard barely glanced at it or the vehicle and just waved them through.

As they drove from the airport they could see the Burj Khalifa in the distance, cutting into the night sky like a knife. It was twice the height of the next tallest building in the city and Shepherd couldn't imagine why anyone would want to live so high above the ground.

'You've been inside?' Shepherd asked.

'Sure. Many times.'

'How long does the lift take, top to bottom?'

'The longest elevator in there runs 140 floors,' he said. 'Ten metres a second. It takes a full minute to get from the ground floor to the observation deck on the 124th floor. And it moves fast.'

As they drove along the main highway towards the tower, it seemed that every other car was a luxury limousine or a million-dollar supercar. There were Rolls-Royces, Bentleys, Lamborghinis and McLarens, and even the regular cars were gleaming and brand new.

After about fifteen minutes, Fallows turned off the expressway and pulled up next to a large grassy park area fringed by palm trees. 'This is Burj Park,' said Fallows. He climbed out and Shepherd and the troopers joined him. They craned their necks to look up at the tower, which from where they were standing seemed to stretch up into space. 'There shouldn't be anyone around in the early hours,' said Fallows. He pointed up at the tower. 'You jump and then turn right over the Dubai Fountain. The fountain is huge, it's nine hundred feet wide and the water goes up five hundred feet, but it'll be off that time of night. You head straight across the fountain and land in the park and I'll be waiting here.' He pointed at a line of stone cubes with marble tops, each about three feet high. 'You'll want to avoid those stones, obviously,' he said. 'You pile into the minibus and I'll drive straight to the airport.'

'What if we're unlucky and there are cops around?'

'I've arranged for two vehicles to ride shotgun. If we are followed, they'll provide a distraction. But the cops in Dubai tend to stay in their nice air-conditioned offices until they're needed.' He grinned. 'Only Emirati citizens can work as cops and most of them are pretty lazy, truth be told.'

'There's no problem with you waiting here?'

'It should be okay but I'd rather you send me a text or something just as you're about to leave.'

'Yeah, I can do that.'

'As soon as you text me I'll text the pilot and within twenty minutes of you landing in the park you should be back in the Hercules and heading to the UK. The plan is to drive this vehicle straight into the plane so that it can't be traced later.' He gave Shepherd a card with a Dubai mobile on it. Shepherd looked at it and handed it back. 'You can keep the card,' said Fallows.

'It's okay, my memory's good. So there'll be no problem with us driving into the airport?'

'No, we come and go a lot. We do a lot of training with the Emirati special forces and we provide bodyguards for several members of the Sheikh's family, here and in London. As you saw, my ID gets me in and out with no checks. The two extra passengers can be concealed in the back. I'm assuming they'll be unconscious?'

'That's the plan,' said Shepherd.

They all climbed back into the van and Fallows drove towards the Burj Khalifa. 'So, there's five of you, we need to get you all in without attracting attention, plus the gear, then get all the bags out because you don't want to leave anything behind,' said Fallows.

'Sure,' said Shepherd. 'We'll need to change into our gear in the flat and have our civilian clothes brought back to the plane. And we'll need blankets or something to keep the passengers warm.'

'I'll get that arranged,' said Fallows. 'Adi's there waiting for you in the flat, and we don't want more than two in the lift at the same time, so we've got a fox, goose and corn thing going on.'

'I guess so,' said Shepherd.

'I figure two of you go up first with suitcases and holdalls. You take out the stuff and put the holdalls in the cases and Adi will bring them to me. The cases go in the van and two more guys take the room card to operate the lift and they go up with more cases. Not long after, Adi can go back up with the last of your guys so then all five of you will be up there. And then Adi brings the last cases back to me. Does that make sense?'

'Perfect,' said Shepherd.

'There's a single CCTV camera in each lift so I'd suggest hats on and heads down. There are more cameras in the hallways but they're easy to spot. Also, I'd suggest you guys switch off your mobiles and leave them in the bus, along with anything of a personal nature.'

They drove along a double-decker road into the Dubai Mall,

and Fallows parked the van close to the Burj Khalifa entrance. Fallows handed Shepherd a keycard. 'That's for the lift,' he said. 'It will also open the door to the apartment but you'll also need a six-digit code which is the month and the year.'

Shepherd looked over his shoulder. 'Sagey, why don't you come up with me?'

As Shepherd and Sage climbed out of the minibus, Fallows pressed the button to open the rear door. Shepherd took out two of the suitcases and two of the holdalls. He and Sage took a case and a holdall each. They pulled on baseball caps and put on sunglasses, then headed towards the lift lobby.

There were two women in headscarves and long black robes with gold trim waiting for the lift. It arrived and they went in. The older of the two slotted in a keycard and pressed the button for the 83rd floor. Shepherd kept his head down as he used his keycard and pressed the button for the 101st floor.

The doors closed and the elevator shot up. It was so smooth that there was very little sensation of movement, and in less than a minute the women were getting off on their floor.

'I don't understand that fox and goose crack,' said Sage as the lift headed upwards again.

'You've never heard of it? It's a logic problem. You have a farmer who wants to cross a river with a fox, a goose, and some corn.'

'Why?'

'What do you mean, why?'

'Why's he got a fox? Is it a pet?'

'It's in the problem because the fox will kill the goose if it gets the chance. So the farmer has a boat, and the boat can only take one thing at a time across the river. How does he do it?'

'Are you serious? He takes the fox over. Then the goose. Then the corn.'

'Yeah, but while he's in the boat with the fox, the goose will eat the corn.'

'Okay, so take the goose over.'

'Then what?'

'Then come back for the fox.'

'Yeah, but if he leaves the fox with the goose, it'll kill it.

'So take the corn over.'

'But when he leaves the corn with the goose, the goose will eat it.'

Sage sighed. 'Kill the goose, then. It's going to get eaten anyway, right? In fact kill the fox while you're at it. They're vermin. Job done.'

Shepherd grinned. 'Yes, Sagey, job done.'

They arrived at the 101st floor and the doors hissed open. Shepherd and Sage kept their heads down as they walked out of the lift and along the corridor to their flat. Shepherd used the keycard and pin number and pushed the door open. They carried the cases and holdalls into a narrow hallway, one wall of which was mirrored. There was a gleaming marble-and-steel kitchen to the left and the corridor opened into a wall of glass with a heart-stopping view beyond it. They were looking down on dozens of skyscrapers and beyond was the desert, a pool of darkness with a blanket of stars above it. They were so shocked by the view that they didn't see the Asian man standing in the bedroom doorway. It was only when he cleared his throat that they realised he was there. He was in twenties, wearing overalls and a peaked cap. There was the logo of a courier company on his breast pocket. He smiled over at Shepherd and Sage. 'Hi, I'm Adi. I'm with Chris. Let me help you with those.'

'That's okay, we can manage,' said Shepherd. 'We'll dump the gear in the bedroom and then Chris says you'll take the bags down.'

'It's a chicken and egg thing,' said Sage.

Adi frowned. 'I'm sorry, what?'

'Ignore him, Adi,' said Shepherd. He and Sage took the bags through to the bedroom. The view from the floor-to-ceiling windows was just as impressive. 'How high up are we?' asked Sage, walking up to the glass and peering down.

'A hundred and one storeys, so about one thousand eight hundred feet. The top is two thousand seven hundred feet high.'

'What do you do if the lifts don't work?'

'I guess they make sure they always work,' said Shepherd. There were three shotguns in one suitcase and two in the other. Shepherd took them out and placed them on the carpet, along with the boxes of Taser cartridges. Sage unpacked the holdalls, removing Kevlar vests, black overalls and slings for the shotguns, which he laid out on the bed. There were two coils of climbing rope in one of the holdalls and he put them on the floor by the window.

Once all the gear had been unpacked, they rolled up the hold-alls and put them in the suitcases, then wheeled them out to the sitting room. 'There you go, Adi,' said Shepherd.

Sage opened the front door to let Adi out. Shepherd sat on a sofa and switched on the TV.

An hour after Shepherd had entered the apartment, the four SAS troopers and the equipment were all in place, and Adi had left with the last of the cases. They had stripped off their civilian clothes and changed into the black coveralls and Kevlar vests, and wore black Kevlar gloves so as not to leave fingerprints. All their civilian clothing had been taken out in one of the suitcases.

They spent half an hour setting up and testing their comms and checking all their equipment, paying special attention to the parachutes, then settled down in the sitting room to watch football until it was time to go. There was little banter, each man was mentally rehearsing what he needed to do.

Time seemed to drag for Shepherd. Waiting was always the hardest part of any operation. Once they were moving the training and the adrenaline kicked in, but prior to that there was nothing to do other than sit and pretend to be interested in twenty-two multi-millionaires kicking a ball around.

Eventually it was time. 'Right guys, rock and roll,' said Shepherd. He pushed himself off the sofa and led the men into the bedroom.

Taylor and Ireland took a coil of rope each. They had identified pipes in the bathroom that could be used as attachment points and they went to secure the ropes.

Shepherd pulled the duvet off the bed.

'Grab the sledgehammer, Sagey.'

Sage grinned. 'Tom Cruise wouldn't let us borrow his laser, then?'

Shepherd ignored the joke and took the duvet and sledge-hammer over to the window. The windows in the Burj Khalifa were made of heat-strengthened and laminated glass. Unlike tempered glass, which would break into countless small cubes, laminated glass tended to crack but remain in one piece, held together by the plastic layer that was baked in the middle.

Coleman and Sage held the duvet up against the window. Shepherd swung the sledgehammer against the duvet and heard a satisfying thump. He swung it a second time, putting more of his weight behind it, and the head of the hammer buried itself into the glass.

He hit the glass hard in all four corners of the panel, then walloped it twice in the middle using all his strength. Then he stood back and Coleman and Sage dropped the duvet. The glass had buckled and cracked and had come away from the frame at several points. 'Right, guys, brute strength is what we need now,' said Shepherd.

Taylor and Ireland came into the room, paying out the ropes. They dropped them onto the floor and hurried over to help. Between them they managed to pry the broken panel out and move it to the side. The cool night wind immediately tugged at their clothes and hair. The men grunted as they dragged the buckled pane along the carpet and then rested it against the wall.

'Right, kill the lights,' said Shepherd.

Taylor flicked the switches to plunge the room into darkness, then he moved to the gap in the window and knelt down. He took a small mirror from a pocket on his coveralls and he held it in the palm of his right hand and moved it through the gap, using it to check that there was no one on the terrace. Then he put his hand out further to check the apartment underneath them. The lights were off. He nodded. 'All clear.'

They moved away from the window and put on their night vision goggles and parachutes, checked their comms again, and then slung their shotguns over their shoulders. Coleman and Ireland each had an extra harness attached to the front of their own.

Taylor clipped a waist pack over his stomach. It contained two hypodermics loaded with the sedative he would be using. He grinned at Shepherd. 'Hot to trot,' he said.

Taylor and Coleman moved the ropes over to the gap in the glass wall. Taylor clipped himself to one of the ropes, threw Shepherd a mock salute, and lowered himself down.

Shepherd went down on all fours and peered out. He watched Taylor lower himself smoothly to the metal cabana and unclip himself.

'Okay, Mustard, down you go,' said Shepherd.

Coleman clipped himself to the second rope and lowered himself down. He joined Taylor on the roof of the cabana. Taylor lay down and used his mirror to check the terrace and the room beyond it. 'The lights are off and I don't see anyone inside,' said Taylor over the radio. There were a few seconds of silence and then he spoke again. 'The sliding doors are open. We're good to go.'

Shepherd went down next, followed by Sage and Ireland.

Taylor did a final check with his mirror and then put it away.

Shepherd lowered himself down from the cabana. There were several sofas and chairs and a coffee table and he bent down to use one of the chairs as cover as he swung his shotgun around.

The SAS troopers climbed down one by one and then Shepherd led them to the gap in the sliding doors. He pulled the door open further and stepped aside to let Coleman and Ireland go first.

There were lights on in the hallway so the two men flicked up their night vision goggles and moved silently, guns at the ready, heading for the kitchen. Sage followed and immediately moved towards the front door. Taylor and Shepherd waited in the sitting room, their guns aimed towards the bedrooms.

The seconds crawled by and then they heard a pop from the

kitchen. 'Hostile in kitchen neutralised,' said Coleman. 'Returning to main room.'

Almost immediately they heard another pop from the front door lobby. 'Hostile down, front lobby,' said Sage.

Shepherd looked at Taylor and nodded. Two down, one to go. Suddenly he heard a noise ahead of him and the door to the bedrooms opened. The light was on behind the door and immediately Shepherd's night vision goggles overloaded and went bright green. He reached to flick up his goggles but before he could, there was a pop to his left.

By the time Shepherd got his goggles up, the bodyguard who had opened the door was on his back, a Taser round embedded in his chest. 'Hostile in bedroom area is down,' said Taylor over the radio.

'Nice shot, Mutton,' said Shepherd.

Taylor went over to the stunned bodyguard, retrieved his round and zip-tied and gagged the man.

Coleman and Ireland returned to the room. Sage arrived a few seconds later. He had also flipped up his goggles.

They had neutralised three bodyguards but as the Major had drummed into them back in Credenhill, there could easily be more so they continued with the protocol that they had rehearsed. Shepherd and Taylor moved down the corridor towards the bedrooms. Sage, Ireland and Coleman followed.

Taylor cleared the first bedroom, the one they had labelled bedroom three, Sage checked the bathroom, and Shepherd checked bedroom number four. Once they were satisfied, they went back along the hall and headed towards the master bedrooms. Shepherd opened the door at the end of the hallway and they all tiptoed into the lobby area. Shepherd, Taylor and Coleman went right, Sage and Ireland went left.

Shepherd reached the first master bedroom with Taylor and Coleman close behind him. He turned the handle and eased the door open. He listened and smiled grimly when he heard slow steady breathing. He didn't know who was in the room, but whoever it was they were sleeping soundly.

He held the shotgun with both hands and moved forward on tip-toe. Taylor and Coleman followed him. The room was in darkness and he flicked down his night vision goggles. The figure on the bed was Mrs Rashid, lying on her back, covered by a sheet, her chest slowly rising and falling. Shepherd aimed and pulled the trigger. The Taser hit her just above the stomach and she went into spasm.

Taylor and Coleman moved either side of Shepherd. Coleman slid open the sliding doors to the dressing area and went to check the bathroom. Shepherd pocketed the discharged Taser round and pulled the sheet away from the woman. She was wearing a pale lace nightdress that had ridden up over her thighs. 'Okay, Mutton, she's all yours,' he said.

Taylor let his shotgun hang on its sling and he rolled the woman over on to her stomach.

Coleman came back from the bathroom. 'As soon as she's out for the count, get her in the harness,' said Shepherd.

Coleman nodded. Taylor unzipped his black nylon waist pack. He took out a clear plastic box containing a hypodermic syringe. He removed a small plastic cap from the needle, sat down on the bed and inserted the needle into the woman's backside. He emptied the contents and slipped the needle out. Mrs Rashid continued to breathe deeply and slowly, then her breathing became shallower.

'Bedroom two, we have a problem here,' said Sage in Shepherd's ear.

'Get her in the harness and out on the terrace,' Shepherd said to Coleman, then he hurried out of the room. Taylor put the used hypodermic in his waist pack and zipped it closed.

Shepherd reached the other bedroom and saw Ireland in the doorway. The light was on so Shepherd flicked up his night vision goggles. Ireland stepped to the side and Shepherd went into the room, his shotgun at his shoulder. Sage was standing in the middle of the bedroom, facing sliding doors that led to the dressing area and the bathroom beyond. Rashid was in the dressing area, wearing blue Ralph Lauren pyjamas, pointing a gun at Sage. It was a Glock 43, often referred to as the Baby Glock, because it was so small. The magazine held just six 9mm rounds so it was mainly a weapon to be concealed in a pocket or a purse and wouldn't be much use in a fire fight. But it was a good enough weapon to shoot grown men who were crowded into a bedroom.

Rashid was half-hidden by the sliding door. If Sage's shotgun had regular ammunition he would have been able to fire through the flimsy door, but the Taser round would simply bounce off. Rashid thought they were in a stand-off but in fact he was the only one with real ammunition in his gun.

Shepherd moved slowly across the room to get a better view of Rashid behind the sliding door. Rashid's eyes widened when he saw Shepherd. 'I should have known they'd send you,' said Rashid. 'Only the best, huh?'

'You need to put the gun down, Joey,' said Shepherd.

'And why would I do that? So that you can splatter my brains across the wall?'

Shepherd shook his head. 'I need you to watch me very carefully, Joey. I'm not going to pull the trigger. But I need to show you something.' He slowly turned the shotgun to the side and ejected a Taser cartridge onto the bed.

Rashid looked at it but kept his gun pointed at Shepherd.

'It's a Taser round. It's non-lethal.'

Rashid frowned. 'You want to Taser me?'

'To incapacitate you and take you back to the UK.'

'To put me on trial?'

'Well I don't think they're planning on giving you a medal, not after the number of people you killed.'

'So why take me back?'

'It's called justice, Joey.'

Rashid sneered at him. 'I know all about justice, Dan. That's why I did what I did.'

'You killed dozens of civilians. Innocent men and women. How is that justice?'

'Your country killed my father. Ruined my life. Ruined my

mother's life. The Brits and the Americans invaded my country and destroyed it. And then Melissa Schofield destroyed my father.'

'Then come back to the UK and tell your story.'

He shook his head. 'No one will listen. No one will care. But they do care about the bombs. They'll never forget the bombs.'

'So you wanted revenge? That's not the same as justice, Joey. Come on, put the gun down.'

Rashid gestured with the gun at the desk by the window. 'There's a letter in there that my father wrote to me. You should read it. The people you work for . . . you should be ashamed of yourselves.'

Sage shuffled to his right, the shotgun aimed at Rashid's chest.

'Stop moving!' shouted Rashid, pointing his gun at Sage. More of Rashid's body was visible now.

'Joey, I'm running the show here,' said Shepherd. 'Don't look at him, look at me.'

Shepherd heard the brush of a foot on carpet behind him and knew that Ireland was moving across the room. Ireland moved to the left, coming into Shepherd's peripheral view.

Rashid pointed the gun at Ireland.

'At me, Joey, at me,' said Shepherd.

Rashid's eyes were wide and he was panting as adrenaline coursed through his system. He had moved slightly while he had been talking and Shepherd could see a good portion of his chest. Rashid was holding the gun one-handed and his arm was shaking. Shepherd knew there was every chance that if he pulled the trigger the recoil would send the round up into the ceiling. Handguns were unreliable at the best of times, even when held with both hands in a stable stance, but with three targets in front of him, even a wild shot could do some damage. Rashid pointed the gun at Shepherd. 'Just let me go,' he said, his voice shaking.

'That's not going to happen,' said Shepherd.

'I will shoot you,' said Rashid.

'And the moment you do, my friends here will both pull the trigger and you'll go down.'

'But I won't be dead.'

'Don't bank on that,' said Taylor who had come up behind Shepherd. 'If you shoot Spider, you're going over the side, Taser or no Taser.'

Rashid's arm was trembling. Even a relatively small handgun like the Glock 43 weighed a pound and a half, and Rashid had been holding it at arm's length for a minute or more. At some point Rashid was going to realise that his right arm was tiring and then he would either bring up his other hand for support or transfer the gun to his left hand. Either way, for a second or two, the gun would be out of play. Shepherd took a quick look to his right. Sage was sighting his gun at Rashid's chest, his finger tight on the trigger. Instinctively Shepherd knew that Sage was also waiting for the transfer.

'No one's going to shoot anybody,' said Shepherd. 'Rashid is tired, I'm tired, we're all tired. Let's just lower our guns and no one need get hurt.'

'I'm not fucking stupid!' shouted Rashid. He brought his left hand up to support his right hand and as he did the gun wavered. Shepherd heard two loud pops, to his left and to his right, followed by the bang of the Glock going off. The two Taser rounds had hit Rashid in the chest simultaneously and the resulting seizure had tightened his finger on the trigger and discharged the weapon. Shepherd felt as if he had been punched in the chest and he took a step back, gasping. Rashid dropped like a rag doll, his head banging against the wall as he hit the floor.

The strength had gone from Shepherd's arms and he let the shotgun fall to his side on its sling as he gasped for breath.

'Are you okay, Spider?' asked Ireland.

'Of course he's okay, how much damage is a Baby Glock going to do to a ballistic vest?' said Taylor. He patted Shepherd's chest. 'Big breaths, Spider. Big breaths.'

Shepherd continued to breathe in and out. The vest had stopped the bullet doing any serious damage but at close range the tiny gun still packed a powerful punch and it felt as if a horse had kicked him in the chest. He loosened his vest and the bullet fell to the floor. He bent down and picked it up, wincing at the pain.

Ireland pulled the sliding door wide open and went over to Rashid and pulled the two Taser rounds from the man's pyjama jacket and put them in his pocket.

'Help me move him,' said Shepherd. They picked him up and laid him face down on the bed. Taylor unzipped the waist bag and took out a second syringe. He uncapped it, sat down next to the unconscious Rashid and injected the full hypodermic into Rashid's backside. It took him almost thirty seconds to empty the syringe, after which he stood up, recapped the needle and put the used syringe back in his waist pack.

'Okay, Paddy,' said Shepherd. 'Get him in the harness.'

Shepherd picked up Rashid's gun and stuck it into a pocket on his coveralls, then went over to the desk and opened it. There was a copy of the Koran and a notepad and two pens, and a cream-coloured envelope with 'Yousef' written on it in cursive writing. Shepherd shoved the envelope into the pocket of his ballistic vest, then headed to the terrace.

'Spider, we've got a problem here,' said Coleman over the radio. 'I think she's dead.'

Shepherd cursed and hurried back to the first master bedroom, where Mrs Rashid was still on the bed. Coleman was standing over her. 'She just stopped breathing,' said Coleman. 'She had a spasm and then went still.'

'Mutton, get in here,' said Shepherd over the radio.

There was no reply from Taylor.

'Mutton, we need you here.'

When there was still no answer, Shepherd hurried back to the other room. Ireland was standing looking down at Rashid, whose whole body was trembling. Taylor was standing by the window, his arms folded. As they watched, Rashid suddenly stiffened and then went still.

Shepherd stared at Taylor in horror. 'Mutton, what have you done?'

Taylor shrugged. 'There's been a change of plan, Spider.'

'What do you mean there's been a change of plan? What's going on?'

'There's no time for a debrief,' said Taylor. 'We need to get out of here.' He pushed by Shepherd and headed out to the terrace.

'Everybody out,' said Shepherd over the radio. 'This operation is over.'

Shepherd hurried to the sliding doors. Taylor was already on the terrace. He pulled over a chair and stood it next to the barrier. In one smooth movement he got up onto the chair, stepped onto the stainless-steel bar above the glass barrier and launched himself into the air.

As Coleman, Sage and Ireland hurried out on to the terrace, Shepherd took out his mobile phone and sent Fallows a message. ON WAY. He waved for the men to jump.

Ireland got onto the chair. He put one foot on the stainless-steel bar, held his right hand holding the ripcord to the side, and jumped. His arms and legs were out in a starfish pattern and within a couple of seconds they heard the rustle of his chute opening.

Coleman was next, followed quickly by Sage.

Shepherd looked over the glass barrier. The four black ram-air canopies were all open. Shepherd stood on the chair, tightened his shotgun sling so that the weapon wouldn't flail around during the descent, took a final look over his shoulder at the apartment, and jumped.

He adopted the starfish position and arched his back to stay stable as he fell away from the building. He counted two and then pulled the ripcord. The chute burst into life, flapped above his head, and then snapped into shape. The nylon shoulder straps bit into his arms as his descent slowed, and he grabbed for the risers so that he had directional control.

He looked down and saw Taylor over the fountain, making his turn towards the park.

Ireland made his turn. Shepherd was moving to the right so he tugged on his left riser until he was going straight again.

Coleman made his turn. Taylor was already over the park, coming in to land.

There was little traffic around and the black coveralls and black chutes would be hard to pick out against the night sky.

Sage made his turn.

Shepherd pulled down on his left riser to keep going straight. He looked down to the right. Taylor had landed and was gathering up his chute. He had landed about a hundred metres from the minibus.

Ireland timed his flare so that he came to a halt in the air and simply stepped onto the ground. Shepherd smiled to himself. 'Flash,' he said.

Coleman landed on the run, then came to a halt and wound the chute around his arms before jogging towards the minibus.

Shepherd looked down between his legs at the giant pool that housed the Dubai fountain. He pulled hard on the right riser and the chute responded immediately, turning him to the right.

He followed Sage who was a hundred metres or so ahead of him.

Taylor and Ireland had reached the minibus and were climbing in. Coleman was running with his chute in his arms.

Sage hit the grass, took two quick steps and then stumbled. He fell and the chute dragged him along the ground before he pulled hard on one of the risers to deflate the canopy. He stood up, grabbed his chute in both arms and ran towards the others.

Shepherd had to concentrate on his own landing. The last few metres rushed towards him and as he pulled hard on both risers, his legs swung up and his forward momentum all but vanished. He flexed his knees to absorb the impact but his timing had been so good that it was like stepping off a chair. The chute began to collapse around him and he pulled it in and held it to his chest as he started running.

Sage was in the minibus now.

Adi was holding the side door open. Shepherd sprinted over and climbed in and sat next to Taylor. Fallows twisted around in the driving seat. 'What happened to the passengers?'

Shepherd glared at Taylor. 'Apparently there's been a change of plan,' he said. 'Let's just get on the plane.'

Adi slammed the side door and climbed into the front passenger seat. Fallows accelerated away as Shepherd stuffed the parachute under his seat.

Fallows drove at just below the speed limit. Shepherd checked the side mirrors and then looked over his shoulder. 'There's a white SUV that looks as if it's following us,' he said.

'They're with us,' said Fallows. 'They'll run interference if there's a problem but everything is looking good and I don't think they'll be needed.'

As Shepherd and the SAS team removed their comms gear, Fallows drove through the gleaming glass-and-steel tower blocks of the financial centre, and then the road curved to the east and they drove over Dubai Creek.

Fallows drove to the General Aviation terminal and the minibus was waved through the gate by a bored uniformed guard who barely glanced at his ID card or the occupants of the vehicle.

The propellers of the Hercules were already turning. The rear ramp was down and Fallows drove the minibus straight up it and into the belly of the plane. The moment he stopped, the load-master began securing it with thick straps and placed heavy wooden boots around the wheels. 'We'll leave you here, guys,' said Fallows, switching off the engine. 'It's been a pleasure doing business with you.'

He and Adi climbed out of the minibus and walked quickly down the ramp. As soon as they reached the tarmac, the ramp began to rise. It clicked into place and almost immediately the plane began to taxi.

Shepherd and the troopers slipped out of their parachute harnesses, took off their shotguns and sat down on the bulkhead seats. By the time they had all fastened themselves in, the Hercules was at the end of the runway awaiting clearance to take off. The engines roared, the massive plane began to roll down the runway, and then it was in the air and they were climbing through the night sky.

Shepherd waited until they were at their cruising altitude and the SAS team were stretched out trying to sleep before crossing the fuselage and sitting next to Taylor. Taylor had avoided eye contact with Shepherd from the moment they had climbed out of the van and had sat as far away from Shepherd as he could.

Taylor's eyes were closed and he was breathing heavily but Shepherd was pretty sure that he was only pretending to sleep. He gripped the man's knee and squeezed. Taylor grunted and opened his eyes. 'What's going on?' Shepherd hissed.

Taylor sighed. 'Like I said, there was a change of plan.'

'Without the Major's knowledge?'

'The order came from way above him.'

'From who exactly?' Taylor averted his gaze and Shepherd gripped his knee again. 'You'll go to prison for this,' he said. 'You murdered two people back there.'

Taylor shook his head. 'I executed two terrorists who had killed dozens of civilians. They deserved it. And it's not the first time I've been on search and kill missions. The Regiment does it all the time.'

'We were supposed to bring them back to be questioned. And put on trial.'

'Like I keep saying, the plan changed.'

'And you thought it acceptable not to tell me or the Major?'

'It was a need-to-know mission.'

'And I didn't need to know?'

'I was told to tell no one.'

'Told by who?'

Taylor sighed. 'Just let it go, Spider. It was sanctioned at the highest level. No one is going to get into trouble for this.'

'Who sanctioned it?'

'It came from the top, that's all I know.'

'The top? What does that even mean? Who gave you the job? Who told you to kill the Rashids?'

'You wouldn't know her.'

'Her? Who?'

Taylor turned to look at him. 'You know I'm leaving the Regiment, right?'

'Yeah, you said.'

'And one of my options was the Pool. I applied a while back and they said they'd keep my name on file. Then they got back to me with this job. To take out the Rashids.'

'What was in the syringes?'

'Plain old potassium chloride. Inject enough of it and you induce a fatal heart attack. Leaves no traces afterwards.'

'You said "her" before. This woman worked for the Pool?'

Taylor nodded.

'Charlotte Button?' said Shepherd.

Taylor's mouth opened in surprise. 'You know her?'

'She used to work for MI5,' said Shepherd. He leaned closer to him. 'Mutton, you have to be careful dealing with her. She's dangerous.'

'She was fine with me.'

'You don't know what you've got yourself into, mate.'

'A better-paying job for a start. She promised me twenty-five grand for this and more to come once I've left the Regiment. First thing I'm doing when I get back to Stirling Lines is to hand in my papers.'

'Well, I hope you have a contract in writing.'

'I do.'

'And did she put down in writing what your job here was and that it was officially sanctioned?'

Taylor shook his head. 'I didn't think of that.'

'She wouldn't have done it, anyway. Seriously, Mutton, you're playing with fire.'

'I'm a big boy, Spider. I know what I'm doing.'

Shepherd patted him on the knee. 'I hope that's true, for your sake,' he said.

He stood up and went back to his seat before taking the envelope from his pocket. He opened it and slid out the letter. The paper was of very good quality, it was thick and slightly rough and had a watermark, probably handmade. There were four sheets and the letter was handwritten in near perfect copperplate. Shepherd had expected it to be written in Arabic, but the first paragraph explained why it was in English.

My dear Yousef, my son, my life. My dear wife would never forgive me if I wrote to you in anything but English, because she wants you to be the perfect English gentleman, I know. I have spent my whole life trying to please her, and that will not change now. I have a problem, my dear son, and there is only one solution. By the time you read this, you will know what that solution is. Do not be sad, do not grieve too much, and support your mother. I have had a good life and I have no regrets, other than that I have no choice except to end it now.

Ireland snorted and grunted and Shepherd looked over but the trooper was only shifting in his sleep. He turned back to the letter.

I have rarely spoken to you about my job, mainly because finance is boring and there were always so much more interesting things to talk about. Books, movies, sport. I always enjoyed talking to you. Perhaps I should have talked to you about my work. But it's too late now. In the course of making a lot of people very rich, I also helped people who were fighting the good fight. People who were standing up to the oppression of Muslims. I moved money around for them, and sometimes I carried out transactions for them. If I had been helping fund the Westerners who invaded Iraq and Afghanistan and who brought about carnage in Libya and Syria, then I would have been hailed as a hero. But by supporting those who fought for the rights of Islamic people, for that I was branded a villain.

Shepherd smiled to himself. He'd never met anyone who had openly admitted to being evil. But Islamic State was truly an evil organisation and anyone who served it or funded it couldn't help but be tainted with its brutality and depravity. Its fighters raped their captives, burnt hostages alive, threw gays off rooftops and hacked the heads off journalists with blunt knives while chanting glory to their God. Rashid didn't like being labelled the villain, but what else was he? Shepherd turned to the next page.

My problem started almost three years ago, when I met a woman at a function at the British Embassy in Berlin. She spoke very good Arabic and said her name was Jennifer and that she worked for the Trade Department, specialising in Middle East trade. That turned out to be a lie. Her name was Melissa Schofield and she worked for MI6. The British Secret Intelligence Service. They run spies. They are like the American CIA, and they are every bit as evil.

Shepherd put the letter down. Melissa Schofield had met Rashid three years before he died? That's not what he had been told. Pritchard had said that she met him the day he committed suicide, to tell him that the Americans wanted to arrest him, and offering him the chance to work with MI6. Had that been a lie? He picked up the letter again.

This woman told me that she had evidence that I had been laundering money for Islamic State. But she said I wouldn't be in trouble if I gave her information about my clients. To my shame I did as she asked. For almost three years I met with her every few weeks and showed her my files. She made it clear that if I didn't help her I would be arrested and sent to prison.

Shepherd's frown deepened. So Ali Aziz Rashid had been an MI6 agent? And Melissa Schofield had been his handler? Why hadn't Pritchard told him? Or was Pritchard also in the dark?

Everything changed today, my son. Everything. Melissa Schofield came to see me. Now the Americans know what I have been doing and they hate me for it. The Americans hate all Muslims. They invaded Iraq. They invaded Afghanistan. They killed Gaddafi to get their hands on Libyan oil. They are the devil. And now the devil is looking at me. The MI6 woman told me that the Americans wanted to take me to Guantanamo Bay to torture me, and then to put me in a Supermax prison. She said they would never forgive me for helping Islamic State. There

*would be no deal, no compromise. Just prison. And if I appeared
in an American court, they would learn about the deal I had
done with MI6. Once Islamic State found out that I had betrayed
them, they would wreak a terrible revenge on my family. On
you, my dear son, and on my beloved wife.*

Shepherd turned to the next page.

*She offered me a choice. If I agreed to help her, if I agreed to
work with her against Islamic State, then she would keep the
Americans at bay. But it was no choice. She wanted me to give
evidence against Islamic State, to stand up in court and explain
what I did for them. If I did that, my dear son, I would be signing
my death warrant. And yours. And my wife's. I told the MI6 woman
that, but she insisted. She only cared about attacking Islamic State,
she cared nothing about me or my family. The warmongers have a
phrase for it. Collateral damage. That's what she thought of us.*

Shepherd shook his head, unable to believe what he was
reading, but knowing that Ali Aziz Rashid had no reason to lie
to his son. The letter was a deathbed confession, and every word
was almost certainly true.

*So this is where I now stand. If I go with the Americans, I die
in prison and my family is killed by Islamic State. If I go with
the British woman, we will all be killed. The British cannot protect
us. There will be fatwahs against all of us and that will only end
one way. So I have only one choice. I will remove myself from the
equation. If I am not here, there is no court case. I will have proved
to Islamic State that I would die to protect their secrets. They will
respect that and they will leave my family alone. So please do not
worry, my son. This is my choice. It is what I want to do.*

Shepherd read through the final page of the letter. It detailed
what Rashid was doing with his money and his property, with
details of bank accounts and safety deposit boxes around the

world. The last words were 'love you forever, take care of your mother' and a scrawled signature.

Shepherd refolded the four pages and put them back in the envelope. He sat staring ahead of him as he tried to process the contents of the letter. Ali Aziz Rashid had been an MI6 agent, and he had killed himself because Melissa Schofield had effectively betrayed him. Shepherd had handled agents before and while they often had to be used, they always had to be protected. So Joey Rashid, and presumably his mother, knew who had been responsible for the death of his father. They would have wanted revenge, against the woman who had betrayed him and the country that she served. From the moment they had received the letters, Joey Rashid and his mother had begun to plan their revenge. A plan that had ended with the deaths of dozens of civilians in Trafalgar Square and the murder of the head of MI6 and her colleagues. He put the letter back into his pocket and stretched out his legs. It was going to be a long flight and he hoped to sleep through as much of it as possible.

The Hercules landed at RAF Northolt, ten kilometres north of Heathrow Airport, at just after one o'clock in the afternoon. Shepherd and the troopers had changed out of their coveralls and boots and were wearing their casual clothing, and they had repacked their weapons and equipment into the suitcases and holdalls.

The plane taxied to the hangars and the pilot cut the engines. The ramp came down and the men blinked as the sunlight flooded into the fuselage. Shepherd walked down the ramp, stretching his arms and rotating his neck. Flying Cargo Class in a Hercules was never a relaxing experience.

A black Lexus was waiting by the hangars with a grey-suited driver standing with his arms folded. As Shepherd walked off the ramp, the driver came over. 'Dan Shepherd?' he called.

Shepherd raised his hand. 'That's me.'

'I'm Dan Shepherd!' said Ireland, raising his hand.

'I'm Dan Shepherd!' said Coleman as he came down the ramp.

'I'm Spartacus!' said Sage.

Shepherd couldn't help but grin. 'Give it a rest, guys,' he said. He nodded at the driver. 'You're here for me.'

'I'm to take you to Thames House, sir,' he said.

'Bloody VIP,' said Taylor. 'How do we get back to Hereford?'

Shepherd pointed to a battered Army minibus on the other side of the Hercules. 'I'm guessing that's your ride.' He fist-bumped the four SAS troopers and promised to take them out for a drink next time he was at Credenhill.

'Hopefully I'll be gone by then,' said Taylor.

'Yeah, good luck with that,' said Shepherd.

'No hard feelings?'

'The jury's still out on that, Mutton.' Shepherd climbed into the back of the Lexus. The traffic was light and forty-five minutes later Shepherd was heading into Thames House. He went straight up to Pritchard's office and his secretary waved him through.

Pritchard was at his desk. He smiled when Shepherd walked in. He looked a lot more relaxed than the last time Shepherd had seen him but there was a wariness in his eyes. 'Take a seat, Dan,' he said, waving for him to sit on one of the two chairs facing his desk, which meant it wasn't going be a long meeting. 'I know this turned into the mother of all screw-ups but there is some good news.'

Shepherd sat. He'd had a brief chat with Pritchard on the way to London but had covered only the bare essentials. Pritchard had been as surprised as Shepherd at what had happened in Dubai and said that any further conversation needed to be face-to-face.

'So I've spoken to our Emirates people and according to them the Dubai cops don't know what to make of it,' said Pritchard. He forced a smile. 'We had a stroke of luck with the Russian bodyguards. When they came to and untied themselves, they figured that the best thing to do would be to get to the airport and on the first flight out. The Dubai justice system tends not to treat foreigners kindly and they'd almost certainly be kept behind bars until they'd proved they weren't involved with the perpetrators. Anyway, the fact that they ran most certainly does make them suspects. They've held preliminary autopsies and the cause of death of mother and son is showing as cardiac arrest. The thing about potassium chloride of course is that hours after the death the levels are no longer elevated. They might well suspect the deaths weren't natural but there's no proof. The method of entry is going to have them scratching their heads, but as things stand there's no way they could suspect any UK involvement.

'In fact if they do start digging, they'll see the Israeli connection and suspect Mossad.'

Pritchard grinned. 'Ah, you heard about that?'

'The muddier the water, the better.'

'Mossad are big boys, they'll tough it out,' said Pritchard. 'And we do owe them one. But at the moment we're in the clear. No thanks to Charlotte Bloody Button.'

'How could she commission the assassination of the Rashids without you knowing?'

'Because she's a devious little minx, that's why. Authorisation for the killings came from the PM's office, non-attributable of course. But Number Ten gave the green light.'

'But the PM wanted rendition. That was the last we heard.'

'Which means something or someone changed his mind,' said Pritchard. 'And I'm guessing that was Penniston-Hill. He obviously decided that a trial would be the death knell for MI6 so figured attack was the best form of defence. He and the PM go back a long way. I think they were at the same Oxford college, but at different times. Anyway, the PM gave the go-ahead and Penniston-Hill briefed Button.'

'The guy who did the dirty deed has been promised a job with the Pool. And twenty-five grand.'

'They got their money's worth,' said Pritchard. 'Anyway, the bombings can be tied up with no mention of the Rashids or the rings they ran around MI6. And we all live to fight another day.'

'And how are you with Penniston-Hill after this? He lied to you and went behind your back.'

Pritchard shrugged. 'I'm not happy, obviously. But if I had been in his position, who knows . . .'

Shepherd reached inside his jacket and took out the envelope he'd taken from Rashid's desk. He dropped it in front of Pritchard. 'Joey Rashid thought I should read this.'

'What?'

'Before he died, he said I should read this. It's the letter his father wrote to him before he killed himself.'

Pritchard picked it up gingerly. 'You've read it, obviously.'

'Obviously.'

'And with your eidetic memory, you'll never forget, will you?'

'No.'

'Do you think I should read it?'

'That depends.'

'On what?'

'I guess on what you would do with the information it contains. You'd never look at Melissa Schofield the same way again.'

'Rashid mentioned her in the letter?'

'Her and MI6. Mentioned at length.'

'And that information would be damaging to the agency?'

'If it was true, yes.'

Pritchard tapped the letter against his hand. 'And who else has seen it?'

'Joey Rashid, obviously. And I assume his mother got a similar letter. Rashid senior left a letter for Melissa Schofield but she never showed anyone hers.'

Pritchard placed the letter on his desk and rubbed his chin. 'What's done is done, right?'

'Turning back time isn't an option,' said Shepherd. 'Last time I looked, anyway.'

'So knowing what's in that letter can't change anything, can it?'

'Not for the Rashids, certainly. Or for all the people who died and were injured in Trafalgar Square. Or for Melissa Schofield and the others who died in the Hampstead house. But that letter would certainly damage MI6's reputation.'

Pritchard shrugged. 'There'll be an official inquiry into what happened at Trafalgar Square, obviously. Mistakes were made, lessons will be learned, etcetera etcetera.' He picked up the letter again. 'Would that inquiry be helped by a letter written by a suicidal ISIS financier? I think on balance, probably not.' He looked over at his shredder and wrinkled his nose. He looked back at Shepherd. 'But who knows what might happen in the future? Probably best if I hang onto it.' He opened a desk drawer and dropped the letter inside. He smiled at Shepherd as he closed the drawer. 'Well then, onwards and upwards.' He flashed Shepherd a tight smile, then went back to studying his screens, his way of telling Shepherd that the meeting was over.

An explosive, action-packed thriller from
Sunday Times bestselling author
Stephen Leather

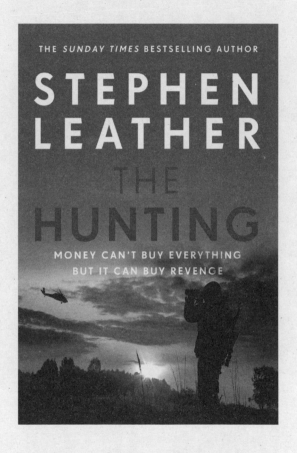

Money can't buy everything
But it can buy revenge

HODDER

**A Matt Standing thriller from
the bestselling author of the
Spider Shepherd series . . .**

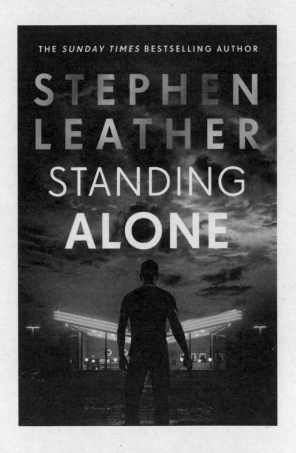

THE *SUNDAY TIMES* BESTSELLING AUTHOR

STEPHEN
LEATHER
STANDING
ALONE

**What makes a good man
become an assassin?**

HODDER &
STOUGHTON